Smoke & Blood

"Blood is thicker than water, but loyalty is thicker than blood."
—Unknown

Chapter ONE

Julien

fter five long years, I was sitting in my cell for the last night. I stared at the tattoos on the backs of my hands. Even in the wash of darkness, I saw them. A skull on my left hand and a rose on my right.

I always looked at them as the balance of life. There were both beauty and death in everything we did. Every moment we lived and breathed was either fueling one or the other. Neither was good or bad. They just were.

As for me? I had more death in me than beauty. More darkness than light. When I left the cold concrete walls of Florida State Prison, I was going to prove once again why I was void of light and beauty. I was going to sate myself with murder. It had been far too long since I created the most intricate art there is.

The art of death.

I took pride in what I did. In the way I did it. Sometimes with a knife. Sometimes with a gun. Sometimes with a syringe full of tranquilizer and a small windowless room where nobody could hear any screaming or pleading.

If it was an indisputable fact that art came from beauty then the same had to be true for death. If not, I made sure it was true. I brought beauty and poetry to death.

Everyone walking the earth was one moment away from dying and sometimes, I was that moment. Sometimes, bad men crossed paths with me and I sent them to hell way before I'd be on my way.

Ironically enough, I wasn't in prison for murder. I always thought that would be my fate. I was the dark and twisted one. My grandmother used to pray for my soul when I was little because more than a few times she found me beating the fuck out of the so-called neighborhood bullies until their mouths were bright scarlet and my knuckles were a mess of my blood and theirs.

She told my older brother, Angel, to watch me and put me on the straight and narrow path because she knew I looked up to him. What she didn't know was that I lashed out on behalf of Angel. All he had to do was point and I would throw my fists in that direction.

When we got older, I wielded knives and guns. It was still the same game though. Nobody fucked with my big brother.

Angel wasn't like me. He wasn't born with screws loose. He was always the enterprising brother. He had grand ideas and found ways to execute them. When he was in middle school and I was in fourth grade, he used Grandpa's clippers to give boys in the neighborhood haircuts. I was his security. Yeah, I was in fourth grade but I was twice as big as the kids in seventh and eighth grade.

In high school, Angel got hold of a fake I.D. and bought liquor with the money Grandma gave him every week. He mixed it with Kool-Aid, poured the concoction into juice bottles, and sold them for ten dollars each. I was in charge of getting money from the kids who promised to pay but didn't.

Every year, he came up with idea after idea and we always had money because of it. He looked out for me no matter what. So, when the time came to look out for him, I did it without hesitation.

Five years ago, Angel started making plans to elevate his petty drug operation selling pills and weed to something bigger. He wanted to move more weight but he needed a cover. He was already a party-promoter so I suggested he get his own club. That way, he could sell his product and wash the money at the same time.

Me and Angel ran the streets of Miami that summer stacking money and selling drugs so we could buy a club together. The same day he finally got a business loan, he got robbed. Angel was never without a gun on him, so he killed the motherfucker. It smelled like a set-up from a jealous motherfucker anyway. When the time came, I took the charge for him and claimed self-defense. It went through in the hearing but I got charged for having an unregistered firearm. I got five fucking years on that bullshit charge.

Angel begged me to keep quiet about it over the years because several times I cursed his ass out for letting me take the hit so he could open his club. I got over it though because we're blood. That's what blood does. It helps. It keeps the heart pumping for the greater good.

During my entire bid, Angel kept money on my books and helped me study gemology. For some reason, I'd always been interested in jewels. He made sure I had all the up-to-date study material and told me when I got out, he'd make sure I got certified. I hoped I did well enough for myself that I could start designing my own fine jewelry pieces. He also promised me that when I got out, I'd have a place right beside him running Rush, his nightclub.

When we had our last conversation before my release, Angel told me he'd have one of his security guys pick me up. I was a little confused because why the fuck wouldn't he come get me after all these years of being locked up on his behalf? Then he told me the guy had been getting too friendly with his wife and wanted him taken care of.

"Can you talk some sense into him for me, Smoke? I'll make sure everything you need is in the glove box." He'd asked quietly on the phone.

"Yeah, I got you," I said.

"I'll roll around immediately afterward and we can finish

talking to him." I knew what all of Angel's codes meant. Talking sense into someone was his way of telling me to do what I did best. Kill. Finishing the talk meant disposal. I was skilled at that too. Can't have one talent without the other. "I need to know your loyalty hasn't shifted while you've been inside, bro."

"How could it, Angel?" I asked, my face impassive but my mind storming and swirling with darkness. All I'd done for five years was sit silently serving time Angel was supposed to serve. If that wasn't loyalty, then I don't know what was.

"I just need to make sure. I told you, I have people out here crossing me. I even worry about Cress sometimes. It's not just you, hermano." He said it as if his words should soothe me but they didn't. I shut my eyes for a moment at the mention of his wife Cress. I could see her sandy curls and champagne eyes. When I opened my eyes again, I was staring at the cold gray brick wall in front of me.

"Cress? You think she's cheating on you?"

"She's not the same little preacher's kid we knew from back in the day, Smoke." His voice sounded heavy and laden with suspicions. "Listen, just talk some sense into my guy when he comes. I'll ride by afterward."

"Yeah, I got you, Angel. I'll see you in a few days."

"Fucking finally, hermano. Can't wait to see you and to bring you into the fold." He told me he loved me then he hung up. At first, the thought of killing his security guy did nothing for me. The entire time I'd been inside, I hadn't killed anyone. I wanted time off for good behavior. They only gave me a month. I took it gladly though. One less month being in that hell hole was a blessing.

Once I sat with the idea and possibilities of how I could kill this motherfucker who crossed my brother, the familiar hum of anticipation heated my blood. I'd been that way since my mother died. Thoughts of murder and killing blanketed my mindscape. Now was no different.

I was supposed to be sleeping. Getting rest for the big day tomorrow. Instead, I was sitting on the edge of my bed thinking of ways to kill Angel's security without leaving blood droplets or spatter. Like I said, I brought art to death and any type of challenge in my craft excited me. I wouldn't be able to sleep until I figured out the perfect way to create art and dispose of the materials.

…

"Don't end up back here, Jean," the release guard said in a rough voice. I looked at him without a word. I had my belongings and I was ready to leave. I stepped through the metal detector then showed my prison ID to the guard standing between me and the outside world.

He looked at it, the corners of his mouth turned down like I'd be using someone else's ID to escape. If I'd wanted to escape, I could have a long time ago. I had several chances but I was smart enough to know that running would only make my problems worse.

"Julian Montez Jean," he grunted and handed me back the laminated ID. I snatched it and shoved it in my wallet. It was the one I had on me when I got arrested and processed five years ago. I couldn't wait to get back into the real world where I didn't have to hear my government name being used as a form of authority over me. I was ready to be Smoke again. "Watch it, boy." He tipped his head back and adjusted his uniform hat to look me in the eye. "I'll haul your ass back in here."

"You can try." A cocky smirk tipped my lips. I meant that shit too. He could try all he wanted to drag me back to that hell hole but I wasn't going. I'd served my time and I was done. He couldn't send me back for snatching my I.D. out of his hands. Fuck him.

I stepped outside the huge metal door for the first time in five years and was escorted off the property. The guards reminded me frequently that as long as I was on Florida State Prison property, I belonged to them.

I sat on the metal bench bolted to the concrete and stared at the trees. They were the same trees that were there when I went in but now, they seemed more alive. Greener. Taller. I stared at them for a long while, watching them blow in the wind while I contemplated if being inside changed me at all. Did it make me appreciate life enough not to take it? Or was that darkness still inside of me?

When I saw a black Audi pull up and stop, my blood hummed with murderous possibilities, and I knew the darkness was still there. Being in prison hadn't changed a goddamn thing. It only put a hold on it.

The Audi's mirror-tinted window rolled down and a smiling face peered out at me. "Smoke? Angel sent me to pick you up. He's right behind me in another car."

"Yeah, I'm Smoke." I walked up to the car and looked around before getting in with my belongings. We pulled away from the building and I was finally putting that place behind me for good.

Once the prison was out of sight, I checked the glove box and saw a small, brown leather bag with a zipper running around the outside. I pulled it out and smoothed my hand over it. I knew exactly what was inside.

"So, how does it feel to be out?" The man driving asked while he focused on the road.

"Great."

"Angel's excited for you to finally be home. He said you've never seen Rush before."

"Seen pictures," I said quietly. Every picture I saw looked amazing. Each year, Rush evolved. Now, it had soft neon red lighting throughout and a bar that wrapped around the entire interior with plush suede seating. Angel had turned Rush into something classy. Nobody would have ever suspected it was the biggest drug operation in Miami.

"It's beautiful, man. And the women…" He made a noise and shook his head while smiling wide and bright.

"Oh yeah?" I lifted an eyebrow and tucked the leather bag against my leg.

"Yeah, man. I'm messing with one of the girls that work the bar and she's bad. Actually, I got a couple of them." I wondered if one of them was Cress. I looked the guy over and didn't see what she'd find attractive enough about him to cheat on Angel after all he'd done for her.

My chest tightened when I thought about Cress. I pushed the thoughts out of my head and stared out of the window as palm trees began speckling the sidewalks.

"You don't talk much, do you, Smoke?"

"Nah." I shook my head and kept my eyes on the road out of my window.

"Well, I guess I should introduce myself. We've been riding together for twenty minutes and I haven't told you my name. Or did Angel tell you?"

"He didn't." I pulled my stare away from the ground rushing beneath us and looked at him.

"I'm Sam. Nice to meet you." I nodded at him and turned back to the window. After another ten minutes of silent driving, my mind started drifting to the feeling I knew would come when I wrapped the fishing line around his neck.

"Did Angel give you a phone for me?" I asked.

"No, he didn't. Sorry." I ran a hand over my chin and nodded. I asked him to pull over to the next gas station so I could piss and he obliged. We pulled into a small station and I hopped out with my bag. When I walked in, the woman behind the counter smiled at me. She was all green eyes and raven hair with way too much cleavage exposed.

My wandering eyes still took a trip down her shirt though.

"Bathroom?" I asked, ignoring her flirting eyes.

"Oh, let me show you."

"You can just point me in the direction. Thanks."

"You're a quiet one. What's your name, sweetheart?"

I almost rattled off my real name. Being inside really did a fucking number on me. "Smoke." I looked around at the gas station snacks and realized not too much had changed in five years. Everything in convenience stores was still trash. My stomach was growling though. It was time to kill Sam and get something to eat. "You know what?" I said, holding up my hand to the busty green-eyed cashier. "I'll find the bathroom myself." I walked to the back and lo and behold. There was the fucking bathroom.

I pushed through the squeaky door and went into the handicap stall to open my bag and inspect everything. Neatly folded up inside were a pair of black latex gloves. Hiding beneath them was my gold switchblade, a reel of fishing line, and zip ties. It was my bare-bones kill-bag. I had a much nicer one at home.

I succumbed to my dark side when I was still a teenager. My first kill was accidental. I beat a guy to death in an alley behind a club. He started talking shit to me first then to my brother. Our fight started in the parking lot and ended up in the alleyway somehow. Angel was by my side throwing punches, then kicking the guy once he was on the ground but something happened. Something snapped inside of me.

His blood looked like paint the way it splashed across the wet pavement. It was glossy and darker than it always looked on TV. It mixed and swirled with the shallow puddles on the ground. I was transfixed. I blacked out and drove my knuckles into his face until it he didn't resemble a human anymore.

Angel had to pull me off when sirens filled the night sky warning us to scatter. The hum and rush in my blood from killing that man sparked a dark candle inside of me. I saw beauty where everyone else saw tragedy.

Angel saw the black hunger inside of me and put it to work. I only took out men and only the ones who were actively trying to take Angel out...or fuck him over. He was all I had. My only family. I wasn't going to lose him.

When I saw everything in my bag was still there as I left it, I left the bathroom and ignored the cashier trying to drum up a casual conversation on the way out. I wasn't much of a talker. I preferred action over everything.

"You ready to ride?" Sam asked, waiting by the car.

"Yeah. We still have a while to go so I'm going to catch a nap." I climbed in the roomy back seat and reclined a little to the side. I was just out of Sam's line of sight. Good.

He started the engine and checked his phone while I scanned the area for cameras on the traffic lights and the shabby gas station. I didn't see any.

I unzipped my bag and slipped my fingers into the cool latex gloves. I flexed my hands then unwound the fishing line while Sam chuckled at something on his phone.

"Girlfriend?" I asked in an attempt to mask the sound of me smoothing out the fishing line.

"Something like that. It's my side piece. She's bad as fuck too, man."

"Oh yeah?" I wrapped the clear line around my hands a few times then examined it, making sure to hold it low so Sam couldn't see.

"Yeah, let me stop bullshitting around. You know how your brother is." He scoffed and it rubbed me the wrong way. I glanced around the empty parking lot and before Sam could throw the car in drive, I sat upright and wrapped the line around his throat from the backseat, pulling hard. He gasped and struggled trying to dig his fingers underneath the fishing line to get a breath so I pulled tighter.

I was too strong for him to overpower and I attacked from behind. He had no choice but to go willingly into the blackness that called out to him. I knew he felt death beckoning when his shoulders fell slack and his body got heavy. My skin prickled in response to the gurgle leaving his crushed esophagus. It was one of the last sounds he'd ever make. It was sad and solemn and it struck me somewhere deep. The same way a sad song hits.

I watched the thick vein in his neck pulse in a last-ditch effort to pump blood to his failing heart. I let the fishing line go and looked around before getting out of the backseat and walking around to the driver's side. I opened the door and Sam's body fell out heavy and limp. I slid my arms under his and pulled him around to the backseat. Once I laid him down in the back, I grabbed everything from his pockets and looked in the trunk for a blanket. I found a thick, gray flannel blanket along with a fresh roll of duct tape. I wondered if Angel made sure they were in there in case I needed them.

I slammed the trunk then walked around to the backseat and draped the gray blanket over Sam's body. Once I was in the driver's seat, the cashier from the gas station came running toward the car. My body went still but my mind fired off a million mistakes I could have made strangling a guy in broad daylight. I hadn't killed anyone in years. Maybe I was rusty. Sloppy.

I rolled down the window, aware that I was wearing gloves in Florida. I flashed a polite smile and waited for the woman to speak. "I saw you hadn't pulled off yet and I was wondering if you wanna exchange numbers or something. It's been a long time since something as tall and fine as you walked into the station."

Relief flooded my body. She only wanted my number. Thank fuck. Even as dark and twisted as I was, I had a moral compass buried somewhere inside me. Or maybe it was just because I adored my mother so much...but killing or hurting women was off the table for me. If the cashier caught me red-handed, my black ass would be going back to prison.

I chuckled at her question and narrowed my eyes in the harsh sun. "I'm seeing someone," I lied. "I appreciate the gesture though." I nodded my head and rolled up the window before she could apologize or say whatever pointless words were about to leave her mouth.

When I hit the gas, a horn blared from behind, making me jam my foot on the brake to see who the fuck was blowing at me. I turned around and saw another black Audi. The person in the driver's seat waved their arms before getting out and jogging up to my car.

"Angel? What the hell, hermano?" I laughed for the first time since being released. I hopped out and greeted my big brother with open arms. We hugged like we hadn't seen each other in five years even though he came to visit monthly.

"I told you I'd be around when you were done talking to Sam." he leaned against the car and sparked a cigarette. Thin gray smoke spilled into the air and the smell of tobacco and nicotine filled my nose.

"And I told you to stop smoking this bullshit." I snagged the cancer stick out of his mouth and stamped it out. He leveled a glare at me then sighed.

"I'm the big brother. I have five years on you and you're still trying to tell me what to do?"

"I'm taller," I grunted, rolling my shoulders and standing up straight. I towered over Angel by a head and outweighed him by at least seventy pounds. He was tall and slim where I was tall and muscular. I worked on my body constantly while I was inside because I wanted the discipline. I wanted physical power more than muscles for show so I wasn't bulky but I could bench press four-hundred pounds easily.

"Yeah, yeah. Listen…let's get out of here." Angel looked at the sparse parking lot then peered in the backseat where Sam's body lay stiffening more by the second. "Damn. You still got it, baby bro." He clapped me on the back then strolled off to his car. "Follow me," he called over his shoulder.

A quiet sour pang echoed in my chest. Damn, no *thank you for handling my dirty work*. Nothing. That was Angel's nature though.

He moved so fast, sometimes he forgot to do the small work like showing gratitude. I had to chalk it up to him still being the arrogant big brother I remembered.

I followed Angel to the Sparkling Dolphin Docks where we used to rent boats with Grandma when we were kids. When I got older, it became easy for me to dump bodies or body parts in the water because it was where the gulf stream flowed. It carried currents as far as Iceland. It was my favorite disposal spot second only to the marsh because that's where the gators were and they always made light work out of the bodies I dumped.

"I figured you'd want to take a boat ride like we did when we were younger," Angel said, dangling a key in the air.

"Of course," I nodded. "You got your own boat here?"

"Several. That's why I'm so glad you're home, Smoke. I can share all this fucking wealth with you, man." He stretched his arm out and I looked at the glittering Miami waters.

"You know money isn't my thing," I told him as I opened the back door of the Audi. "What are we doing for clean up?" Usually, I would have had the body wrapped in plastic or rolled up in a carpet. Something...anything besides a flannel fucking blanket that could fall off at any time.

"You're going to have to make it work, Smoke. I have access to three boats docked here. This place still doesn't have cameras."

"What?" I looked around and saw very visible cameras attached to the roof of the building. "So those are dummies?"

"Yup. To keep inspectors off their ass. They don't work though.

I talk to the clerk, Vicky all the time. Only one of the cameras even films anything. It doesn't record though. They have no way of running it back. It's old and cheap and fucking perfect."

"You got any more blankets at least?" I huffed, eyeing the six-foot-tall man in the backseat.

"Two more. You can wrap him up while I take this call. It's Cress." He waved his ringing phone at me just long enough for me to get a glimpse of Cress's face as it flashed across the screen. She didn't have sandy curls anymore. Her hair was straight but everything else was still the same.

Pouty pink lips, cherubic cheeks, and almond-shaped eyes the translucent color of champagne made her look young and innocent. I blinked away her face and looked at dead Sam in the backseat.

I could wrap him up with two more blankets. I didn't want to risk using any sort of ties that would mold the blankets to his body because it would look suspicious as fuck to be carrying something that shape and weight onto a boat. I didn't give a damn if they had cameras or not.

When Angel got off the phone, he grabbed two more blankets from the trunk of his car and tossed them to me. I went to work trying my best to drape them over Sam's body. Once I had him positioned right and the blankets looking as little like a body as possible, I hauled the dead weight over my shoulder.

"Goddamn Smoke, you been in jail hitting the weights heavy," Angel remarked with a loud laugh.

"It's not like I had a lot of other things to focus on," I said, clenching my teeth together. The weight of a dead body wasn't technically more than the same body when it was alive but it damn sure felt like it. My muscles started to burn once we walked up the ramp and onto Angel's boat...well, one of them.

"Thought you'd like this one. Named her Beauty and Death. I was thinking about you." He lit a cigarette and walked onto the boat after I dropped the dead body on the floor. I waited for my heart to stop pounding then I looked at my big brother.

"Thanks, Angel."

"The boat is yours if you want it." He tossed the keys at me and I caught them in the palm of my hand.

"My own boat, huh?" I lifted an eyebrow at him and he smiled. He looked exactly like his father. I'd never met him before but I'd seen so many pictures when we were growing up. Our grandmother raised us for most of our lives and Angel's father was her son. I had a different dad and Grandma let me know it every chance she got.

"Yeah, you need something to use for disposal. Why not?"

"Damn, and here I thought this was a gift for serving five years for you. Or for killing this motherfucker." I sent my foot into Dead Sam's ribs. "As soon as I was a free man." Angel pushed a hand through his glossy black hair and blew out a puff of smoke in my direction. I clenched my teeth to stop toxic words from pouring out because I knew it wouldn't do any good.

"I'm sorry, Smoke. I fucked up. I'm so excited to see you that I haven't thanked you for everything you've done for me. It's not

17

like I haven't been thanking you all along though. Making sure you never wanted for anything while you were in there. Making sure you got your little gemology books so you could learn about diamonds and sapphires and shit."

"When did I neglect to appreciate that, Angel? I'm saying my first few hours out and you already have me cleaning up and killing."

"I'm sorry," He chuckled, taking a long drag then pushing the smoke from between his lips. "I thought you loved what you did." He gestured to Sam. I scoffed and started the boat's engine, kicking up the smell of warm salty water.

"Never said I didn't. I'm saying it feels like you're putting me to work instead of saying a simple fucking thank you first." I pulled away from the dock slowly maneuvering farther into the water before gunning that shit.

"Okay, Smoke. I'm happy to see you. Thank you for handling Sam for me. Thank you for everything. I wouldn't be where I am now if it weren't for you." He sat down and finished his cigarette in silence.

That was all I wanted. I wasn't hard to deal with but I appreciated gratitude and loyalty. I was a simple man.

"I have something else for you...with my ungrateful ass," Angel said from his seat as he stared out at the water swishing past us. He pulled a thick white envelope from his pants pocket. I took it from him while the boat coasted on the small waves.

Inside was a thick stack of money. I lifted my eyes to Angel's, a question on my face. "Five-grand," he said. I looked at the stack of money again and chuckled. I told my brother money wasn't important to me but it damn sure helped, especially since I was fresh out of prison.

"Thanks, Angel."

"I told you, I got you, Smoke. You might feel like I'm not appreciative but I'm always there for you. Who else is there for you like me?" He was right. I didn't have anyone else.

"Nobody," I said with a sigh.

"Right." He stood beside me and we looked out at the water together. "Now, after we take care of this piece of shit, we're going home. You're going to take a hot shower and wash the stench of prison off you. Then we're going to sit down and break bread after that, I'm going to take you to Rush. It's just as much your brainchild as mine. Then we'll talk about your welcome home party. Cress is going to plan it. She needs something to do." He grimaced when he mentioned her. I didn't understand how he could have a woman like Cressida and grimace at the mention of her.

"What's up with y'all?" I quizzed, looking at the water.

"Nothing. Ever since she had Nasim she's been different. I can't put my finger on it. I don't like that shit though." He lit another cigarette and took a long hard pull.

"Cress? Little Cress?" I had to shake my head because thinking about Cressida Erickson doing anything that went against her moral code was laughable. She'd been strait-laced since I met her at her father's church in seventh grade. I was a grade above her but the moment I looked at her, I was in love.

Or I thought I was in love. I didn't know shit about feelings and emotions when I was that young. I had no idea that something lacy and delicate like love wasn't meant for someone dark and gnarled like me.

Back then though, I thought Cressida could do no wrong. She was golden. Literally. Her name meant golden. I was obsessed with her in middle school and I looked her name up online to see what it meant. I was pretty pathetic.

I even asked her out once. It was the summer Angel started working as a party promoter for the local clubs. He was busy moving drugs and he didn't have a lot of time for me anymore unless it was the weekend and I was helping him move weight.

Cress and I went to the carnival and I spent all my money playing every game just to impress her and win her something. I lost all of them but at the end of the night, I won the basketball toss. I told her to pick whatever prize she wanted. She had her champagne golden eyes on a silver mood ring in a display case with other silver-plated jewelry and trinkets. I'd never seen someone be so proud to wear something so cheap.

I tried to kiss her at the end of the night but she gave me her cheek and told me it was wrong to kiss on the first date but since she liked me, she let it slide…a little.

Knowing she grew up to be shady enough to cheat on Angel was crazy. She didn't even want to have a boyfriend when we were in school. Her parents were strict and made her focus on her schoolwork. Even back then she was shooting for Spelman.

"Like I said, Smoke," Angel flicked ashes over the side of the boat. "Cress isn't the same little girl she was when we knew her from around the way. I guess being married to me combined with all the money we have now has changed her. Every other week that bitch is flirting with some motherfucker. Shit drives me crazy."

"Didn't she just give birth to Nasim eight months ago? And since when did you start calling Cress out of her name?" I frowned, killing the engine. We were raised to respect women above all else and that's what I did. I didn't hit women, call them out of their names, or cheat on them. If I was going to fuck multiple women, I let it be known.

"Shit. My bad, Smoke. I didn't know it bothered you so fucking much. I call her what she acts like. She's mine. Remember?" He narrowed his eyes through the haze of cigarette smoke and cracked a crooked smile. "You don't still have that little stupid ass crush on her, do you?"

"Nah," I shook my head and motioned to Dead Sam with my chin. "Grab his feet."

"I'm paying you to dispose of him. Go ahead and do your job." He tossed his cigarette butt over the side and locked eyes with me. I wasn't in the mood to fight with Angel. He was clearly on some weird-ass power trip and I didn't do power trips. I'd have to learn how to navigate this new version of my brother. He was high-strung and offended by every goddamn thing.

When I saw him pull a small vial of white powder from his pocket and tap out a tiny mound on the back of his hand, I knew why he was so paranoid and high-strung.

"Coke, hermano? Are you fucking kidding me?" I laughed

because that shit had to be a joke. He knew better than getting high on his own supply. Biggie taught us both that shit at the same time. We both knew The Notorious B.I.G.'s *Ten Crack Commandments* by heart. He was fucking up.

"I don't deserve to live a little?" He grumbled before hitting the bump of coke on his hand. He sniffed it then pushed out a sigh before doing another bump. "Dump that worthless piece of shit in the ocean and let's go. I don't like leaving Cress home alone for too long. Plus, I want her to talk to you and figure out what you want for your party." I didn't know if I wanted to talk to Cress if she'd changed as much as Angel said. It would make me look at her in a different light and I liked the image of her I had in my mental memory box.

"Come on now, you know better than this shit though," I said about the cocaine.

"I know I do what the fuck I want, when I want. You haven't been home in a while, Smoke. Your big brother is the fucking king of Miami. All the competition we had before you went in? Other motherfuckers bitching about turf and shit? They work for me now. I run everything. So, if I want to party and sniff a little coke, don't chew me out about it. It's hard being the king."

He sniffed and wiped the white residue from his nose. I shook my head and grabbed Dead Sam from the floor of the boat then eased him in the water so he didn't make a splash.

Angel and I started back to dock in silence. I didn't know what to make of him now. He looked like my brother. He sounded like him too. Something was off though. His energy had shifted. I hadn't picked up on it when I was inside but maybe I only saw what I wanted to see. Maybe I was focused on staying alive. Whatever the reason, I cursed myself for not noticing Angel needed help.

Now that I was home, I was going to help him kick that nasty ass habit. Miami didn't need another coked-out king.

...

Chapter TWO

Cressida

I laid my son, Nasim, down once he was full and knocked out in my arms. I eased away from the crib, grabbed the baby monitor, and went back to the living room where my best friend, Bree, was waiting.

"You sure you don't want a glass of wine?" She poured herself a glass of the full-bodied Malbec and hummed happily bringing the glass to her nose.

"No, I'll have a glass after I put Nasim down for the night. I still have to pump though. This milk is too precious to pump and dump." I squeezed my boobs through my shirt and flopped down on the couch beside her.

"I can't believe as big as that boy is, you're still breastfeeding him."

"He's not nursing anymore." I shrugged. "He gets it in a bottle. Nas wouldn't take my boob right now if I offered it to him on a silver platter. He's too grown."

"He's too damn grown to be drinking titty milk," Bree laughed. "I'm just messing with you, Cress. Lighten up." She nudged me with her elbow then took a sip of wine from her full glass.

"You know that glass is too full. The wine can't breathe like that."

"Let me stop you right there, Cress. I'm not trying to let the wine breathe. I want to drink the wine. Not sing love songs to it."

"Uncouth," I smirked playfully. We laughed together and I absorbed that moment like a sponge. I knew soon it would be over. Soon, Angel would come home and I had no idea what mood he'd be in. His brother, Julien, was getting out of prison today and that meant he could be over the moon excited or he could be wildly bitter and angry.

"You okay?" Bree asked, studying my eyes.

"I'm fine," I said nodding and tucking a stray chunk of ochre hair behind my ear. "Just thinking about Angel bringing Julien home today."

"Who?"

"Smoke. Angel's brother." I forgot that I was the only person who called him by his real name. I liked it. It was musical.

"Oh yeah, that is today, isn't it? That man is fine as hell."

"Who, Julien?" I laughed a little and spun my dainty mood ring around on my finger.

"Yeah, girl. I've seen pictures." She wasn't lying. Angel was always bragging about Julien to anyone who would listen. He went on and on about how his little brother took a five-year bid for him like that shit was commendable. I always thought Julien was stupid for going to jail for a crime he didn't commit. The gun that killed the guy who robbed Angel five years ago was Angel's. Not Julien's. He should have never done that time. It took him away from...everyone.

"So, if I turn into a ho when Angel comes up in here with Mr. Tall Dark and Handsome, don't act brand new. Let me shine."

"You can have all of that," I laughed, shaking my head.

"You said that like you're competition. You're married, Cress. Let the single ladies have this one."

Like Angel could hear us talking about him, the alarm beeped and he walked in. I smelled the cigarette smoke and saltwater before he even hit the living room.

"Speak of the devil," Bree muttered before taking another gulp of wine.

"Devil?" Angel boomed. Just from the tone of his voice, I could tell he was high.

Fuck.

I raked shaky fingers through my hair and gave my mood ring a spin. "I'm motherfucking Angel Delgado. *Angel*," he said again. "It's right in my name. I can't be the devil." He rounded the corner and I took him in quickly then my eyes immediately went to the familiar hulking stranger behind him. He was bigger than I remembered but to be honest, I hadn't seen him in more than five years.

Before he went to prison, I didn't see much of him. We were both doing our own thing. I was in my first year of college and he was running behind Angel, as usual. So this was the first time I'd seen him in about seven fucking years.

I couldn't stop looking at him. He was so...tall. He'd always been taller than Angel but now the height difference was insanely noticeable. More than the height was the bulk. Julien was thick, dense cuts of muscle under smokey honey brown skin. His hair and beard were a little long and scraggly but his high cheekbones and sharp jawline still stole the show.

"Besides, would the devil bring this motherfucker home in one piece?" He slapped Julien's back a few times and laughed but there was no smile on his little brother's face. He was all stone and scowl.

Same old Jules.

I swallowed to loosen my tight throat before smiling politely. I stood up and smoothed my hands over my black blouse then fluffed my hair. "Hey baby," I said, kissing Angel's cheek. He pressed me against him, his hand forcefully at the small of my back.

"A kiss on the fucking cheek?" He said in a low grumble that only I could hear. My heart thumped in my chest but I put a smile on my face.

"You smell like smoke," I said through barely parted lips. The entire moment was stiff and stretched so thin that even a pin drop would pop everything.

"So the fuck what? When your goddamn husband comes home, you kiss him." My eyes blinked so rapidly, everyone in the room was a blur of clothes and colors. I wondered if anyone else sensed that danger was ripe in the air. Or if they knew one wrong move on my part would end with something being shattered or a hole being punched in the wall.

I leaned in and kissed Angel's lips, trying to put my all into it so he wouldn't think I was putting on in front of our company. When I pulled away from my husband's tobacco-stained lips, I caught Julien's mahogany brown eyes peering at me. His face was impassive but I knew something was churning inside him. I just didn't know what it was. He probably thought I was stupid for marrying his brother.

I cleared my throat and pulled away from Angel a little. "Hey, Julien. Good to have you back." My smile was bright and pulled too tight across my face. I hoped nobody noticed.

"What's up, Cress?" He kept his eyes trained on mine for a brief second, then looked around the house. Like I was fucking Medusa or something. Still, the way my name sounded coming from him was...

"You know he hates being called Julien. Call that man by the name I gave him." Angel's smile was back and deceptive as ever.

"Sorry about that. Old habits." I grinned. "Welcome home, Smoke."

"That's more like it," Angel boomed. He moved over to Bree and I pushed out a quiet sigh of relief. "Smoke, this is Bree. Cress's friend."

"Cress's best fucking friend. Nice to meet you, Smoke." She

held out her hand and Julien took it gingerly before giving it a quick squeeze then shoving his hand in his pocket. I'd never seen Bree look more disappointed.

"Nice to meet you, Bree." Julien glanced at her then went back to surveying the living room. "Yo, Angel, where's Trinity? She's never too far from Cress." I tried not to look at Julien like he'd grown three new heads. It wasn't his fault. He didn't know I wasn't speaking to my big sister anymore. Or rather, she wasn't speaking to me.

"Trinity?" Angel growled. "That bitch ain't welcome in my fucking house and she knows it."

"You gotta chill with calling women bitches," Julien scolded. His chiseled jaw flexed. My heart leaped into my throat as I watched in horror at their exchange.

"Yeah, what-the-fuck-ever. Trinity isn't welcome here. Is that better?" Angel scoffed before falling into the plush white armchair. Julien didn't respond. He remained stone-faced and quiet. "Cress, take Bree and Nasim and do something with yourself for a few hours. I'll give you some money."

"I just put Nas down. He's sleeping," I stammered, blinking at him in disbelief.

"Yeah, where is my nephew? That's who I really want to see." Julien smiled a little for the first time and I saw how pretty his lips and teeth were. I indulged for a few seconds in the sight of his smile.

"He's sleeping," I said, looking at my husband.

"I don't care. I need y'all up out of here for a while. I need to talk to Smoke alone."

"Come on, girl. All I needed to hear was money. I'll keep her out all night if you want, Angel," Bree laughed. She tugged on my arm but I wouldn't budge.

"As big as this house is you can't just talk to Smoke in another room?" Knots constricted my throat, tying tighter and tighter the longer Angel's eyes bored into me.

His dark brows crashed together and he stood up, staring me straight in the eye. He was only a few inches taller than me so his height wasn't intimidating. Not like Julien's. I didn't need Angel's height to intimidate me though. He was strong and he was nasty when he was high or when he didn't get his way.

"I said take your ass out of the fucking house, Cress. Don't make me ask again." His teeth were pressed together so hard his cheeks shook. I was on thin ice and I knew it.

"Chill," Julien said holding his hand up toward Angel. "We can talk anywhere. You don't have to put them out." It was the most I'd heard him talk in seven years.

"Nah. We can't talk anywhere. I like my house empty when I talk business." His cold, dark eyes were still focused on me.

"It's fine." I swallowed, stepping out of arm's reach. "I'll go get Nasim and that way you can see him." I looked at Julien and smiled before heading out of the living room and up the steps. When my smile finally faded, my cheek muscles twitched from holding on to my mask for so long.

I walked into Nasim's nursery and peered at him in his crib.

A soft knock on the door behind me, made me jump. "Sorry. I just wanted to see my nephew." Julien's voice made my shoulders drop.

"Come in," I said quietly ushering him inside.

"Damn, little Cressida Erickson had a baby." He looked like he was scared to get too close. He had that clueless look that most men have when it comes to handling babies and children. "I can't believe how big he is." Julien's deep voice pushed vibrations through my stomach. Like a million fluttering wings all at once. Only, it wasn't sweet or romantic. It was terrifying and I wanted no parts of it.

"Yeah. He's eight months old."

"Not until tomorrow," he said still staring at his nephew. An unintentional smile crept across my lips before I extinguished it.

"You've been keeping track." I cleared my throat to disperse whatever that sound was in my voice.

"Of course. He's my nephew. My blood."

"You want to hold him?" I asked, scooping my big boy up from the crib. He stirred in his sleep before opening his bright hazel eyes to look at Julien.

"Oh...I don't think I should." He shook his head and took a step back.

"You're his uncle. Hold him. You won't break him. He's big and strong like you." I could have left off that big and strong part. I scolded myself quietly then offered Nasim to Julien. "Come on, Jules."

"For a little while," he said, finally caving. He held out his arms and Nasim went to him without any trouble. He even smiled and babbled for his uncle. "Wow...look at you, buddy." He gave Nas a squeeze then pressed a kiss to his forehead. "I'm your uncle, Smoke."

"Uncle Jules," I corrected, giving Nasim my finger to grip.

"Nah. Smoke." He looked at me, his eyes hardening a little. What the fuck did I do to make him look at me like that? I ignored the expression and took Nasim back before Angel started fussing downstairs. "He's a handsome boy," Julien said with a nod.

"Thank you."

"Still can't believe little Cress had a baby."

"Well, it would help if you stopped calling me little Cress. I'm not her anymore." Growing up, Angel and Julien were the older guys I thought were so damn fine. It was hard for any of the girls in our neighborhood to choose which brother was better looking. I always leaned toward Julien but I got sucked into Angel's bad-boy persona. If only I knew then what the hell I know now...

"Yeah, I heard. A lot of things have changed." He glanced at me then shook his head before leaving the nursery.

Something about our interaction made me feel empty and on fire at the same time. What the fuck had Angel told him about me? I sat Nasim down on the floor to crawl around while I got his diaper bag together.

The look on Julien's face kept playing on a loop in my mind. It was almost like he didn't know me anymore. I guess he didn't though. We hadn't seen each other or spoken in seven years. That's a long time. Maybe he was different too.

Downstairs, Bree waited for me by the front door waving

Angel's credit card between two fingers. "Hubby handed over the card." Her eyes glittered and I tried to smile through it but I knew my husband. He only gave me enough money to shop. Not enough to leave him. He set spending limits and determined which stores I could go to.

In order to hide my stupidity, I grinned and took the card from Bree. There was no way in hell I could tell her I basically had a child's debit card that Angel controlled fully. I slipped the card into my wallet and adjusted Nasim's bag on my shoulder.

"Ball out, baby," Angel strolled around the corner with a smile that stretched from one ear to the other. He was so handsome. Olive skin, dark eyes, thick black hair that he kept perfectly coifed, and that mega-watt smile. Any woman would have killed to be with him. Shit, they didn't have to kill to be with him.

Since I gave birth to our son, he fucked any beautiful woman who wanted him. "I already called the driver. He's in the driveway." Angel leaned over and kissed my forehead before opening the door. I stiffened under his lips then stepped toward the open door.

"Thanks, babe." Another fake smile. More sore cheeks to keep the façade in place. "Love you. You and Jules...I mean Smoke have fun." The driver strapped Nasim into his car seat while Angel watched from the open front door.

Once I was inside, I let my head fall backward as I pushed out a heavy sigh. "You okay, Cress?" Bree asked.

"I guess." I kept my eyes trained on Nas who was strapped into the middle seat while Bree sat in the third row.

"You guess? What's up? Things seemed tense between you and Angel back there."

"He's fucking high. I hate when he's high. And Jules coming home is going to put him in a weird space."

"Why though?" Bree asked from behind me. "That's his little brother. I thought he would be happy to have him home. Smoke is literally all Angel talks about."

"I know but it's…strange. The relationship between them has always been different. Jules looks up to Angel. Treats him like a god. Especially after their grandmother died. He's big on family."

"Sounds like you know a lot about Smoke," she said. A hint of accusation in her voice.

"We were friends back in the day." I twisted the mood ring around on my finger and stifled the beating butterfly wings in my belly. "Anyway, Angel has this weird obsession with Jules. He loves his brother but only in the way Angel knows how to love."

"And how is that? Because Angel seems like he loves pretty big and pretty hard. I mean, look at how he's treating us to this impromptu shopping spree."

"You know how Angel is, Bree. He's a narcissist." She never agreed with my assessment of Angel as having narcissistic personality disorder. Bree was easily swayed by Angel's grand gestures. Not me. Not anymore.

"He's not. I keep telling you he just works a lot. He's stressed out and you need to be there for him. You know the business he's running isn't easy. Plus, he has a ton of motherfuckers gunning for him. That's probably why he's so happy that Smoke is home." Angel was only happy about Jules being home because it meant he had someone else he could manipulate.

"I guess." I shrugged my shoulders and wiped a puddle of drool off Nasim's chin. "All I know is, things are going to be stressful as fuck with Jules being home."

"They'll be fine. You just worry about being a good wife and mother. Take care of Angel and you know he'll take care of you." I could hear the smile in her voice and I knew it was time for me to be quiet and suffer in silence like I'd been doing for the past five years.

"Yeah...I know," I said softly, staring at my son. I swear, if it weren't for him, I would have left Angel. Now I was stuck because my best friend in the fucking world believed the phony mask my husband wore. My sister wasn't speaking to me anymore. I didn't have any money of my own, and my parents loved Angel like he was their biological son.

During my shopping spree, I mostly bought things for Nasim while Bree had no problem filling her bags with shoes and clothes on Angel's dime. I didn't care. Mentally, I was somewhere else. I was terrified of the mood Angel would be in when I came home.

I barely spoke the entire ride back to the house. I mainly listened to Bree go on and on about how fly she was going to look in the new shoes she bought while she was at work. She worked as a bottle girl at Rush and they all had to wear red leotards. Some of them had cute little skirts that flared out when they spun around and some wore shorts barely long enough to cover their ass. All of them had to wear red bottom shoes. Now that Bree had a new pair, she was going to flaunt it in the other girls' faces. She lived for the flare and flash.

"Okay girl, I'm going to sneak off before Angel realizes that he funded a shopping trip for me and Nas and not you." Bree smiled at me then hugged me while I balanced a sleeping Nasim on my shoulder.

"Call me later," I told her. "I'm sure I'll have an earful for you between Angel and Jules."

"Cress, just be good to your man and everything will be fine. Stop stressing so much. It's bad for my godson to see you like that." She kissed the top of Nasim's head and looked at me, something looming in her brown eyes. She wanted to say something. I knew her well enough to know when she was holding back. I didn't prod her though. I let her go and I walked into my version of hell.

The thick smell of smoke hit me first and I cursed under my breath. Every time I tried to tell Angel the smoke was bad for the baby, he cursed me out. I tried to keep Nas away from it at all costs. I'd leave whenever Angel started smoking heavily, but I needed to feed him and I wanted him to be able to play in his own goddamn room.

I tipped my head toward the ceiling, hearing the thump from whatever music Angel and Julien were listening to. I looked down at Nasim and checked to see if he was still knocked out. Thankfully, he was. I laid him in the pack and play in the living room then went upstairs to tell Angel I was back.

The closer I got, the more noise I heard. There was giggling coming from behind my closed bedroom door. The same bedroom

I shared with my husband. I shut my eyes for a moment to gather strength from somewhere.

My hand shook as I turned the knob. I knew what I was going to see when I opened the door but I was hoping for some other outcome. Anything else.

When I walked in, Angel was on our bed with two naked women taking turns sucking his dick. Some sick and twisted part of me watched for a few beats. Something masochistic held my eyes open when I wanted to turn away. I stood there until he noticed me.

It seemed to take forever before his heavy head lifted from the pillow and his burgundy red eyes cracked open to see me standing there, trembling with anger. "What's up, Cress?" He slurred before letting his head fall back to the pillow.

"In our bed, Angel?!" I shouted, tossing my hands in the air. My heart thundered in my chest as anger and embarrassment took over my veins. "You dirty motherfucker!"

I can't lie and say he'd never cheated before. In the eight months since having our son, he'd cheated more times than I could count but it had never happened in our house. Not in our fucking bed. It was always at the club or somewhere I couldn't see and I had to just rely on my intuition or hearsay from the people in our circle. Angel had never been this bold before.

I hated it. I hated the way it stung and burned like sand whipping across my skin. My chest was so tight it felt like it would pop and I heard my heart beating furiously in my ears.

The two women scrambled off the bed and grabbed their clothes while I hurled curse words at Angel like projectiles. "All the shit I let you get away with and this is what you do? You bring these dirty bitches into our house where our son sleeps and you fuck them?"

"I didn't fuck them," Angel countered, sitting on the side of the bed casually naked like we weren't in the middle of a fucking crisis. Well, maybe it wasn't that deep for him since he'd been fucking around on me since I had Nasim. I was the stupid one.

Angel took one pull of his lit cigarette then stood up, his dick still glistening with stranger spit. I turned my head and caught one last glimpse of the two bitches as they scurried out of the bedroom.

"I'm taking Nasim and leaving," I said, my voice shaking like a leaf. I pushed past Angel and went into the closet to grab the bag hidden deep behind clothes and shoes.

"Leaving? You're not going anywhere, Cress. Stop being fucking stupid." When I looked over my shoulder, I saw him sliding on a pair of silk black pajama bottoms. "Put that shit back. You're crazy if you think you're leaving me and taking my son." He reached around me and snatched the bag.

In the next second, his powerful fist was in my hair, dragging me, kicking and screaming out of the closet. My scalp was on fire. Every pore on my had screamed for relief. I tried in vain to pry his fingers from my hair but he was too strong.

"Angel, stop!" I shrieked.

"You think you can walk out on me with my son, Cressida?" He shoved my head to the floor and it hit with a thud. Fear blared to life, blooming in my belly like a dark flower.

"You had two bitches in our bedroom, Angel. This is out of hand." I blinked away the tears and tried to hold his gaze even though I was terrified.

"No, what's out of hand is your stupid ass thinking I wouldn't notice you flirting with Sam when I wasn't around. Did you fuck him, Cress? Did you let him inside your pussy like a fucking whore?" He knelt over me, his warm breath reeking of smoke and liquor. My body seized. Every muscle locking up. My breaths came in quick puffs as I kept my eye on Angel.

"Sam?" I asked, a frown creasing my face. "I've never flirted with Sam, Angel. Never." It was the truth. Sam was the main security guard. He was around me more than the others so I spoke to him more often. That was it.

"You're lying!" His long fingers curled around my throat and squeezed until black dots floated in front of my eyes. "I decided to give you a taste of your own medicine. Show you how it feels to be married to a fucking slut." He let my throat go with a shove and I gasped for air, trying to scramble away from him. I managed to back against the wall and pull my knees up to my chest. "Now maybe you'll appreciate the fact that I fuck my bitches outside of the house." He crawled over to me and I turned my head away from him when he got close. On the nightstand by the bed, I saw a small pile of powdery white cocaine. I glanced at Angel and saw white residue around his nostrils.

I knew it. I fucking knew he was high out of his mind. My stomach lurched. I prayed that today wouldn't be the day he finally hit me. He'd choked me, shoved me, and broken things around the house but he'd never hit me and I was terrified of what it would mean once he did.

"Now, stop being such a goddamn hypocrite." He tugged on my hair then thumped my head against the wall repeatedly. "If you can fuck other people...so can I. And I'll do it right in your face because I pay for this house. I pay for the cars and the clothes and the motherfucking shoes, Cress." My head ached with every thump against the wall. "I pay for your fucking life!" He boomed and spittle sprayed across my cheeks.

Tears leaked from my eyes as he forced me to look at him. He dug strong fingers into my cheeks until my lips puckered.

"Yo, what the fuck are you doing, Angel?" Jules rushed into the bedroom and yanked Angel's shoulder until he stumbled backward and away from me.

"Get the hell off me, Smoke. I'm talking with my wife. *Mine*. She's learning what happens when she cheats. Doesn't feel good, does it, Cress?" He sneered wiping the sweat from his brow.

"Did you hit her?" Jules asked, his teeth clenched so tightly I thought he'd grind them to dust.

"No. I didn't fucking hit her. You know me better than that. She's just in her feelings because she got a taste of her own medicine."

"I never cheated on you," I said, tears collecting in my voice.

"Whatever, bitch." Angel shook his head and moved closer to me, on the floor. "I know what I saw."

"You didn't see anything because nothing happened," I said inching to the side.

"Cress, you okay?" Julien asked. Our eyes locked for a moment and I'd never felt more ashamed of my situation before. My ribs cracked and flaked off like pieces of dust in the wind. I folded my arms across my chest defensively and avoided his gaze.

He had to think I was stupid. I felt stupid. I looked stupid. Sitting on the ground, face red, hair a mess while Angel yelled and degraded me like I was nothing. I hated that Julien had to see me like that. He had to see what my life had turned into.

"I'm fine. Can you leave?" I asked, misplaced venom in my voice. I knew he was only trying to help but I couldn't function past my embarrassment.

"Watch how the fuck you talk to my little brother, Cress. Apologize." Angel grabbed my arm, his fingers curling around my bicep while he forced me to my feet. "I said apologize!"

"Chill, Angel. She's good. She doesn't need to apologize to me. I'm leaving. I'm out." He turned without giving me a second glance and walked out of the bedroom. Angel didn't even bother to shut the door before he yanked me over to the bed and pushed me down.

"I-I have to get Nasim. He's sleeping downstairs." The glassy, vacant look in his eyes was almost worse than the dark shadowy look. I pressed my hands against his bare chest when he hovered over me, forcing my legs apart. "Angel! I have to get the baby!" I pushed against him but he was like stone. Heavy and unmovable.

"If he's sleep. Let him sleep. I need to show you who you belong to." He was so rigid pressed against my thigh as he slopped wet, inebriated kisses along my neck. Bile burned the back of my throat as I struggled against him.

"I belong to you," I said, lips quivering. Tears slipped into the hollows of my ears as I tried to convince him he didn't need to fuck me.

"You goddamn right, bitch." His words slurred together as he tugged at the waistband of his pants. I regretted wearing a skirt. I regretted coming upstairs and flipping out on him. Now, I was pinned on my back, about to be raped by my own fucking husband. "Why the hell do you have on panties, huh? Did you wear them when Sam fucked you?"

"I never fucked him, baby." I tried pleading with him in my sweetest voice but his eyes kept fluctuating between anger and vacancy. There was no getting through to him. I pressed my lips together and swallowed, trying to force the bile back down my throat.

Angel was done listening to me. He'd checked out and now he was going to do whatever he wanted to me and it didn't matter what I said or how much I begged him not to.

I felt his dick slide against my underwear and I tensed, still pushing against his tattooed chest. His hands fumbled lazily, trying to tug them aside. I braced myself when he finally managed to pull them over. Fabric and thread popped and tore as he pulled violently at the thin material between my legs.

In a last-ditch effort to escape, I pushed my ass back causing Angel to slip a little. He growled then pinned my thighs to the bed so I couldn't move while he tried to force himself inside of me.

"Please don't!" I screamed so loud my throat caught fire. "Angel, please! I love you," I sobbed, trying anything I could to make the madness stop. He was in a trance. The coke had him so high out of his mind I doubted he could even hear me.

He slid his erection against me, hard and uncoordinated, missing my entrance. He jabbed at me again and pain shot through my core. He jabbed and jabbed, never entering me, but causing pain every fucking time.

"Shit, Cress. You know I love you, girl." Wet sloppy kisses covered my lips over and over until my top lip started to numb from the coke residue on his mouth and tongue. "Fuck..." He let out one long groan before he came all over my thighs and panties. "You're mine. I need you. Don't ever leave me, okay?" His eyes shut before he collapsed on top of me, snoring.

He never even got inside of me. He still managed to make me sore. I tried to wiggle from beneath Angel's limp body but he was twice my weight. I was trapped. Literally and metaphorically. Trapped.

...

Chapter THREE

Julien

ngel waited for Cress to leave with Nasim before he
called over a few girls to end my unintentional five-year
celibacy stint. I didn't know he'd disappear with two of
them on his own to teach Cress a lesson about cheating.

When I saw how broken she was, huddled on the floor, against
the wall like that...I wanted to help her. To tell Angel to back the fuck
up. Especially after her declaration of innocence. I could tell she was
telling the truth because I had a built-in lie detector in my veins.

She pushed me away though. She didn't want my help so I left Angel and Cressida to work their marriage issues out amongst themselves. It wasn't my place to interfere.

When I came back upstairs after seeing the girls out to their Ubers, I passed Angel's bedroom and saw him knocked out on the bed. I would have kept walking but I saw movement underneath him. Something squirming. Then a shock of sandy brown hair and a silver mood ring.

"Cress?" I called out quietly. If they were in the middle of something I didn't want to interrupt.

"Jules?" Whenever that nickname came out of her plush mouth...the nickname only she called me...it brought back memories of the golden Cressida I used to look at with stars in my eyes. "Help...please." Her tiny voice reached out and cracked something inside my chest. I stepped inside the huge bedroom and crossed the open sitting area. From the looks of it, Angel passed out on top of her. Her breathing was labored and she looked like she was about to pass out.

I shoved Angel with ease and he rolled over flat on his back, still snoring. I noticed the pile of coke on the nightstand and shook my head. Was Cress sniffing coke in here with him?

She sat up and pressed her hands to her chest. It was red and mottled as she sputtered and coughed, crawling out of the bed. She slid on the floor and I saw sticky white glaze coating her thighs and skirt. My shoulders tightened and my nostrils flared as I turned my head.

"You okay?" I asked.

"I'm fine," she snapped, sniffling and pulling her skirt down. I was tired of her random catty attitude. Angel was right. Cress had changed. I passed a hand over my face and walked to the bedroom door.

"You sure?" Something wouldn't let me leave her crumpled on the floor like a piece of paper.

"I'm fine." Her voice broke. I watched her raise a trembling hand to her nose and I caught sight of the silver mood ring. I rubbed the back of my neck and walked over to her with heavy feet. I bent down and took her arm in my hand to help her stand. "Get off of me!" She sobbed, batting at me, landing a few good hits to my shoulder.

"Hey, calm the hell down, Cress. I'm helping you up. That's all." I released her arm and she straightened herself, wiping away the tears rolling down her golden cheeks.

"Sorry. I'm so used to the way Angel handles me that..." She shook her head and looked up at me. I still towered over her. I looked at the top of her head while she stared at Angel passed out on the bed and remembered how I'd get lost in her sandy galaxy of rioting curls. Even with it straightened, I liked looking at the varying shades of gold and caramel falling around her shoulders. I looked at my brother passed out on the bed tearing my eyes away from Cress's hair.

Downstairs, Nasim let out a loud cry that made Cress jump into action, rushing across the bedroom. "Clean yourself up," I said, holding my hand out. She pressed into it, her full firm tits against my palm. My face remained placid but my dick jolted to life. I dropped my hand and she swallowed.

"I need to go to him."

"I'll get him. You clean up." I looked down at her rumpled skirt then back into her eyes. They were still the clearest hazel I'd ever seen.

"Jules…you don't have to."

"He's my nephew. I got him." I walked out of the room before my dick stiffened anymore. Thankfully, holding Nasim calmed my involuntary lust. I understood why parents broke their fucking backs to give their kids the world because looking into my nephew's hazel eyes made something warm spark in my chest. I'd do anything for him.

I didn't even know if I was holding him right, but he'd stopped crying so I guess I wasn't doing anything wrong. "Hey lil man," I cooed. I fucking *cooed*. I'd never cooed at anything before in my damn life. "Can you stand up?" I asked, sitting on the floor with him. I stood him on his feet and he gripped my fingers in his chubby hands. "See? Look at you. I knew you could do it. Your daddy told me you weren't ready yet but I knew better." I smiled while I watched him balance on his feet while holding my fingers for leverage.

"Oh my god…look at him." Cress's soft voice came from over my shoulder. In a heartbeat, she was on the floor beside me. She smelled like honey and spice. I inhaled again and caught a hint of cinnamon on her skin. She was wearing different clothes now. A satin white blouse and a pair of jeans. Her hair was pulled up in a loose twist and her face was clean and fresh.

"I can't believe he hasn't sat down yet. He hates standing up for too long," she told me. I stole a quick look at her and noticed finger-sized bruises ringing her neck. The sight of them pissed me off.

"That's because Uncle Smoke is helping him." When I looked at Nasim, he smiled. It was bright and gummy.

"Uncle Jules." She smiled but she didn't look at me. Instead, she stared at Nasim while she twisted the silver mood ring around on her finger. "Thank you for helping me out upstairs." Her words were rushed, quiet, and coated in shame.

"It's nothing. Did he pass out on top of you?"

"Yeah. Usually, when that happens, he wakes up but I guess he was just…really tired." Her slender throat flexed when she swallowed.

"Tired? I know Angel's on coke, Cress. You don't have to cover for him." Nasim made a loud, happy sound then dropped to his knees and crawled over to the playpen grabbing the side, and pulling up. "Oh shit, look at him." I beamed with pride.

"Jules," Cressida nudged my side and I tossed her an apologetic look. "It's bad enough Angel has a nasty mouth around him."

"My bad." I couldn't stop marveling at my nephew standing up. I mean he was using the playpen for balance, but it was still amazing. "Can I ask you something?" I stole another glance at her when I shouldn't have. I didn't need to see her lush, deep pink lips or the copper splash of freckles dancing across the bridge of her nose and the apples of her cheeks. I knew her eyes were the color of champagne and her smile was a bright star in the sky. I didn't need to look at her again. But I did…

"Um…sure." She shrugged.

A million questions popped into my head to ask her. What the fuck made her change? Did she ever finish school? Did she cheat on Angel?

"Before I talk to Angel about his coke habit...tell me now, are you on that shit too?" I watched Nasim gumming the side of the playpen and blowing raspberries in the air and my chest squeezed. Maybe I was capable of love. I damn sure felt something when I looked at that little boy. I looked at the backs of my hands. At the skull and then the rose.

Beauty. Death. Love. Hate.

Maybe I was capable of them all?

"What?" Cressida's gasp brought me back to the present moment. "You think I'm using coke, Julien. Are you fucking kidding me?"

"Hey, watch your mouth. My nephew is right there." I pointed and Cress's laugh caught me off guard. It caught her off guard too. She blinked with wide eyes when the sound popped out of her mouth. "Ah, I still know how to make you laugh." I wet my lips and looked at her.

"I guess some things never change." She waved at Nasim when he looked at her from the other side of the room. "To answer your question, Jules...no. I'm not using coke." She fluttered long thick lashes that framed her almond-shaped eyes.

"Good." I nodded my head.

"What did Angel tell you about me?" The words kind of spilled out of her mouth like she had to work up the nerve to say them.

"Nothing," I said with a shrug.

"Don't do that shit." She aimed her pointer finger at me and

I caught sight of the mood ring. I checked her other finger. The fourth one on her left hand and noticed the rock sitting there. It paled in comparison to my carnival prize. Just like my skull and rose tattoos, Cressida's rings represented beauty and death. Her wedding ring represented beauty. It represented a happy, loving life. The tarnished mood ring represented death. The promise of a flower that never bloomed. A life that never grew. My skin prickled as I tore my eyes away from her outstretched finger.

"Don't do what?" I asked, staring at Nasim.

"Don't be short with me, Jules. You do that when you're avoiding something. You shut down. You get short."

"I'm not being short."

"You are. You won't say more than four words at a time." She was staring at me. Even though I wasn't looking at her, I felt her champagne eyes boring into me. "What did he tell you about me? Because you're treating me differently."

"I'm not."

"Oh my god, Julien. If you hate me now, that's cool. Let me know upfront so I can try to avoid you." She slid away from me a little and took the warm vanilla-cinnamon that clung to her golden skin. The pull to talk to her was intense. I hated it.

The entire time I was locked up, I didn't need to talk to anyone. I was a lone wolf and I liked it that way. The only person I spoke to was Angel. He kept me up to date on everything going on with Rush and the operation. He also kept me updated on things with him and Cress but now that I knew he was using coke I wondered how accurate his assessment of Cress was. Cocaine was infamous for making people irrational and paranoid.

"He told me you'd changed. That you've been flirting and cheating on him. That you fucked Sam." I eyed her, wanting to see her expression. She rolled her eyes then let out an icy laugh.

"He's fucking insane." She paused then said, "Pretend I didn't say that." Fear inched across her pale brown pools.

"Why the fuck are you so scared of him?"

"I'm not," she said swallowing and biting into that plump, bottom lip. My dick throbbed with the threat of getting hard even though I'd spent hours fucking some random girl who didn't mean anything to me. Not that Cress meant anything to me but still...

"He can be a little much sometimes," she said nervously.

"Is he abusing you, Cress?" Anger spilled into me. A knocked-over glass of red wine on a white carpet.

"No!" She squeaked, shaking her head and putting on a fake smile for Nasim. "He's never hit me." She was telling the truth but it was still wrong. My mind wouldn't let me believe her fully.

"He just yells at you and passes out on top of you when he's high, huh?"

"I don't want to talk about it, Jules. Just know he hasn't hit me yet."

"Yet? You planning on him hitting you, Cress?"

"No...leave it alone, please. Just know none of the stuff he said about me is true. I'm not cheating on him. I never flirted with Sam. I've never touched him." Hearing her say that pissed me off but I wasn't mad at her. I stood to my feet because I had to disperse some of the energy collecting in my bones. It was dark and angry.

Angel had me kill his head of security all for a fucking suspicion that he couldn't back up. I was livid. I didn't get mad like normal people though. I smoldered and plotted. I'd never plot to kill Angel but we were going to have a fucking talk.

"Are you okay?" Cress stood too but she only reached my shoulder.

"Yeah." It was a lie. She knew it because she pushed her lips to the side. I watched her do it. I stared at her mouth without any shame for a few beats.

"So, you're lying. Julien, look at me." She reached up and gripped my jaw in her hand. The smell of vanilla and cinnamon pulsed at her inner wrist.

"I don't want to talk about it," I said before pushing her hand away from my face. If she lingered there for too much longer, it would start to unearth things I'd buried years ago. Those types of things had to stay buried because life was different now. Cressida was Angel's wife. Not his girlfriend or some chick he was fucking. She was married to my brother. She had his kid for fuck's sake.

I didn't screw family over. Not like that. Angel was my brother and even thinking about Cressida in an inappropriate way was fucked up. So, I couldn't look at her curvy frame and the way having a baby had done her body good. I couldn't look at how full her tits were or how I could see the faintest outline of her nipples through the blouse she had on. I couldn't look at any of that shit because Cressida was married to Angel.

"Tit for tat, huh?" She smacked her lips together and started picking up toys that Nasim had pulled down.

"No. I just don't want to talk about it."

"Why not? Is it business stuff?" Her voice dropped to a quiet hush.

"Still nosey, I see," I muttered.

"And?" She smirked a little and her eyes twinkled playfully. Those fucking eyes were going to haunt me in my dreams tonight. Cress poked my chest with her pointer finger and I looked down at that damn mood ring. I caught her dainty wrist in my hand and held it up so I could examine the old ring.

"Why do you still have this?" The smile left her eyes and she slipped her hand out of my grasp, shoving four fingers in her back pocket. Her slim shoulders rose and fell as she aimed her gaze at the floor. I wanted to keep staring into those pale amber pools. It was my quiet indulgence. Nobody had to know Cressida's eyes were my addiction.

"It makes me think about better times, I guess." I skimmed her body, watching the way her narrow waist flared to rounded hips that she definitely didn't have in middle school or high school for that matter. "Don't tell Angel you gave it to me. He doesn't know. He thinks it's just something I have a sentimental attachment to from back in the day."

"He doesn't know I won that for you after spending all my money on those rigged games at the carnival?" The memory made me smile a little.

"You did spend all your money."

"Hey, I had sixty bucks on me and I didn't win that damn ring until the last game."

"You barely won the game. I think the guy who worked the booth felt sorry for you." She walked closer to me and bumped me with her hips. A quick jolt surged through me at the brief connection. Evidently, I still had some nuts to bust because every time I was close to Cress, I thought about fucking her. I fought the thought for as long as I could but the pull she had was stronger than ever.

"Nah, I won that shit fair and square," I chuckled. I grabbed her hand again, pulling it from her pocket, and stared at the mood ring. "What's red mean?" I quizzed, staring at the way the color morphed from jade green to scarlet.

"Excited or passionate," she told me in a breathy voice that made my dick hard as fuck.

"Are you excited?" The question jumped from my mouth because I had no idea how to hold things in when they were begging to come out.

"No." Her long lashes fluttered when she looked up at me. "This thing is old. It goes crazy sometimes." She didn't move her hand from mine and I didn't let go. I should have let go.

"Old, huh?" I wet my lips because the longer I stood near Cress, the more my mouth turned to cotton. "I guess it is pretty old."

"It is. Sometimes old things still work though." Her eyes were locked onto my mouth like heat-seeking lasers.

"True."

"You're doing it again, Jules."

"Doing...what?" My thumb skimmed the silky skin on the back

of her hand.

"Being short. What are you hiding?" Her eyes flicked back and forth over my face. Studying. Prying.

"Nothing." I looked her hair over and said, "I liked it better curly." I let her hand go so I could reach out and tug the ends of her hair. It was such a quick action but it made my dick ache. I could grab a fist full of golden strands and pull until she cried out. Until her mouth hung open and I got a glimpse of her pink tongue. Until the warmth from her breath scraped my neck.

I blinked away the rush of thoughts and stepped away from her. She stepped closer. "Well, Angel likes it straight. So it's straight."

"What does Cressida like?" I tipped my head to the side a little and mapped out the splash of copper freckles on her face.

"Cressida likes to keep the peace." She held her head down and I hated how the weight of fear held her hostage. I had no idea what her marriage with my brother was like but something wedged deep inside begged me to find out. Something wasn't right between them.

Cress cleared her throat a little tucked a lock of hair behind her ear. "I um…like your tattoos." She took my massive hand in her tiny one and brushed the pads of her fingers over the rose tattoo. "This is new. So is the skull."

Seven years ago, I had my forearms covered in tats. Now, I had two full sleeves down to my fingers. My chest was still untouched but now that I was out of prison, I'd fix that.

"Yeah, I got them before I went inside," I told her. "Beauty," I said pointing to the blossoming red rose that covered the entire back of my hand. "And death." I pointed to the skull.

"That's so macabre."

"That's life, Cress. There's beauty in the macabre aspects too. You can't relegate beauty to just the roses. The skulls and bones need to be appreciated too."

"I think that's the most you've talked since you walked through the door today, Jules." She took my other hand and studied the skull. "Do you still find beauty in the bones?" When she looked at me, something buzzed between us. Something buzzed inside of me. It was the beautiful hum in my blood that happened before I killed someone. The same one that screamed beauty and art. I looked at Cress and saw all of those things.

"I'm a monster. Bones are the most beautiful to me."

"You're not a monster, Julien." She shook her head and traced the outline of my skull tattoo.

"That's sweet but I know what I am. I know who I am."

"You're Julien Jean. Jules. My *friend*. Not a fucking monster or whatever dark shit Angel tells you so he can use you."

"He's not using me," I frowned. Hearing her say that put my lust back in check. Angel wasn't using me. He was used to being the center of attention though and I didn't give a fuck about things like that. I wasn't shallow. If anything, I was too deep.

"Okay…" she said holding her hands up. "All I'm trying to say is you're not a monster."

"I kill people, Cress. Bad men. And I love it. I'm fucked up and dark."

"Deep down you're…"

"The deeper you dig, the darker I get." I didn't want to leave any room for her romanticized view of me to flourish. I knew who I was and I wasn't making excuses or trying to hide it. Cressida knew what family she married into. She knew the darkness that ran through us like a vein of onyx. There was no covering my bones with roses.

"Yo, yo!" Angel swayed into the room. His mood was on one hundred and I knew he was still bouncing from the coke he did earlier. His pupils were dilated black spots. He tossed on that charming smile like no other, slapping me on the back.

"Look at my man Nasim. He's rolling around this room. What did you call it, Cress?" I asked, folding my arms across my chest.

"Cruising," she said, fidgeting with her mood ring.

"Yeah, look at him cruising. You said he wasn't ready when you came for visitation earlier this month," I chided.

"Shit, I guess I was wrong," Angel grinned then bent down to pick Nasim up in his arms. "Look at you, boy! You'll be walking before the end of the month." He turned his too-wide smile to Cress. "He's a grown man now, baby. You're going to have to stop that bottle feeding, breast milk shit. My man is ready to eat. Right, Nas?" He munched his son's fingers causing giggles.

Cress's shoulders crowded around her ears while she folded her arms across her body in a semi-hug.

"He's only eight months. He's transitioning to solids now. He already eats apple sauce, oatmeal, and fruits and veggies but he still needs breast milk."

"I said he's done. Wean him." Angel said it with finality before handing Nasim over to Cress and motioning for me to follow him. Before I left the living room, I locked onto those champagne orbs and indulged in the flare of heat that crackled between us.

"What's up, hermano?" I said once Angel and I were alone in the kitchen. He grabbed a decanter from the ornate liquor cabinet tucked in a nook near the fridge and set it on the counter.

"I know your D.A.R.E. graduate ass won't try any coke but do you want a drink?" Angel's eyes were off. Something jagged and dangerous lurked there.

"Yeah, I'll take a drink." He poured two glasses and slid one toward me. I didn't need to know what I was about to drink. Only that it would take the edge off my thoughts about Cress.

"You thought about when you want to have your welcome home party, Smoke?"

"I don't need a party. I'm good."

"My little brother is home after five years and you think I'm not going to go all out? I have the hottest fucking club in Miami. Shit, the hottest club in Florida and you think we're going to sit at home and watch Netflix? Nah. We're partying. Let's do it this weekend. I'll do half-price drinks and full-price drugs." He chuckled and held his glass up. We toasted then he knocked his back like it was a shot.

"You need to chill," I laughed.

"Nah, you need to stop babysitting that drink. Being in the pen made you soft, Smoke."

"Soft?" My nostrils flared. "Was I soft when I killed Sam like you asked me to?" I knocked my glass back too then set it next to Angel's empty one. A small gasp from the doorway turned my head. Cress stood there with Nasim on her hip, wide eyes tunneling into me. Shit, now she knew Sam was dead, and after our talk in the living room, I was sure she knew why.

"Cressida, what the fuck are you doing in here? You heard me say I wanted to talk to Smoke alone. Goddamn, I swear they make these bitches stupider by the day."

"I'm sorry. I was grabbing a bottle for Nas. He's hungry."

"He's off bottles now." Angel's voice rose on a sharp angle that made Cress wince. She said he hadn't hit her but she was damn sure acting like a battered woman. Nothing about that shit set well with me.

Our mother would have flipped the fuck out if she even *thought* Angel was hitting his wife. She'd been abused before by Angel's dad and she told us both to never hit women. I took it to heart but I didn't know if my brother did.

"Give him some of that baby food but he's not a fucking newborn. You saw him cruising around the living room. He's growing up."

"Okay...but what am I supposed to do with the bottles I've already pumped?" Frustration inched in on Cress. She pressed her lips together in a line and narrowed her eyes at Angel. He pushed away from the island and stormed over to the fridge. After tearing the door open, he grabbed bottles of what I assumed was breast milk and started emptying them down the drain one after the other while Cress made a strangled noise.

"Angel, stop! Do you know how much I had to pump? That was enough milk for today and tomorrow!"

"And? You think I give a fuck? I told you I wanted him weaned now and that's what I meant. Fuck your milk. I don't want you babying my goddamn son."

"I'm trying to give him the best possible start in life. He needs my milk during his first year of life. Even better if it's the first two years."

"What? Nah. No. We're done discussing this shit. Matter fact." He moved past me taking long strides out of the kitchen. I followed because I didn't like the tension. I didn't know if this was their normal behavior toward each other or not but if Angel put his hands on Cress, I was going to put my hands on him.

Angel stormed into Nasim's nursery and snatched Cress's breast pump off of a shelf near the crib. "Angel, cut that shit out," I said, trying to grab the pump out of his hands.

"Fuck that! I said I don't want my fucking son drinking out of a bottle anymore. I said he's done with breast milk. What I say in this house goes. Fuck Cress and whoever else doesn't agree. As long as I pay the bills in this motherfucker, what I say goes!" He slammed the pump against the wall sending pieces flying.

Nasim let out a startled cry then grabbed Cress's shirt. Angel picked up the pump and smashed it against the wall again and again until it was a broken pile of junk on the carpet. Silent tears streaked Cressida's face while she sat in the rocking chair to soothe Nasim.

"Clean this shit up, Cressida. Don't just sit in this chair babying him when I leave. Fucking dumb cunt." Angel looked at me like he was waiting for me to say something to him. I would but not in front of Cress.

I didn't know how the hell to broach the topic of his drug use but it had to be addressed. He was out of fucking control. There was very little of the Angel I knew in there. It made me wonder if he was sober when he came to visit me in prison because I never saw him waver from the big brother I'd always known. Now was a different story.

Once I knew Angel was out of the room, I knelt on the floor and started cleaning up the breast pump pieces while Cressida sat rocking Nasim and crying quietly into the top of his sandy curls. I wanted to say something to her but I had a feeling she'd snap at me to leave it alone.

At least I understood her mood swings more. I hated the way they came about but I understood them.

...

The pictures Angel showed me of Rush didn't do the place any justice. The club looked small from the outside with its exposed brick exterior and red neon sign touting the club's name in cursive letters but inside was a different story. Rush boasted a sprawling inside with crystal chandeliers hanging from the ceilings and a bar that spanned the entire inside perimeter of the club. Plush couches and booths clung to the edge of the space on a raised platform while the inner ring was sunken and had red LED lights running along the edge. When I stepped down into the inner ring, the dancefloor seemed to open up before my eyes. It was a huge space where the lights from above didn't pulse or strobe but the lighted floor under your feet did.

"This is the coolest part about Rush," Angel said. He'd told me about the dance floor but he always finished up his description by saying I had to see it to believe it. He was right. He pulled a remote from his pocket and pressed a button. The lights in the club went down and the red light turned up creating a bloody, smoky glow in the air. I was right at home. "Move around the dance floor," Angel said, lighting a cigarette.

"You know I don't move around on dance floors, man. Not my thing."

"Goddammit, Smoke. Just move. You can even walk around on it. Just try it." He let out a big sigh and shook his head like he always did when I was being difficult and it showed me that some of my brother was still in there buried under stress and a mountain of cocaine.

Begrudgingly, I moved around, walking from one spot to another. The floor lit up under my feet. Colorful pressure point orbs followed my every step. It was honestly cool as fuck.

"Damn, how much did something like this cost?" I quizzed. Angel hopped up on the raised edge of the dance floor and shrugged, blowing out a puff of smoke.

"Couple of million for a space this big."

"Shit, Angel. You have that kind of money?"

"That's what I'm trying to fucking tell you, hermano. Your big brother is the king of Miami. I run this shit." He unclipped a sleek walkie-talkie from his belt and spoke into it. "Yo, Boogie. Bring down the gift I got for Smoke."

"On my way, Angel," the gravelly voice on the other end answered.

"Boogie is my right-hand man. The one I told you about." Whenever Angel came to visit, he never used anyone's real name because he knew the feds were listening to everything he said and watching everything he did. So I knew stories about people but I didn't know their real names.

A dark-skinned man with a silvery gray beard and a bald head came over carrying a slim black box in his hand. "Thanks, Boogie. By the way, this is my little brother, Smoke." He gestured to me. I slapped hands with Boogie and said hello. "Now, I was going to wait until your welcome home party to give you this but since you don't want a party, I'm giving it to you now. I'm still throwing the party though." Angel cracked a smile then handed me the box.

Inside were ten different rings. Some were solid gold with a simple geometric design and others were diamond-studded. The clearest diamonds I'd ever seen in person. Some were ruby studded and a couple were sapphire studded.

I was in awe but I really couldn't wait to get them under a gemological microscope so I could classify the carats and exact clarity. I plucked the ruby and gold skull ring up first. That shit was so fly I knew it would be the one I never took off.

"I know you love skulls. I also know you'll spend hours looking at all the jewels and shit in those rings."

"These are dope as fuck, Angel. Thank you." I slid the ruby skull ring on my middle finger and continued to examine it. Angel even thought to have a small gold rose anchor each side of the skull. Needless to say, it was my favorite of all the rings.

"Boogie, show Smoke around the club. I'm going to make a few calls. I'll be right back." Angel disappeared up a long staircase lit with red lights that seemed to swallow him in their glow.

"Nice to finally meet you, Smoke. Angel always talks about you," Boogie said as we moved around the club.

"Thanks." I followed him listening to him explain the different rooms and how ordering drugs worked during open hours. The bottle girls took the orders and certain menu items came with specific drugs. If someone ordered an Angus burger, seared and extra pink, it meant they wanted molly. Ordering a Rush margarita with extra sugar on the side meant cocaine. I cataloged all the extra orders in my mind quietly while Boogie talked. He knew that shit like the back of his hand. I understood why he was Angel's right-hand man.

"You don't talk much, huh?" Boogie asked, eyeing me after the grand tour was done.

"Nah." I shook my head and looked around the club.

"Exact opposite of your brother." He chuckled. "The only place I can't take you without Angel is the storeroom. He's been paranoid as shit about it lately. Me, him, and the head of security are the only ones allowed back."

"Sam?" I quizzed.

"Yeah. You met him already?" He inquired.

"Something like that."

"Well, I'm not sure how long Sam will be on the entry list for the storeroom but we're the only three people Angel approved and I'm not trying to ruffle his feathers right now."

"Why won't Sam be on the entry list anymore?" I asked. We were sitting in one of the plush suede booths along the wall.

"He's on Angel's bad side right now." I could tell Boogie didn't want to divulge too much and I understood why.

"Because Angel thinks Sam is fucking Cress." I sighed, running a hand over my face.

"Oh, so he told you about that shit?" Boogie's shoulders relaxed a bit and he pushed out a quiet breath.

"A little. What's your take on it?" I rested my elbows on the table and leaned forward so I didn't miss any of what Boogie was about to say.

"Cressida is a good girl. She's worried about being a new mother, not fucking anyone behind Angel's back. He can't see that though."

Hearing Boogie say that confirmed that my gut feelings were still intact. I didn't think Cress would cheat on Angel. Once I saw he'd picked up a nasty coke habit, I knew where the paranoia stemmed from. I wondered how else he'd been terrifying Cress. I didn't even want to think about all the violent shit Nasim had witnessed in his short life.

"Honestly, I think Angel needs some help." Boogie glanced around the mostly empty club and then looked into my eyes with sincerity. "Your brother is digging himself into a hole he won't be able to get out of. I feel like I can talk to you about it because well… you're his blood."

"What kind of hole?" I asked. My eyes darted to the red illuminated stairs my brother climbed.

"He's breaking the number one rule. Don't get high on your own supply. His habit is outrageous. I'm worried about him."

I tapped my finger on the glossy tabletop and said, "Me too. I'm going to talk to him about it. I just need to get settled in first." I didn't plan on coming home to Angel's drug problem or him mentally and emotionally abusing Cress. It's amazing the shit you can hide from people in plain fucking sight.

"Keep this conversation between us but let me know if you need anything, Smoke."

I assured Boogie that our conversation wouldn't reach Angel and I meant it. Angel was my brother but if I told him that his right-hand man was worried about his stupid ass, he'd get paranoid and try to set up a hit. I didn't need another innocent man's blood on my hands. Killing Sam knowing he didn't do anything still didn't sit well with me.

"Smoke, you ready? We got business. We need to roll out." Angel flew down the steps and over to where I sat with Boogie.

"Business?" I asked, looking at my watch. Another gift from Angel along with a new phone and new clothes. The only thing missing was a fresh haircut. "Isn't Rush about to open the doors?"

"Yeah. In an hour. I'll circle back around but I want to get this shit taken care of. I finally got eyes on one of the motherfuckers who hasn't paid what he owes. His count for pills came up short. I gave him twenty-four hours to correct it and he hasn't. Now, he's hiding but I found him. I always find them." A wild glint in Angel's eyes let me know I wasn't the only dark and twisted brother.

"The little scrawny white boy who kept talking shit about having your money?" Boogie asked.

"Bingo. It's always the gringos." Angel motioned for me to follow him and I stood, tossing a peace sign up at Boogie before catching up to Angel and hearing about the second kill I was about to make in less than twenty-four hours since I'd been out of prison.

…

Chapter FOUR

Cressida

The front door beeped at four in the morning. Heavy footsteps thudded through the house and the sound of Angel's slurred words rose toward me. I was just getting Nasim back to sleep after he cried for hours on end because he didn't have his bedtime bottle. When I tried to offer him milk straight from the tap, he refused. I tried to hand express the milk engorging my breasts but I could only get out about four ounces. It wasn't nearly enough. I needed my pump.

I wanted to cry angry tears every fucking time I thought about the way Angel smashed my favorite pump to pieces. It would have been easy to buy another one but he got an alert any time I spent money. He had such a tight leash on me, it was hard to do anything without him finding out.

I always find out...

His voice rang in my ears like the forked-tongue hiss of a snake. I shuddered then stood to my feet, moving to cut the light off in Nasim's nursery. I didn't want Angel coming in and seeing me. I wasn't in the mood to talk to him. Hell, I didn't want to look at him.

I hated times like this. When I was utterly disgusted by Angel. When I loathed him and wanted to get out of the prison he kept me in more than anything. I tried like hell to leave over the years but he caught me every time. I was always stupid enough to believe his silver-tongued lies.

The one time I got the nerve to leave for good last year, I packed my bags and went to my sister Trinity's house. She took me in like she'd done every other time before. She fed me and gave me a safe place to sleep where Angel couldn't get to me without going through her. She was my therapist. My savior...or so I thought.

I found out I was pregnant while I was staying with her and I knew I had to tell Angel. I could have gotten an abortion and never said a word to him but the way my parents raised me wouldn't allow my morals to operate that way. I commended women strong enough to do what they needed to do no matter how tough it was. I wasn't that strong.

My father was a preacher. My mother was the first lady. Trinity and I were supposed to wear matching halos. We were supposed to be the epitome of the fifth commandment.

Thou shalt obey thy mother and thy father.

In my mind, if I got an abortion, I'd be fast-tracked to hell and my family would shun me. I'd never tell a soul, but I didn't want Nasim when I found out he was growing in my belly. I'd just found my backbone. Trinity was so proud of me for finally leaving. I wanted to keep making her proud but I knew better.

I tied my healing to her and that was a mistake from the start. I couldn't tie my healing to anyone. I had to do it. But I was pregnant and I had to think about my unborn child. There was no more thinking solely for myself.

When I told Angel I was pregnant, he showed up at Trinity's house and begged on his hands and knees for me to come back home. He cried. He swore he'd be a better man for our son. Then he proposed.

How could I say no?

He'd already gone behind my back to get my parents' approval. He said the magic words to them. He didn't want our child to be born out of wedlock. He wanted to do the right thing. That's all they needed to hear to shove me into his arms and tell Trinity to stop fighting my battles for me.

Just like that, I was back with Angel for good. I had a ring and a baby. My parents got a shiny new church out of the deal. A church where they were both pastors. A church three times bigger than the little one Daddy preached at when Trini and I were little. My father gave me away and married me to Angel. My entire family was there…except Trinity.

I knew I'd broken her trust. I didn't bother reaching out to her except to tell her when Nasim was born. She came to see him but after that, she stayed away and I missed her every fucking day. I hated myself for letting her down. I hated myself for believing Angel's lies.

It showed me that men can have nervous breakdowns, make the grandest of gestures, grovel and suck your goddamn toes all while lying to your face. I learned that lesson late, and now I was trapped. I spent most of my time drowning in self-loathing.

"You in here, Cress?" Angel's voice was soft. Quiet. Apologetic. I thought I would be able to hide out in the dark nursery until he passed out in bed.

I squeezed my eyes shut in the dark and swallowed the tears. "Yeah. I just put Nas down." I walked into the hallway and closed the nursery door behind myself.

One look at Angel let me know he was high as fuck. His pupils were blown wide and dark as sin. I said a silent prayer that he wouldn't wake Nasim up then prepared to go through the routine of forgiveness and reassuring him that everything was fine between us. God, I was tired of that shit.

"You know I'm sorry about earlier, right?" He said, touching my hair. I caught sight of the fine white dust settled between the grooves of his fingerprints. Anyone else would have overlooked such a tiny detail. Knowing when Angel was high or not meant the difference between a night spent in fear and a normal, quiet night for me.

"I know," I said, trying to lighten my voice. Inside, I was screaming at him. Cursing him the fuck out for pouring out my breast milk.

"Sometimes, you do stupid shit and it pisses me off then I fly off the handle and you know how I get when I'm a little high." He dragged his thumb down the center of my chin. His hands smelled like the smoke from Rush. "I promise to do better but you have to promise to listen more. You test me around every corner when you know I'm only looking out for you and Nas." His large palms scooped my face up, making me look into his nearly black eyes. "I'm going to fix this milk issue tomorrow morning. We'll all get back to normal. Or our new normal while Smoke stays here."

Hearing him mention Julien made me remember when I walked in on the tail end of a conversation I shouldn't have. The conversation where Julien admitted to killing Sam. He told me he was a monster but even knowing what kind of shit Jules did, I didn't think he was a monster. At least not one I was scared of.

Did that make me a monster too? Or someone capable of seeing the good in them?

"You're so fucking beautiful. I haven't told you that lately, Cress." His lips pressed against my forehead and all I could think about was running blindly into the night with Nasim strapped to my chest. I wanted to put as much space between me and Angel as possible. He'd never let me leave though and if he ever did, it would be a trap. He'd find me and kill me. God knows what would happen to Nasim.

"Thank you." I nuzzled against his touch when I wanted to revolt.

"I'm serious. You're so beautiful. Even if I fuck other bitches, they don't hold a candle to you. That's why you can't ever leave me. I'd be lost without your beauty, baby." He took a step back and looked at me. Black grease slicked my skin where ever his eyes wandered. I suddenly regretted wearing a lacy racerback tank top and tiny black shorts.

"Shit, I wish I weren't so tired. I'd fuck you right against the wall." He bit his bottom lip and shook his head at me regretfully. I hoped he fucked some girl at Rush so I didn't have to deal with him.

"You're too tired?" I faux pouted, folding my arms across my chest. I was honestly stopping his probing eyes. I was only putting on an act to seem interested. It would make my life easier.

"Yeah. Tonight, at Rush was crazy. Then I took Smoke with me on a job to hit that kid who stole from me."

"Did Jul— I mean Smoke…kill him?"

A full smile bent Angel's lips as he regarded me. "Baby, you have to see Smoke in action. When that boy gets a knife in his hand, it's like watching a conductor at the head of an orchestra. He moves so fast. That little fucker didn't know what hit him." A yawn slipped out and he shook his head. Disheveled black hair fell into his eyes. So many women would kill to have my spot and I'd give it up gladly. I didn't give a fuck how gorgeous Angel was.

"I'm going to bed before the sun comes up. Bring your beautiful ass to bed in the next five minutes, Cress."

"Okay. I'm just going to get a glass of water." I smiled. I needed to put distance between us. I was already tired of him.

"We have water in the mini-fridge. Come on." His voice didn't have an edge…yet.

"You know I like water out of a glass. I'll be right back." I knew when he hit the bed he would pass out if I was beside him or not. I moved down the steps and into the kitchen. Every damn step I took made my swollen breasts hurt.

If I could get out even a few ounces, I'd feel some relief. In the darkness, I grabbed a glass, lifted my shirt, and started gently massaging my engorged breast.

"Cress?" The disembodied voice came from the dark corner where the table was. I nearly jumped out of my skin. I tugged my shirt down and swallowed.

"Jules? Is that you?" I snatched my shirt down and let out a few curse words under my breath.

"Yeah, sorry if I scared you."

"Why the hell are you sitting in the dark?" I hissed.

"I might be a little drunk," he confessed. "I haven't had a drink in five years. It's hitting me quick."

"Lightweight," I teased.

"Wow. Little preacher's kid Cress is giving me shit about being a lightweight?"

"I keep telling you, I'm not little Cress anymore." I folded my arms over my aching breasts.

"You're definitely not little Cress anymore." His voice was low and rough and it made me throb. He wasn't little Smoke anymore either. "Let me get the fuck out of your way. I'll go to bed," he said.

"You can stay. I need to hand express some milk but..." I made a frustrated sound and pressed my palms against the counter.

"What's wrong?" He actually sounded like he cared. I wasn't used to that from Angel. When he asked what was wrong, it was because I was annoying him.

"For some reason, I can't seem to express more than a few ounces. Earlier, I almost spilled everything I expressed because I couldn't hold the damn cup and pump." Until I felt tears burning my eyes, I didn't realize how much I was stressing over pumping. Jules seemed to dissolve my guard.

"Hear me out, Cress. I'm not a pervert or anything like that but I can hold the cup for you while you pump. I'll close my eyes."

My heart stuttered in my chest at his words. Not because it was a kind gesture but because I was suddenly aware of how fine Jules was. How tall and thick he was with his perfect muscles and tattoos. Dammit. I couldn't pull my boobs out in front of him...but Christ they hurt.

Even though there was nothing sexual about Jules holding a cup for me while I pumped, my body felt like a giant antenna. Anticipation charged through my blood at the thought of lifting my shirt and baring my breasts in the dark with him. All six-foot-something-inches and two-hundred something pounds of him. I sank my teeth into my bottom lip and tried to quiet my body.

"Are you sure?" I asked, collecting myself.

"I wouldn't have offered otherwise."

"Okay," I blurted quietly. "Close your damn eyes." I heard the chair scrape the floor as he stood. His footsteps came closer, then I saw the fresh white cotton of his t-shirt and the glint of a chain around his neck. Must have been a gift from Angel.

"I'll be a gentleman." He smiled. Those fucking lips...they looked so soft. "I won't sneak a peek." The faint smell of expensive liquor lingered on his breath but it didn't turn my stomach like it did with Angel. With Jules, I wanted to suck the cognac from his lips and tongue.

Fuck.

Stop it Cressida.

Angel would kill me and Julien if he even thought I was attracted to his brother.

"You know your brother would flip out if he knew."

"For what?" He chuckled. "It's not like I'm hand-expressing you." The thought made something warm zip through me. What the fuck was wrong with me? "I'm closing my eyes now. Just put my hand on the cup and I'll hold it still for you."

I watched his eyes fall shut and I paused a beat to study his features. He hadn't had a haircut yet so his dark hair was thick and wavy. It was just at the point before his hair started to curl and spiral outward. I traveled down the bridge of his bold nose and stopped at those lips.

I shook my head and took his hand in mine. I lingered a

little, dragging my fingertips over the thick veins in his tattooed forearms. The dense muscles beneath his smooth skin flexed in response to my touch. I guided his hand to the glass on the counter and his fingers gripped it tight. The skull on the back of his hand stared at me, reminding me I couldn't indulge. Not only was he my brother-in-law, but my husband would kill me. I just had to keep repeating that to myself.

"Tell me when to let go."

"Okay. Keep it just like that." I lifted my shirt and began pumping my engorged breasts one at a time. "God this is embarrassing," I groaned listening to the way my milk squirted into the glass.

"It shouldn't be embarrassing. You're doing what you have to do." He was quiet for a while then he said, "I'm sorry Angel broke your pump. That was fucked up. He had no right."

"You don't have to apologize for what your brother does, Jules." I must have been more relaxed this time when I was hand expressing because I filled up the glass and still had more milk coming down. "Shit. Hold on, I need another glass."

"Damn, Cress. You need a bucket instead?" Jules joked, cracking a smile. It was such a beautiful smile.

"Shut up. I guess I'm more relaxed now because earlier I got about four ounces. Nas was pissed."

"I bet. You try to give me three ounces of food and I'd be pissed too."

I sat the empty glass on the counter and began squeezing

my breasts again. I watched Jules to see if he really had his eyes closed. I even paused to wave a hand in front of his face. He was true to his word.

When I was finally done, I felt ten pounds lighter and my breasts didn't ache anymore. I pulled my shirt down and let out a sigh of relief. "All done," I told Julien. "You can open your eyes."

"Everything good?" He quizzed. He only looked me over briefly but the way he lingered on my breasts and hips made me burn with both desire and self-consciousness. Did he think I'd gotten fat after having Nasim? Did my boobs look funny? Uneven? They did that sometimes if I went too long without pumping. Like today.

"Yup. Thank you so much, Jules."

"You're welcome."

"Now I have to figure out how to hide the milk from Angel. Before y'all left today, he also took the liberty of tossing out all my frozen milk too."

"What the fuck? I need to talk to him." He moved over to the kitchen table while I poured the milk into two eight-ounce freezer bags.

"Don't bother. He's not going to listen. He doesn't listen to anyone but himself." I shook my head and looked around for somewhere to hide my milk. Jules got up and went to the freezer. He pulled out a carton of ice cream and sat it on the counter beside my milk. "Put the bags in there."

"You're brilliant, Jules!" I was way too excited to stash my milk in an ice cream container. "Wait, how'd you know that was in there?"

"I might have been rummaging for food. I haven't had good ice cream in five years. I went straight for the good stuff. I ate like half the carton. There's plenty of room."

"Your greed saved my life." I laughed as I plunked full bags of milk inside and closed it up.

"Saved your life? I thought you said Angel didn't hit you."

"He doesn't." I put the carton back in the freezer then hopped on the island, swinging my bare legs. "He's just…"

"Abusive in every other way?" Jules sat beside me on the island. He was so close I felt his body heat and smelled the faint hint of deodorant and whatever lotion he had on that made his skin glow like smokey honey.

I stared at the backs of my hands, looking between Jules's mood ring and Angel's wedding and engagement rings. I found myself wishing I'd chosen the path of the mood ring.

"Angel is…"

"Not who you thought he was when you married him?"

Ugh, why was he doing that? Peering straight through the perfectly crafted excuses I'd trained myself to spew out over the years. Every time I said this shit around Bree, she never batted an eye. She went along with it. Jules was calling me out around every corner. It made my stomach tighten.

"It's probably the coke. If he gets off that then…" It was the start of another lie.

"Maybe the old Angel would come back?" He took my hand in his, touching the mood ring. It betrayed me by turning bright red.

Jules had hope for the old Angel but I didn't. I wasn't in love with the old Angel either.

"It wouldn't make a difference if he did," I said with a simple shoulder shrug. Jules's fingers traced the mood ring over and over. My nipples tightened under my shirt with each pass.

"Why are you with him, Cressida?" My name on his lips was sinful and rich. His gritty, deep voice let loose that damned legion of butterflies with their steel wings, beating inside my belly.

How did I tell Julien that I was with his brother because he went to jail? Because he was something to do to numb the confusion and pain I was in during that time?

"I…love him." I tried to spit the lie out but it fell flat on the floor. A stain on the truth.

"Lying ass," Jules said, letting my hand go.

"Okay, I'll answer your question truthfully but promise me you're still the same Jules you were before you went inside. The one who'd guard a secret with his life. The one who marched to the tune of his own drum."

"I'm still him, Cress. I'd never mention what we talk about to Angel." He stared into my eyes and I had to press my thighs together…hard. Something in those deep brown eyes unraveled me.

"Please don't. I've created a careful balance in our marriage and if it got destroyed, I don't know what would happen to me or Nasim."

"You have my word, sweetheart." A string tugged at something solid in my core. He pressed his palm to his chest and gave me those sincere dark eyes that I didn't realize I missed.

I nodded my head and looked down at the floor. A sweep of

golden hair hid my face, thankfully. "I never loved him. I started dating him because…my parents liked him. Plus, he showed up to church every Sunday and they knew he was about to open Rush. In their eyes, he was a smart, god-fearing businessman on the come up."

A laugh flew out of Jules's mouth as he shook his head. "Your parents clearly didn't know the real Angel."

"Exactly. Angel was cool but he wasn't what I wanted. I was just too afraid of my parents to do anything about it."

"So, you let them steer your life?" Jules asked.

"Basically." A frown weighed my lips down. "And I couldn't tell them about the guy I'd liked since middle school."

"Oh yeah?" He turned to look at me. "What was wrong with that guy? I mean if you liked him since middle school why not give him a chance?"

"Because when I was in middle and high school I wasn't allowed to date. I had to keep my nose in the books. Books before boys, because boys bring babies," I recited from memory. Daddy gave me and Trini the same speech all the time. He was serious too. We couldn't date until we were in college. "By the time I graduated high school and was in my first year of college, the guy I liked got locked up. He took the fall for someone he loved. It was stupid."

"Damn. That hurts," he chuckled with his fine ass. It was crazy to me that Angel had never been to jail a day in his life. He'd been pampered by everyone in his family and was considered the pretty boy between him and Julien but the presence Jules had was overwhelming. Sitting on the island with me in just a white t-shirt and a pair of jeans, he was sexier than his big brother. Swag oozed from him and he didn't even try.

"Well, it's true. He was stupid but noble nonetheless."

"He was doing anything to save his brother." Jules played along with my faux anonymous conversation and I appreciated him for it. Admitting that I stupidly stumbled into a marriage with the wrong brother was too much to say outright. "That's what you do for family. Even if it means missing out on a great girl because of it." A sad smile lifted his lips and he brushed my hair behind my shoulder.

The knot in my throat was massive and barbed. I leaned into his touch ever so slightly. Not enough to be inappropriate but enough for him to notice. I didn't know how much he cared. Everyone thought Smoke was dangerous but, in my opinion, Julien was far more dangerous than Smoke even though they were one in the same.

"I wish he stuck around," I said.

"I'm sure he wishes the same thing. It's gotta make a man feel a certain way to see the only girl he ever liked married to his brother."

"I'm sure I wasn't the only girl he liked." I smiled down at my knees.

"A girl like you? I'm sure you were the only girl he liked. If he's anything like me…" He slid a finger down my arm and goosebumps told on the way he made me feel. "He fucked countless girls but he only liked one."

"Well, that makes me feel like shit," I exhaled.

"Don't. I'm sure the guy you liked is cool with being your friend." Another finger sliding against my warm skin. This time on my thigh. Fuck. I was going to melt into a sugary puddle right on the counter. There would be so much of me melted that I would ooze onto the floor.

"You don't think it'll be hard being friends?" I asked in a hush.

"Hard as fuck. But necessary. I'm sure he doesn't want to hurt his brother and turn the one girl he liked into something she'd regret." He brushed his tattooed knuckles along my cheekbone.

He hopped off the counter and stood between my open legs. My heart dropped to my knees. He pulled his pristine white t-shirt off and underneath was a thin, ribbed, white tank top that molded to his chiseled muscles and bunched around his trim waist. I almost drooled.

"Julien," I said, barely audible over the roaring in my ears.

"Put this on and I'll answer your question." He licked his lips then let his eyes wander down to my chest. I was leaking milk through my shirt.

Goddammit.

I took his shirt and put it on over mine while cursing. Jules laughed a little and shook his head, taking his place beside me on the counter. "I'm so sorry," I said pulling the warm cologne-scented shirt over my head. "I thought…"

"I know. It's cool. I was just being a gentleman, Cress." A gentleman who was in a tank top with glorious muscles and vibrant tattoos on display. "Now, what did you want to ask me." He clasped his big hands together and I honed in on the intricate rose tattoo.

"Oh, yeah…um. Why does Angel insist on everyone calling you Smoke instead of your actual name? I like Julien. It's beautiful." I nudged him with my shoulder. My wandering fingers reached out to touch the ruby skull ring on his finger.

"He never told you that story before?"

"Nope. Angel is tight-lipped."

"You know we have different dads, right?"

"Yeah. I know that much." I gave a short nod.

"Well, Angel is five years older than me. Mom had him when she was young. His dad's parents made them get married. My mom's parents didn't want her marrying his dad but his parents were paying for everything including a one-way plane ticket out of Columbia."

"So, they let her go ahead with the marriage," I said quietly. Jules nodded his head.

"She was miserable when she got to America. Angel's dad was controlling and abusive."

Hearing that made my muscles stiffen.

Like father, like son.

"She started getting close with a guy at her job. He was her escape. They eventually fell in love and..." He held up his hands. "I was conceived."

"Seriously? That's how it happened?"

"Yup. When Mom found out she was pregnant with me, she told Angel's dad she wanted a divorce. He wouldn't sign the papers. So she went to work one day and didn't come back home. Angel was with Grandma so when my mom got off, she went to pick him up. She planned to leave the country with my dad. She wanted to go back to Columbia to her parents."

I couldn't stop listening to his story. I'd never heard it before because Angel didn't talk about his mother at all. It was an off-limits topic and I knew better than to push.

"Grandma told Angel's dad that Mom was planning to run back to Columbia."

"Damn, she ratted your mother out like that?" I sighed.

"Yeah. It was fucked up. Angel's dad decided to sign the divorce papers and my mother went to live with my dad. She was going to give birth in America so I could be a citizen then she was going to take us all back to Columbia for a while.

Angel's family hated my mother. They called her out of her name for cheating on Angel's dad and getting pregnant while she was still married. They hated her even more for falling in love with and having a baby by a black man." He shook his head and paused for a minute like the memory still cut him deeply. "When I was born, Angel's dad took him and told Mom that she wasn't leaving the country with Angel. He told her she could take the smoke baby but leave his son."

"Are you fucking kidding me?" I blurted, narrowing my eyes.

"Nope. Angel called me Smoke every time we saw each other. He rarely called me by my name. I was so young that I didn't understand the insult. Angel didn't understand it either but it stuck."

"Jesus, Jules. That's not okay." It made me hate his nickname even more. "If Angel's grandmother was his dad's mom, how did you end up with her after your mother died?"

"She was the only relative that would take both of us. She hated me though. She called me Smoke too. Told Angel all the time how handsome he was because he was olive-skinned with silky black hair while I had smokey brown skin and curly hair. I was always the black sheep."

"All because you were mixed?"

"Yeah. Then there's the whole bastard child thing too. Grandma never let me forget that. She'd pray for my soul every Sunday in your dad's church because she didn't want me to go to hell even though my existence was an abomination." The sadness in his voice broke me inside.

"This is going to sound weird but…can I give you a hug?" Tears blurred my vision.

"You don't have to ask. You're the only girl I like…remember?" He hopped down from the island, tall and broad then stood between my legs again. That time it wasn't because he was going to give me his shirt.

I reached up and pushed my fingers through his almost wavy, almost curly hair then hooked my arms around the back of his neck, pulling him close. My lips and nose brushed against the side of his neck and I caught a whiff of soap and lotion and the last remnants of Rush that usually repulsed me when I smelled it on Angel. On Julien, it smelled like heaven.

His strong hands fixed on my waist and he pulled me right to the edge of the counter so I had to balance some of my weight against him. I was trying not to press my breasts against him because my tank top was wet and I didn't want to soak through his shirt but he pressed me against him. Against his impossibly hard chest and abs.

Julien's hand slipped down to my hips and he gripped them tighter the longer we stayed embraced. I spread my legs wider for his bulk and he pulled me even closer so that my ass was barely on the counter. My pussy was soaked.

That hug was so wrong. I refused to pull away though. I needed the connection. I needed it like I needed air. I inhaled his warm scent and he let his head drop, burying his nose in my hair. I thought I was going to come just from that lingering hug.

"I'm so sorry you were raised in such fucked up circumstances," I said trying to bring myself back to the present moment and ignore the lustful fog swirling around me. "I can't imagine anyone ever treating Nasim differently just because I'm black and Angel is Columbian. That's insane to me."

"I'm okay, Cress." His deep voice rumbled in his chest and the vibrations pushed through to my ribs, soaking into my heart.

"Still…it's fucked up. You didn't deserve that." We fell quiet again, still locked in that embrace. My thighs pressed against his sides and he pulled back abruptly. I knew it was too much but it had been so long since I'd been hugged and touched like I mattered. Like I meant something to someone.

"Thanks. I'm going to go to bed now before…" His words trailed off and I wondered what he wanted to fill the blank with. He jabbed his thumb over his shoulder and nodded at me before turning quickly and walking out of the kitchen.

I sat in the dark silence for a while before getting up enough nerve to go upstairs and lay beside a man I hated.

Just like I thought, when I got upstairs Angel was passed out. He barely got out of his shirt and he still had on the same pants. I peeled Jules's shirt off and folded it up, placing it in the bag I kept packed and hidden in the closet. I changed into a cotton nursing tank and eased into bed beside Angel.

The weight of choosing the wrong brother settled in my stomach like rocks. I hated myself so much. How could I be so fucking stupid? I should have waited for Jules. The sour taste of regret collected in my throat. Spikes of disappointment stabbed at me until tears leaked from my eyes. I wet my pillow with silent shame until I fell asleep from exhaustion.

…

The sound of Nasim crying and babbling in his room woke me up at seven in the morning. I looked to my side and noticed Angel was gone. He left me a note that said:

Cress,

Me and Smoke went out to do some business. I left you money for lunch and shopping. Be home by noon. I have someone coming to the house for you.

Angel

I rolled my eyes at the note and went to grab Nasim. When I reached inside his crib, I saw one of his blankets covering something boxy at the opposite end. My eyes narrowed as I balanced him on my hip. "Hey, baby boy. Mommy's here." I kissed his tear-soaked cheek and he settled down, grabbing at the scarf I'd tied my hair up with. With my free hand, I tugged the blanket off the thing in Nasim's crib.

It was a new breast pump with a note stuck to the top. A smile crossed my face. Angel actually fixed something he said he'd fix. I put Nasim on the floor to crawl around while I grabbed the breast pump and examined the note Angel left.

Cress,

Hide this one.

Jules

I blinked over and over at the neat, blocky handwriting and then looked at Nas. "Did uncle Jules come in here earlier?" I asked like he'd answer me. The smile on my face grew until my cheeks hurt. *Jules* got me a new pump. Not Angel.

Of course Angel wouldn't get me a fucking pump. What was I thinking? How the hell did Julien sneak this pump past his brother? The man didn't miss anything. Every time I tried to sneak something past him, he caught me and I paid for it dearly. He restricted my money to pennies or he yelled at me and called me everything but what my parents named me.

I wanted to call Jules but I didn't have his number and I didn't want to give Angel any reason to be suspicious. I went through the house checking all the rooms to make sure I was alone, then I fed Nasim a small bowl of oatmeal before opening my pump and putting it together.

It felt so good to relieve my breasts. Nasim was happy to get a bottle at snack time.

Jules had me floating on a cloud from that simple gesture of kindness. Okay…and that hug from last night.

···

Just like Angel said, someone came by the house at twelve. I made sure to call Bree over in case I needed moral support for whatever Angel set up. "Girl, you're paranoid. Angel isn't going to do anything to hurt you. It's probably a massage or something. Shit, if he was my man, I'd sit back and be pampered. Let him take care of you, Cress."

"I am but I'm always on eggshells around him," I told her.

"Have you talked to him about the coke? That's the only real problem I see."

"You don't see everything," I muttered, heading to the front door.

"Oh my god, Cress…is he hitting you?" Her arched eyebrows pulled together in the middle of her forehead as she scanned me for visible bruises.

"No. Angel doesn't hit me." Bree pressed a palm to her chest and pushed out a rush of air.

"Thank god because it would be hard helping you kill him." I shook my head at her but silently thanked God I had someone to talk to who cared.

When I opened the door, a tall, slender man dressed in a plaid shirt and khakis smiled at me. He was rolling a black suitcase behind him that made me uneasy. Why the hell did Angel have to get rid of Sam? I was used to having at least one security guard I could call on.

"Hello, Mrs. Delgado. I'm Dr. Ortiz. Your husband said he told you I was coming by."

"Doctor?" I said, folding my arms. "And you're here why?"

"To see you. Excuse me," he said politely as he stepped his long legs into my house without an invitation. "Your husband expressed concern about your mental health surrounding nursing your son, Nasim." Dr. Ortiz looked over his shoulder and I did too. Two of Angel's men marched up the steps and into the wide-open foyer, flanking the doctor. My pulse quickened. Fear set in as a million questions popped into my head.

This wasn't the first time Angel had a doctor come to the house and see me. The last time he did it, he had a gynecologist come remove my IUD while Sam and another security guy stood guard. It was one of the times I left him only to come back after he'd shoved piles of broken promises and gifts down my throat.

"Hello, Mrs. Delgado. We're here to make sure everything goes smoothly," one of the taller-than-skyscraper men said. That did nothing to ease my fears. I felt like a cornered animal ready to break out and claw my way to freedom.

"What the fuck is going on?" Bree snapped loudly. I was terrified but having my best friend by my side made the situation a little more tolerable. "Why does Cressida's little ass need two big guards and a doctor?"

"We answer to Angel. Not a fucking bottle girl." The guard sneered at her, his top lip curling in disgust like Bree was some piece of shit on the street.

"Fuck you!" She spat. "I want to know why y'all came busting in here talking about making sure things go smoothly."

"Mrs. Delgado," Dr. Ortiz smiled at me, locking onto my eyes. "Let's go have a seat and I'll let you know what's going to happen."

"You can tell me now. Right here," I said, trying to keep my voice calm and even. Nerves jittered through my body, ping-ponging back and forth. I pushed my hand through my hair and then curled my fingers into tight, nervous fists at my sides.

"It's better discussed calmly. Ma'am, can you leave?" Dr. Ortiz turned to Bree and she rolled her eyes before flipping him off.

"The hell I am. Cress is my best friend and if something is going on with her medically, I'm going to be right there for support."

"Why don't you guys take her into the kitchen to get something to drink?" The doctor eyed the security and they obliged, picking Bree up by each arm and hauling her off cursing and kicking, into the kitchen. "Let's go into the sitting room, shall we?" His voice was so quiet and smooth like he wasn't barging in my house and forcing something down my throat.

Fear continued to mount inside of me until my steps were stiff and slow on the way to the living room. I sat on the couch with this doctor I'd never seen or heard of before and looked at him, waiting for an explanation.

"As I said before, Cressida, Angel is concerned about how breastfeeding is affecting your mental health. He said you were stressing over pumping and feeding your son."

"I'm not stressing over it. He wants me to stop giving Nasim breast milk and I told him that at his age, he still needs it. That's it. I don't need whatever anti-depressant he's trying to put me on." Angel had done that before too. Had a doctor give me anti-depressant pills because I wasn't happy enough being his wife and the mother of his child.

"Oh, you misunderstand, Mrs. Delgado. I'm not here to give you pills. I'm here to give you a shot of Dostinex." I blinked at his words wondering when they were supposed to make sense.

"And what is that?" I asked, a humorless laugh rolling off my lips.

"It's a medicine called Cabergoline that suppresses milk production." He opened his rolling suitcase and inside were all sorts of individually wrapped syringes and glass bottles of medicine. My blood went cold.

"No. Absolutely not." I stood up and rubbed my slick palms on my pants. "You can leave now and take those men with you. I'm not getting a shot to dry up my milk."

"It's to help you not stress about producing enough milk."

"I produce more than enough! Angel is trying to control me. Why can't any of you people working for him understand that?" I tossed my hands in the air.

"Calm down, Mrs. Delgado. We're all working for what's best for you and Nasim."

"You're a fucking doctor! You know my son still needs my milk."

"He's eight months old. His diet should be varied now. He doesn't need to solely rely on your milk for nutrients."

"He eats a varied diet. This is ridiculous. You can leave now. I'm sorry you came for nothing."

"Oh, you don't understand, Cressida, your husband said you're to get the shot no matter what. I'm sorry." His apology was hollow while his eyes flashed remorse.

"Cress!" Bree's frightened voice came from somewhere else in the house right before the two hulking guards came into the living room. "You can't do this to her!"

"Please, hold her tight. I just need her arm. The shot is intramuscular," Dr. Ortiz said, donning latex gloves and tearing into a sealed syringe. My heart pumped fear and sweat dotted my brow and trickled down my spine. Angel's men dug their strong fingers into my arms and without any effort, carried me, legs swinging to the couch.

I fought the guards until my heart thumped through every part of my body. I fought them until I was out of breath and my voice came out as a hoarse creek. I fought them until my eyes burned from tears.

Dr. Ortiz still gave me the injection to dry my milk up. He gingerly cleaned my arm with alcohol, tapped the bubbles from the syringe, and eased the needle's point into my sensitive flesh while I sobbed. I was done breastfeeding my son even if it wasn't my choice.

What I wanted never mattered. I was living in Angel's world and what he said was law. I was his prisoner and it was all my fucking fault. I hated myself even more after they left. I lay curled up on the couch in a ball.

Bree tried her best to soothe me but I couldn't form words. I didn't want to talk. I just wanted to hold my son and apologize to him that I wasn't being the mother I'd planned. I wanted to apologize for the fact that I believed his father's bullshit and lies.

I couldn't keep pitying myself though. This shit had to stop. I had to get away from Angel by any means necessary.

...

Chapter FIVE

Julien

I'd been a free man for three weeks and I was finally starting to unfurl and shed the chip I had on my shoulder. I sat Angel down my first week out and told him that he had to change his habits or he was going to fuck himself over. I also told him I didn't like the way he was with Cress especially around Nasim. He didn't like anything that came out of my mouth but I didn't expect him to.

After our talk, I noticed he slowed down on the coke, and well...I didn't know how things were between him and Cress because she'd been quiet and so had Angel. I was running with him so much that whenever I was home, it was night time and Cress was nowhere to be found. I started wondering if she'd been avoiding me after the talk we had that night. The one where I came so close to betraying Angel and fucking his wife.

If I didn't believe in death before dishonor, I would have let myself slip that night. I would have kissed Cress's full pink lips and left bite marks on her neck and those perfect fucking tits. Shit…If I had one, I would have sold my soul to mark the tops of her breasts so if she wore a low-cut shirt, everyone would know who she belonged to.

My dick had never been as hard as it was that night. I was sure of it. When I left Cress and went to bed, I jerked off twice and came hard thinking about her. Thinking about how soft she'd feel wrapped around my cock. How tight and warm and wet…

She wasn't mine though.

Even thinking about Cress like that was dangerous. I had to keep my mind on making my own money. I was cool with being on Angel's payroll as his number one hitman but he kept telling me he wanted me in on the deals with his cocaine connect in Columbia. According to him, it would make more money. Money that didn't come from him but the kingpin. I could use it to have my own business. Maybe even get certified in gemology so I could study under a jeweler and make my own pieces. I couldn't tell if I was too eager or if I was ready to start my own life.

A life that didn't include Cressida Erickson.

What the fuck did I even want from her besides sex?

Raw. Punishing. Void-of-morals sex.

I mean...I did like talking to her. It felt good to converse with someone who listened and offered valuable input.

I pulled in a deep breath then walked over to the Bluetooth speaker and turned the music down. Biggie's husky deep voice became muted and the muffled cries of the man tied to the chair across from me became loud and clear. Full of fear and adrenaline.

Sweat trickled down the side of his face mixing with the impressive gash I put along his cheekbone when I hit him with my rings on. He strained against the plastic zip ties holding his wrists and elbows to the arms of the chair.

I plucked my 24-karat gold knife, a gift from Angel, from the table to my right and his muted screams hit a crescendo that made the hairs on my arms stand on end. My blood hummed and I stood there absorbing the feel of it.

Wrong. Dark. Evil.

I couldn't help myself though. It was like an addiction to drugs or food. I craved the sound of screams and the slick of red blood. I relished in knowing that I was plucking a problem out of Angel's life like an ingrown hair. We had a level of teamwork that was unmatched.

"Are you going to tell me who you've been feeding information to?" I asked the guy as I flipped the knife over in my latex-gloved hands. The lights in the small room glinted off the blade with a wicked brightness.

More muffled screams and pleas.

One of the cooks in Rush had been caught feeding information about Angel's operation to the competition. We didn't know who he'd been talking to or how long he'd been selling us out so I was called in. I was asked to extract details. So far, I was an hour into extraction and it looked like my guy wanted to sing.

I loosened the gag in his mouth and let it fall around his throat while I cupped my hand to my ear. "A suit-wearing motherfucker," he spat out around the blood in his mouth. I'd already knocked a couple of his teeth loose with my hands alone. Once I brought my knife out, much more damage would be done.

"I know you have a name for the guy." I stooped down to look at him. Sweat, tears, and blood slicked his face. There were black gaps where his front teeth used to be. His once-pristine chef's uniform was now splattered with crimson.

My blood thrummed again.

It was such a stark but beautiful contrast looking at the red mix with the white. Studying how the cotton wicked up the first spots of blood but then drowned in the viscous life force. I wanted to sink the tip of my blade into him and watch more blood drown out the white.

"Smoke...please," he panted. "I won't say anything if you let me go. I swear to god..." I stood up and made a single slashing motion across his chest. Deep enough to slice through his uniform and to the flesh beneath. He wailed, curving his spine forward while the slow spread of blood mottled his white cotton smock.

"Okay! Please don't kill me!" But he knew I was going to. I couldn't let him live after this. Besides, I wanted to watch the beauty of his blood as it soaked into his clothes.

"What's his name, man? Just tell me so we can get this over with. I'm tired. I want to go to sleep." I let out a yawn while he sobbed for his life. Tears and begging meant nothing to me.

He picked this particular path for himself. He wanted a dangerous life. He wanted the role of betrayer. It wasn't like Angel wasn't good to all his staff. This guy had more than enough money and access to whatever drugs he liked to put in his veins. All Angel asked for was loyalty in return.

It's how we were raised. You didn't have friends or employees. You had family. Blood. And if someone dishonored that…well there's me. That lone moment between life and death. In my eyes, losing your life over dangerous lies and dishonor was a fitting consequence.

I'd never hurt anyone innocent and that's why Sam still weighed heavy on my mind. I couldn't rightfully say I had a conscience because I highly doubted monsters like me came with a Jiminy Cricket voice lodged in the recesses of their brain or soul or where ever the fuck a conscience resided. I did have regrets though. I guess that's as close to a conscious as I was going to get.

I turned my attention back to my friend zip-tied to the chair and waited for him to give me a name so his agony could be over. Finally, with a labored breath, he said, "H-His name is Man."

"Man?" I turned my lips down and nodded. "Who can I contact about Mr. Man?"

"I don't know! I swear. I only know who I talked to. I'd never be able to meet with Man. He's like a ghost." He blurted out who his connect to Man was and I turned up Biggie's *Who Shot Ya?* on the speaker.

The screams that rang out were muffled under the bass-heavy beat as I plunged my 24-karat gold knife between his ribcage. I angled it upward and watched blood rain from the gash. I took in the abstract way scarlet ate up white before dripping on the floor then I tugged my knife out of his body and he slumped over. Silent.

With a satisfied sigh, I walked over to the door and pulled it open. I expected to see Angel waiting on the other side so I could tell him I needed help with clean-up. Well, I didn't *need* help but he felt like having other people help, they were indebted. They couldn't snitch on anything happening inside of Rush because their hands were dirty too. I liked to work alone but I didn't bitch about it too much.

"He went back to Rush," Boogie said when he saw my eyes scan the area for my brother. "I'll help you with the cleanup. We need to get him out of here." Boogie looked past me into the small, concrete room and shook his head. "Snitch-ass motherfucker." He pushed the words out through gritted teeth then walked in, donning the same black latex gloves I wore.

"I got a lead on a guy named Man. I haven't heard Angel mention him. You know anything?" I asked as we worked in tandem to pull up the taped-down sheets of plastic on the ground.

"Man? Nah. I don't know a Man."

"I'm guessing it's an alias," I said cutting the zip ties and letting the body fall heavy to the floor. Boogie wrapped the guy up and I secured the duct tape and more zip ties. When we were done, it looked like nothing happened…besides the body-sized heap of plastic by the door. I finally peeled off my gloves and Boogie grinned a little.

"You barely got a drop of blood on you."

"That's the point, right?" I asked.

"Yeah, but it's still amazing. You cut this motherfucker deep and you didn't get a drop on you. Anybody ever tell you that's talent?" A proud smirk tipped the side of his mouth up.

"Not exactly."

"It is. I've cut people and it's messy. You get blood in places you wouldn't think to look." He lugged the plastic-wrapped body through the doorway and paused to take a breath. "I see why Angel uses you. Besides the fact that you're his brother. You're a damn good hitter. No gun. No noise. No bullshit. If I had an operation, I'd keep you at my right hand."

"Hopefully, Angel moves me from hitter to partner. I love what I do but I'm ready to move forward."

"Yeah? Forward to what?" We worked together pulling the chef's body out of the room and into the trunk of an innocuous Nissan parked in the back of Rush. We'd been buried in the deep storage room beneath the club. Even the heavy bass from the dancefloor couldn't be heard down there.

"I have goals," I told him, slamming the trunk.

"Of course you do. I forgot how tight-lipped you are. Another good quality, Smoke." He looked at me like he was evaluating me for a job then he slid his smiling mask back in place and said, "You talked to Angel about his habit, didn't you?"

"Yeah."

"I figured." He passed a hand over his silver beard then shook his head. "He just changed his schedule. Same shit. Different timeline."

"Wait...he's still using heavy?" I knew Angel hadn't stopped. No coke head was going to stop cold-turkey and still have access to it.

"Heavy as fuck, Smoke. Why you think he bailed when you were getting ready to make the hit?"

"Can't say I'm shocked." I flared my nostrils. I didn't say anything else to Boogie, I headed back inside of Rush and up the red stairs to Angel's office. It was high above the dancefloor. A glass box nearly suspended in the air where he could peer down at everyone.

When I got to the top of the steep climb, I met Bree, who looked frustrated outside of Angel's closed office door. "What's up, Bree?" I asked, looking at her pinched expression. She smacked her glossy lips and tossed a hand in the air.

"Hey, Smoke. I can't get your brother to come to the fucking door." She fixed brown eyes on the closed door. "I know he's in there fucking some bitch." Her delicate jaw twitched and I swore I saw a sheen of tears on the whites of her eyes. At least Cress had Bree in her corner.

She had me too but I couldn't get too close.

I put my hand on her shoulder and she looked down, skimming over the gold and diamond rings. "I'll talk to him." I found myself saying that shit more and more. I was starting to wonder who was the older brother.

I sent a pissed Bree back down the steps to work while I knocked on the office door and waited for Angel to answer. "It's me," I said over the music pumping below. The door opened in seconds.

My big brother stood before me with white residue around his flared nostrils. His pupils were wide and dark and his irises were wild. He flashed me a smile as he adjusted his open belt.

"Smoke, what's good? The job done?" The naked woman behind him handed him a lit cigarette before fixing her red Rush uniform. I stared at her, not because her tits were out or because she was pretty. I stared at her wondering if Cress was at home taking care of Nasim while her husband was at work fucking someone else and sniffing coke up his nose.

"It's done," I said, watching the unidentified woman dress then leave after blowing Angel a kiss. Once she left, he sat on the corner of his desk and exhaled gray smoke. The bass from the music pulsed all around us. *Mercy* by Kanye West boomed through the walls while bodies below on the colorful dancefloor moved almost in sync to the song.

"What's up with you leaving? I thought you were watching the door for me." I leaned against the far wall and crossed my arms over my chest.

"I had...pressing matters to attend to." He let out a chuckle.

"You came up here to fuck and do coke, motherfucker?" My brows furled together while I glared.

"You got the job done, right?" He snapped.

"I got the job done but you weren't where you said you'd be."

That rubbed me the wrong way. We were blood brothers. At the very least, he was supposed to mean what he said when he said it. I was supposed to be his best fucking friend.

"My bad, Smoke. Goddamn. What do you want me to do? Grovel?" I saw anger inching in on him and I restrained myself. Normally, any sign of anger pissed me off enough to slam my fist into someone's mouth. Angel wasn't someone though. He was my brother. I didn't treat him like I did everyone else. If he were anyone else, he would have been on the floor.

"No. I want you not to take off so you can fuck a bottle girl and do coke, Angel." My voice was an even, deep tone.

"I'm sorry, Smoke. You happy?" He sneered.

"Not really. Why the hell are you cheating on Cress? She's at home with Nas right now and…"

"She's *my* wife!" His voice exploded and my fingers instinctively flexed into a fist before I shook it out. Even when we were kids, I let Angel's mouth run away with him when he spoke to me because I knew I was bigger than him. If I punched him, I'd break something. So, whenever we got into it, Angel talked his shit and I let him get it out because I knew he couldn't handle my blows. I didn't hit back with my mouth like him. I was about action.

"Who knows what the fuck Cress is at home doing. Fucking bitch," he muttered, rubbing the back of his neck.

"Watch that shit, Angel. She's the mother of your child. You goddamn wife. What the fuck is your problem?"

"What's yours?" He fired back. "You get out of jail and think you're a fucking saint, Smoke? You're a murderer. You're a goddamn machine. You don't have a soul. Why are you so concerned about my morals when you don't have any? Huh?" He sat behind his desk and my eyes fell on the small mound of coke in front of him. He pulled out a tight straw made from what looked like a hundred-dollar bill and inhaled the line of coke laid out in front of him. He groaned then relaxed against the high-back leather chair.

"I have rules," I told him. "Not morals. I have a code."

"Fuck that, Smoke. I don't have to follow your rules. I'm the big brother. Remember that? I'm the one paying you and taking care of you."

"Then let's end that shit, Angel," I said moving toward his desk, anger narrowing my eyes. "You said you wanted to make me a partner in this organization. Let's do it."

"You know I have to run it past the Columbians." He pushed a hand through his hair.

"Then let's do it. Unless you want to keep me under your thumb for moments like this when you can rub shit in my face."

"Fuck you, Smoke. I'm trying to ease this process along. You've been out for three weeks. You think you're going to come in here and shoot to the top of the ladder that easily?"

"Yeah, I do. Especially since I did five motherfucking years inside for you!" My voice was a clap of thunder that settled Angel and made him eye me cautiously.

"Okay," he huffed, finger-combing his black hair. "I'm going to Columbia tomorrow and..."

"Tomorrow? Why the fuck didn't you tell me?" I was on my feet and so was Angel. He moved around the desk and looked up at me. He had to feel the anger rolling off me in waves.

"Because I run this shit, Smoke. Me. Not you and me. Just me… for now." He cleared his throat and moved over to the floor-to-ceiling window that offered him a prime view of Rush below.

"What time are we leaving?" I asked, already knowing the answer.

"It's a solo trip, hermano."

"Don't fucking *hermano* me, Angel. You should have told me. All the loyalty I've put into Rush—into you—I deserve to be at the helm with you. Rush was my fucking idea anyway."

"Smoke, I told you I'd bring you in. The Columbians love loyalty like yours but I have to make sure the timing is right. Just… let me do this shit. I know what the fuck I'm doing. I've been doing it for five years." His jaw flexed when he looked over his shoulder at me. "You're my hitter. I need you helping me out until I get you in good with the Columbians. Matter fact…" He snapped his fingers then walked toward me. His movements were jerky. "I need someone to keep an eye on Cress. You know, since Sam is unable to." A dark smirk bent his lips.

"Keep an eye on her for what? She's grown."

"Because I can't trust that bitch."

"Yo, I swear to god, Angel…you got one more time to disrespect her and…"

"And what, little brother? You Dr. Phil now? You think you know my marriage? You think you know my wife? Just because you were her friend when y'all were in school? Because you had a little crush on her and she wouldn't let you even sniff her pussy?" He laughed in my face and something inside of me snapped. I rushed him and pinned him to the glass.

"Watch the way you talk to me, Angel."

"Or what, Smoke?" He growled, baring his teeth at me like an animal. "Huh? You want to fight me? Your blood? Is that the savage shit you learned in jail? Get the fuck off me." He snatched away and I let him go because my vision became blurred with the image of putting my brother through that pane of glass. "I need someone to watch Cress like I said." He straightened his shirt and sat down to do another line of coke. "Someone I trust not to fuck her when she does what whores do and opens her legs." He sniffed a few times then wiped his nose when a rivulet of pink-tinged mucus rolled from his nostril. He was doing too much. He was going to kill himself. "If she tries to fuck you...kill her. I'm tired of her shit."

"What?" My face twisted under the weight of his words. Normally, I followed Angel's orders. I did what I loved and what helped him out. I couldn't kill Cress though.

I wouldn't.

"You heard me. I'm tired of her doing shit behind my back."

"Yo, you're tripping hard, Angel." I wouldn't even dignify that conversation anymore. He knew goddamn well I wasn't going to kill Cressida. He was too high to think straight which meant there was no point in me being in his office.

"You heard what I said, Smoke. I meant that shit. Now, you

need to go home because she's there alone and who knows what the fuck she's doing. She's scheduled to Facetime me in ten minutes. I bet you the bitch won't even pick up the phone."

"Scheduled?" I almost laughed.

"I keep her on a schedule," he said.

"You need to fucking chill with that shit. I've barely seen her in weeks. It's like she's hiding in the house."

"She's depressed. About what, I don't fucking know because I give her the world. Ungrateful…" He swallowed whatever insult he had on his tongue because the look I gave him would wither a fucking tree. I was tired of hearing him disrespect her. "Call it an early night here and go check on Cress. Shadow her for a while and lay low until I can make moves with the Columbians. Besides, with me being out of town, I know she's going to run wild in the streets. You're the only one I trust around her, Smoke."

He was a bad judge of character because I wanted to fuck his wife. I wouldn't but goddamn, I wanted to.

"I'll keep an eye on her," I told him just to shut him the fuck up. I knew I didn't need to babysit Cress. Angel just wanted me out of his hair for a while because he didn't like what I was saying.

"I'm going to get you in with the Columbians," he said after another line.

"Yeah, okay, Angel. I'm out." I couldn't stand to watch him get high as a fucking kite and spew more nonsense. He barely noticed I was gone because his nose was in a mound of coke. I just hoped I didn't hear about him overdosing in his office tomorrow morning.

...

When I walked into the house, I heard Nasim fussing upstairs and wondered why he was still up. He'd been going down at ten and it was nearing midnight. I only knew his schedule because sometimes I'd hear Cress on the phone with Bree or her mother and I'd catch pieces of conversation.

I was going to pour myself a glass of rum but I wanted to check on my nephew and hell...after the night I had, I wanted to see Cress too. She wasn't mine but I could at least look at her and let her presence soothe away the tension.

"Everything okay?" I asked from the nursery doorway. I mapped out Cressida's curves beneath the colorful silk kimono robe she wore. My chest tightened then popped, heavy with something warm.

"Jesus, Jules." She jumped so hard it startled Nasim and he started fussing again. "What are you doing here? You're usually at Rush with Angel."

"Well, I'm here now." I stepped in, towering over her, and took Nas into my arms. After a few fussy seconds, he settled against my chest. "What's up, Nas?" I asked, bouncing him the way I'd seen Cress do a million times. She stood back, arms folded, eyes tired.

"He's teething," she told me.

"Oh yeah? Come on, I got something for him." I walked out of the nursery and heard the soft sound of Cress's feet padding behind me, down the steps, and into the kitchen.

"What are you doing?" She asked, standing on her tiptoes to see over my shoulder. I was facing the counter, cracking open the bottle of rum.

"Putting some of this on his gums." I shook the bottle at her and she frowned at me.

"No, Julien."

"Come on. Trust me. I'm not pouring him a shot." I sat Nasim on the counter and he grabbed for me, fussing a little bit. Drool covered his little chin while he tugged at his earlobe.

"That's so old school."

"It's old school but it works," I told her pouring some into the cap of the bottle. "You trust me, sweetheart?" I looked at her and she swallowed, running delicate fingers through golden strands. Her hair nearly matched her brown sugar skin. I tried not to get caught up in her freckles and champagne eyes. It was a tempting trap to fall into though.

"I don't know," she said quietly.

"Have I ever given you reason not to? Plus, you think I'd hurt my nephew?"

He should have been my son but my chest ached thinking about it so I dropped the thought. What the fuck was that feeling? It was like being hit hard. I hated whatever the hell it was.

"I know you wouldn't hurt him." She glanced at Nasim on the counter and heaved a sigh. "Okay…just a little."

I washed my hands then dipped my finger in the cap and rubbed the rum on his sensitive gums. He smacked his lips and licked the liquid before frowning at the taste. I rubbed on more and he babbled. "Jujuju," he said, smiling up at me. Cress gasped and slapped her hand over her mouth.

"I think he's trying to say your name, Jules!"

"You think so?" I eyed my nephew with his big hazel eyes and sandy curls just like Cress's used to be. I didn't see much of Angel in him at all.

"Yes! Nas, say it again. Uncle Juju?" She rubbed my shoulder and that small touch sent a jolt to my dick that I had to control before I got hard at an inappropriate time.

"Fuck no. He's not calling me Juju."

"Jujujuju!" Nasim clapped and grinned at me and Cress.

"For real, Nas? I thought we were cool, man." I picked him up and he clapped his hands together then tugged at my gold chain. "See, he's fine. He's happy again. Nothing a little rum can't fix."

"Thank you, Jules. I was too nervous to do it. I don't know why. I'm just...stupid sometimes," she said, shaking her head.

"Says who?" I asked.

"Nobody, I just..."

"You sound like Angel. Don't let him get into your head, Cress." We went upstairs and I walked around the nursery holding Nasim while she sat in the glider chair watching me intently. "I'm not going to drop him. You don't have to watch me like that."

"It's weird seeing him so happy with someone else."

"I'm his uncle. We have the same blood, right buddy? If you can't be comfortable with me, who can you be comfortable with?"

I dropped a kiss to his soft curly hair and he made a happy sound before laying on my chest. It took a few laps around his room before he was nodding off.

I didn't want to put him down. His solid weight felt good in my arms. I kept stealing sniffs from the top of his head and the small space between his neck and shoulder.

"Do they all smell this good?" I asked, lifting my eyes to Cress's.

"Yeah," she laughed softly. "It's how they trick you into having more."

"No bullshit."

"Jules," she scolded with a smile quirking the corners of her lips.

"He's sleeping," I reasoned.

"I know. You can put him down. He's knocked out."

"Just a few more seconds." Another kiss. Another sniff. It was weird but his soft, clean scent made me want to move mountains for him.

I laid him down in the crib and looked at Cress. "You did good with him."

"Thanks. Sometimes it feels like I'm failing him miserably already." She laughed but it was a sad sound.

"Have a drink with me, sweetheart." My fingers slid through her hair because I was greedy and I couldn't help myself.

"I can do that. I need…something," she scoffed, turning the light out in the nursery. We went downstairs and I poured her a glass of rum. We sat on the couch in the living room and Cress settled beside me, tucking her feet under her body. Her silk robe fell open and I ate up the length of her toned legs with my eyes.

"You need to lighten up. You're too hard on yourself," I told her after a few drinks from my glass.

"I don't know how *not* to be hard on myself," she said with a shrug. Silk slipped off her shoulder and I noticed she didn't have on anything underneath. Her skin was smooth and golden brown. I wanted to taste every inch of it.

"Start by telling yourself you're a good mother to Nas."

"I'm glad you think so. I can't even give him my milk." She pressed her hand to her chest then let out a choked cry. I put my glass down and without thinking, I pulled her close to me for a hug. "Did Angel tell you what he did?" She looked up at me with watery champagne pools.

"No. What did he do?" I felt myself tensing up already.

"He sent a doctor and two of his men to the house a few weeks ago. Security held me down while the doctor gave me a shot to dry up my milk." Tears knifed into her words as she dissolved into sadness in my arms.

Something swelled so big inside of me. So prickly and hot that I thought it would swallow me alive. I was livid with Angel but something else was there too. Something softer.

"Cress." I smoothed her hair down and gripped it in my fist for a moment before tipping her chin up. "I'm sorry. I'm so fucking sorry he snatched something like that away from you." I wiped the tears falling down her face and fuck if she didn't lean into my touch. The growing feeling at the base of my spine was consuming me again. "You don't deserve the shit he's doing to you."

"What do I deserve then, Julien?" She laughed like the idea of her having someone better than Angel was a joke.

"Someone who won't abuse you and control you."

"He doesn't abuse me," she snapped.

"He does."

She wouldn't hear me though. She shook her head and broke away from my embrace. Her cheeks were flushed and the tip of her nose was red from crying.

"I told you, he doesn't hit me." Her words were pointed and meant to pierce but they crumbled instead.

"And you know there are other forms of abuse. You're too smart to hide from it, Cressida. Now you're letting him get inside your head. You're starting to believe that bullshit he feeds you. The last thing Nas needs is to see his mother being controlled and abused. You want to raise another Angel?" I asked her seriously. A sobering look flickered in her eyes.

"No. *Hell* no."

"That's what you're going to do if you keep letting this happen."

"I can't leave him, Jules. He will fucking kill me. You don't think I've tried?" Her hands shook as she brought the glass to her full pink lips. "My sister won't speak to me anymore because I fucked up. I came back to Angel one too many times and now I'm alone. I can't even be real with Bree because I'm afraid she'll think I'm stupid for staying too."

"Nobody thinks you're stupid. Stop fucking saying that." I felt helpless hearing her talk down about herself like that.

"Maybe it's me then. Maybe I feel stupid. Maybe I feel like a failure as a mother because I'm not giving Nas the best version of myself. Maybe I feel lonely and ugly and…" Her mask finally fell apart and she showed me the real Cressida. The depressed, scared, vulnerable Cressida.

My chest cracked open for her.

I reached out and slid my palm against her cheek, catching remnants of salty tears until my fingers curled around the back of her neck. Her crying stuttered. Her lips were swollen and puffy from shedding her emotions. I studied how perfect they were. How pink and plump they were. How they glistened when she licked them.

"You're not ugly, Cress. You're not any of that shit. Listen to me." Our foreheads nearly touched as she peered at me through wet, spiky lashes. "You're beautiful. So fucking beautiful and smart." My blood hummed as I spoke. My thumb stroked her skin. It was warm and silky smooth. I caressed her jawline then let my fingers drop, slipping down the delicate line of her neck. "Angel should be kissing your feet. He should be making you feel as stunning as you are." Cress blinked and drew in a shaky breath.

"Is that what you would do if…" She didn't have to finish her question. I already knew what she was going to say.

"If…" I nodded.

"Julien, I always wished it was you. Angel was never supposed to be more than a date and…" She looked down at how close we were then back up at me. "Just know I always wished it was you."

When she touched my face. My dick got so hard I could barely concentrate.

I was going to combust if I didn't take over those perfect pink lips with mine. If I didn't crash into her mouth and taste her salty, tear-stained kisses. My grip on the back of her neck tightened. Probably too much. Too hard. I didn't know how to be gentle when everything was screaming at me to take.

Claim.

Own.

She gasped and those fucking lips parted giving me a glimpse of white teeth and a waiting wet tongue. "Fuck...Cress," I growled. Still gripping to the back of her neck. Still torn and confused.

"You feel it too," she breathed her lashes fluttering ever so slightly.

"All the time." My dick ached as I stared into her eyes. Pools of clear gold. "We can't," I told her.

"I know." Her words sounded pained coming out. Like not indulging in what we both wanted was physically hurting her. I knew the feeling.

"So we won't." I shut my eyes and rested my forehead against hers. I had to talk myself down or I would fuck Cress so goddamn hard. I'd fuck her with everything I had locked inside of myself.

"We won't. It would just make life harder." She sniffled and gulped then pulled her forehead away from mine.

"Right. I couldn't betray Angel like that." Even though he seemed increasingly okay with putting me off and treating me like I was a stranger instead of the brother who did five years for him.

"Me either," she said. I let the back of her neck go and made my spine straight. I was going to need more rum. Cressida was making things churn inside of me. She was walking through me with a lit match knowing my blood was gasoline.

When she looked up, her eyes pierced me. It was swift and intense. I swallowed hard to unstitch my tongue from the roof of my mouth. I didn't feel like this around women. I didn't feel like this around anyone for any goddamn reason. My thoughts stayed on my goals and my family. Now, looking at Cressida with her velvet skin and ochre hair, made me feel wild.

I didn't like feeling wild. I was calculated and precise. My brain didn't allow for wild and unhinged.

"Deal. We won't move any further than friendship," I finally said even though the words singed the roof of my mouth and left soot on my lips. I reached out after a few quiet beats and slid two fingers beneath her robe, right at her shoulder. I watched it slip down baring one honey shoulder with a delicious tan line where her bra would have been if she wore one. "Why the fuck are you naked under this robe, Cressida?" The pads of my fingers danced down the middle of her chest. My feather-light touches made goosebumps blanket her skin.

"I was home alone with Nas. Why would I need clothes?"

"What if Angel came home?" She and I both knew I wasn't asking about Angel because I was concerned. I was asking about Angel because how the fuck could he come home to her wearing only a robe without fucking her senseless?

How could any man?

How could *I*?

"I'd get dressed before he stumbled upstairs," she told me, her breathing labored. My long fingers rested on the knot tied at her waist.

"You don't let him touch you?" My voice was thick and low while I grappled with my code. My rules.

Death before dishonor.

"I hate when he touches me. I always hope he's too high or he's already fucked someone else before he comes home so he won't need me." The confession must have burned coming out because she wet her lips and looked away from me for a moment. She couldn't stay away for too long though. Her eyes found mine and I tugged at the knot. It fell open easily and I took in the sight of her perfect tits. *So* fucking perfect.

I could tell some of the fullness left since her milk dried up and she tried to snatch the robe closed so I couldn't see. She muttered about new stretch marks on the sides of her breasts since they were going back to their normal size. I didn't care about shit like that.

"Stretch marks that show you gave Nas the best possible start at life? Can I kiss them?" I asked, pushing her hand away from the robe. Her nipples were an exquisite mesh of mauve and sable brown. Her areolas tightened pushing her nipples out more, making me ravenous.

"We said we wouldn't."

"Then why are you letting me look at you?" I squeezed her stiff nipple between my fingers and she bit her bottom lip. "Why are you letting me touch you, Cress?"

"Because I can't remember the last time I felt seen. Wanted. Desired." Tears, full and ripe resting on her waterline, begged to fall but she refused to give in. She couldn't hide the patchy pink color invading her cherubic cheeks though.

Did she have to look so goddamn innocent?

"Is that all? You need to feel desired?" I asked, alternating between pinching and caressing her nipples. With my other hand, I gripped my stiff dick through my jeans. As painful as it was to sit beside Cress, touching her like that, I couldn't pry myself away. I should have. I knew better than touching my brother's wife. She knew better than letting me. We were both in over our heads.

"No," she shook her head and a soft river of hair fell over her shoulder brushing one pebbled nipple.

"Then tell me why you're letting me look at you and touch you like this when you know it's wrong." I was barely holding on to control. Everything in me roared.

"Because I still want you, Jules. I've always wanted you. Even when we were in middle school. Even when you walked me home after the carnival and I kissed your cheek." I moved to cup her breasts while her breathing continued to grow shallow.

"Tell me what you really wanted to do, sweetheart."

"I wanted to kiss your lips. I wanted to stand on my tiptoes and wrap my arms around your neck while we kissed for hours... forever."

Fuck.

Hearing such a sweet admission made me even harder and I didn't know that was possible.

I let my hand move down her stomach. It was soft with the slightest pudge beneath her navel. The perfect V of her pussy stared back at me. It was smooth and waxed except for a landing strip pointing to her clit.

I slid my hand between her thighs and made her open her legs. The fresh scent of her pussy, slick and wet hit me and I felt logic bending and snapping inside my head. That smell…it was so perfect. I needed to feel it. I needed to *taste* it.

"That's what I wanted too," I told her, my voice slipping further into the abyss. Deep and hungry. "That's what I want right now."

"Me too." She squirmed when I traced her soft landing strip. I knew she was anticipating my touch where it mattered most. I stared at her perfect pussy on display for me. So wet and inviting. Her clit was a swollen, thick nub nestled between her plump pussy lips that begged for my mouth.

I knew when I touched her clit and heard that sharp moan, I wasn't leaving Angel's living room without putting my dick in his wife. My fingers were smeared with Cress's wetness. I rubbed her pussy again, letting my fingertips brush her clit.

"Jules," she whined, bucking her hips. I used to hate that she was the only one who called me Jules but now I loved it. I craved it. I pulled my hand away from her hot, wet cunt and licked her arousal from my fingers. She was so fresh and slick on my tongue. I knew after that small taste I wouldn't be able to walk away. She watched me with her legs still open, the perfume from her pussy pushing me to betray my brother.

I reached behind me, tugging at my shirt and pulling it over my head. The second it hit the floor, Cress's hands were on my chest, touching and groping. I unbuckled my belt then unzipped my jeans, breathing a sigh of relief once my hard dick was free.

"Shit, Julien." She gawked at it, wide-eyed but needy and hungry. I felt the same way looking at her.

"You can handle it, sweetheart." I pushed my jeans down and kicked them off then I stroked my cock while I looked at her. "You're so fucking beautiful," I muttered. I leaned over and kissed her lips like I'd been wanting to do for more than a decade. I sucked on her bottom lip then sank my teeth into it. I wasn't sweet or gentle. I don't know if she was hoping I would be, but I couldn't be. Not right then. I'd wanted Cressida since I was in seventh grade. I wanted to hold her hand back then but now I wanted to hold her throat. I wanted to fuck her until all she could remember was how I felt inside of her.

Not Angel.

Nobody else.

Just *me*.

"Jules, please fuck me. I've been dreaming about feeling you for so long."

"Wait," I said gruff and demanding. "I need to taste you, Cress. You smell so goddamn good." I lowered to my knees and pressed her thighs open, groaning at the wetness kissing her there.

"Your pussy is so fucking wet, sweetheart." I breathed her in and committed her scent to memory because I had no idea when I'd be able to taste something so sweet and fresh again. I knew after we were done tonight, guilt would swarm me. I'd deal with it then but right now?

I needed to eat.

I lapped up her juices first, slipping between every crevice just to hear her moans because goddammit they were addictive. I kissed and sucked my way to her clit. I teased it first, flicking then I got hungry and couldn't hold back the savage side of me. I wrapped my lips around her, sucking and groaning into her slick heat. She tasted so good. It was a flavor unique to her and I couldn't get enough.

I slid my arms beneath her legs, making sure to keep her open so I could suck her pussy until she came. Holding her like that was like gripping a live wire. She moaned and wiggled beneath my mouth, fucking my tongue, rolling her hips, calling for God, Jesus, and whatever other deity she could spit out.

When Cressida came, she tensed up, arching her back and raking her nails through the close-cut waves of my hair. I deepened my suction keeping it gentle but firm. I wanted her to explode in my mouth like Fruit Gushers.

While her legs shook and trembled, I slid an arm from under her so I could probe her opening with one finger. She was so wet and leaking silky cream from her perfect pussy. I had no idea little Cress had been so hungry and horny. I loved her nasty like this.

Uninhibited. Raw. Free. It was my favorite version of her.

While I teased her plump clit with my tongue, I pulled her wetness out, coating my finger in it. I looked up to see her stomach contracting with each pass of my tongue and insertion of my finger.

I'd spent years dreaming about the way I'd fuck her if I ever got the chance. The ways I'd make her come for me...*on* me...wrapped around me. It was like watching my fantasies play out in real life. I pulled my mouth away from her pussy and watched her come over and over while I finger fucked her.

Each time I pulled out of her, I licked my fingers clean while she shook. Her pretty face was flushed and wet with tears and sweat. Her perfect hair was a mess of fine strands rioting on her head in a halo of sandy brown, caramel, and gold.

"You're beautiful," I said tasting the last traces of her pussy from my fingertips. By now, my dick was so thick and hard there was a physical ache in the pit of my stomach.

"So are you, Jules." The hunger in her eyes while she watched me stroke my dick turned me the fuck on. "Please..." It was a breathy plea falling from her pouty lips.

"Please what, Cress?" I moved closer, pressing my lips to her neck and savoring more of her sweetness. I licked her skin while I rocked my rigid dick against her pussy lips. It felt like she was French kissing my cock. I was so close to exploding cum all over her.

"Fuck me, Julien."

"Tell me how long you've fantasized about this dick." I pressed my teeth into the crook of her neck and she gasped, lifting her hips to slide against the head of my dick. I let out a hiss of air and bucked against her, stretching her tight hole.

"For years. So fucking long." She let out a cry mixed with pleasure and pain. I couldn't pull back and ask if she was okay because something in me knew how she wanted it. How she needed it. "Don't be gentle with me," she panted, sliding her nails up and down my back while I bit and sucked on her neck.

My hips crashed into her in one motion and she let out the most beautiful, erotic scream. I paused before moving another inch. Shit, Cress was so tight I didn't know if I *could* move another inch.

The pained whimper she let out was like a honeyed rose petal. Beautiful. Sweet. I needed more. Before she could fully acclimate to my size, I pumped into her again, feeling my dick throb in response to the pressure she squeezed me with. I didn't think I would even fit inside her tight little pussy without splitting her in half.

"Julien!" She moaned, squeezing her eyes shut and letting her head loll on the pillow. Her nails dug into my flesh while her full hips moved in a frantic circle like she needed my dick. Like she would die if she didn't get it and I felt the same way about her. I wanted to bury myself inside of her but she was such a tight fit, I'd have to take what I could get.

I pulled out slowly and looked between us at how wet my cock was and how good I looked slipping in and out of her. "Look at that shit," I said, easing my dick back inside watching her pussy eat up my inches. "Look at how pretty your wet little pussy is, Cress." One deep thrust followed by a high-pitched howl, and I was inside her.

Goddammit.

The couch made deep scooting noises on the floor while I fucked Cressida violently. The cushions threatened to slide from under our bodies but neither of us gave a damn.

My teeth bit a trail along her neck up to her jawline then I sucked her earlobe in my mouth. I wanted to taste all of her. I knew every part was delicious.

"Fuck, Julien! I'm about to come," she warned, her body going stiff as an orgasm ate up her words. She rolled her full pink lips between her teeth and pushed out a satisfied moan. Feeling her grip and pulse around my dick was something to get drunk on.

"Wet this dick up, Cress. I want to feel you come all around me."

"Mmm, you feel so good. So deep, Julien." She pulled me down to kiss my lips while I fucked her slower so I could savor the feeling of how warm and perfect she was. I couldn't hold on for much longer though. Familiar pressure mounted at my core and I knew I had to pull out no matter how much I wanted to fill her up with cum.

In one swift motion, I pulled out right before my climax. Cum splashed up her stomach, stretching to her tits. I didn't come that hard my first day out of prison. I don't think I *ever* came that goddamn much.

While I marveled at how much come Cress pulled out of me, she was busy swirling it around on her golden skin, making a loop around her navel before licking her fingers clean. She did it over and over until most of my orgasm was gone from her stomach.

"Shit, sweetheart. You can't do nasty things like that."

"What if you make me want to do nasty things?" Her eyes were brimming over the top with lust. It was a gorgeous fucking sight.

"Then that makes you a nasty girl, Cress." I stood up, still wet from Cressida's pussy and still coated with sweat. I ran a hand over my face and looked down at her. She was just as beautiful naked as she was fully clothed. I couldn't lie and say I didn't love the nude view though.

"Oh, and you don't like nasty girls?" She sat up, blinking innocent almond-shaped eyes at me the color of liquid gold. Drops of cum were still clinging to her skin, dotting her chest. I stared at them like small badges of honor.

"I love nasty girls," I said taking her chin in my hand and making her look up at me. "I don't know if you can handle being the type of nasty that I like though." I wiped away a drop of cum from her chest with my thumb then swiped it across her bottom lip before feeding it to her.

Cress was about to unlock something dangerous inside of me. I wasn't a possessive man when it came to women because I'd never felt anything for them besides an incessant need to fuck them and hear them. I wanted more with Cressida.

I wanted to bend her in the bedroom…break her. Snap her in fucking half. I also wanted to hold her and kiss her in public. I wanted to wake up beside her and grab her from behind while she was in the kitchen. Thinking about it made my blood warm again.

"As long as it's you, I can handle being as nasty as you want me to be," Cress said, licking her lips and chasing my flavor. Hearing her say shit like that made my dick twitch.

"Just for me?" I quizzed, cocking an eyebrow up. I saw her catch on to the true meaning behind my question.

"Just for you. I could never be this way with him," she said, casting her eyes down. "Whenever he even holds my hand, I'm hollow inside. With you though? I feel…seen. I feel full. The way you made me feel just now? I've never felt like that before." Her throat dipped. "I didn't know I could feel like that."

"Neither did I," I confessed.

"I need more of that feeling." She slid off the couch and onto her knees while she looked up at me. All I needed to see was her lick those pink lips and my dick was standing to greet her again. "I want you to have more of that feeling, Jules." She stroked my dick with her small hand, sliding up and down my shaft, skimming her fingers over the veins snaking beneath my skin until she reached the head of my dick. Thick and hard.

Cressida sucked my dick on her knees in her colorful silk kimono robe while I watched her messy head of ochre strands bob up and down, slurping. Her mouth was so hot I couldn't help thrusting into her throat. She pulled back and gagged a little but then my hungry little Cress went right back in. Sucking until I hit the back of her throat and her eyes watered. Saliva dripped from her chin and down her chest. God, she looked sexy like that.

I gripped a fistful of her hair and fucked her face while she looked at me. "Goddamn, Cress you're such a nasty little girl."

"Mmm-hmm," she mumbled around my dick.

"Did you sit in church thinking about choking on my dick when we were in high school? Because I thought about eating your pussy so many times." She made a long noise before deep throating me and I saw stars. A roar tore from me when I shot down her throat. I felt every beat of my heart like a pulse of light in my body.

When Cress popped off my cock, she sat on the floor, back against the couch, satiated. A lazy grin slightly bending her lips. She chased a lone drop of cum with her tongue and I watched every millisecond.

I knew what just happened between us was fucked up. I shredded my moral code. Now I was past the point of return. I should have told Cressida that we couldn't ever do that shit again. I should have told her I was drunk or caught up in the moment but I didn't.

Instead, I sat beside her on the floor after pulling my underwear on and held her against my chest. It felt like I'd unlocked something ancient inside of me. Something that had always existed but remained chained behind iron and steel. Now, it was roaming free and I knew it would ruin my fucking life.

...

Chapter
SIX

Cressida

What. The. Fuck.

Seriously, what the fuck had I just done? What had Julien and I just done?

We were sitting beside each other after he fucked me and I could still feel him humming through my body. He was everything. He was too much and not enough and...I needed *more*.

I needed more of my thighs pulsing and my pussy aching from stretching to fit him. I needed more of his deep gravelly groans and dirty mouth. I needed more of that dull ache from the space behind my earlobe where he licked and sucked and bit.

I pulled in a slow breath while I laid against his chest with his fingers stroking my hair. "I know what just happened was wrong," I said. A million pounds of guilt fell on my chest from my vows to Angel to our sleeping son upstairs to my lifetime of church. "I promise you I've never cheated on Angel before." Like cheating on him now was any better and with his fucking brother no less. I pinched the bridge of my nose. Still, no matter what my guilt-ridden brain said, I wanted more.

"I know. I believe you. I feel fucked up too but at the same time…" Jules's voice trailed off and he let one blocky shoulder rise and fall. "I wanted that to happen for so goddamn long, Cress. I know you did too."

"I did." I twisted the mood ring around on my finger then looked down at it. Red. It was always red around Jules. "I want it to happen again."

"Shit, me too." He tugged on my hair and made me look up at him. Those deep brown eyes tunneled through me. "Over and over and over…" He dipped his head low and kissed the top of my head. It felt so good. Every time he touched me, it felt good.

"And over, and over," I whispered. I hated the war inside my head. One second, I wanted to lose myself in Jules and the next, I wanted to forget I ever fucked him.

But for what?

It wasn't like my marriage to Angel was solid. I wasn't happy and as much as I hated admitting it, he was abusing me.

"We gotta think about Angel though, sweetheart."

"Think about him for what?" I snapped, sitting up. "He had his men come in our house and hold me down. He had a doctor come in here and give me a shot without my consent. He never thinks about me."

A heavy sigh came from Jules as he pulled me against him again. His affection made me dizzy, especially since I knew he didn't give his affections freely or easily. He was quiet and closed off most of the time. I sensed sadness and darkness in him, even when we were younger. I was still drawn to him and everything about him. Even the dark parts.

For someone as calculated as him to show tenderness and affection was serious. I didn't take it lightly. I knew it meant I was more to him than something thrilling to do or someone to fuck. Especially since he betrayed Angel, and to Jules, family and loyalty were everything.

"You're right. I can't argue with it from your perspective but for me? As his little brother? I know I fucked up. Something like this can't be fixed," he said, grimly.

"Why would you want to fix it?" I asked him honestly. "Angel isn't that great of a big brother."

"I know." His eyebrows crashed together, heavy and dark like a storm cloud over his face. "He's still my blood though. We're not supposed to fuck each other over."

"You know what I think? I think you've made the same mistake

I made years ago with Angel."

"Oh yeah? What's that?"

"You keep expecting him to have the same kind of heart as you. You still haven't seen him for who and what he really is. At least you can still get away from him. I saw his true colors too late and now I'm stuck." Reality sank into me hot and heavy, filling up the space inside that was warm and fluttery for Jules.

"You're not stuck. You can leave him. Take Nasim and start over." His words caressed me with fantasies.

"Do you know your brother?" I laughed and it was frosty as hell.

"Maybe I don't know him anymore." I saw the struggle in his eyes and I recognized it. Sometimes I'd sit with that expression for hours wondering how Angel could wear such a convincing mask all the time. I knew seeing Angel for who he really was would be jarring to Jules. He idolized his big brother. In his eyes, Angel could do no wrong.

"I'm not here to change the way you see Angel. He'll do that for himself but…watch him. Pay attention to the things he shows you."

Why didn't I take my own advice years ago? I wouldn't be stuck now. I tried to shake the feeling because there was nothing I could do about it.

Jules looked at me for a long moment packed with unspoken words but I understood them all the same. "I'll keep my eyes open," he said. I could tell he weighed every word before he spoke. I admired a man like that. Most of them shot off from their mouth without thinking. "Let's keep this between us, Cress. I haven't unpacked any of this yet and…"

"Say no more. I don't know what just happened between us but I do know that the last person who needs to know is Angel."

"You *know* what just happened between us," he said incredulously, stroking the sore, sensitive spots on my neck. Each time his thumb brushed against a bruise, my body tingled and pulsed. "We did what we've been dying to do. I guess no matter how fucked up something is, when you're drawn to it, there's only a matter of time before you act on it."

"How long have you been wanting to?" I asked quietly, taking his big hand in mine. I examined his fingers. How long and sturdy they were. How close-cut and clean his nails were. The way the low light in the living room glinted subtly off his ruby skull ring. Every ring on his smooth and calloused hands was unique and beautiful. Just like Jules.

"Ever since I saw you in church that day. I still remember bitching when Grandma told us we were going to a new church but I shut the hell up when I walked in and saw you sitting in the front row with Trinity." An understated smile brushed across his full lips. "Your hair was wild and curly. I couldn't tell if your head was big or your hair was fluffy. That's the first thing I noticed."

"Fuck you, Jules," I laughed, shoving him. He caught my wrist in his hand and pulled me close. The feeling of his hand wrapped around me, demanding my closeness, made me dizzy. Jules was strong and silent in all the areas Angel was loud and weak. True confidence didn't announce itself and Jules never announced himself. He just showed up. Silent. Reliable. Real.

"It's true. You did have a big ass head though, Cress."

"Whatever. I grew into it." I touched my head lovingly then smiled at him.

When was the last time I smiled so genuinely and easily?

"You grew into a lot of things, sweetheart." He ate every inch of my new, softer curves up then licked his lips and smiled. I was useless after that. Jules had the prettiest smile. It consumed me like it always had.

"So did you," I fired back.

"Thank you. I think."

"It was definitely a compliment." I tried in vain to smooth my frizzy hair down but I knew it wouldn't work. I just needed something to do with my hands. "Can I ask you something?"

"What's up, Cress?"

"Why'd you come home early from Rush? Did you and Angel get into it?" I traced the rose petals on his tattoo while I listened.

"Something like that." He cleared his throat. "He's still using coke at the same rate. Never cut back or anything. He just gave me the run around so it would look like he slowed down. Then I had a hit tonight and he was supposed to be outside the door to help with clean up since I've been handling all his hits alone lately. When I opened the door, Boogie was there instead." His eyes flashed something that looked like anger, but I couldn't tell because he was so good at cloaking his true feelings.

"Where was Angel?"

"His office." Julien's words came out short and I knew that meant he was hiding something.

"Let me guess, fucking some random bottle girl or one of the bartenders?" I scoffed, tossing my hand in the air. I caught Jules's eyes and he sighed.

"If you know he's like this, why the fuck..." He shook his head and let the rest of his words fall off a cliff.

"I have Nas to worry about. I'd like to keep my life too, Julien. Everything isn't cut and dry."

"I get it. I guess I just want better for you. You don't deserve this kind of treatment, Cressida. Angel thinks your cheating on him. He's paranoid and projecting."

"He always does that shit. He cheats on me with everyone in Rush except for Bree but in his mind, I'm the one fucking around." I grew quiet because I wanted to take a page from Jules's book and weigh the next words about to come out of my mouth. "That's what got Sam killed, isn't it?" Thinking of Sam's life being wasted like that twisted my stomach in knots.

"Yeah." Jules shook his head and sighed. "I was so hungry for a kill that I didn't examine the situation. Angel told me Sam was fucking around with you and I took his word at face value. He's my brother..."

"Fuck. I knew that's why he ordered the hit. I mean, I didn't know before I walked in on your conversation with him but once I heard you say that you'd taken care of Sam, I knew why."

"I'm not proud of that kill," Jules said matter-of-factly. Like he'd given someone too much change back or something equally mundane and annoying. "I hate kills that don't make any sense. Sam was innocent and now, I have to eat that forever. I call rare hits like that thorns."

"Thorns?" I said, curiously. The more Jules talked, the more tangled I got in him. He was the single most complex man I'd ever known. I wanted to dig and dig until I hit his core. I was afraid of doing something stupid like falling for him though.

If I fell for Jules, my life would be over and so would his.

"Yeah. You can't take the rose without taking the thorns too. I see death and murder as something artistic. A person's last moments of life are fleetingly beautiful. I get to witness it over and over and it's still something I can't quite put into words. But everything beautiful comes with a dark side. A painful side."

"The thorns," I said knowingly.

"Yeah. The ones that stick with you as a single prick of pain forever."

"How is sitting with you in the dark, half-naked, and talking about murder and death so fucking soothing? My father would burn me at the stake if he could hear me," I chuckled.

"Soothing?" Jules's soft lips dropped kisses along my exposed shoulder. "Talking about this shit is soothing to you?" He sounded shocked.

"Yes. I think it's because listening to you describe anything is soothing. Also, getting to hear your inner-thoughts is fascinating. It makes me...tingle, I guess."

"Is that right?" Shock gave way to intrigue. "I think I like making you tingle."

"Mmm, I like it too." Our conversation fell away to scraps as I straddled him and peered into his deep brown eyes. Eyes that held a beautifully dark soul even though he denied having one.

His lips were so soft. I wanted to kiss him forever. I rocked against his stiff dick and he groaned. I ate up the deep sound, licking into his mouth with my tongue, exploring him every way I could.

"You want to get fucked again, don't you, Cress?" His fingers dug into my hips and he moved me the way he wanted, grinding against my pussy, making me hot as fuck. My skin was dewy from trying not to give in to all the things he made me feel.

"Yes," I panted, shrugging my robe off. I wanted to be naked in front of Jules. I wanted him to see every part of me because he made me feel beautiful and sexy. Maybe it was a shallow feeling or maybe I was so deprived of real desire and passion that I was starving.

There wasn't one of Angel's men that hadn't tried to fuck me behind his back but I brushed them off. I didn't want them. Julien was different. He'd always been different. The kind of desire and affection he gave couldn't be found anywhere else and now I had a taste of it and I was addicted.

"Play with your pussy for me," Jules instructed while I was on top of him, kissing and licking his neck. He tasted so good. So *him*.

I leaned back and slid my hand down my stomach until I reached my clit. I inched backward on his lap a little so he could watch the show and he definitely did. He watched me unashamed, biting his bottom lip and shaking his head at the way my body moved for him.

He reached in his boxer briefs and pulled his thick, heavy dick out, stroking it while he stared at me. I moaned, needing to feel him stretching me again. "You know how bad you are for making my dick this hard again, Cress?"

"Am I bad?" I asked, my voice trembling from working myself up.

"So fucking bad. You know we can't keep doing this shit." A clear drop of pre-cum beaded at the tip of his beautiful cock. I wanted it on my lips.

"Can we think about that in the morning? Right now, I need you. I need your dick." Hearing my breathy voice coupled with Jules jerking off inches away from me, had me on the razor-thin edge of an orgasm.

"You need this dick?" He pushed my hand away from my pussy then grabbed me by the throat and pulled me down to his lips. The kiss was possessive and hard. It made me gasp for breath that he stole in the very next beat.

"I need it," I heard myself begging against his warm mouth. We were outside of ourselves. I'd never felt so free to be me.

"Then ride this shit. I want to watch you stuff your little pussy full of all this dick, Cressida. I want to watch it stretch you until you shake." He lifted me without so much as a hiccup and thrust upward while he lowered me on his stiff cock. I braced myself on his hard shoulders, digging my nails in when he entered me.

Once he was inside me, my legs shook and my biceps twitched as I pushed down, trying to take all of him. "Bounce," Jules commanded before slapping my ass. "Treat my dick like a stripper pole, Cress." I was trying to fill myself up with him but he wanted me to slide up and down.

"Like this?" I quizzed, bouncing my ass on him to a slow rhythm.

"Yes," he said, clenching his teeth together. "Faster." His strong hands squeezed my ass hard while he drove into me from below. He was so unforgiving. So damn ruthless. He knocked the air out of my lungs with ease.

"Oh my god," I babbled almost incoherently. I tossed my head back, baring myself to Julien while his hands explored my skin. The feeling was just rough enough to send static buzzing across my arms and shoulders. My nipples pebbled for him and god, he took notice. He pulled my breast into his mouth, sucking and flicking my nipple while I gasped and moaned on top of him.

"Goddamn, Cress. I'm about to bust hard. You gotta slow down." He sounded so pained. I knew that no matter how much I wanted him to fill me up, I couldn't risk getting pregnant by him. I slowed down and rocked my hips while Jules pushed out a slow breath.

"Your pussy is so fucking good and that's so fucking bad, sweetheart." He bit a tender trail across the tops of my breasts and I moaned, rocking forward then back.

"Bad?" I quizzed, watching him lick and suck his way back and forth across my chest.

"So bad. Because now I know I can't stop fucking you even though I should." I stopped his flow of words with my lips on his. Our tongues slid against each other then took turns exploring while

I stayed still in his lap. I wanted to feel every inch of him inside me even if I couldn't sit all the way down on it.

"We'll stop after tonight, I promise."

Nip. Bite. Suck.

"Shit, then let's make it last as long as possible."

Bite. Suck. Nip.

The hungry way we kissed each other bordered on frantic and obsessive. I drowned in how freeing it was. How reckless and in-the-moment it felt.

Jules flipped me on my back and slowly drilled into me while my thighs bracketed his sides. I dug the heels of my feet into his ass and pushed him as deep as he would go. When I looked down and saw the way he pulled out then slid back in, my body trembled.

His strokes came harder. Heavier. His hips crashed into me while his dick drove deeper. Every thrust sent my moans closer to God. Shit, every thrust sent *me* closer to God.

"Fuck me harder, Julien." I knew he was already plowing into me but I wanted him harder and deeper even though it was physically impossible. I wanted him to burrow so deep, I felt him with each beat of my heart.

He grunted, fucking me so hard, tears dripped down the sides of my face. He bowed his head and kissed my neck while he pumped into me furiously. He was like a goddamn machine.

"Oh god. Julien…I'm…"

"Come for me again, Cress. Make that pretty pussy squeeze my dick. I want to look down and see that shit." He stared between our bodies, looking at where we were connected and I came. It was a wave of electricity I wasn't ready for.

My muscles went wooden and my breathing staggered in and out but my pussy? Oh my god. It was breathing and beating on its own. Jules watched in awe.

"Damn, Cressida." He jerked his gaze to mine and all I could do was hold his stare with watery eyes. He started fucking me again, this time with measured stiff strokes that sent jolts careening through my core. My name had become a whispered chant on his lips while he lowered himself to kiss my neck and bite my shoulder.

When he came, he pulled out quickly and let his orgasm splash all over my stomach. I watched his dick bob and pulse until every drop was spilled on my flesh. Once he was spent, I let my head fall with a soft thump on the arm of the couch.

With heavy eyes, I looked around the living room and noticed the blue glow from the clock above the TV. It was two in the morning.

"I have to check in with Angel." Saying his name brought down a hailstorm of unwanted reality. It must have had the same effect on Jules because his expression went from open and relaxed to tense and void of emotion. I wanted the passionate Jules. The affectionate one. I missed him already.

"Check-in?" He frowned. "He said something about that shit when I was at Rush."

"Yeah, while he's at work, I have to check in every two hours. If I don't, he gets pissed. Even when I call and he doesn't answer, he gets pissed."

"That shit is obnoxious, Cress. The more of Angel's bullshit I see, the less I feel like I know my own brother." He leaned over and kissed my forehead.

"I don't know if it means you don't know him now or if it means you never knew the real him."

Jules stood up, towering with muscles laid carefully, brick by brick and smokey brown skin glowing under the low lights. Every thought tumbled out of my head and landed in a heap on the floor. The dark lines of his tattoos shadowed his sculpted arms and bordered his shoulders like armor.

"You keep looking at me like that and I'm going to fuck you again."

"I wouldn't be mad."

"I don't want you to miss your check-in." He disappeared out of the living room and I let the sting of his words sink in. I knew he didn't mean for what he said to scathe but it did anyway.

When Jules returned, he had a washcloth in his hand. He wiped my stomach then handed me the robe from the floor and watched me put it on. It felt like we were being forced out of the Garden of Eden. For a couple of hours, we had something so fresh and beautiful. Now, we were hurtling back toward reality and it was bleak.

I tied my robe extra tight. Probably too tight. Jules brushed my hand away from the tie and tipped my head up, his fingers resting on my chin. "We'll talk in the morning, Cress."

"Okay," I said. I heard the sadness in my voice and wondered how long it had been there? How had I desensitized myself to the pain I lived through daily?

"I'm serious. Angel will be in Columbia so…"

A frown crashed into me. "Columbia?"

"Shit, he didn't tell you?"

"Hell no. I don't know why I'd expect him to tell me anything. It's not like he would have asked me to go with him. He likes to keep me locked in this…beautiful golden cage." I tossed my hand in the air and gestured to the house.

"If he offered to take you…would you go?" Jules studied my face and I knew he was looking for a specific answer but I didn't have one to give him.

"I wouldn't have a choice," I told him honestly. Something hot and stony flashed in Jules's eyes but he buried it almost immediately. "I gotta go, Jules. Thank you for tonight." Popped up on the balls of my feet and touched the side of his face. His low-cut beard tickling the palm of my hand. I didn't expect him to cover my hand with his, holding my touch against him.

"Thank you, Cressida." Then he brought my hand to his lips and pressed the sweetest kiss there. When he let my hand drop, my stomach went with it. I wanted to crawl in bed beside Jules and lay my head on his chest. I wanted his tattooed arms to wrap around me and keep me safe.

Knowing I could never have something so simple, sliced deep. I grappled with my feelings as I climbed the steps and went to my room. I had to clear the emotion from my eyes and face because Angel studied me and would pick up on any significant change. He already thought I was cheating on him all the damn time. I didn't need to add fuel to the fire. Even though his suspicions had come true.

"What the fuck took you so long, Cress?" Angel's face filled up the screen on my phone and I forced a tired smile. The mask I wore daily felt like stone.

"Sorry, Nas is teething and was cranky. I had to calm him down and put him back to sleep." It wasn't a complete lie. The timeline was off though. Fear clogged my throat as I looked into the dark, dilated pupils on my phone.

The way he stared at me, flitting his eyes over my face made me feel like he could see the way his brother fucked me. I pressed my aching thighs together involuntarily, trying to savor the sensations Jules made me feel.

"See? He's getting more teeth. So, weaning him was good, right, baby?"

"Uh-huh." I had to give Nasim formula since I couldn't nurse him anymore. He still needed milk. He wasn't even one yet. It was pointless explaining that to my husband. All he cared about was validating his irrational thoughts.

"I'll be home in a little while. Smoke in the house? I sent him home."

"Yeah, he came in a couple of hours ago." My skin heated at the mention of Jules. I tried not to give it away on my face, but it was hard. The way he made me feel was still fresh in my mind.

"I told him to watch your sneaky ass. I trust him around you. I couldn't trust Sam." Anger flickered in his dark eyes. He blew a stream of smoke toward the screen and narrowed his eyes through the haze. "Be on your best behavior, Cress. I know how much you like fucking around on me."

"Angel, I've never cheated on you." It was the honest to goodness damn truth well…until tonight and I didn't know why he couldn't understand that. He kept me on a tight leash. I couldn't spend money without his approval, I couldn't drive myself anywhere, I could only hang out with Bree, and I wasn't allowed to go back to school or work because I needed to take care of Nasim. When exactly was I going to have the time to cheat on him?

"Whatever, bitch. Sometimes I wonder why the fuck I plucked you out of that run-down church and gave you a better life. All you do is stress me the fuck out with your stupid ass. Look, don't try anything dumb. Smoke is there and he'll be there when I leave town tomorrow too."

"You're leaving town?" I feigned shock, pushing my brows together.

"Don't worry about where I'm going. I'll be back on Monday. At least with Smoke watching you, I know you'll keep your goddamn legs closed."

Frustration and anger inched up my spine. I wanted to hurl hurtful words at him then take Nas and run blindly into the night.

Would Jules stop me from running?

My mouth went dry.

"Okay, Angel." I looked down at the bed and smoothed a hand over the blanket. I listened to my husband rant and rave in disjointed paragraphs for a little while longer before he let me get off the phone.

I went to check on Nas but saw Jules standing in the nursery, peering into the crib. I didn't make a sound. I just stared. It was so foreign to see anyone other than me, Bree, or my parents around him. Jules reached a gentle hand into the crib and touched Nasim's curls then took a step back. I wished I could climb inside his head and hear his thoughts because I knew he was steeped in them after what happened. Maybe he was thinking that Nasim should have been his son. Or maybe it was my thought alone.

I struck the thought down as soon as it cropped up again. It was so incessant.

I crept back to the bedroom and waited until I saw him leave the nursery before I went in to check on my son. I didn't want to risk running into Jules and trying to pry myself away from his energy or his touch. He said we'd talk in the morning, so that's what would happen.

...

Chapter SEVEN

Julien

"Here." Angel handed me a stapled packet of papers to flip through while we stood in the living room. The same room I fucked his wife in. He sat on the couch in the spot where I sucked and licked Cressida's pussy until she came all over my tongue. Images flashed vivid and nasty in my mind.

"What's this, hermano?" I asked.

"Instructions for how to watch over Cress while I'm gone," he answered. Angel was packed and ready to leave for Columbia and I can't say I was sad to see him go for a little while. "The list of stores she can spend money at. A list of pin numbers and passwords so you can check her spending. A list of phone numbers that should be in her phone. The names and tags of all the cars in the garages and all the cars she's allowed to ride in. A list of foods she can and can't eat along with her expected caloric intake and how many calories she should burn daily."

A laugh tumbled from my mouth as I looked at my brother. "You're fucking kidding me...right?"

"No." His eyes were stone.

"You expect me to check up on a grown-ass woman like this? Yo, Angel what are you doing to your wife?" I knew I had no room to talk to him about his marriage after what Cress and I did last night. Truthfully, I didn't want her with him anymore. I didn't know what the alternative was though.

Her being with me instead?

I wasn't relationship material. I was a lone wolf. Nobody could look inside of me and find something to love. Good girls like Cress didn't love monsters like me.

"I'm keeping her stupid ass in check. She doesn't have the goddamn brain to take care of herself. I don't need her stress-eating and getting fat or not eating enough and getting too skinny. She represents me. She carries the Delgado name." He glanced at me and smirked, arrogance washing over him. "No offense to you, Smoke. You're not a Delgado. Not that there's anything wrong with being a half-breed. Shit, Nas is a fucking half-breed."

"Don't call my nephew that bullshit." I curled my fingers into my palm, ready to punch him in the fucking mouth.

"You seem to forget who owns what around here." He stood and we were bumping chests. "Nasim is my son. Cressida is my wife. I don't need you protecting them from me. I know what's best for my goddamn family. Until you get a family, don't say shit to me about how I handle mine!"

Without warning, my fist connected with Angel's mouth. The sound of knuckles cracking into lips and teeth felt like the loudest noise in the world.

Angel's hand flew to his mouth to inspect his swelling, bloody lip. I pulled my punch and didn't throw it as hard as I could but he was losing his goddamn mind yelling at me like we were kids.

"What the hell is going on down here?" Cress's voice was frantic as she rushed into the living room. While Angel's head was bowed in pain, she glanced at me quickly and I made the slightest head nod, telling her to go to her husband.

She rushed over, pressing her hand to his back while trying to examine his face. He kept turning away from her though. "Get your ass back upstairs!" He boomed and lifted his open hand in the air, poised to strike. Fear clouded Cress's pretty face and rage swelled up inside of me. I stepped in front of her, arms folded, my stare laser-aimed at Angel.

"Do it," I growled. I dared him to violate everything our mother and grandmother taught us about how to honor women. He knew he was fucking up because he lowered his hand and sniffed, straightening his spine.

"Cress, take your ass upstairs. This is a matter between two men and it doesn't concern you."

"Are you okay?" She asked, her hand on his back but her eyes on me.

"I said go!" Angel snapped. I don't think he realized that question wasn't for him. I'm glad because it would have caused more trouble and I didn't want to have to fuck my brother up, but I would for her.

Cress scrambled out of the room leaving me and Angel standing face to face. His nostrils flared. One was noticeably larger than the other. "What the fuck was that, Smoke? You choosing some bitch over your brother?" Hearing him call Cress out of her name, again and again, dragged hot needles across my skin. I wanted to lay Angel out on the floor for that shit alone.

"She's your wife. You need to respect her. Do you think Mom and Grandma would be cool with the way you talk to her and treat her? You were about to hit her because she was checking on your bitch ass." I jabbed two stony fingers into his chest and he stumbled back.

"*My* grandmother wouldn't be proud," he admitted quietly. The way he emphasized that it was his grandmother wasn't lost on me. It stung because I knew Grandma loved Angel more. She always did. He was her biological grandson and I was just the smoke baby. The half-breed.

"Then cut that shit out. I'm not going to let it happen. I don't disrespect women or children and I don't allow it to happen in my presence."

"Your presence? Who the fuck are you, Smoke?" He scoffed before sitting on the couch and lighting a cigarette. Smoke filled the space as he spoke.

"I'm your brother, motherfucker. I should be able to call you out without you losing your shit. We made a pact when we were younger, Angel. We said we'd always have each other's back and do anything for each other as long as the other one was loyal and real. You're not being real with yourself." Standing in his living room, in his house after fucking his wife and telling him he wasn't being real, hurt. I wasn't being loyal or real either.

Angel was quiet for a while. Words and thoughts piled up between us like old newspapers. Finally, he broke the silence and said, "You know if anyone else in the world punched me in my fucking mouth, they'd be dead on the spot."

I didn't respond because he was looking for a confrontation. I dented his ego and pride. No man likes that but I didn't give a fuck. The way he was treating Cress was out of line.

"Smoke, you're the only other person in the world that I trust. Why do you think I'm letting you keep watch over my wife and son? Why do you think I'm making moves so you can be my right-hand man and help me run Rush and the entire drug game? I love you, man."

"I love you too, hermano. I just need you to understand, we're not kids anymore and I'm not going to look the other way while you fuck up your life and relationships. I don't know what your men tell you but I'm going to keep it one-hundred. You gotta stop using coke and you need to stop abusing your wife."

"Abusing?" Now his voice was raising and his eyes were turning shadowy.

"You heard me, Angel. You were about to hit Cress. How long before you follow through?" Silence flashed between us for a few seconds, then Angel blew out a plume of gray smoke and stood up.

"We need some time apart to cool off, Smoke. Maybe I need to clear my head and reevaluate some things. It's good that I'm leaving today."

"You need to hear me and not run away."

"I hear you, goddammit. Now, you hear *me*." He held the cigarette pinched between his thumb and pointer fingers. "You're my baby brother and I love you but if you ever hit me like that again, we're going to have real problems."

"And I welcome them," I said, tipping my chin up, putting even more distance between the top of his head and mine.

"This is how I know even though we have different fathers, we have the same blood. You have my heart in there." He thumped my chest with his cigarette-free hand. "I trust you with my life because you're willing to call me out on my bullshit. I trust you with my wife and son's lives because you're willing to protect them at all costs. You're a real one, Smoke. I might want to bash your head in sometimes but you always keep me straight."

I didn't respond. I nodded my understanding at him. I wished I could say the same things to him but I realized I didn't know Angel the way I thought I did. My view of him was shifting from the way a little brother looks at his big brother to something else. I couldn't put my finger on it.

Before Angel left for his flight, I asked him if I was also in charge of Rush operations while he was gone. He gave me a full novel about how to take care of Cress but nothing about the club. "Boogie is holding down Rush while I'm gone. Answer to him."

"You don't trust me or something, hermano?"

"I do. But before you can stand-in as a boss for Rush, you need to be smarter. Right now, you're not." He was gone after that and I was left standing there wondering what the fuck just happened.

I was supposed to be sliding into position as Angel's right hand. He was supposed to give me more control as time went on until we were equally yoked. Angel knew damn well I was smart enough to oversee Rush while he was gone. He just didn't want me to. It settled inside of me like a feather and a brick resting on a scale. The feather being the Angel I thought I knew growing up and the brick being the Angel in front of me now.

"Did Angel leave?" Cress's voice sounded from behind me and I turned around to see her with Nasim balanced on her hip. His chubby hands were fisted in her hair while he grinned.

"Yeah, he just left. Everything okay?"

"Everything is fine. I just thought he'd want to say goodbye to Nas. I guess I was wrong." I still saw remnants of sadness and fear etched on her face and in her champagne eyes. I hated it.

"Your mom watches Nas when you need her to, right?"

"Yeah, why?" She switched Nasim from one hip to the other

and his hands went from her hair to her shirt. I took him in my arms to give her a break.

"I want you to take a minute to yourself today, Cress. After what happened last night…" I cleared my throat because thinking about last night while she was standing in front of me was making my dick hard. Instead of focusing on how good she tasted or how sweet her moans were, I focused on Nasim in my arms, babbling and smiling. "I know you need time to unpack things and think. Let your parents keep him for today." I sat the squirming eight-month-old down on the floor in the foyer and he immediately pulled up to a standing position, using my pant leg.

Cress smiled down at him while I studied the soft curve of her cheek and the love in her eyes when she stared at him. It created an inconceivably deep need inside of me. I tried to push it away, but when I looked at how motherhood settled on her head like a crown, I couldn't fight the pride swelling in my chest. I ignored the other thoughts starting to crowd in. Thoughts about when I'd have my own family. Was I even capable of having a family? Monsters like me didn't have a wife or kids or a house with a fucking picket fence.

"I don't know, Jules. It's short notice and…"

"And Angel told me they live in the neighborhood."

"Did he also tell you they're the only ones allowed to watch Nas? I can't get a nanny or a babysitter because he doesn't trust that I won't hand Nas over and run away somewhere." Disdain colored her pretty face.

"Without Nas? You'd never do that. It's just one more thing he uses to control you. I'm not trying to do that. I just see how stressed you are. When's the last time you were alone?"

"Alone?" She laughed at the word like it was foreign.

"Yeah, Cress, alone. Just you in the house. No handlers, no security, no Bree, and no Nas."

She blinked her eyes repeatedly, then stared at me like she didn't know the answer to my question. Finally, she let her slim shoulders rise and fall. "I don't remember the last time I was alone."

"Alright, let's fix that shit. Call your parents and tell them you need them to keep Nas. I have some shit to take care of for a few hours but I'll be back later because we still need to talk."

"I don't know, Julien. It's such short notice and I don't want them to think I don't like spending time with my son." Her pouty lips tugged downward.

"Nobody said you don't like spending time with him. He's a cool ass kid. You're still human though. You can't be Nasim's mom twenty-four-seven. You gotta remember how to be Cressida." I reached out and touched a lock of her golden-caramel hair.

"Is it bad that I felt like myself last night when I was with you?"

I shook my head in response to her question. So many thoughts were fighting a war in my head...in my chest.

I watched her throat flex when she swallowed and imagined biting her there. When I traced the curve of her neck, I noticed muted bruises from last night.

Fuck. I was so sloppy.

What if Angel had seen those marks? I passed a thumb over one bruise near her collarbone and she shuddered. "I used concealer. You marked me up pretty good," she said with a soft smile.

"I'm so sorry, Cress. I wasn't thinking."

"Don't be sorry." She grabbed my hand and pressed my fingers to her neck. "I'm not."

"I'll be more careful next time," I assured her.

"Will there be a next time?"

"We'll talk when I get back." I wet my lips with my tongue and stared into her eyes. They were deep pools of possibility and they were dangerous as hell.

"You said we'd talk this morning and now you're running off to do work. Like Angel." A sad smile curved her lips up before she took a step back and grabbed hold of Nasim right before he fell to the floor. She scooped him up and looked at me. "I'll call my parents."

"I know I said we'd talk this morning but I have to take care of something important." I passed a hand over my freshly-cut hair and sighed. I hated letting her down but I did need to take care of something. It had been weighing on my mind since last night.

I watched Cress walk off with Nas and my chest felt warm again. I rubbed the spot between my pectoral muscles and shook my head. That woman was working some kind of magic on me and I couldn't decide if I liked it or not.

Once Cress was out of earshot, I called Boogie hoping he'd be as real as I thought he was. I didn't have any friends but I knew real when I saw it and Boogie was a real one.

"What's good, Smoke?" He answered after a few rings.

"Yo, Boog. I need to talk to you."

"Meet up?" He asked.

"Yeah. You at Rush?"

"I'm at my crib. Come through. I'll text you the address."

"Cool. I'll be there." I ended the call and waited for his information. Once I had it, I told Cress goodbye and kissed the top of Nasim's head before leaving.

Since I'd been home, Angel gifted me cars, money, and clothes but I wanted to get that kind of shit on my own. I was a grown man and getting gifts and a paycheck from my older brother was starting to sour on my stomach. Being his equal was one thing but being his employee was rubbing me the wrong way.

I pulled up at Boogie's house and was shocked at how understated it was. He lived in a condo about ten minutes from the beach. The neighborhood was quiet and clean.

He met me at the door and I nodded at him before we slapped hands. I stepped in and noticed the inside of his house wasn't as understated as the outside. Hardwood floors stretched throughout the space and expensive art hung on the walls. It was like stepping into a boss's den.

He led me to the living room where he sat in a plush leather chair. I sat on the matching couch. "What's up, Smoke? Everything good?"

"Nah." I relaxed and flexed my fingers, staring at the ruby skull ring. "I need to take care of something sensitive," I said looking into his eyes.

"Something or someone?" Boogie asked. I leaned forward,

resting my elbows on my knees.

"Someone. Two someones. I didn't go to anyone else about this because it needs to be discreet. You don't have to do anything but provide information." I continued to study Boogie's eyes because I could sniff out weakness. If Boogie wasn't who I thought he was and I had to kill him, I wouldn't hesitate.

"Someone inside the operation," he replied knowingly. I nodded and waited to see what his response would be. I wasn't going to further compromise myself if he wasn't with it or if I detected even a hint of immoveable loyalty to Angel. "Okay, I'm down. I trust you, Smoke." His eyes told me he was being genuine so I continued.

"I need the names of two of Angel's men. Security. They came to the house a few weeks back and did some foul shit to Cress. I don't play that shit." I relaxed again, resting my ankle on my knee.

"What happened?" Boogie asked.

"I'm not getting into the details right now. Can you get me their names?"

"Yeah. Of course. Angel only uses a handful of guys at the house."

"Cool. Get me that information by this afternoon."

"You know," Boogie said, running a hand over his silver beard. "Don't take this as me being disloyal but you got a better head on your shoulders than Angel. I'm trying to figure out how someone as clean as you got caught up on a gun charge." A true laugh flew out of my mouth.

"I took the fall for Angel," I admitted with a nod.

"I knew it. Ain't no way in hell someone like you would ever get caught on some bullshit charge like that. Guns aren't your weapon of choice."

"Nah. I like knives. Makes the artwork classier."

"Noted," Boogie chuckled. "You need help with the job?"

"No. I got it. I want this one all to myself. You get me those names." I stood up to leave but first, I asked Boogie a question. "Yo, did Angel leave you in charge of Rush while he was gone?"

Boogie cracked a smile and shook his head. "Nah. Rush is automated at this point. Unless Angel is gone for months, Rush doesn't need anyone to run it. Just oversee it. I was told you were doing that."

"Oh yeah? News to me," I scoffed before heading toward the front door.

"So, you're not overseeing things?"

"Fuck no. I was told to answer to you."

"What the fuck? Seems like Angel is giving us the runaround. No disrespect to your brother." He held his hands up and I waved him off, shaking my head.

"No need for the disclaimer. I noticed the same thing. I don't know who the fuck Angel is anymore." Thoughts fired through my head rapidly which meant my words became scarce. "Call me when you get those names, Boog."

We slapped hands and I went back to the house so I could have a much-needed talk with Cress.

Chapter EIGHT

Cressida

efore I walked into my parents' house, I took a deep breath and readied myself to be annoyed. I tried to limit my interactions with them because they seemed to love my husband more than they loved me. It made my world feel even smaller.

Even though I was grateful Mom and Dad agreed to watch Nasim for me, I was on pins and needles wondering what they'd say. How they'd judge me.

The front doors swung open and my mother grinned at me

with perfect teeth. Everything about her was perfect. She was used to never having a hair out of place. She had to project a certain image being First Lady of the church.

"Cressida! It's so good to see you." She took Nasim from me without so much as a hug and walked into the house. I followed her, balancing Nasim's bags on my shoulders. "You'd think we'd see you every Sunday especially now that Angel blessed us with our own church. There's no excuse but you seem to find one every week." She sat on the couch with Nas in her lap and he squirmed to get down and cruise.

"I just get overwhelmed sometimes and need to take a breather."

"Every weekend, Cressida? Come on now. The Lord needs your butt in that seat in your tithes in the basket."

"Angel sends money every month, Mom." He had a recurring tithe coming out of his account weekly. It kept my parents quiet and out of the way. I hated it.

"I know he does but money doesn't replace your heart being in church and open to God." I shut my eyes against her voice for a minute and breathed.

"Is that my grandson I hear in here making all that noise?" Dad walked into the room smiling at Nasim.

"Sure is. He's getting so big. Angel told me you weaned him off breast milk," Mom said, eyeing me.

"I didn't wean him. Angel did."

"Oh…well, father knows best." A fake smile stretched her lips tight. "You really should thank God every night that you have such a caring and smart husband like Angel."

"Amen," Dad said, nodding. "A wife is nothing without her husband to guide her. How are you, Cressida?"

Lonely. Aching. Trapped. Terrified.

"I'm fine."

"Fine? That's it?" Mom scoffed. "You're in that beautiful house with your son and your husband. You should be telling us how blessed and highly favored you are." That's the only answer Mom would ever accept from me. Even when I was single, she wanted to know that I was blessed and highly favored. Like nothing in my life was ever supposed to be wrong.

"You know, Cressida, you sound a little ungrateful. Do you need me to pray for you? Or maybe pray for Angel because it can't be easy for him working as hard as he does and having a wife who still finds something to be ungrateful about," Dad said with faux concern in his voice. If only they knew their beloved Angel was running drugs around Miami and was gunning for the spot as the top kingpin of Florida.

"No, Dad," I said, my words clipped. "I never said I was ungrateful. I said I was fine and you two made it a big thing. I'm fine."

"Watch your tone, Cressida. You know better than to talk to your father like that." Mom turned to Dad and rubbed his knee before handing Nas to him. "I'm going to make you some tea, honey. Can I get you anything else while I'm up?"

"No thank you, Sarah. I'm fine."

"You sure? I can fry some more bacon or…"

"I'm fine. Let me spend some time with my grandson." Dad started talking about taking Nasim fishing and to all these other places and I tuned out.

"Did you hear me, Cressida?" Dad's voice faded back into my mind and I jerked my eyes to him. "I said is he walking yet?"

"Oh, not yet. He's almost there though. He's been cruising for weeks. He started the day Julien came home."

"Julien?" Dad frowned at me, not sure who I was talking about.

I cleared my throat and said, "Smoke. Angel's brother."

"Oh…" Recognition clouded his features before disgust settled in. "The one who just got out of prison."

"Yeah, him." I tried not to sound too excited or happy about Jules being home because Dad would sniff it out.

"Didn't he used to have a crush on you when you were in middle school?"

…And high school and probably up until he took the charge for Angel.

"Yeah, he did."

"Well, I'm glad it never worked out. You don't need that kind of man in your life. You did good marrying the honest, hard-working brother."

"I never meant to marry Angel. We went on a date and…"

"And God took over from there," Mom said, walking into the room with a mug of steaming hot tea for Dad.

"You guys took over from there," I said, masking the sour tone of my voice with a soft chuckle.

"You're darn right we did. We knew Angel was going to be a successful man and once that brother of his was locked up, we knew if we didn't marry you off to Angel, that…Smoke boy would come sniffing around when he got out."

Little did they know, that Smoke boy still came sniffing around when he got out and good lord did he ever catch what he'd been chasing. My temperature started to rise just thinking about Jules and the way he touched my body. The way he said my name and caressed my skin.

"You let that boy around Nasim?" Mom asked, crossing her legs.

"I do. That's his uncle. Why wouldn't I?" A frown creased the space between my brows.

"Because he's a jailbird. I don't want my grandson to be influenced by a man like that." My mother shook her head and shut her eyes, her lips moving in silent prayer. Dad bounced Nas on his knee and I was swimming in a world of disbelief.

"Like what? Julien is a good man," I said indignantly.

"He *killed* someone, Cressida." Mom's harsh scold ruffled my feathers. I twisted my mood ring around a few times and paced my breath.

"You don't know the whole story but it's not worth discussing."

"You're right about that," Dad grunted. "That boy will have to repent when his time comes. The Lord will surely forgive but that doesn't mean he's meant for you."

"I never said he was meant for me. I said he's Nasim's uncle and he has a right to be around him."

"He doesn't need to be around anyone in my family," Mom huffed.

"Listen, I gotta head back home so let me put Nasim's food away and get out of here," I said, standing. I couldn't handle feeling like I needed to defend myself from my own parents. They called themselves Christians but they were so judgmental. They didn't know a damn thing about Julien yet they were assassinating his character like he was Lucifer himself.

I walked into the kitchen and started putting away small containers of food and snacks for Nas while he was with them. At least they treated my son better than they treated me.

"I'll help," Mom said, standing beside me and digging through my tote bag. The silence between us was thick and gnarled. It wasn't a smooth and natural silence between two people who were at peace with each other. It was bitter.

"Cressida, is everything okay? I mean at home. Do you need counsel?"

"I told you, I'm fine." I pressed my hands against the countertop, soaking in the smooth coolness.

"That's just it, baby...fine isn't okay. You can tell me anything." She took my hands and looked into my eyes. Hers were the same light hazel as mine. Her sandy brown hair was sleek and identical to mine though she was starting to gray at her temples.

I wanted to fall into her arms and cry like a little girl but I'd been burned one too many times by my parents. They took Angel's money and extravagant gifts and looked the other way when he neglected me and Nas or when he tried to control everything I did.

Still…standing in the kitchen with her holding my hands made my stomach wobble and my eyes burn. Something about my mother offering understanding made me want to break. Maybe if I told her I was being abused she would understand better. Maybe I needed to use plain language and not dress it up like I was coached to do by Angel.

"Angel…he um…" I rolled my lips between my teeth while my eyes watered. "He abuses me, Mom." Shock took over her eyes.

"What? Abuses you? Cressida, why didn't you tell us he's been hitting you?" Was that a flicker of compassion I saw in her eyes?

Not being one to lie outright, I said, "He doesn't hit me." My mind couldn't help replaying the moment his hand raised at me this morning after him and Jules got into it. I winced inside thinking about what would have happened had Julien not stood in front of me like a wall. A solid mass of muscle and anger, daring Angel to lay a hand on me. It was the only time I'd ever felt protected.

Mom's perfectly arched eyebrows pulled together. Fine creases disrupting her smooth forehead. "What do you mean? If he's not hitting you, he's not abusing you, baby. You can't throw around words like abuse if it's not true."

"There's more than one way to abuse someone. He controls everything I do from what I eat to how I spend money to…"

Her hand in the air was a silencing slice. "That's enough, Cressida! I won't stand here and listen to you talk bad about the man who gave you this beautiful life and that beautiful baby boy in there. What I hear is an ungrateful little brat who doesn't know how to submit to her husband.

Angel sounds like he's leading the way a strong man of God should lead. You on the other hand don't know how to follow." She aimed her outstretched pointer finger at me. "Angel is a blessing to this entire family. You need to learn how to serve him quickly before another woman does. I swear, Cressida if you divorce this man, I will never forgive you." She sucked in a breath and smoothed her hands over the pristine blouse and skirt she wore. "Now, go home and take some time to read your bible. For your maker is your husband," she quoted a line from the book of Isaiah. "Don't you forget that. You go home and read it over and over and fall to your knees, thankful that God saw fit to bless not just you, but all of us, with Angel." With that, her face turned to stone and she finished putting Nasim's food away.

I couldn't even look at her. I was disgusted. Not only with my mother and father but with myself. How the fuck did I let things linger this long and get this bad?

Before I left my parents' house, I kissed my son and told him I'd be back to get him. I didn't even know if I wanted him around Mom and Dad absorbing their toxic energy. It would be a long time before I let them keep him again. Jules was right though, I needed time to be me for a little while.

...

Back at home, I blasted *The Miseducation of Lauryn Hill* as loud as I could to drown out the confusion and pain rocking me. It felt weird being home alone without security, Nas, Bree, or Angel.

There was nothing for me to rage-clean because the housekeeper had been there already and made everything sparkle.

I sat in my room, staring at the runaway bag I had packed and ready to go for me and Nasim. I kept it under the stash of Always pads in the back of the closet because I knew Angel would never look there. I was right. Even if he did somehow stumble upon it, I had a layer of pads on top of everything else in the bag.

What he wouldn't see were the clothes and toiletries I had stashed there or the list of numbers to shelters and domestic violence organizations or the envelope of cash at the very bottom. I packed light because I'd need more things for Nas than for myself. I sat there, fantasizing about running away in the morning when I picked up Nas.

My string of scenarios was interrupted by the doorbell ringing. I froze for a second then rushed to look at the camera trained on the front door. It was so unsettling being home alone that anything startled me.

When I looked at the camera, I saw Bree standing there, phone in hand. I let out a rush of relief and went downstairs to let her in. She came into the foyer and we hugged then she pulled away to look at me.

"You okay, girl?"

"I'm fine," I said, moving into the kitchen. "It's just so weird being here alone. When the doorbell rang, I almost jumped out of my damn skin."

"Why are you here alone?" Bree asked, looking concerned.

"Angel went out of town and I let my parents watch Nas."

"What?" She blinked at me. "Wow." She cleared her throat and said, "So who does Angel have staying with you from security? Is Smoke here?" Her questions caught me off guard. I took a moment to contemplate her words before I answered.

"Julien will be back later. Angel didn't send any security to stay with me. I'm not a child, Bree."

"I know, I'm just used to someone being here when Angel leaves." She forced a smile then went to the wine chiller and grabbed a bottle. "Want a glass?"

"Not really." I started to tell her that I wanted to stay clear-headed for my talk with Jules but something made me bite my tongue. I went with it.

"What's up, Cress? You're not pregnant, are you?" She laughed but her eyes told me she really wanted an answer.

"Hell no," I blurted. I'd never make the mistake of getting pregnant by Angel again. I knew my cycle well and I avoided him like the plague when I was ovulating. I played sick, pretended to take care of Nas, anything to avoid fucking him.

"Oh, okay girl just making sure." She flashed a smile then opened the fridge, peering inside.

"Is everything okay with you, Bree? You seem a little high-strung. Well, more than usual," I laughed a little.

"I'm good. Just wanted to lay eyes on you when I heard Angel was out of town." I felt her eyes examining my neck then tumbling down to my chest. I concealed Jules's bite marks pretty well but the way Bree was staring made me feel like each bruise was a red exclamation point. "Y'all must have had a good night."

I thought about the way Jules fucked me and my throat tightened.

"It was okay." An awkward silence blanketed the moment and I didn't know how to shift things. Something was guarding my tongue and heart against Bree and I hated it but I couldn't force a genuine interaction. I was probably too stressed after what happened at my parents' house.

I talked about it a little with Bree but left out the most damaging part about my mother dismissing Angel's emotional, mental, and financial abuse. The entire time I talked to her, she half-listened and half scrolled on her phone. Every now and then, she'd toss out an occasional auto-pilot reaction but that was it.

Was I so immersed in motherhood that I was dull when I didn't have Nas as a buffer or topic of conversation? Jules's words came back to me after Bree made up an excuse to leave.

I needed to learn how to be Cressida. Not Nasim's mom or Angel's wife and I had no idea how to do that.

...

Chapter NINE

Julien

Boogie came through with the names of the security guards that were at the house and held Cressida down while a doctor injected her with something against her will to dry her milk up. He was starting to move up the ranks in my mind. So far, he'd proven to be more loyal and dependable than my goddamn brother. It was a shame.

I wasn't stupid enough to kill the men in Rush's sub-level where I did most of my kills for Angel. Instead, I found another spot. I preferred places without windows. Somewhere that looked abandoned. Somewhere with rich smells and sounds where nobody would look twice if they saw someone in an all-black hoodie, black sweatpants, and hiking boots.

I took one of Angel's cars to a small, abandoned mom-and-pop diner in the middle of nowhere. I'd scouted the place out one night when I was driving around Miami, zoned out with Jay-z's *The Black Album* thumping through the speakers. I listened to Jay when I plotted and Biggie when I executed.

The place was overgrown and had boards haphazardly nailed over the windows allowing slits of dusty light to fall through the cracks A few miles down the road was a dead-end, and past that was an undisturbed marsh, thick with wildlife. Even as I pulled up, I heard the croaking song of frogs and birds and the hissing of insects. I got out and took a deep breath, inhaling humid air.

Muffled grunts came from the backseat and I knew the guy I had stashed back there was waking up. It was easy to lure both men. A handshake and back pat turned into having a drink in the receiving area of Rush laced with Rohypnol. They both knew they'd fucked up when their eyes grew heavy and their speech slowed down, looping around vowels until they were nodding off, chin to chest.

Having a coked-out drug lord for an older brother had its perks. I had access to tons of deadly substances. Before, I had to take motherfuckers by force or by pressing a needle into their necks.

I was able to walk both men out to Angel's car and pass it off by laughing and telling whoever was around that they couldn't handle their liquor. Nobody questioned it. Now, one was in the backseat and the other was curled up in the trunk.

I grabbed the grunting man from the backseat and hauled him over my shoulder. He was heavy as fuck but I bench pressed four-hundred pounds easily, so I handled it. In twenty minutes, I zip-tied and duct-taped both men to rusty steel chairs in the diner.

I sat my Bluetooth speaker on the grimy counter covered with plastic tarp and chips of falling drywall from the ceiling. While they both struggled and woke up from their slumber, I searched for the perfect killing song. Something so disgusting and dark it would send me to a place full of shadows and black water.

Dead Wrong by The Notorious B.I.G. and Eminem flooded my ears and I shut my eyes against Biggie's thick, deep voice while he rapped about the most heinous things known to man. My eyes snapped open when I heard the heavy scraping sound of metal chair legs scooting across the plastic-covered floor. A scowl deepened on my face as I sighed.

"Where the fuck are you going, man?" I asked with a shrug. "You're trapped." I walked over, my gleaming sharp knife extended. I sliced the tape from his mouth while his friend watched in horror. I disregarded his facial hair and the skin underneath, slicing it with the razor-sharp blade.

Blood leaked from his skinned lips and chin. "What were you saying?" I asked, letting the tape fall to the plastic under my feet.

"Smoke, what the fuck are you doing?" He growled, blood coating his once-white teeth.

"I'm about to kill you," I said.

"Angel ordered a hit?" I didn't respond. Instead, I walked over to the other man tied to the chair and snatched his tape off with my hand.

"Smoke, don't do this man." See, he pled for his life a little. I liked when they did that because they had to know I wasn't going to have a change of heart. I wasn't going to let them go. This was the end of the line for them.

"What's this even about! We did everything Angel asked us to." The bloody one asked, his voice wobbling as the pain from having patches of his skin cut off set in.

"Fuck Angel!" I roared. I didn't even know that would jump out of my mouth but I suppose it had been coming for weeks. Fuck Angel.

Muscles in my neck and shoulders flexed as I contained my outburst. I pushed out a breath and shook my head. I had to get my anger in check. It was hard when I thought about how these two bitches held down a nursing woman against her will. There weren't too many things that triggered anger inside of me, but mistreating women and children did it. It turned me into a raging monster because I couldn't help thinking about my mother getting abused by Angel's father. How scared she must have been. How heartbroken she was.

I walked over to the one with the bloody face and flared my nostrils. The smell of his metallic blood hung faintly in the air. That familiar hum flowed through me and I knew I had myself back in check. It was like flipping on a switch. A deadly fucking switch.

"Y'all motherfuckers have no code. No honor. No loyalty to anything other than money," I said, squatting down so he could look into my eyes and see his last moments reflected in my irises. I wondered if skulls danced in my eyes or maybe it was roses since I found poetic death and murder so beautiful.

"Just tell me what we did, Smoke. We can fix it," he reasoned, tears streaking his cheeks and mixing with the blood smeared along his jawline.

"Nah. You can't. You went to someone's house, walked in, and held them down against their will."

"Cress?" The other one said. My head turned at the mention of her. Something dark and viscous pumped through me. "We...we were just doing what the boss asked us to do."

"And I'm making it right. Putting the scales back in balance. You should never harm a woman or aid in her being hurt. What the fuck kind of monsters are y'all?" I stood up and shook my head. "You fucked with the wrong one." I dragged the sharp tip of my knife down the center of his shirt, drawing small amounts of blood as I opened the cotton, exposing his skin.

"What the fuck are you doing?" The bloody one tried in vain to get loose.

"You helped Cress lose something precious to her so I'm going to return the favor." His friend watched in horror with wide eyes. I never got tired of that terrified look. Now he knew how Cress felt.

I ignored the rest of the questions and pleading. I let their voices melt together in my mind like red and blue on a white canvas. I was the black vein of smoke swirling between the colors.

With one quick swipe, my blade took off the bloody one's right nipple like slicing the top off a tomato. His high-pitched scream rang over the music in the background. The sound of his friend vomiting added an extra splash of orange to the canvas in my mind. I took his other nipple of and it flopped into his lap, a slab of skin leaving behind a bloody patch.

I let him groan and scream in anguish before moving over to the next man. I repeated slicing his shirt open and taking off his nipples one at a time, letting them fall to the plastic. His screams were a beautiful bloom in my ears. Their voices hummed together. A duet I relished.

When I was tired of the sounds, I plunged my knife in the space just above the bloody one's collarbone then dragged it upward, opening him and letting the rest of his life force spill over his shoulder. It soaked his sleeve as his heavy head lolled. I walked over to the other man, not bothering to wipe the knife before staring into his eyes.

I remained silent while I gave him the same fate as his friend. A sliced jugular. I liked going for the right jugular because it tended to be slightly larger than the left. An easier target.

They both bled out over the next half hour into black buckets I placed at their fingertips to catch the rivulets of warm crimson flowing from them. It would make clean up much easier later on.

While I waited for them to bleed out, I sat alone with my thoughts as Biggie and Jay-z took turns playing in the background.

I didn't like the man Angel turned out to be. I didn't like what the past five years had done to him. Or maybe it was like Cress said,

I didn't know him like I thought I did. Maybe I was finally seeing the real him. The thought dragged barbed wire through my chest.

I turned my eyes to the black buckets and noticed only drips of blood falling from their fingertips. It was time to clean. That part of a kill was therapeutic for me. The strong smell of bleach and peroxide to break down the blood enzymes. The sweeping sound of the scrub brush. The crinkling of the thick plastic. The noise the duct tape made when I pulled it from the roll. It all was an act of meditation. It was a quiet moment for me to reflect on if I made the right decision.

Every kill had always been the right decision. I weighed things on a scale inside myself. If the kill didn't balance those scales perfectly, the kill wasn't right. Like Sam. I knew damn well my inner-scale wasn't balanced. I was too hungry. Too eager to please Angel and to sate my blood lust.

I had to atone.

Once I had the bodies of the dead men stacked neatly in Angel's trunk, I drove home to wait out the sun. I liked to dispose of bodies when the sun went down. I liked the cloak of night. It made things much easier.

When I walked in, I heard music coming from upstairs. Erykah Badu's *Baduizm* played, the iconic song *Didn't Cha Know*, and my head bobbed. I felt the lyrics somewhere deep inside. "Trying to run but I lost my way." Yeah, that was me all the time. I felt lost right now. I felt like I had to guard myself against my own brother.

I walked upstairs quietly, peering in the bedroom. Cress

was standing at the foot of the bed looking at a pile of clothes contemplatively. Her sandy hair was a riot of looping spirals all over her head, sweeping her shoulders. That was the Cressida I grew up knowing.

I found myself smiling while watching her. My eyes inched down her curves then back up. She was wearing a white crocheted halter top that tied in a soft bow at the nape of her neck leaving her shoulders and back exposed. Her smooth golden skin had a dusting of faint copper freckles along her spine. If you weren't staring and dissecting her, you'd never notice them. The skirt she wore had deep emerald green palm leaves all over it and swept her bright pink toes. She was a goddess.

I don't know what alerted her to my presence but she turned to the doorway, shock registering on her face. She pressed her hand to her chest and blew out a breath. The song skipped to *Next Lifetime* and I wondered if Erykah was singing out my life.

"Jules, hey." She smiled and walked close to me, hesitation evident in her stiff posture. She didn't know if she should hug me or not. I chose for her and pulled her into my arms. She disappeared against my broad, solid frame. Her eyes fell shut. Thick dark lashes resting against her cherubic cheeks. How could I not kiss the top of her head? How could I not squeeze her tighter?

"You okay?" I asked into her wild curls.

"Now I am. I was kinda going crazy in here alone. So, I decided to get things together to give away to a women's shelter. I don't need all these clothes and shoes." She walked over to the bed, gesturing to the heap of designer shit.

"That's noble," I said. I sat on a clear spot of bed and looked at her. "I like your hair."

"Thank you." She blushed while folding a shirt. "I took a shower and I heard you in my head telling me you liked it curly, so I washed it and let the curls come back. At least until Angel gets back."

"But how do *you* like your hair?" I asked, tipping my head to the side. Why the fuck didn't she have on a bra? She was scrubbed clean, which meant every damn mark I put on her skin was on display. Bold and brazen for me to see.

"Curly," she said with a sure nod. "It's less maintenance, believe it or not."

"It's nicer to pull too," I noted, staring at her. I watched those plump pink lips quirk up and goddammit I wanted to suck on them. I hadn't been around her for ten minutes and my dick was hard and I was thinking about stroking her curls and sucking on her lips. This shit was out of control.

"Oh my god, Julien," she laughed, holding her hand over her mouth. "You can't say things like that. We haven't talked about what happened between us." She flashed me a look and I sighed, begging my cock to go down.

"You're right. I'm sorry."

She stopped folding clothes and looked at me. My chest felt warm again. "You're different," she said. "Lighter. What did you do while you were gone?" Now her eyes were narrowing as she tried to figure out the answer to her own question.

"Took care of some business."

"You're being short, Jules," she sang, waving a finger in my direction.

"What do you want me to tell you, Cress? You're not interested in the details."

"How do you know that? You haven't told me anything."

"You have to push, huh?" I asked, wetting my lips. Her eyes fixed on my mouth and my dick threatened to stiffen again for her.

"I do. I told you, I like hearing you talk about everything."

"Even the fucked up things?" I asked curiously.

"Yes, Jules. I know you probably think I'm a squeamish church girl but that couldn't be further from the truth." She shook her head and sat beside me on the bed. It wasn't good enough. I pulled her into my lap and wrapped my arms around her waist. She smelled fucking divine. I had to steal a taste so I licked a short trail along her bare shoulder.

Goosebumps flowered on her skin. I couldn't stop my dick from turning rigid beneath her weight. "Tell me," she whispered, her hand on my jaw.

"I made two kills." I fell headfirst into her champagne pools the way I always did.

"Hits for Angel?" She asked, lifting a finely arched eyebrow.

"No. This was independent."

"Okay, so who was it? I know you don't kill unless it's a job or they deserve it."

"You know that, huh?" I squeezed her sides then slid my nose along her throat, hungry for her. I wondered how wet her pussy was.

"I do. So, tell me, Julien." Fire jumped to life in her eyes and the warmth in my chest spread. It wasn't as jarring as it used to be. Now, it felt like a relief. Like aloe on a burn.

"You have to keep it to yourself," I implored.

"Are you forgetting that I'm forbidden to speak to anyone outside of my parents, Bree, you, and staff?"

"I know but these two murders were Angel's men. He didn't order the hit but they needed to go." Cress was all wide eyes and curiosity like a kitten.

"Who?" She almost whispered. That look she had. The look of hunger and need. The look of acceptance and sincerity. It was almost too much. My fingers curled around her slender neck then I tugged her close to me. Close enough to suck on those perfectly sculpted lips, slipping my tongue into her mouth.

"I need to know you're loyal, Cress," I said seriously.

"You know that already. You know it and you feel it," she told me, pressing her hand against my sternum. "Stop acting like it's empty in here. It's not."

"I don't know about all that but I damn sure feel something when I'm around you." Another kiss. Slow and smoldering while I possessed her mouth. Then when I pulled away, I said, "I took out the two motherfuckers who held you down while the doctor gave you that shot." It was out in the open now. A detonated bomb. "I don't know what made me do it, Cressida but I couldn't handle knowing what they did to you. I couldn't handle knowing there were two men on his team who were okay with making a woman do anything against her will. Something like that doesn't sit well with me. What they did was fucked up and it's even more fucked up that Angel put the order out."

I let my words hang in the air so she could absorb them fully. It felt like forever before she said something and everything contained inside my ribcage tightened. It felt like I could barely breathe waiting for her next words.

What the fuck was Cress doing to me? I wasn't the same man I was when I walked out of prison. My chest warmed at the sight and thought of her. I became furious when anyone harmed her or spoke ill of her.

"I-I don't know what to say, Julien." Her voice was so soft and quiet. "You did that for me?"

"Of course. You know I got you." I lifted her head, making her focus on me. Only me. "I'd protect you with my life." The declaration of truth came out of nowhere. It was raw and unfiltered and I didn't take it back. I was a man of my word and I meant that shit.

"I've never had anyone protect me before." I didn't know why tears were rolling down her cheeks, but I wiped them as they flowed. I usually relished in pain but not like this. She was aching somewhere deep and I wanted to close the gash left there by everyone else.

"You've never had *me* before," I told her, tugging on a springy lock of curls.

"Do I have you now?" She asked. This was the talk we needed to have. The talk that would lay everything on the table.

"Is that what you want? Do you want to have me?" I knew my answer already, I just wanted to hear hers. I had no idea how I was so sure of something so wrong. Cressida didn't belong to me. She wasn't free for me to want. I couldn't keep her.

I needed her though.

She was a powerful force pulling at me even when I wasn't around her. When I was at Rush, Cress was on my mind. When I was tucked away in the guest room, researching becoming a certified gemologist, she popped into my thoughts. She popped into my thoughts when I was doing the most mundane things like brushing my teeth or getting my hair cut. At first, it was annoying as shit but now, I'd come to expect it.

Her silence made me feel open in a way that was foreign to me. I didn't like it. It made me not want to play fair. She was still on my lap, warm, soft, and smelling like vanilla and cinnamon. So, I inched her long, sweeping skirt up her legs until it was a pool of gauzy fabric around her hips.

She didn't have on panties. I felt the soft, smooth skin between her thighs and got so hard it hurt. I spread her thick pussy lips and grazed her clit with my fingers. Her gasp was sweet and quiet.

"You're not being fair, Jules."

"I know. Now answer me. You knew we needed to have this talk." She squirmed around so much I thought I would come in my fucking pants. I gripped her hip with my free hand to steady her.

She was so wet. It was killing me not to pin her to the bed and suck on her pussy until my face was soaked.

"I want you too, Jules but I'm scared. I don't know what that means and I don't want Angel to hurt you. I don't want to be the cause of a rift between you two." She stopped talking to let out a moan. That time it was louder and needier.

Shit, I didn't want there to be a rift between me and Angel either but there seemed to be one growing despite what I wanted. Even if things were all good between us, I could never turn a blind eye to the abuse he was making his wife suffer through. I could never ignore the way he swooped in and took her once I was in jail.

Took her?

She was never mine. I took her to the carnival once and won her a mood ring when we were in fucking eighth grade. That didn't entitle me to her but still…there was a connection. One that I had never felt again after that night under the stars. She must have felt it too because she still wore the ring.

"I'll figure that out. Just let me know if you want this to keep happening."

"I want it," she panted, working her hips in circles even though I tried to hold her still. "I want it so fucking bad, Jules." A pause and then, "I want *you*. Not just the…*amazing* sex." She covered my hand between her thighs with her own. "But you."

"You sure about that, sweetheart? I come with demons and darkness."

"Over the past five years, darkness has become my favorite

color." Her eyes fell shut and her body tensed. She was getting wetter with each fevered stroke of her swollen clit. Her words drove me crazy. They made me feel accepted and seen but she had no idea what wanting me meant.

"You sure about that?" My voice was gruff and in stark contrast with Cressida's soft skin.

"I'm sure, Jules." She fucked my fingers faster. I'd never seen anyone so needy. She let out a whimper as her body stiffened against me, her legs trembling involuntarily. She drew in ragged breaths as she gave in to the currents of an orgasm.

She was so damn pretty. So perfect. So...*mine.*

Angel had no right keeping someone like her caged while he abused her and made her feel like nothing. He was raised better than that but maybe the demons of his father were too powerful to escape. What Angel had for Cress wasn't love. It was possession.

"Is that what it's supposed to feel like?" Cress's voice brought me back to her sitting in my lap with her legs splayed open.

"What do you mean, sweetheart?" I asked, kissing her jaw and pulling my fingers from her slippery pussy. I licked off every sweet drop of her while I listened.

"When you come. Is it supposed to feel *that* good every time?" It took a minute for her question to filter through my mind but when it did, astonishment took hold of my features. I raised my eyebrows and gawked at her.

"When you're fucking with a man who knows what he's doing...yes." I slid her off my lap and beside me. Even though my dick was aching for her pussy, I had to ask this next question. "Cress, was Angel your first?"

Color crept high on her cheeks as she stared down at her hands. Her red-tinted mood ring stared back. "First and only...until last night."

"Fuck." I stared at the ceiling realizing that I was deeper into this shit than I'd anticipated. Of course Angel was her first. She was a church girl. Her parents kept her on a short leash. He was her first real everything.

I understood it but I hated everything about it. It was wrong. That was supposed to be me. Angel had no idea what kind of woman he had. I doubted he even cared.

"It was never good," she said looking up at me. "I kept hearing that the first time hurt but after that, it felt so good and I kept waiting for it. Waiting for the so good part. It never came. I've never been as wet with him as I am with you. I didn't know my body could even do that. I thought maybe I was broken."

My dick throbbed in reaction to her words. I reached out, smoothing a large, wide palm over her chest, skimming up to her delicate collarbones.

"You are not the broken one. He shouldn't have been your first." I looked her up and down, hungry for every part of her. "I should have."

We fell into a kiss that made her whimper against my mouth. I speared my fingers into that thick, beautiful mane of curls and tugged hard. "I don't know how to be gentle with you, Cress."

"I don't want gentle. He tries to be gentle and I hate it."

"Because he doesn't know what the fuck he's doing" A war raged in my mind. One between loyalty to my blood and loyalty to whatever this was blossoming between me and Cressida.

With my hand at her throat, I pushed her back on a pile of clothes and settled between her open legs. I found the tie at the base of her neck and pulled it, freeing her perfect tits. I pushed down my sweatpants enough to let my dick out then pulled her tight mauve and brown nipple into my mouth, circling the areola with my tongue while she moaned under me. She raked her nails over my short hair while I licked and sucked on one nipple then the other.

While I feasted on her breasts, my hips bucked against her slick heat. The swollen head of my cock kissed her cunt over and over, driving both of us insane. I couldn't take any more teasing. I thrust inside her tight walls and groaned at how she squeezed my thick dick.

"You were so ready for this, Cress. Goddamn." I had to look down and watch the fucking grip she had on me. I crashed into her, hard, pushing her long legs back toward her ears. Slippery wet noises filled the space singing along with her moans and my groans.

Her pussy was so good. It was fucking perfection. I wanted to swim in it forever.

"Jules!" She squeaked while I hammered into her as deep as her tight little cunt would allow.

"That's such a good girl, sweetheart. Take this dick." I slid my thumb along her bottom lip and watched her tongue chase me.

"I need it," she cried, pressing her nails into my back. "Oh my god, Jules. Fuck me harder."

"You like it rough, Cress? My sweet little church girl likes getting pounded?" I drilled deeper, feeding her the inches that wouldn't fit comfortably. She howled in response, squeezing her eyes shut while we made the bed squeak and groan.

I fucked her like the monster I was. Pounding. Grunting. Stroking violently until sweat coated my brow and Cress sounded hoarse.

I gripped her neck and choked her while I dug into her slippery pussy and stayed there, letting her walls suck my dick. She licked her lips and lifted her hips, hungry for everything I had to give her. When she came, I watched her face melt. Her plump lips opened on an O before she called my name and shook. I let out a hiss of air when she started squeezing and throbbing around me.

I pulled out quickly and came all over her thighs and still pulsing pussy. My eyes fell shut and stars danced on my eyelids.

Fuck.

Was I going to come that hard every time?

How many more times would there be before Angel found out?

Once the lust and hunger cleared from my brain, I tucked my wet dick away and went to the bathroom to get a warm cloth so I could clean her up. "Don't move," I told her.

"What are you doing?" She asked from the bed. I didn't say much, I let my actions speak. I cleaned her gently washing away the traces of my seed. She acted like I was an alien. "Are you...*cleaning* me?" She had a smile in her voice that I heard clear as day.

"Yeah. I can't let you lay there with my cum all over you. I mean you look fucking beautiful but I assume you want to walk around at some point." We laughed together.

"I'm just not used to it."

"Yeah, I kinda figured. I might be a monster, Cress but I clean up my messes." When I was done, she sat up, straightening her halter top and tying it around her neck again.

"You're an anomaly, Julien Jean." She smiled when she looked at me and not many people did that. They took one look at the tall scowling guy with tattoos and went the other way.

"How?" I quizzed.

"You find beauty in murder. You're practically a recluse. Brooding is your second language. You fuck like a savage…yet here you are, wiping me so gently. Cleaning me like I'm some precious treasure."

"You are." The words came out with ease because they were true.

"I'm not a precious treasure," she laughed. I could see the years of demolition my brother did in her eyes. I saw it in the way her smile slipped when I complimented her. I saw it in the quick twist of her mood ring and fidget of her left foot on the rug. In the way her shoulders rose around her ears ever so slightly.

He'd broken something that used to be strong in her. He taught her how to self-destruct so that when he wasn't around, she made herself feel less than. I kissed her forehead, then her eyelids while her breath came in rapid inhales and exhales like tears were brewing under the surface.

"Who taught you how to hate yourself, Cress?"

"I…I don't know. Angel, I guess. He taught me how to shrink to survive." Her words were a whisper.

"But he got it wrong. You can't shrink to survive. You have to overcome and that means growing." I slipped a lone finger along the line of her shoulder. "I had to grow when I was locked up. I had no choice. I had to make myself grow to accept the fact that I was sitting in a cage like an animal for something my brother did."

Cressida looked up at me through thick lashes. So beautiful and angelic. I touched the apple of her cheek and my chest burned warm and bright. There'd never been anything bright inside of me before.

"You talk about prison like a badge of honor." She frowned, shaking her head.

"Because I did something noble. I laid myself on the sword so Angel could fly high with Rush. He was always the star between us. He was the one with a future. I was the quiet one. The evil one, like my grandmother used to call me."

"*His* grandmother, Jules. She was Angel's grandmother. Not yours. Don't attach yourself to her like that. Every time you bring her up, you're telling me how she said something fucked up to you as a kid."

Her words were quiet blades sliced across my skin. I knew they weren't meant to be but that's how they felt. "I never claimed she was my favorite person in the world but I learned to respect her while she was alive."

"Did she ever learn to respect *you* while she was alive?" More sharp blades. "Who's to say you didn't have a future, Jules? Some old woman who hated you and loved Angel? Of course she couldn't see your potential. She couldn't see how smart you are or how deep your mind runs. She couldn't see how charming and strong you are." She bit her lip as if to stop the onslaught of words but I wanted more of them. I wanted all of them.

It was the first time I'd ever stood in the sunlight and the warmth wasn't as bad as I thought it would be. I studied Cress's eyes and wondered why the fuck I left for Angel when I should have stayed for her. Even if it was only to see where things could have gone between us.

Now, she was Angel's wife and the mother of his son. He was her first everything. He gave her a life I could never give her.

Why the fuck do I want to give Cress a life? Why would that thought seep into my brain? She was Angel's wife. She was my sister-in-law.

But fuck…I wanted her so bad.

"You seem to think pretty highly of me." I didn't want to smile but I couldn't help it. She made me smile no matter how foreign and stiff it felt.

"I do. You give me a lot to think highly of." She shrugged.

"Trust me, the feeling is mutual, sweetheart." I followed the swirls of fine hair around her hairline with my finger. The sun slipped down into the earth with a golden yawn making a halo behind Cress. There she was.

My golden girl.

I slid my fingers down the bridge of her nose then outlined her plush pink lips. It was a moment when most men would have asked if they could kiss her. They would have said something beautiful. Not me.

I crushed her lips with mine, taking what I wanted. What I needed. What belonged to me.

She responded with a soft moan. I let it roll on my tongue like velvet before deepening the kiss and pressing my hard body into her soft curves. My dick was thick and stiff, pressing against Cress's thigh. I'd just cleaned her up and I wanted her again.

My mouth dropped to her breasts as my teeth marked her, scraping against golden silk forcing gasps and whimpers from that perfectly formed mouth. I went back to her lips and sucked, nibbled, claimed.

No matter how much I tried not to make her mine, everything inside of me growled that Cressida belonged to me. Not Angel. I didn't know how I managed to fool myself when I was locked up. I made myself think I'd be able to live with Angel and Cressida because I couldn't hold on to a thread of something sparked in middle school. I was grown now and that time had passed. Life happened.

But...

I was there, between her legs. Fucking her. Making her moan. Making her come all over my dick. Listening with every cell in my body while she talked and cried.

My gut told me she was mine. I couldn't ignore it. The call was too loud. Too strong. Whatever was growing between us was charged and powerful. It was stronger than blood.

We fucked again while the sun went down and I knew I was steadily heading toward an inevitable ending. I pushed the thought in the back of my mind and allowed myself to be with the only woman I'd ever wanted. For the moment, my guard was disassembled and on the ground in pieces. I felt warmth and brightness and all the things I never thought I deserved to feel.

I needed that. So, I indulged.

"Fuck," I groaned, sliding a hand down my face. I'd fallen into Cressida so hard that I neglected my phone and the two bodies in Angel's trunk.

"What's wrong?" She sat up beside me, the crisp white sheet the only thing covering her perfect breasts. We'd long since shoved the piles of clothes out of the way. The huge bed was now encircled by her skirts, blouses, dresses, and shoes. The way I fucked her required space.

"I have to finish cleaning up," I told her, sliding on my black sweats and searching the floor for my tank top and black t-shirt. I found them near the nightstand and pulled each one on.

"I'm coming." She scurried from the bed and snatched up her clothes.

"No, the fuck you're not, Cress." I pressed my large hand to her bare chest, sitting her down involuntarily.

"I want to see what you do," she said, a frown creasing the space between her brows.

"I don't need to corrupt you any more than I already have." I shook my head and looked at myself in the mirror. Something was different. I didn't focus on it for long. I had shit to do.

"You're not the one who corrupted me. Your brother did that all by himself. Who do you think taught me how to live with dark thoughts? Who do you think showed me that I'm alone in the world? You honestly gave me a new perspective, Jules."

"Me?" I asked, shocked.

"You. You've shown me that living with a coward is far more dangerous than living with a killer."

Shit, I couldn't argue with words like that. She was right. I was a lot of things but a coward wasn't one of them. I couldn't say the same for my older brother. Not anymore.

When I caved and told Cress she could come with me, she hopped up with such a big smile that I never wanted to tell her no again. I'd say yes to whatever she asked as long as she smiled at me like that.

I rubbed away the warmth barreling through my ribs and tried to ignore the thoughts growing like weeds in my brain. Cress was so happy in her little world of warmth that she didn't even realize how dangerous she was for me. She was loosening the screws and nails driven into something I'd spent my entire life protecting.

"You took Angel's car?" She asked as she clicked her seatbelt into place.

"Yeah. I wasn't risking my tags being seen by anyone. It's an unauthorized hit." I knew several of Angel's men looked to me for direction more than they looked to him but that didn't mean I had more pull with his men than he did. I needed to tread lightly. I couldn't trust anyone.

Cress understood and left it alone after that.

While I drove, the air between us came to life with deep conversations. She told me how tight Angel's hold was on her and how she tried to force herself to love him after they got married but it didn't work. She said there was always a connection missing. She told me how her parents were no help because they only cared about what Angel could do for them and their church and how even with Bree, she had to keep up a guard.

The more she told me horror stories about my brother that I never would have believed before I got out, the more I realized I didn't like him. If he and I didn't have blood ties, I'd never associate myself with him. It was a jagged realization that rocked me.

I was quiet while I loaded the two bodies onto the boat and pulled away from the dock. Once the rush of the water was the only noise I could hear, my shoulders relaxed a little. Cress inched closer to me, placing her small hand between my shoulder blades.

"You've been quiet. Did I say something on the way here?" Concern and a little bit of fear shaded her champagne eyes.

"You didn't say anything," I told her. "You don't ever have to worry about saying something that will piss me off to that extent. I don't use the silent treatment as punishment." I sucked in a deep, saltwater-filled breath and looked at the blanket of navy and stars stretching out before me. "I'm thinking about a lot of heavy shit."

"Like?" She tipped her head to the side and a charge of bright golden curls covered half of her face. I pushed her hair back, sinking into the lush feel of her spirals.

"Like the fact that Angel isn't who I thought he was."

"Who did you think he was before this?" She quizzed, one eyebrow lifting.

"A man. Maybe not a man I agreed with on everything, but still a man." My gaze dropped to the tops of Cressida's breasts. Golden and supple and dotted with concord bruises. My dick jolted at the sight of them. Did she have to wear a sundress on the boat? Of all places to wear a pink sundress, she chose at night in the middle of the almost black water.

She was a welcome contrast to the isolation I usually had with me. She was bright when everything else was dark. I slid my hand around to the small of her back feeling the flare of her hips starting at my fingertips.

"You gave him way too much credit," she laughed mirthlessly, narrowing her eyes.

"I know now."

"You're thinking about something else too because..."

"I'm being short."

"Yup." She rubbed the back of my neck and I rained soft kisses along the crook of her arm. She was soft and warm there and she smelled like soap.

"I want what's mine," I said simply. "And I can't stop thinking about it."

"Are you talking about Rush and the operation?" She asked, a frown folding her face.

"Rush?" I laughed." I don't give a fuck about Rush or the drugs or the money."

"Then what are you talking about, Jules?" I slid her so close to me that our sides touched and I could see the subtle emerald flecks dancing around the rings of her irises.

"You." My hand moved to touch her cheek. The warmth I kept fighting off, spread from my chest to my throat. Even my lips tingled with it. I leaned forward and Cress met me halfway, stretching her neck upward to catch the kiss I dropped on her full lips.

"I think I've known I wanted you since that night at the carnival." She whispered with her hand pressed to my jaw.

"Me too. I could have dealt with any interruption and still picked up where we left off but I hate that Angel was the interruption."

"Me too." She nodded our foreheads pressed together. "Look, if this is too much for you, I understand, Julien."

"No. It's not too much." I couldn't put into words what I knew had to happen. Not yet. It was still a fresh wound and resigning to it would be one of the hardest things I ever had to do. "My mind is already made up, Cress. I don't share what belongs to me. You belong to me and I know that's not the acceptable way to say it or whatever but I don't know how to be soft and romantic. I don't know how to use pretty words to explain myself." I killed the engine and let the water settle then slosh against the sides of the boat. "I probably shouldn't say you're mine. I should say something more poetic or politically correct but fuck all that shit. I don't know when it happened but...you're home for me, and I know I'm home for you too." I pointed to her then at myself. It was as close to romance as I could offer. She gave me so much warmth and kindness that I had to reciprocate. Cress deserved that and so much more. I didn't know how to give it to her but I wanted to learn.

...

Chapter TEN

Cressida

It was eerily quiet standing beside Jules on the boat yet the moment between us was charged with static. I felt it buzzing beneath my skin, collecting at my joints and making them weak. Jules didn't do romantic proclamations or long showy speeches but what he said about me being home for him and vice versa…I understood it.

He cared about me. He wanted to be with me and he wasn't going to let Angel stop it. Nerves clouded my throat knowing that my husband wouldn't let me go especially to be with his brother. This meant war. I knew it and so did Jules. That's probably why he was so quiet at first.

Instead of pointing out to Julien that what he said was his way of expressing how deeply he cared, I hugged him. Tiptoes pressing into the floor beneath me while my arms locked around his neck.

"I hear you," I said. I kissed his jaw and he looked at me like he didn't know what to say or do. How closed off was he that even the simplest show of affection took him by surprise?

I wondered if he saw that he was as much a victim of Angel's mental and emotional abuse as I was. Only he'd taken it from his brother and grandmother. The only person to love him unconditionally was his mother and I saw the shining light she left him with. It came out in his respect for women and children. It came through in the fact that as dark as he was, he had morals.

After we'd coasted for a few minutes, Jules reached down and hauled one of the tightly wrapped bodies over his broad shoulder. His muscles flexed beneath his t-shirt and I couldn't stop thinking about how strong he was. Here he was tossing a dead body into the dark water and all I could think of was how fine he was.

He was nothing like his brother and maybe it was shallow but Julien's dick was longer and thicker than Angel's by miles. I was going to split myself in two if I kept fucking him the way I was. I was addicted though.

"That's it, huh?" I asked after the second body was slipped into the water without so much as a splash

"That's it. The stream will take the bodies so far away from Florida, if anyone finds them, they'd have no physical way to trace them."

"Wow," I said, disbelief twined around my voice. "And you did this because they came in and held me down? You didn't have any other beef with them?" The wind whipped my wild golden curls around covering my face then freeing it.

"Nah. No other beef. I draw the line at holding women down against their will." He grew quiet then looked at me. Whenever he locked those mahogany eyes on mine, a key turned inside of me.

Jules said, "I draw the line at holding *you* against your will." His fingers were a feathery brush against my chin. Goosebumps washed over my arms and shoulders in response.

"You didn't have to do that," I told him, finding my mood ring and twisting.

"I did. I need every motherfucker inside Angel's operation to know not to fuck with you. I can't get that message across with meetings and arguments. I don't argue." Something about the grit of his voice made my thighs press together seeking out some sort of relief from the way my clit throbbed. I was insatiable when it came to him.

Every word he spoke was so goddamn sexy. I knew when I heard him speak for the first time in seven years that he was more man than Angel could ever be. He wasn't the alpha every TV show or book portrayed. Jules was the alpha every TV show and book warned you to stay away from.

He was the alpha-villain.

Something pulsing at my core needed to touch his darkness to understand my own. Before Jules came back into my life, I didn't feel my thoughts of killing Angel and running away were dark. They just...were. Now that Julien was back, I had a name for those thoughts. The ones that whispered in my ear when I watched Angel sleeping. Thoughts of driving a letter opener through his throat or setting the house on fire with him in it before running off with Nas.

Those were my dark thoughts.

They were my bones. Bones deserved love too.

"I like that about you, Julien," I said, cutting off my thoughts before they ran away from me. "I like that you don't argue or ask questions." Wind whipped my sundress behind me, molding the soft fabric to my waist, hips, and thighs. Jules devoured every inch of my body. His eyes were two x-ray beams peeling my clothes off.

"Does my little Cress have a dark side?" He smirked and I loved every arrogant second of it.

"I'm not little Cress anymore. I keep telling you that." I huffed, folding my arms.

"Right. Now you're the Cress who likes the fact that I do what I want when I want...huh?" He was closer to me now and my heart was pounding like the sea at the shore. I tipped my head upward to look into those intense eyes.

"Exactly," I said in a strong voice. He dipped his head low and he was so close I could feel the warmth of his breath on my lips. My tongue wanted his so badly, the roof of my mouth ached. Heat prickled the back of my neck and inched down to my spine.

How the hell was he driving me insane like this when we weren't even touching? Everything Jules did made me pulse with hunger and need.

When he wet his full lips with his tongue, I felt my breathing stutter. He really was a beautiful man with his smoked honey skin and dark wavy hair. I reached up, unable to keep my hands off him, and stroked the ocean of jet-black waves that he liked to wear cut short in a faded Caesar. My fingertips skimmed the shell of his ear before resting for a second on the sparkling diamond in his earlobe.

I'd never wanted a man so fucking bad. I'd never wanted anything or anyone as much as I wanted Julien Jean. He was pure addiction. I understood what addicts must go through when the object of their addiction calls out because right now in the shadow of Jules, I was helpless.

"So...if I take what I want right now, would you like it?" He asked, his deep voice scraping every throbbing part of my body. His hand was at my throat, squeezing enough to reduce my airflow but not hard enough for me to black out.

Everything. Pulsed.

My clit was a heartbeat between my legs thumping and begging for attention. *His* attention.

Jules didn't say another word. My slight nod was enough consent for him to spin me around and bend me over the boat's wheel. He pushed my dress up hastily and I didn't complain because the faster he got to my needy pussy, the better. I pushed back on him and he growled before slapping my ass hard. A pained, but aroused moan fell from my mouth.

"You," he said, pressing his warm, thick dick against my bare ass. "Are mine. Fuck whoever doesn't like it. And fuck my brother for mistreating you and stealing you while I was away." A grunt then a thrust and he was inside of me so deep I gripped the front of the boat, moaning to the waves below.

I was so wet for him that he slid in effortlessly. Each slow pull back and hard push inside made me drunk. Jules's chilly fingers found my hot, swollen clit and grazed it at first making my pussy clench around him. He let out a hiss of air then buried his dick deeper, making my toes curl.

"Jules!" I cried out pushing back against his punishing strokes. With one hand he massaged my clit and with the other, he yanked the braided straps of my dress down so that my breasts popped out. He squeezed my nipples and my clit at the same time. It was just enough pressure to make me explode. I couldn't hold it anymore and I didn't want to.

My legs shook and my eyes fell shut, closing out the stretch of night sky before me. I muttered his name like a chant while I unraveled. I was dripping with arousal. It slipped down my thighs with every stroke. He moved his hands to my hips and pulled me back so he could drive deeper.

"Take that shit, Cress. Take all this dick." He slapped my ass again and a delicious jolt surged through my core. Another orgasm. "I want to watch you come all around my cock. Let me watch your pretty pussy suck my dick."

Almost at his command, my body pulsed. Squeezed. Throbbed. My climax nearly suffocated me. I sucked in little sips of night air to keep my lungs inflated.

Jules was still fucking me relentlessly but I felt when his movements became stiffer. "Goddamn, Cress," he groaned. "Your pussy is so fucking tight. I'm about to..." He pulled out a little and I knew he was getting ready to come on my ass but I wanted to feel him inside of me. It was selfish and insane but I needed it. I was addicted to the way he made me feel. So when he tried to pull out, I pushed my ass back on him, swallowing his load inside me.

Oh my god.

He felt so good beating between my walls. He was helpless. The noises he made were pure fucking heroin. I made him sound like that. Me.

"Fuck..." He dragged the word out while he flooded me.

"Yours," I panted. "I'm yours." His rough hand gripped my throat, standing me up. He slid out of me and spun me around so I faced him, strands of curls slicked to my face from sweat. My skin cooled in the breeze, making my nipples tighten.

"Are you mine, Cress?" He asked in a deep growling tone. What other answer was there besides yes? His cum was trickling down my thigh while my body hummed his name. It surged through my blood and heated every inch of me.

"I've been yours since middle school, Julien." My lashes fluttered as I focused on his face. Finely sculpted high cheekbones, smooth skin without one blemish. Sleek, dark brows furled together in contemplation. Brown eyes so pure and honest and intense…and that mouth. That magical, perfectly formed mouth.

He nodded at my admission and let my throat go so he could touch my hair. For someone who claimed not to have a heart or emotions, he made me feel so loved and cherished. When he went to tuck his still-wet dick away, I put my hand on his wrist, stopping him.

"I want to suck your dick," I told him, lowering to my knees. It was the first time I *wanted* to do it. Angel always forced himself on me and I hated it but with Jules. The desire flowed easily. Shit, he made everything flow easily. I wondered if this was the difference between being with a coward like my husband and being with a real man like his brother.

Jules's fingers tugged at my hair once I was on my knees, making my eyes meet his. I prayed he didn't tell me to get up or that I didn't have to do it if I didn't want to. I wanted to feel empowered for once. If I wanted to get on my knees and suck the flavor of my pussy off his dick, then I didn't want him coaxing me out of it.

"I want you to look at me. I need to see those pretty champagne eyes while your mouth is full of my dick," he said wearing a smirk sharp as a knife. My stomach flopped. Of course he wouldn't be nice and romantic. That wasn't my Julien. He was rough and dark. He was my alpha-villain.

I took him in my mouth, relaxing my jaws and inching him in. He was so thick and long that it took some finessing to fit him comfortably without gagging. When he thrust further into my mouth, all hopes of not gagging flew away with the night breeze.

Heat prickled my face as I bobbed up and down on his cock trying to take as much of him as I could. The noises he made pushed me to go faster, slurping and moaning around his girth while I felt him slicking my inner thighs.

"Play with your pussy, Cress. Let me see," he commanded. "Spread your legs and let me see how much sucking my dick makes you come." I moaned again and did what he asked. I'd do almost anything Jules asked me to. He had me wide open.

The more I touched myself, the more Jules groaned and thrust deeper down my throat. Pressure swelled fast in my core and before I knew it, I was trembling from the intense wave of climax that crashed into me. My eyes fell shut for a moment and Jules yanked my hair, making them snap open again.

"Eyes on me, little Cress." He caressed my cheek then rubbed my ears all while biting his full bottom lip. I wanted to swallow him whole. "Fuck you look pretty on your knees...choking on my dick like a good girl." He gathered my thick bouncy curls into a ponytail in his hand and fucked my face until his movements became jerky and his dick throbbed in my mouth stiff and thick. Warm jets shot down my throat with a few spurts landing on the back of my tongue. Jules tasted fresh and familiar. I savored his cum in little salty drops until I'd milked every last ounce from him. When I popped off his cock, I chased his flavor with my tongue.

"Bring your sexy ass here," he said, pulling me up and pressing his lips to mine. His tongue slipped into my mouth and I moaned. I'd never felt so inebriated by someone before. He made me feel like

I was soaring.

When we got back home, I ran the shower and asked if he wanted to get in with me. My stomach twisted in knots waiting for his answer. I'd just fucked and sucked this man until my knees were weak and I was having anxiety about asking him to shower with me. I was so damn backward.

Showering together was more intimate than fucking though. There was something tender about it and Jules wasn't tender. I waited for his answer, standing at the kitchen door, toeing the floor.

"We did get pretty nasty on the boat, huh?" He said, his intense eyes peering down at me.

"We did."

"You go head, Cress. I have some shit to take care of." His words barely landed before I nodded and excused myself. I was so damn stupid thinking he'd break down his barriers and be soft for me. Julien Jean didn't yield. He didn't bend. He didn't take showers with his brother's wife.

I stepped into the hot spray of water and pushed out a slow, chastising breath. Why did I ask him to take a shower with me?

Stupid, Cress. So fucking stupid.

While I was busy beating myself up in the billowing steam clouds around me, the bathroom door opened and sucked all the muggy air out, replacing it with a chilly breeze. I wiped the condensation away from the shower door and saw Jules in a rivulet-distorted glimpse. He was naked. Completely. Butt. Naked.

"You gonna open the door for me, Cress?" He asked. His rough deep voice squeezed my insides. I slid open the shower door and he stepped in. A tall skyscraper with chiseled muscles under honey skin. I was finally getting to admire him without a stitch of clothing on and he was magnificent. His chest was a clean sculpted stretch of muscle untouched by tattoos. Expertly laid abdominal muscles like golden bricks led to the sinewy slashes at his narrow hips guiding my eyes to his thick dick. It was soft and I was still turned on. Julien had the prettiest caramel dick I'd ever seen. His shaft was so fucking thick and the veins snaking down toward his perfectly formed head made my mouth remember the way each one felt under my tongue.

I could stare at him all damn night.

"I...I thought you weren't getting in with me," I finally said, after taking inventory of every inch of his naked body.

"I told you I had something to take care of. I never said I wasn't getting in." He frowned. His strong arm hooked around my back, pulling me against him. He was so warm. So hard. Speaking of hard...I glanced down to see his dick stiffening. It poked my thigh as it stood.

"I know but..."

"I'm here now, Cress. Turn around and let me wash your back." He spun me around and slid the washcloth up and down my back sending tingles along my spine.

"You don't seem like the shower-together type," I told him, scooping my thick curls over one shoulder.

"I'm not." His big hands traveled down to my ass then my

thighs and hips.

"So why are you in here with me? You could have just lied and pretended you had work to do."

"I don't lie and I definitely don't lie to you." Now he was washing my shoulders, massaging as he went along. My muscles sang his praises. We settled into a comfortable silence for a moment and it felt good. My brain sighed with relief. I didn't realize until that moment in the shower with Jules that I was in a constant state of stress when Angel was home. I was in survival mode so often that I didn't know how to just be.

When Jules was around, I got to just be. It was awkward but welcome.

"This is so foreign to me," I said.

"What? Having someone wash you in the shower?" He turned me to face him then he soaped up my breasts and stomach. I noticed his erection had settled down and he was just washing me without expecting or demanding sex in return. I was in awe.

"Yeah, and having someone just do something nice. Something I asked them to do."

"I'm not Angel, Cress. I might not be a good guy but I'm not my brother."

"I can tell. It's refreshing."

"Refreshing," he chuckled like it was an absurd word to use in reference to him.

"It is." A knot swelled in my throat. I tried to swallow around it but it was hard.

"What's wrong?" Jules asked.

"Nothing." But I was lying my ass off. The stinging tears in my eyes told on me immediately. I didn't know how to explain the feeling coursing through me.

"You're lying. Let's not do that shit, Cress. Us being together is already stressful enough. Let's not add lying to each other to the pile."

"I'm sorry," I said, tucking damp curls behind my ear. "I'm not used to anyone caring this much about me." I looked at the water washing down the drain so I didn't have to look into those too intense mahogany eyes.

"Sometimes," I said, sniffling. "Your brother makes me forget I'm a person."

"You can't be with him anymore. You and Nas have to get the fuck out of here. You don't deserve to be treated like this."

"How? I can't leave him. He'll kill me."

"Let me think about it. I'll figure something out but you can't keep doing this shit. You're better than the way Angel treats you." He let a few silent beats pass then said, "I don't know how to be what you need, Cressida." While he talked, I washed him, soaping up his skin and watching rivers of suds and water run down his perfect abs. "I don't know how to do dates and flowers and shit but…you make me want to learn." He turned around and I slid the washcloth over his broad shoulders. Standing on my toes a little to reach the back of his neck.

"I do?" I blinked in disbelief.

"You do. I don't know what that means but I want you to teach me. I know this warmth in my fucking chest is because of you. I know that I feel happy around you when I haven't felt happy since my mother was alive. I know I'd kill a motherfucker where he stood for you and Nas." He rested his palms on the slick shower wall and let his head drop like the weight of admitting he care was so heavy.

"I care about you too, Jules." A soft smile curved my lips. The water washed away the soap on his skin and he turned to look at me. Those intense brown eyes roving over my face and body. It wasn't sexual though. He was really looking at me and seeing who I was. He was seeing my truth.

"I guess that's what all this is huh?" He asked, tipping my chin up.

"Yeah. This is what it feels like to care about someone." I touched the side of his face feeling his close-cut beard under my fingertips. I left light scratches down the side of his neck and he shut his eyes against the sensation.

"I think I *really* care a lot about you, Cress. Not just you, Nasim too." He skimmed my bottom lip with his thumb. I saw the sincerity in his eyes. It was forged with fire. I knew he would protect me and Nas with his life and unfortunately, I knew it would come to that once Angel found out.

"I know," I said quietly. The kiss we shared after that was so full. He held me like I'd always belonged to him and I started wondering if I had. If it was possible to stake a claim to someone years ago and never give it up. That's what it felt like.

When we were out of the shower and dressed, Jules and I sat in the living room sharing a blanket and watching Half & Half on

Netflix. Well, Half & Half watched us because we couldn't stop talking. It was so easy with him. The laughs came easy. The playful banter came easy. The silence came easy too.

"Why couldn't it have been like this from the beginning?" I asked, holding Jules's skull-tattooed hand in mine.

"Because sometimes we have to walk through darkness to appreciate the light," he said. Of course he'd say something stoic and profound.

"What happens when the darkness comes back after this weekend?" I quizzed.

"What do you want to happen?" He asked, curiously.

"In a perfect world, he'd come home. I would talk to him about how unhappy I am and tell him I want a divorce. He'd respect me enough to let me go and I could move on...with you. He'd be upset and put distance between us but he'd eventually calm down." Even I had to laugh at that shit. Jules laughed with me.

"Nah, that's not how he sees things. You know it. I know it. Bottom line is you want to leave him, right?"

"Yes," I said giving an emphatic nod. I'd never wanted anything so badly in my life. My biggest mistake was marrying Angel but I'd never regret Nasim. He was the only bright spot that came from that fucking monster.

"Then I'll make it happen. I just need to know if you trust me." I looked into his eyes and seriously weighed that question because I didn't want to lie. I didn't want to tell him I trusted him if I didn't. When I stared at him though, all I saw was trustworthiness and sincerity.

"Yes. Of course, Jules. I trust you with my life."

"Good. Because you know I'd never let anything happen to you. I'd die first." My chest squeezed at his words. "Try to steer clear of him when he gets home and let me figure everything out. I won't let him hurt you." He pressed a kiss to my forehead then pulled me against him. I rested my head on his chest and stared at the TV. For the first time in a long time, I felt safe and protected.

…

I woke up to cheesy scrambled eggs, toast, and bacon in the morning. Jules was in the kitchen shirtless, cooking for me. I rubbed my eyes and blinked a few times to bring everything into focus because I couldn't believe my eyes.

"You can cook?" My sleep-heavy voice creaked out. He looked over his shoulder at me and flashed a perfect smile.

"A little bit. I'm mostly a prison chef but I can throw down with breakfast food."

"Wait…you didn't make anything like scrambled ramen noodles, did you?" I teased, walking up to him. He lifted his eyebrows then nodded, impressed.

"You got jokes? I can make noodles taste like scrambled eggs though. Your man is a noodle expert."

"My man, huh?" I bumped him with my hips and he grabbed my waist, hugging me, then kissing my forehead.

"I thought we already established last night that you belong to me. At least that's what you said when I had my dick in you." His teeth sank into my neck and I moaned a little.

"Did we establish that? I might need a refresher." In the next second, I was on the countertop while Jules pushed the pan of scrambled eggs off to the side so they wouldn't burn.

His hard body pressed against the hottest spot between my legs, and I couldn't help grinding, trying to relieve some of the pressure building at my core. My hands were all over him, roaming over perfect thick cuts of muscle and beautifully drawn ink, slipping past the drawstring on his cotton pajama pants until I found what I was looking for. It was so hard and warm and heavy in my hand.

I stroked his velvety shaft to the tip of his crown working out precum as I went, smearing it around the head of his dick while he groaned and bucked against my hand. "You better not have on any panties," he said in a low voice against my ear.

"I don't," I purred, inching closer to the edge of the counter.

"Good girl. I need this pussy." He slipped two fingers inside of me with ease and massaged something deep inside of me that made my back arch. I was always soaking wet for Julien. He slipped his fingers out then licked them while he stared at me. "Free for me to suck and fuck whenever I want to." When he looked at me, I saw something flicker. Like an ancient thing coming to life again. I nodded my head in response to him and lined his dick up with my entrance. I needed him inside of me.

Without any more words between us, Jules thrust hard and quick inside of me, burying himself to the hilt. My toes curled and the heels of my feet dug into the top of his perfect ass. "Shit, Cress," he groaned, fucking me harder and faster. More decadent pressure mounted between my hips, swelling while he pumped, hungry and feral inside of me.

My eyelids fluttered before I called out for God. How was it possible to feel his dick in my soul? I let his long, thick cock punish me over and over until I thought I would be swallowed whole by the need to release.

"Jules!" I whined, fucking him back, working my hips like a madwoman.

"Fuck me back, baby. Make my dick disappear in that tight little pussy." Our bodies seemed to know exactly what to do. They fit so perfectly. Our movements were harmonious and flawless and...oh god, I was coming.

It happened so suddenly. So abruptly. I didn't have time to prepare. I was a spool of passion pink ribbon rolling down a hill. Unraveled by a force as old as gravity itself.

"Oh my god. I'm coming." I almost whispered it. Hushed words of passion and desire muttered against the side of Julien's neck.

"Fuck...me too," he groaned, shutting his beautiful eyes. "I know I can't keep fucking you raw like this, Cress but... goddammit. Your pussy is amazing." He thrust mindlessly inside of me out of some pure carnal need. I felt it too and I felt the electricity eating up my body each time he slid out then back in.

Jules dropped soft kisses along the curve of my neck, telling me that he didn't want what we had to end. I listened while he pulsed inside of me, my foolish mouth agreeing and uttering the same things back to him.

We were spiraling out of control and neither one of us wanted to turn back.

"Tell me you remember where home is," he said after a stretch of silence. My long legs were still wrapped around him, not wanting him to pull out. I loved being full of him.

"You're home, Jules. You." I pressed my pointer finger into his granite chest.

"I'll always be home for you, Cressida." I think I melted. Right there on the counter. I kissed him because how the fuck could I not? He didn't see it but I damn sure did...

We were freefalling for each other.

The way it should have been before he left.

A hot lump of coal sank into the pit of my stomach. My life could have been so much easier with Jules. I knew he felt the same way.

We ate breakfast and talked like we'd been doing since he came home. Talking to him was so easy. It was becoming my favorite thing to do. I loved peeling back his layers and studying him. He loved making me laugh and listening to me pour out all my pain. I'd never felt closer to anyone. Not even Trinity.

After we finished eating, and Jules started washing the dishes, the doorbell rang. "I'll get it. You stay here," he said, drying his tattooed hands on a kitchen towel. I told him he didn't have to hand-wash the dishes but he insisted. He said it helped calm him down, like meditation. I wasn't mad at the view I had of him while he washed them, so I didn't complain.

When Jules grabbed a gun from a concealed space behind

a mirror in the foyer, a chill raced down my spine. I forgot that he wasn't just my Jules. His brilliant energy wasn't just mine to consume. He belonged to the world he immersed himself in. While I'd staked claim to a part of him, another part would always be steeped in darkness and I had to accept that. It didn't mean I shied away from him though. Even then, I followed him needing to see.

"Cress, go back in the kitchen," his tone left no room for disobedience. I turned on my heel and hurried back to the kitchen. I understood why he grabbed the gun. With Angel's business, it was hard to tell if the person coming to visit was friend or foe.

While Jules answered the door, gun in hand, I headed upstairs to put on something more presentable than an oversized sleep shirt and no panties or bra. Angel would have killed me if I was seen lounging around the house like that.

I put on a white blouse and a red skirt that showed off my legs. I pulled my curls on top of my head in a fluffy poof and hurried downstairs. Before my foot hit the last step, I heard Bree questioning Julien like a detective.

"There you are. I had to make sure you didn't run away from home without telling me." She pushed past Jules and walked over to me. "You look cute. Got on more clothes than Smoke." She let her eyes roam up and down his shirtless body.

He eyed her, face impassive, and said, "I live here. Do I need to wear a uniform?"

"Um, Cress lives here too and so does my nephew. They don't want to see all of that." She looked him up and down once more and a blanket of hot prickles fell across the back of my neck. She sure as hell seemed like she wanted to see it. "I'm just saying, it's inappropriate for you, a grown-ass man with all those muscles, to walk around a married woman without a shirt on."

I opened my mouth to call her off but Jules silenced me with a single pointer finger in the air. "You live here too?" Jules asked in that eerily quiet way.

"No," Bree said, smacking her lips.

"When you move in, I'll put a shirt on." Then he walked off leaving her blinking furiously.

"You're an asshole, Smoke!" She shouted after him. She was met with silence. I swallowed my laughter and moved into the living room while Bree fussed about Jules behind me.

"How do you live here with him? He's a dick. He's fine as fuck but he's a dick."

"He's nice," I said, trying not to let a grin consume my face. "He's quiet. Stays to himself." I shrugged and sat in the armchair, crossing my legs.

"Mmm...well, he needs to stay to himself with a shirt on. Does he walk around like that while Angel's home?"

"I barely see him when Angel's home so I wouldn't know."

"I bet he doesn't. He's trying to flex because he's watching you while his brother is in Columbia."

"How do you know he's watching me?" I quizzed. I hadn't had a chance to fill Bree in on things since Angel left early yesterday morning. Plus, the last time she was around, the energy between us was strange.

"Why else would he be here without Angel? You know your husband likes to keep a close eye on you."

"True," I nodded. "How'd you know he was in Columbia?" My brows creased together knitting a frown on my face.

"Everybody knows he went to Columbia. Anyway, Cress...I have news." She waved off my line of questioning and moved closer to the edge of the couch so I wouldn't miss a word of what she was saying. Her eyes were round and full of excitement as a slow smile engulfed her face. Something was off though.

"Okay, what's up?" I asked. Her excitement was contagious. Instead of telling me like a normal, non-dramatic person, Bree pulled something from her purse and slapped it in my hand. When I looked down, I saw a positive pregnancy test staring back at me. Shock was an understatement for what I felt.

"Bree, oh my god!" Finally, happiness took over and I threw my arms around my best friend. My only friend. "This is amazing and if you're happy then I'm happy but..." The question hung in the air, unavoidable. "Who is the father? I haven't heard a word about you being with anyone. Hell, you haven't even talked about fucking anyone."

"Damn, do I have to tell you everything? Clearly, I've been fucking." She laughed but her words felt barbed. They left behind a sting.

"Clearly, but *who* have you been fucking?"

"Some guy. It hasn't been deep at all which was why I didn't feel the need to talk about him. Things are going to fucking change now though." Determination found its way to her soft brown eyes. "I haven't even told him yet. I wanted to tell you first."

"I'm honored," I chuckled. "So, who is this guy? Is he going to flip out? Do you need me to do anything?" I couldn't help her once Angel was back home because he'd make sure I was locked down. I hated when he came home from an out-of-town business trip. He was so over the top and even more controlling than usual. After Jules punched him in the face before he left, I knew he'd be in a pissy mood.

"He's one of Angel's guys." She drew her shoulders up around her ears a little and gave a sheepish smile.

"No wonder you didn't want to tell me. Which one?" I asked, scrunching my nose up. I hoped it wasn't one of the guys Jules dumped in the ocean. My stomach twisted at the thought.

"Not telling. Not yet." She sighed a little then checked her watch. "Shit, I need to go pick something up from Rush. Let me go. I'll call you. Kiss Nas for me." Just like that, she was out. It was out of character for her not to stay and talk for a couple of hours but I let her go without prodding. She didn't seem like she wanted to give up any information anyway.

...

Chapter ELEVEN

Julien

A ngel left on Friday morning. Now, it was Sunday afternoon and I hadn't heard a word from him. Nothing about when he was coming home. If he needed to stay longer. If I needed to prep for a huge shipment coming in. If things needed to be taken care of at Rush. Nothing. There was no communication. For someone who wanted to slowly pull me into his organization, he was treating me more like security and not a soon-to-be partner.

Shit, since I'd been fucking his wife, I didn't need to be a part of his organization. The principle of it all still pissed me off though. I was big on integrity and keeping promises. Angel was failing at both. He was showing me over and over that he was only looking out for himself.

Cress tried to tell me that he'd manipulated me the same way he did her but I was being hard-headed. It hurt to see the truth about my big brother. It made me question my entire life up until this point.

I kept replaying childhood moments in my mind. The way he always had me beat people's ass on his behalf but he never returned the favor. The way I suggested the idea of Rush to him and he ran with it but never gave me credit. He put money on my commissary in prison and helped me when I got out but other than that, he'd been noticeably neutral.

How had that slipped by me for thirty damn years?

My thoughts were broken apart by a phone call from Boogie. It was almost time for Rush to open so for him to call me meant something was happening.

"What's up, Boog?" I asked. I'd been registering online for the Professional Gemologist Certification Program. I was ready to move forward with what I wanted to do instead of blindly following Angel around. He was making it abundantly clear that he had no plans to pull me deeper into his organization.

"We got a situation," he sighed into the phone.

"I'm listening."

"Got another couple of guys overheard talking about jumping

ship to Man's operation. I wouldn't even bother you with this shit but too many people heard them talking about it. You know we have to do something." Boogie sounded reluctant. It was unusual for him.

This guy, Man, had been inching in on Angel's operation for about as long as I'd been home. I hoped we wouldn't have to go to war over it but this was the second time Angel's men had been caught being disloyal. Honestly, I didn't give a fuck about their loyalty to him anymore. I was starting to lose my own.

"You sound like you don't want to do anything, Boog." With a breath caught in my throat, I clicked send on my application and shut my eyes.

Applying for the gemology certification program was the first thing I ever remembered doing that was solely for me. Applying to finish my studies had nothing to do with Angel or his vision. It was all me. A buzz flowed through me and I allowed myself the smallest of moments to soak it in.

"I don't want to do anything but..."

"Your hand feels forced because other people heard them talking," I said, finishing his thought.

"Exactly." Boogie's voice was hesitant. He still had something to tell me. Something he didn't want to say over the phone. "You free to come to Rush? We got twenty minutes before doors open."

"Yeah. I'll be there." I hung up and went into the kitchen where Cress was having a drink. She had a rough conversation with her parents about them keeping Nasim a little longer. She missed him though. I saw it in how quickly her smile faded even after I'd made her laugh. She needed to get her mind off her anxiety.

I stood in the kitchen doorway watching for a few moments. The sadness my brother gifted her, was tightening around her like a boa constrictor. I knew it didn't matter how much we loved being around each other, until she was free from Angel, she would always carry that sadness and I hated it. She didn't deserve that shit.

"Hey, Cress. You feel up to going to Rush? I have business to handle." My voice made her head jerk up and in my direction. Her eyebrows drew together as she studied me.

"Rush? Isn't it about to open?" She asked, still confused.

"Yeah. I have some business to take care of and I don't want you home alone. You're going to sit here and sulk about Nas still being with your parents."

"Am not." She poked her full lips out and folded her arms across her chest. So convincing.

"Right. Come on, Cress. Get that ass up and get dressed. We're going to Rush."

"Angel doesn't let me go unless there's a function and he needs me on his arm."

I paused and tipped my head to the side to look at her. "I'm not Angel. Get dressed. Let's go." There was a silent beat between us and I saw Cress weighing things in her head before she nodded and stood, finishing the rest of her drink.

She told me that she didn't know what to wear because she didn't want it to look like she was on a date with me but she didn't want it to look like Angel wasn't taking care of her either. She opted for a denim dress that stopped just above her knees and a pair of pink and white sneakers that probably cost more money than I could comprehend. When she met me in the foyer, I looked up from my phone and licked my lips. I would have preferred to lick Cressida though. She looked like a fucking snack.

The lightweight denim clung to her body, molding to her waist then flaring out just a little to skim her hips and thighs. She put her wild curls up in a neat bun and wore small emerald studs that made even a denim dress look expensive.

"I like those earrings," I said. "I mean…I like it all. You look sexy as hell. The emeralds bring out the green flecks in your eyes though."

"Thank you, Jules." She grinned and it was such an innocent and sweet expression. That annoying ass warm feeling hit me hard in the chest. I wanted to make her smile like that all the time. She was so damn pretty, she deserved to smile all the time so everyone could see her beauty. Not just me and Nasim. "Also, did you just say the word *flecks*?" She laughed into her palm and I sighed heavily, pulling the front doors open.

"Isn't that what they're called?" I asked once we were in the car. "The sparkling pieces of color I see every time I look into your eyes. They're emerald and jade sometimes. I can only see them when the light hits you just right. That's when you look the most beautiful because I can see every *fleck*," I said emphasizing the word. "Every freckle. Every little spark of light." I looked at her for a few moments longer then started the engine.

Cress sat beside me silently for a long while. Finally, she said, "I think I love the word flecks now. Pretty sure that word just made me have an orgasm."

"Oh yeah?" I laughed. "If I knew all it took was the word flecks, I would have said that shit a long time ago."

"Can you say it tonight?" She purred as I pulled around to the back entrance of Rush. The line to get in was already wrapping around the corner. It was insane. "Over and over?"

"Definitely," I told her, sliding my hand up her silky-smooth thigh. Thinking about sliding inside her had my dick hard already. When she got out, I sat there for a little while to get my erection under control. I was going to fuck her before we left tonight. I already knew it. It was unavoidable. She looked too damn good and I was addicted.

Boogie met us at the back door, eyeing Cress with shock. "What's good, Miss Delgado?" He finally flashed her an all-white smile against the midnight of his skin.

"Boogie, call me, Cress…please." She still smiled at him but I felt the discomfort wafting from her. She hated being a Delgado. I wanted to change that for her.

"Okay, Cress. How you been?"

"I'm doing good…now." She glanced up at me and I felt the heat from her eyes on the side of my face. I tried not to look at her in return but I wanted to. The warm thing growing in my chest wanted to look at her. I fisted my hands at my sides so I wouldn't touch her the way I wanted to. Shit, I was even addicted to her in public.

This was bad.

"What brings you out of the house?" Boog quizzed.

"I'm watching her for Angel and I didn't want to leave her at the house alone." I had to answer for her and say something feasible even though I hated saying I was watching Cressida. She was a grown woman. She didn't need me or anyone else to watch her while Angel was gone.

"So, what did you have to tell me that you couldn't say over the phone?" I asked, switching topics. I noticed Cress stuck close to my side while we walked through the receiving area where the club accepted large orders of food and alcohol. The steady and loud hum of all the appliances working simultaneously muted our voices. It's where Angel and I sometimes came to have private discussions.

"You knew I had something else to say, huh?" Boogie chuckled, shaking his head. "I swear, Angel doesn't give you enough credit." He glanced at Cress. "I don't think your brother would want her to hear anything."

"And I don't think Angel is here. She stays." My expression remained closed and left no opening for a discussion. Boogie nodded then continued.

"The issue isn't only that there were a couple of guys talking about jumping ship. The issue is that when the other men heard, they agreed and started probing. Asking questions about Man's operation and how much of a cut they got. We can't just kill off several men at a time. That shit is going to raise eyebrows, Smoke." He rubbed the back of his bald head.

"It will…" I nodded in agreement. I knew my brother though, especially with him being erratic. He wouldn't care how many motherfuckers we had to kill as long as it meant he was still top dog. The only difference was that now, he no longer had my undying loyalty. Our blood didn't make our bond unbreakable.

"I'd like to handle it before Angel gets back in town. Has he called to say when he's coming back?"

"I thought he'd been in contact with you," I said, a frown wrinkling my forehead.

"Nah. I haven't heard from him. I thought he was keeping you up to date. All I've been doing is showing up and making sure Rush opens and runs smoothly. Figured I was the flunky and you were the inside guy." He laughed but there was a sharp edge to the tone of his deep voice.

Cress stepped between us with her beautiful soft smile and said, "You two mind if I go inside while you talk? I want to see if I can catch Bree." Both me and Boogie nodded.

"Nobody will bother you. Head up to Angel's box," I told her. "The code is 5693."

Once she left, Boogie jumped right back into our conversation. "We need to talk, Smoke." The heaviness in his voice gave me pause. I knew he wanted to tell me something serious. He stood right beside the walk-in freezer because it hummed the loudest and distorted voices and words. I stepped closer.

"What's going on?"

"I don't have many people I consider my friend. Motherfuckers are too fake nowadays." I didn't respond but I listened, nodding. "I notice that you're the only man around here who stands up to Angel. I saw him briefly before he flew out for Columbia and his lip was busted. I asked him about it and he said it was a little sibling rivalry."

I waited to see where this conversation was going. I didn't know if he thought he needed to check me for hitting Angel but I hoped that wasn't the case because as much as I liked Boogie and considered him a friend too...I would knock some fucking sense into him. I watched him closely for a while before speaking.

"Where are we going with this?" I quizzed.

"What I'm saying is...I know Angel is your brother but he's going downhill." Boogie frowned then pulled in a breath to settle his thoughts. I remained quiet.

I did agree with him that my brother seemed to be going downhill rapidly. The drug usage, the superiority complex, the abuse, and disrespect of Cress. That wasn't the Angel I knew. Or maybe it wasn't the Angel I wanted to see. Either way, he needed to be stopped.

"Rush and the entire operation is in danger of going under. I don't want to see that happen and I know you don't either."

"Honestly, Boogie...the drug game is cool but it's not my passion. It's not where my heart is. That's always been Angel's thing. He wanted to make money fast. That's how he did it. I'm just the muscle."

"Nah, that's how he treats you but you're his fucking brother. Why aren't you at his side, growing this thing into an empire?"

"Because that's not what I want. I told you."

"Even if it's not what you want, it's what should have been *offered* to you." His frustration was visible in the way he shook his head. "He offered but you know Angel...follow-through is his downfall."

"That's a part of my point. He's letting too many things slip. Most of his men want to jump ship. If he doesn't get control of his shit, it's all going to crash and burn."

"Then what do you suggest, Boog?" I folded my arms across my chest and waited for an answer.

"My honest answer?"

"When have I ever wanted anything else?" I quizzed.

"I think the guys aren't wrong about wanting to leave the operation. I could see if things were in pristine condition but Angel is digging a hole that none of us are going to be able to get out of. He's dipping into the supply heavy and he's so fucking coked out that he's starting to accuse everyone that works for him for stealing when it's him. He's the problem. I can't kill these men for wanting better from a failing organization."

Things quieted between us for a few beats then I said, "I agree."

I was tired of playing the henchman while Angel blew through his coke and kept me at an arm's length. I stroked my chin and scoffed. "Let's go see this Man motherfucker everyone keeps talking about. Clearly, he knows what he's doing and our men want inside of his organization. The least we could do is sit and talk to him."

"About...what?" Boogie chuckled. "He's the competition. He's already taking over West Palm Beach. Those rich kids are inhaling his coke and guzzling the pills."

A smirk tugged at one side of my mouth. "Exactly. He's up and coming and hungry maybe he's what we need to get everything back on track."

"Smoke, you know that means you're opening Angel up to get killed. We don't have staff meetings in this business. There's no action plan to put Angel on. If we can't handle it then..."

"If we can't handle this shit internally, which I've tried talking to him and so have you...then we need to seek help elsewhere. Either way, there's only one option for Angel." Boogie and I locked eyes and a silent understanding flooded the space around us.

"Are you sure about this, Smoke?"

"Isn't that why you wanted to talk to me about it? Angel's running Rush into the ground. He's off the goddamn hinges. You and I both know there's no cure for that except a bullet." I hated saying that out loud and about my brother no less but it was a thought that had been snowballing in my head ever since I kissed Cress.

Angel had to die.

And I had to do it.

Bile rose in the back of my throat at the thought of killing Angel. I was supposed to be his protector. He was the one destined for great things while I was the trouble maker. Never in a million years did I think my darkness would expand wide enough to swallow him.

"I didn't think it would be that easy to get a concrete answer out of you."

When I studied his face, he did seem taken aback by my

reaction. I had to give him a little clarity since he came to me with something so deep and personal. He knew I could have killed him where he stood if he spoke the wrong way about Angel. He took a chance anyway and that spoke volumes about his bravery. The only thing that gave me pause was…if Boogie noticed the distance growing between me and Angel, then everyone else did too.

Including Angel.

"My brother has been on my mind heavy since I got out and realized how different he was. I've seen a lot of shit that doesn't sit right with me. It's more than the drug problem. Angel has a people problem. As in he doesn't know how to treat them." My jaw ticked thinking about my brother abusing Cress mentally and emotionally. It was only a matter of time before the abuse became physical and I would slit his throat before I let him lay a finger on her.

"Are we talking about people or one person in particular?" I didn't answer him for a few moments. I had to let the thoughts in my head roll around for a little while. He had to have been hinting at Cress. Boogie was a smart man and didn't miss much.

If he was hinting at Cress then I would tell him the truth. My mind was made up about what had to happen with Angel and there was no moment I feared more than the stand-off I knew would come between me and my brother. If I could still look my plan in the eye and carry on with it then there was no reason for me to be afraid of what Boogie would think once he knew I wasn't just Cressida's brother-in-law.

"The statement was meant for everyone in his life but of course

I'm thinking about someone in particular," I said.

"Listen, Smoke, I'm not going to try and pretend to know what's going on with you and...this *person* you're talking about but I can almost guarantee they're better off with you."

"Agreed," I said, giving a short nod. "So, how soon can we set up a meeting with Man?" I moved the conversation back toward business because even speaking about Cress hypothetically made my chest squeeze and thump.

"Man is elusive. Nobody I've talked to even knows what he looks like or where he stays."

"Well, the motherfucker isn't a ghost so he can be found. You work on it from your end and I'll do the same. Let me know what you come up with. We need to move fast though. Neither one of us knows when Angel is coming back."

"I'm sure that's how he wants it," Boogie grunted, shaking his head. "I'll see what I can do, Smoke."

"I need you to do it. Not see what you can do. This is serious, Boog." He nodded his understanding then we slapped hands. We agreed that this was something best kept between us. There was no need to involve anybody else working for Angel. We didn't know where everyone stood and we didn't need any leaks.

After our talk, I headed through the crowded light-up dancefloor and up the red-illuminated stairs leading to Angel's office. A few of the bottle girls lingered in front of the open door, laughing and talking. Inside, I saw Cress sitting on the red couch in Angel's office, while Bree talked a mile a minute, holding a gold tray in her hands. She was supposed to be on the floor serving bottles but she was up here with the rest of her friends chatting.

"We have a packed house, ladies," I boomed, walking inside the office. "Get y'all asses back to work. This isn't social hour." They all muttered and smacked their lips but they started moving.

"I like all that bass you got in your voice, Smoke." One of the bottle girls with long loose curls purred at me while she stood in the doorway.

"I bet you do," I said tossing her a subtle smirk. I couldn't let on that I belonged to someone else because then, she'd press me for answers. I also couldn't let on about me and Cress. Not now.

"I'd probably like it a lot more in the bedroom." She winked at me and I shook my head.

"Get back to work," I said, flicking my chin toward the door. Below us, a sea of moving bodies danced in tune to the bass-heavy song blasting through the speakers. The music was muffled inside Angel's office but I felt the vibrations through the floor.

"I'm ready to go home," Cress said. Her expression was closed and her voice was quiet.

"What's wrong with you?" I held my hand out for her and she grabbed it standing up.

"Nothing. I'm just ready to go." She folded her arms across her chest and avoided my eyes. Something was definitely wrong.

"Don't lie. I can see through that shit." When I went to touch her face, she turned. It was slight but I saw it.

"I'm fine, Smoke."

My eyebrows shot up to my hairline. "*Smoke?* Oh, okay. So, you're mad then," I couldn't help chuckling. I knew it would piss her off but she was so fucking cute when she was mad.

"You're laughing? Seriously?"

"I'm sorry," I laughed again, grabbing her hand. "Are you pissed because I barely flirted with the bottle girl? I know that's what it is, Cress."

"You admit you were flirting then." She pursed those full pink lips together.

"Are you jealous?" The thought of Cress being jealous of any woman for any reason didn't sit right with me.

"No...I just realized in that split second that I didn't want to see you talking to any other women." Her guard cracked and fell away in flakes as she looked up at me. "I know it's stupid because we're not even together and what we're doing is..."

"Who said we weren't together?" I asked, my brows drawing together at a point on my forehead.

"I know what we said while we were fucking but..." I shut her up with my hand gripping her throat. My thumb and pointer finger rested behind her ears as she gasped from shock.

"I mean what I say. No matter what's going on when I say it." I crashed against her waiting mouth and stole a kiss from her. It was possessive and rough.

Cress was mine.

End of fucking story.

"Jules, the door is still open," she whispered but I could still hear her over the music. I walked over and closed it before clicking the lock into place. Cress moved to the huge pane of glass overlooking the dancefloor and stared down at it.

"I don't want things to go back to normal." I stood behind her, trying to fight the urge to put my hands on her hips...my lips on her neck. "I don't want to be his wife anymore." When she looked at me over her shoulder, those big champagne eyes peering into me, I felt my chest swell so much I thought it would pop. I had to make sure she got what she wanted. Not just for my own selfish reasons but because it was what was best for her and Nasim.

"You don't have to be," I said, moving a chunk of curls behind her shoulder.

With trembling lips and tears in her eyes that she refused to let fall, she asked, "How am I supposed to leave a man who would kill me?"

"You let me handle it. That's how." I couldn't help the burning urge inside my chest that told me to touch her. She was mine.

I dug my fingers into her soft hips, pulling her round ass against my dick. I was rock hard in less than a second. "You're not his wife anymore. You never really were." I spoke with my lips against her ear. Cress's body sagged against me, her curves sighing against my muscle.

"We're in a giant glass box over top of thousands of people, Julien. You can't whisper in my ear and hold my hips like this. We're in the middle of Angel's den."

"More like the devil's fucking den," I muttered against her smooth, clean-smelling neck. Her laugh was soft and silky. My dick ached for her.

"When he gets home, I want you gone. Can you stay with Bree for a while?" I dug my erection into the softness of her ass, pressing her against the glass. She shook her head and I got a whiff of floral shampoo.

"I don't want to stay with her. Something is off with her."

"I'll put you up in a hotel then," I said, inching denim dress over her round hips. She tried to tug it back down but she couldn't get it out of my grasp.

"Jules," she scolded.

"What?"

"We're in Angel's office. Everyone down there can see us."

"They're dancing. They're eating. They're doing fucking drugs. Not looking at us."

"His men..." She gasped mid-sentence when I cupped her pussy. It was so warm and soft against my palm.

"Want to jump ship to another organization. They have bigger shit to worry about than me fucking my woman."

"But anyone could see and..." I rubbed her stiff, swollen clit through her silky black thongs and she became a tangle of moans.

"Let. Them. Watch. Then." I bit her earlobe, trailing down to her neck, letting my tongue follow my teeth. Nothing was stopping me from getting inside of her right then.

Was it stupid?

Probably.

Did I give a fuck though?

No.

I yanked her thongs down and they fell in a wet pool around her ankles.

"If you tell me you don't want me to fuck you and claim you as my motherfucking woman right here in his office. Over his club. In front of everyone he puts on a show for, then I'll stop." I freed my dick and pressed against her warm skin. Pre-cum smeared against her perfect golden ass and I growled at the sight of it. I fisted her wild curls in between my fingers and watched her breath fog the crystal-clear glass. "Tell me to stop, Cress." I rocked against her, sliding my cock up and down her pretty ass.

"Don't," she begged. "Don't stop, Jules." That was all I needed to hear. I gripped my dick at the base and pushed into her.

She was so fucking wet.

So tight.

So hot.

So...goddamn...fuck...

"Oh my god, Julien," she whined, bracing against the glass. "You feel so good. Fuck. Me." Her voice was a sultry, thick growl. The hairs on my forearms stood on end.

"I knew your little ass wanted this dick." I punished her pussy suspended above Rush and I didn't care who looked up and saw. I didn't care who ran and told Angel.

The worst part about losing my trust wasn't the physical death that would follow but the psychological freeze-out that came before. Angel was earning both rapidly. I knew I was disrespecting him. It was the highest form of disrespect but I couldn't make myself care. That's how I knew the bond between us was frayed. By the time everything was said and done, it would be severed.

"I want it. I need it," she cried while I drilled into her.

"And I need this fucking pussy." My chest ached and my tongue burned until I pushed more words out. "I need *you*, Cressida." I pulled her hair and slammed into her, making her stumble forward until she was smashed against the glass beneath me. "What the fuck are you doing to me?" I groaned in her ear as pressure stacked higher and higher in my core. The buzzing, humming need for release filled me up from the bottom to the top.

An orgasm shot out of me. Thick and hot. I was amazed at how much cum Cress could pull out of me. It didn't matter how many times we fucked, I still came for her every goddamn time.

"Fuck, Cress." I dipped my head until my lips brushed the shell of her ear. "I love you." I had no idea where the words came from but the minute they hit the air, I felt like I could breathe. Like I'd just taken my first real breath after having the weight of trauma and darkness lodged in my chest forever.

Her pussy squeezed and milked my cock in pulsing beats like she had a heart between her slick walls. My body shuddered at the sensation prickling my skin. I held her hips to slow her involuntary movement, pushing back against me and, groaned.

"I love you too, Jules." Her voice was thick with emotion and when I pulled out of her slippery heat and looked at her, I saw the crystal tears clinging to her lower lashes. "I know I shouldn't and everything about this is dangerous but...my heart can't help the way it's always felt about you." She stared at me and I knew I had to make this right for her. I had to take away the threat of danger and give her stability. I had to bring the sunshine back to her life or she would fracture like a diamond under too much pressure.

Cress stepped out of her thongs and I bent to scoop them up. I pressed the wet fabric to my nose and breathed in the fresh, clean scent of her. The apples of her cheeks burned a soft pink color that made her eyes shine.

"Your pussy smells like my favorite meal," I told her.

"That's what you say after we confess our undying love to each other?" She laughed.

"I'm sorry, I have no idea what the hell this moment is supposed to be like. Am I fucking it up?" I tucked her thongs in my pocket and ran a hand over my close-cut waves.

"No, Jules. You didn't fuck it up." She popped up on her tiptoes and pressed a kiss to my lips. "Somehow, this is all so…you."

"I don't know what the fuck I'm doing, baby." My arms circled her tiny waist. "You know I've never been in love before." The words were clunky coming from my mouth but when I said them, my heart seemed to thump to life. Like speaking the truth resuscitated the lifeless organ. "You're going to have to teach me. I might fuck up a lot."

"You're perfect, Jules." Her palm slid against the side of my face and the warmth made me feel seen and heard. "I love you just like this. Dark and moody. Awkward and quiet."

"Awkward? I'm cool as shit, Cress."

"You're awkward because you're always quiet and whenever you do talk, it's something cryptic and deep. I love it though. I don't think I've talked and laughed this much in forever."

Hearing her say that brought back the unavoidable reality that even though we loved each other, I was a killer. I wasn't a nice guy. I would never fit in with her family. I wasn't a good Christian man and I wouldn't provide a quiet uneventful life for Cress and Nasim.

Even when I eventually became a jeweler making my own luxury pieces, I knew death and murder would always be a part of me. It was my art just as much as gemology was. I didn't see myself parting from either.

"What's wrong?" She asked, her brows crinkling from a soft frown.

"I realized I can't give you the kind of life Angel has. Even once he's no longer in the picture and it's just me, you, and Nas, I won't be able to stop being who I am."

"I never said I wanted you to stop being who you are. I know the real you."

"Cress, my life isn't a fairytale. I like killing motherfuckers. I'm not a serial killer but I don't handle disputes with strongly-worded arguments. My retaliation is final." When I stared into her eyes, I looked for the fear I saw in everyone else. I looked for the uncertainty and the judgment.

I didn't find it.

"I know," she said after a deep breath. "After everything I've seen and been through with Angel, the kind of man you are doesn't scare me, Jules. I'm not blind to it either. It is what it is. I

DANIELLE JAMES

know you'd never hurt me or Nasim. I can't say the same for your brother. I don't give a fuck what you do to people who earn your wrath. I care about how you treat me and my son." Her slender throat flexed when she swallowed and I let my eyes fall shut.

"Shit, we're really doing this."

"Yeah. Really." She paused then said, "We're insane. We could get killed."

A laugh fell from my mouth and Cress looked at me like I had two heads.

"Stop looking at me like that. Who exactly is going to kill us?" I wasn't completely comfortable or happy about the fact that I had to kill my only brother, but I knew damn well there would be no competition. Angel wasn't a killer. That's why he had me.

The more I removed Angel from the pedestal I placed him on, the more I realized he wasn't strong or brave or any of the shit I used to think when I was younger. The truth was staring me in the face the entire time. Angel was a coward and a user. He used me and now he was using Cress and I was going to put a stop to it all.

"You know how Angel is. He's not in his right mind," Cress said with concern lacing her words.

"You're right about that. I'm not scared of him though, because I know how he works. If he was a killer, he would have never let me defend you and punch him in the fucking mouth before he left. He would have put me in my place. Instead, he got pissed, talked shit, and left. Like I said, let me handle him." I saw the trepidation in her eyes and I knew once I told her Angel had to die, she'd protest.

Not because she was in love with him but because he was Nasim's father. Cress knew as well as I did though, Nas was better off without a father like Angel. Unfortunately, the death of his father, my brother, and Cress's husband would have to come at the end of my knife.

...

Chapter TWELVE

Cressida

The sound of my phone buzzing and skittering across the nightstand permeated my dreams. When I cracked my tired eyes open, the screen was illuminated in the darkness. Jules was beside me breathing rhythmically with his arm tossed around my middle like a heavy log.

I grabbed the buzzing phone and turned my back to Jules so the light from the screen didn't disturb him. Angel's face flashed across the screen and my blood ran cold.

What if he was home?

I stumbled out of the bed and went to the bathroom, turning on the light and nearly blinding myself. "Hello? Angel?" I whispered with the phone to my ear.

"What's up, baby? Miss me?" He was high as shit. I could tell by the jerkiness of his words and I could hear the crooked smile in his voice. Hearing him in my ear made my bleak reality come crashing back down. I was playing house with Jules when I knew things had to go back to normal at some point. Angel wasn't going to stay away forever.

"Hey. When are you coming home?" Sleep was still twisted around my words even as my knee bounced up and down. I sat on the edge of the tub, pinned the phone to my ear with my shoulder, and twisted the mood ring around on my finger.

"I'll be there in the morning. I want to see you and my son. Smoke been taking good care of you?"

Images of Jules between my legs, fucking me until I was hoarse crowded my mind. We fucked everywhere in the house. We even fucked in Angel's office. I blinked away the images and pressed my legs together because even when I was on the phone with my damn husband, the thought of Jules touching and fucking me drove me insane with desire.

"Yeah, I guess. If you can call it that," I grumbled, feigning irritation.

"You don't sound too happy, Cress. What's up?"

"It's just like having you here, Angel. I'm stressed. I can't go anywhere without your brother needing to know everything and...I don't know." A sigh floated from my mouth and I could almost see Angel smirk with satisfaction.

"Well, then he's doing what the fuck he's supposed to do. He's there to keep an eye on you because you're too goddamn stupid to take care of yourself without me there." Anger and resentment burned through me like a thousand red-hot needle points.

After being with Julien for days, I started to feel appreciated. I started to feel like I mattered and like my life didn't have to be so hard and sad all the time. He made me feel like things could be different for me and Nas. It felt like my entire life changed in the span of a weekend. Now, I hated Angel even more than I thought was possible.

"Look, I'll be home by eight in the morning. Tell Smoke I'll hit him up when I land." The call went dead and it wasn't until I put the phone down that I realized my hand was shaking.

I stood to my feet and looked at myself in the mirror. My curls were an escaped riot of golden and caramel. My sleep bonnet had slid to the side while I was in bed.

My hair.

Angel would lose his shit if I had curls when he got home. My stomach dropped and I hated myself for how terrified I felt. When I was with Julien, I wasn't scared of anything. Now, normalcy was inching in on me and I felt suffocated by it.

I snatched the satin bonnet from my head and my hair sprung out in wild coils sweeping my shoulders. Most of my curls had clumped together disobediently and I had to pluck them apart gently with my fingertips. If I didn't straighten my hair, I didn't know what kind of wrath I'd face in the morning.

I plugged in the flat iron and waited for it to heat up while I examined my face in the mirror. I traced the faint bruises along my neck and the tops of my breasts. My skin still hummed from the memories of Jules's mouth on me.

When Angel got home, all the safety and warmth I felt would evaporate. I knew Jules said to trust him and to let him take care of Angel but fear was scorched into my bones. I rubbed the smooth surface of my mood ring and nibbled on my lip.

Once the flat iron was hot, I began straightening the kinks and coils from my hair. With each small section of straightened strands, pressure swelled in my chest. Anxiety mounted quickly, blurring my eyes with tears so that I couldn't see what to do next.

"Cress, what's wrong?" Julien's sleepy, deep voice startled me and I jumped, knocking the flat iron into the sink with a clatter.

"I have to straighten my hair before he gets home. He almost hit me before he left, what if he does it this time?" I sat the flat iron on the sink again and pressed my palms against the cool marble, trying to pull in a steady breath.

"You talked to Angel?" His big hands rested on my hips and my anxiety started to recede.

"Yeah. He'll be home by eight in the morning. I have to straighten my hair and make sure I pick up Nas from my parents' house and..."

"Listen to me, Cress." His voice was strong and rough. "I told you, I won't let Angel hurt you or Nasim. I won't let him even see you. Let's get you checked into a hotel and I'll take it from there."

"He said he wants to see me and Nas when he comes home."

"And I said he won't lay his fucking eyes on you." Jules made me look at myself in the mirror while he held me from behind. "I might not know how to love like they do in books and movies, but I know how to protect. I know how to show you the way you should be treated. I know how not to hurt you." He dropped kisses to my neck and tightened his grip on my hips. My stomach fluttered and twisted while I watched his thick lips kissing and sucking a trail up and down my neck and shoulder.

How did he manage to unravel every ounce of fear and uncertainty coursing through me with only a few kisses? I allowed myself to melt into him while Angel faded into the back of my mind. I hated that he even occupied space there.

"I'm scared of him, Jules. I always knew I was but after being with you, I realize how fucked up my so-called marriage is. Now I feel fucking stupid because I allowed this for so long like it was normal." I felt so weak and foolish. What kind of woman got caught up in an abusive man she didn't even love?

Me.

I did that. I put my life and my son's life in danger and for what? There was no reason to cling to Angel but there I was letting terror rule my every move.

"You're not stupid," Jules said, frowning at me in the mirror. "You're scared for your life. Even if I hadn't gotten out of prison, you wouldn't have lived in fear forever, Cress. One day Angel

DANIELLE JAMES

would have done something that pushed you over the edge and you would have left him. I'm helping to expedite things because I can't stand around and let the woman I love get abused."

There was that word again. It shivered through me and settled in my heart light as a feather but vast as the universe itself.

Julien Jean loved me.

He was the alpha-villain.

The one man I wasn't supposed to fall for or even be around but dammit if I hadn't fallen for him. He was supposed to be the monster. The dark and twisted one. He made me smile though. He was the one I couldn't stop thinking about. Even when he was locked up, he occupied space in my mind and heart.

Silence crowded around us like a blanket. He held me for a while until I settled down and my heart rate slowed to a reasonable thump. Even though I knew there was a shit storm swirling around me, I felt safe.

"I look a hot mess," I laughed, seeing my partially straightened hair in the mirror.

"Nah, you always look beautiful. Your hair is a little fucked up but you're not your hair." He chuckled then took a chunk of springy curls between his fingers and said, "Show me. I'll help you."

"You?" I barked out a laugh and he eyed me incredulously. "I'm sorry," I snickered into my hand. "You're not the flat-ironing type, Jules."

"I'm not the fall-in-love-with-my-brother's-girl type either but...here I am." He tugged on a lock of my hair and I blushed, looking down at the flat iron. I showed him how to take small sections of curls and turn them straight and after the first few tries, Julien did really well to my surprise. His fingers were unsure but gentle as we both worked through my head full of curls.

"I wish you didn't feel like you had to straighten your hair for that motherfucker," Jules said quietly as he pulled the iron down the length of my hair letting it fall to the middle of my back.

"I'm terrified of him. I saw that wild look in his eyes before he left. If you weren't here to step in, I know he would have hit me."

"I know you've told me before but why the fuck are you with Angel? How did you go from the carnival with me to down the aisle with him?"

My shoulders fell and I studied the backs of my hands. "It was stupid. I missed you and I was mad at you all at the same time. I couldn't believe you got caught up and went to prison. When I saw Angel in church one Sunday, we talked and he told me what happened to you. He invited me out for lunch and I went." I paused a beat, letting my thoughts form then fall away. "I honestly think I went to hear more about why you got locked up. I went from being pissed to being worried to regretting all the times I never let you kiss me." My throat tightened with emotions that had been buried in a subconscious graveyard.

"Angel asked me on another date and I accepted because once my parents found out about the first date, they pushed for a second. Then he told my naïve ass I was pretty and it made me feel sexy. I was a dumb virgin. I knew nothing.

My mother and father never told me how men lied to get between your legs. They never told me that what I had was special and not to give it away to the first man who sold me pretty words and even prettier promises.

I knew I didn't love Angel but he made me feel better while you were gone. I never thought I'd be bullied into getting married and living a life I never wanted. Looking back..." A sad laugh fell from my lips. "I was so blind. I took one step after another that pushed me right into his trap." My eyes connected with Julien's in the mirror. "I never want to be that naïve and stupid again."

"Naïve, yes. Stupid? No. Besides, being naïve isn't an excuse for Angel to treat you the way he does. You know how many women fall into abusive relationships, Cress? Women who aren't naïve. Women who've heard every trick in the book. Women whose fathers and brothers have told them the game and how it's played and they *still* get stuck in abusive relationships. Don't blame yourself for Angel's brokenness."

His words reached inside and brushed away some of the pain and suffering. I didn't understand how Jules called himself a monster when the opposite was true. He was such a beautiful dark soul.

He was the rose and the skull.

I was silent as I watched this huge, statue of a man delicately flat iron my hair and make sure he didn't burn my ears or forehead. I was stunned that people would look at Jules and see anything but a tortured and brilliant soul. How could they not see the tenderness, the strength, the brilliance?

"I think we're done," he said, giving my hair a once over. His long thick fingers slipped between silky ochre strands of hair. "You look beautiful, baby." He kissed the top of my head and hugged me tight from behind. His arms around me made me feel safe and grounded. Like I could face anything as long as I faced it with him.

I could even face Angel.

He dipped his head low and brushed away a curtain of freshly straightened hair, then his lips connected with my neck. Electricity hummed under my skin, crackling and pulsing until I felt my heart beating in each fingertip. My core tensed then relaxed repeatedly until I was soaking wet between my thighs.

"Jules," I said my voice stretched thin from desire and lust. "Make love to me." Our eyes found each other in the mirror and I saw something dark and possessive. It reminded me of Angel's eyes but it was different when Jules looked at me.

I saw love.

I saw protection.

I saw *home*.

"I don't know how to make love, Cress." He slid the tip of his nose along the curve of my neck and I felt goosebumps prick the surface of my skin, making me shiver. "But I know how to fuck. I know how to make your pretty pussy come over and over until I feel your clit throb while I'm buried inside of you." He slid my nightshirt up around my hips then freed his hard dick while he pressed against my bare ass. "Can I fuck you *and* love you, Cress?" His warm, soft lips kissed a line up and down my shoulder while my hips mindlessly worked in circles.

That's what he'd reduced me to.

Lines and circles. Buzzes and hums. Moans and cries.

I was deconstructed when I was with him. I was able to find pieces of myself that I didn't even know existed.

"Yes, Julien." My eyes fell shut and I bit my bottom lip.

"Can I make your pussy rain all around my dick?" He slapped my ass with his thick erection and I gasped. "You feel how hard you got me?" My breathing came in ragged exhales while my nipples tightened beneath the thin cotton of my shirt. Jules cupped my pussy while the heel of his hand moved in slow, torturous circles, pressing down on my clit.

He eased one thick finger inside me, then another, curling them both forward and rubbing. Rubbing until my moans became fevered, fogging up the mirror in front of me.

"Goddamn, I can smell you in the air. That pussy needs my tongue. I need to taste how fresh and sweet you are." Then he was on his knees, pushing me over the sink so that my ass was in his face. He tapped my left leg and I lifted it, resting it on the cool sink.

Julien's lips and tongue connected with my sensitive pussy and I dropped my head on a low and throaty groan. My hand flew to the mirror, splayed out flat so I could balance myself while he ate me out from behind. He was beyond starving at that point.

He licked, sucked, growled, and groaned into my pussy like it was his first and last meal. Like he'd found salvation between my thighs and there was nothing greater.

Like...

Oh my god...

My body convulsed in jerky motions and I lost sense of everything except the pulsing emanating from my core. I came so hard that it took me by surprise. Every thought I had stacked up high in my brain tumbled to the floor, shattering along with my sanity.

"Mmm, Cress. So fucking good." The vibrations from his deep voice and the soft tickle from his facial hair doled out cruel and delicious shocks that zipped through me at lightning speed. My legs were useless. My knees were marshmallows. My thighs were jelly.

Still, he stood behind me, his face glistening with my juices, easing his stiff, fat dick inside my entrance. I whimpered when I knew he was only halfway in, biting my lip and trying to catch my breath. With a forceful thrust that stole my breath away, he crashed into me and I melted.

Oh my *god,* I melted for him like coconut oil in July.

He was right, he didn't know how to make love. He only knew how to fuck. He only knew how to choke, grab, slam and stroke. He only knew how to claim me with every dangerous buck of his hips and each dull ache his teeth left behind.

I was wrapped up in heaven and who knew it would be laced with spikes of pain that made my body sing. I squeezed my eyes shut but I felt Julien's big hand gripping my face.

"Nah, open up, baby girl. Look at how pretty you are when you're full of my dick." He rocked his hips and inched deeper inside of me when I felt like I didn't have any more space left for him. My mouth hung open on a moan as I watched the mirror. As I watched Jules. He'd tugged his shirt over his head and tossed it down. His tattooed arms were flexed while one hand held my waist and the other wrapped around my throat.

His sculpted face was warped in a frown while he watched his thick dick slide in and out of me repeatedly. I whimpered as his hips connected with me creating a symphony of applause.

"You're so goddamn perfect, Cressida."

"Oh god, Jules...I'm about to come so fucking hard." I was sure my legs would slide off my body like sweet oil. They felt useless. My body jolted suddenly then came the involuntary shaking and convulsing. The only thing I could concentrate on was not falling on my face.

"Mmm, damn," he grunted, thrusting deeper, hammering the nail all the way in my coffin. "Your pussy is so tight. So fucking wet and warm." Then he shot into me, deep and hard. "Mine," he growled, pinning me to the sink while my thighs continued to tremble.

"I'm yours, Jules." I panted, staring at my dewy skin and satiated eyes.

He slid out of me slowly, hissing along the way then turned me to face him, his fingertips pressing into my jawline. "Do you really believe that, Cress? That you're mine?" His eyes begged me to say yes. I couldn't think of one way I didn't belong to him or that he didn't belong to me. The thought of him flirting with one of Rush's bottle girls burned me the hell up earlier.

"Yes," I said, nodding emphatically. "I know I'm still scared of

Angel and I'm still his…"

"Don't say it, please." For the first time since knowing Jules, I saw pain flash in his eyes. "I know you're still legally married to him but I can't stand to hear you call yourself his wife. It feels like something is clawing at my goddamn heart." I skimmed my thumb over his knuckles and traced the outline of the skull on his hand.

"I know how things look right now but my heart and everything else belongs to you. I trust you."

"Good. Then you'll trust me when I tell you that I have to kill Angel." His voice was low and quiet when he spoke but his words were explosions in my mind.

"*Kill* him?" I stammered, my mouth going dry.

"I've tried talking to him. Boogie has tried talking to him too but he's driving Rush into a hole and he's hurting you."

"And lying to you," I said finishing his statement. I watched his temple flex and his nostrils flare. It was only for a second but I saw it. He hated that Angel had hurt him. He'd never admit it but Angel was the only person who mattered to Julien.

"Yeah," he grumbled. "The point is, Angel can't go on like this and logic is beyond his grasp." Each word he spoke was careful and quiet. I knew he had to have contemplated every angle of his plan. He wouldn't kill his brother without damn good reasons.

"I guess I never…I never thought about the end game. I've always fantasized about killing Angel or him dying or getting killed over drugs but thinking about it as a reality is…"

"I know it's a lot for you. He's Nasim's dad and losing your father hurts," he said, looking down at the backs of his hands. Jules knew firsthand how painful it was to lose both parents. He knew the road Nas would have to walk.

"I don't know how to explain this to him when he gets older. What if something goes wrong and you get hurt or worse? What if..."

"Cress, chill. I got this. It's not something I'm looking forward to but I've never missed my mark." Even though I knew he had to be torn up about ending Angel's life, he didn't show it. His exterior was as unruffled as it always was.

"How soon? Like how soon are you going to do it after he gets back?" My caution had morphed quickly into anticipation. A dark pulse thumped through my body, spreading like inky vines. Jules glanced at me, a smirk warming his handsome face.

"Looking forward to seeing your husband die?"

"Looking forward to killing your brother?" I shot back. Jules turned the corners of his full lips down and nodded.

"Look at you firing back." His smile was full of pride and it made me tingle all over. He draped his long arm around my shoulders and kissed my temple. "I don't know what you're doing to me, Cress but I'm not mad at it. I just hope I'm not rubbing off on you the way you're rubbing off on me." The rough pads of his long fingers swept through the silky hair at the nape of my neck, then he gripped me there and a spike of heat tore through me.

"What's so wrong with you rubbing off on me? Maybe that's what I want." I dragged my nails through his soft facial hair. "Maybe I need some confidence and pessimism. Maybe I could use a little darkness."

"I don't want to do anything to dull your light. That's one of the things that made you stand out to me all those years ago in your parents' church. You lit that place up like a fucking Molotov cocktail. Your sandy curls and pretty champagne eyes and those goddamn lips." He couldn't help leaning over and drawing my bottom lip into his mouth before sweeping his tongue against mine. He pulled back and said, "I wanted to do that when I first saw you."

"I don't think you could kiss like that in middle school, Jules."

"You're probably right. Maybe it's a good thing I waited, huh?" His fingers skimmed my inner thigh and a sea of heat washed over me.

"Definitely." I reached up and met him with another kiss. I couldn't compose myself. I could never compose myself around Julien. I had to touch him. Smell him. Taste him.

We made our way back to the bedroom and I gave my hair a shake. I'd already gotten used to the wild curls and I missed them. Like Jules could sense my thoughts, he tugged my straightened hair and smiled. "You're sexy either way, Cress." He paused for a moment. "Am I really rubbing off on you?"

I took a second to study the tattoos covering his muscular arms. I ended on his skull and rose tattoos and sighed. "Yes, but I told you I don't look at it as a bad thing. You're not rubbing off on me in the sense that I'm talking like you and taking over your style. You're rubbing off on me in all the ways that make me more confident. That make me realize I'm worth more than Angel tells me. I don't know, it's like you came along and now I can see myself better.

I can see how special I am. That's why the thought of Angel coming in here and talking to me like I'm stupid and taking away my freedom is making me sick to my stomach. I can't live like that anymore."

After a stretch of comfortable silence, Jules took my left hand in his and slid my wedding rings off, cupping them in the palm of his hand. "You don't need these anymore. Throw this shit in the trash." I noticed him examining the diamonds, turning the rings over in his palm.

"I have to wear my rings when Angel gets home, Julien." I loathed the icy fear that inched up my spine when I thought about the hell Angel would raise if he noticed my rings were gone.

"I told you I'm putting you and Nas in a hotel. I wasn't bullshitting. Go pack."

My head shook from left to right involuntarily. "He's going to find us. You know your brother has people everywhere. Even in hotels."

"So I'll put y'all somewhere he can't reach you. He's not omnipotent." He was on his feet in the next second, heading to the closet. I rushed over to him, placing my hand on his shoulder. He was a block of marble beneath my fingers.

"Look at me," I said softly. "You're going to start a war if he shows up in the morning and I'm not here with Nasim. Especially if you tell him what's going on between us." I twisted the mood ring around on my finger and gazed at Jules with wide eyes.

"I'm not going to tell him yet. Let me handle Angel and let me protect you and my nephew. Pack some clothes and whatever else you need." I watched his jaw tick and noticed the indignation in his brown eyes.

He was protecting me with his life and I was still scared. Angel was so deeply rooted in my mind that even when he wasn't around, he haunted me. I hated it. I could not fucking live like this anymore.

What kind of mother was I to my son if I lived in fear on purpose? I was being given the chance to run and I had the goddamn gall to fuss back and forth about it. Battered woman syndrome was real. Angel had remote control of me and it made me sick to my fucking stomach.

While my gut still trembled in fear, I stepped forward into the closet and began pulling down clothes I'd need. I didn't know how long I'd be in a hotel so I made sure to get my runaway bag.

I was finally going to leave him.

God, I hoped Julien put a bullet between Angel's motherfucking eyes.

...

Chapter
THIRTEEN

Julien

After I found Cress a boutique hotel to stay in that was outside of Miami, she seemed to calm down enough to get some sleep. I was too consumed to sleep though. Angel would be home in a matter of hours. I had to get Cress and Nas out of Miami before then.

I also had to hit Boogie up to see if he was able to get any information on Man. The way my mind had been racing all damn night and morning helped me come up with a plan to take Angel out and hand Rush over to Man. Shit, he was on the kingpin come up anyway and I didn't want anything to do with the organization after seeing it destroy Angel.

I looked down at my hands, at the gold rings he gave me when I first got out. I would keep them even after he was gone because they'd remind me that I could accomplish even the toughest tasks. I feared nothing and no one. Not even my brother.

I'd started mourning his death already in my head even though I still had a while to go before he was lying at my feet cold and bloody.

I had to let him know his power had been stolen. I had to show him that he'd fallen from his pedestal and that someone else was going to take his place. He needed to see the fucking monster he'd become. I wanted Angel to watch everything he thought he worked so hard for crumble in front of him. Karma needed to lodge her stinger deep in his chest before my blade ever sliced his skin.

While Cress slept, I took her phone and wrote down her parents' address. I'd pick Nasim up for her and get them safely to the hotel while I waited for my brother.

While I was in the kitchen programming the coffee maker to start a pot in a half-hour for Cress, I saw the instruction manual Angel left for her sitting on the counter. A ripple of disgust snaked through me and I felt the familiar hum in my blood. The hum of bloodlust.

I pushed out a sigh and looked down at my hands. I knew what needed to happen but it wouldn't stop me from talking to Angel before killing him. I had to see if there was any shred of my brother left.

I grabbed the papers in my hands and tore them in half. How

the hell did any real man lock his woman down like that? It was only a matter of time before Angel turned into his father and started beating Cressida's ass. I'd die before I let that shit happen.

Shaking the thoughts from my head, I checked the clock, grabbed my keys, and went to get Nasim. On the way there, I couldn't help wondering what was next after Angel was dead and out of the picture. How did we explain things to Nasim? I told Cress I'd handle it when the time came but he was already so smart and starting to walk and talk.

Thoughts bounced around in my head until I pulled into the driveway. I looked in the backseat and made sure I secured the car seat and had Nasim's bag. I remembered grabbing it but I couldn't be too sure.

I walked up to the door and it opened before I could ring the bell. I recognized Cress's father right away. He hadn't changed much over the years except for the silver hairs at his temples. I nodded my head at him and said, "Good morning, Mr. Erickson. I'm Angel's brother, Julien. I'm here to pick up Nasim for Cress." I realized it was the first time since I'd been home that I didn't introduce myself as Smoke.

After being with Cressida all weekend, my outlook on everything changed. Two fucking days changed my life. It sounded so heavy but the truth is never light. I thought Cress was killing me the way my chest felt every time I was around her but it was my heart. I thought I'd gotten rid of it a long time ago. Turns out, it was dormant.

"I know who you are. *Smoke*." He gritted my name out like I was trash. I already knew the Erickson's hated me. Most people did. They saw nothing when they looked into my eyes and I guess it scared them. Shit, they had no idea how it felt to walk in my shoes and *feel* nothing.

"Cressida sent me to pick up Nasim. Angel will be home in a couple of hours and wants to see him." I stood with my hands clasped in front of me, waiting for Mr. Erickson to go get Nasim's things. He didn't budge. Instead, he stepped outside and closed the door behind him.

"Listen here, Smoke. I know what kind of nonsense you're into and I don't want it around my daughter or my grandson. Angel might see something in you but I see right through you. I see the darkness. I see the evil." He blinked up at me as if he had special x-ray vision then said, "I don't think the good Lord gave a man like you a soul. You're the devil's right-hand man, aren't you?"

"Sure. That's me. I got horns and everything." I gestured to my head and smirked. Mr. Erickson's face trembled with anger and frustration as he narrowed his eyes. He looked over everything from my head to my toes, taking in my tattoos, rings, and the understated gold chains around my neck. I definitely didn't look like I was there for bible study.

"I don't know why an upstanding man like Angel keeps someone like you around. You're probably running drugs out of Rush and using in front of my grandson."

"Check this shit out, Mr. Erickson," I said taking a step closer to him. "Nasim is my nephew. We're blood. So, if you think for a second, I would put him in danger, you must be rolling blunts with pages from the bible. Also, you must be blind if you can't see that Angel is the devil's right-hand man.

All the shit you accused me of? That's what he does. I follow orders and mind my motherfucking business. Now, go get my nephew ready." I spoke from between clenched teeth and a tight jaw. I was losing patience quickly. It didn't matter who Mr. Erickson was. He didn't get to judge or disrespect me without getting checked. I wasn't going to put my hands on him unless it was warranted but verbally putting someone like him in their place worked just as well.

He stammered for a few seconds before tossing some dry ass bible verse at me, then he went inside. No doubt in my mind he was calling Cress or Angel to double-check my story. Either of them would have confirmed though.

When the front door finally swung open again, Mr. Erickson held a sleeping Nasim in his arms. His little head resting on his grandfather's shoulder. I took my nephew and he barely budged. It made putting him in the car seat easy.

"Thank you." I nodded, taking Nasim's bag.

"I'm not dignifying that with a *you're welcome* because you're not. You're not welcome here or anywhere else where my family is. God will deal with you."

"Yup, that's what I keep hearing." I tossed Nasim's bag in the passenger side and got in without another word to Mr. Erickson.

When I got back to the house, I didn't see any signs that Angel was back early but I did see Cress wringing her hands in the doorway, watching out for either me or Angel.

"Oh my god, you went to get him," Cress pushed out an anxious breath and with trembling hands, took Nasim from my arms when I walked in. He lifted his head upon hearing her soft voice and looked around. Seeing his big hazel eyes made me smile.

Shit, I'd smiled more in the past weekend than I had in the past five years. Now that I knew what the warm feeling circulating through my chest was, I knew I loved the hell out of Nasim. My heart exploded with warmth when I looked at him.

"Yeah, did you think I was going to run off with him or something?" I chuckled but Cress's eyes were stony. "Cress, I'd never take him from you. I'm not like that."

"I know. I know, Jules I'm just…scared right now. Not of you but of…him." She glanced down at Nasim, trying not to say his father's name out loud.

"Don't be," I said, smoothing a hand over Nasim's sandy curls. I took my phone out and made a call to Boogie while Cress looked through Nasim's bag to make sure she had everything.

"What's up, Smoke? I got the hotel suite paid for and ready for Cress." When I told him I wanted to get Cress away from Angel and away from Miami, he jumped to help. He told me he always thought Angel abused Cress and how fucked up he felt for her.

"Good. I'm about to head that way to drop them off." When I ended the call, Cress gawked at me.

"Drop us off? You're not going to the hotel with us?" She

blurted once she saw I was off the phone.

"I can't. I need to be here to deal with Angel. Plus, the fewer people see me with you, the better. I need to handle this shit without worrying about you and Nas." I tucked a silky chunk of hair behind her ear.

Cress had a stronghold on me so seeing her big eyes staring at me like her brain was full of contradicting thoughts, made me wish I could reassure her more. I wanted her to know I'd never do anything to put her or Nasim in harm's way. I'd kill to keep them safe.

I ran a hand over my face and heaved a sigh. "I'm going to have Boogie take care of you and Nas." Panic creased the space between her finely arched brows.

"Boogie? He's Angel's right-hand man. He's going to tell him where we're at." Her voice was turning shrill. Fear was eating up her logic. I hated Angel for what he'd turned her into.

"He's on our side. Trust me. I don't believe in too many people but I trust Boog. He's a good guy...well, as good as you can be in this kind of business."

"I don't know, Jules. He's been so close to Angel for so long." Her words were broken apart by the doorbell. We froze in silence while Nasim played on the floor, happy to be home.

"I'll get it," I told her. "If it's Angel, I won't let him near you or Nas. Make sure your bags are ready." I gripped the pistol I always had tucked into my waistband and went to the front door. I knew who it was before I even opened it. I sighed and put my gun away.

"What's up, Bree?" I muttered.

"Uh-huh, where's Cress?" She rolled her eyes and walked in, ignoring me completely. I walked around her, blocking her path again. "Move, Smoke."

"No. You don't get to walk up in here like you pay the mortgage. Cress is busy."

"Busy?" She scoffed then folded her arms across her chest. "Look, I'm pregnant and still very much in my first trimester so my emotions are all over the place. Move before you get cursed out."

"No. You can call her later."

I wanted Cress to have friends. I wanted her to have a normal fucking life but for some reason, Bree rubbed me the wrong goddamn way. She acted like she owned everything in Angel's house. Like she had some kind of claim to it and Cressida was just visiting.

I refused to let her move beyond the mouth of the foyer and I hoped Cress didn't come around the corner because the faster I could get Bree out, the better.

"Who the fuck do you think you are, Smoke?" Her lips were flapping a mile a minute but nothing important came out. I checked the clock on my phone in the middle of her rant and saw that in less than an hour, it would be eight o'clock and Angel would be home. I wanted to have Nasim and Cress out of Miami by then.

"You got all your bullshit out now? Good. Leave," I snapped.

"Is Cress even in here? I'm trying to make sure you haven't tied her up or something crazy like that." She pressed her hand to her stomach, which was still flat, and glared at me.

"She's here. She's busy. Like I said."

"I'm not moving until I see her, Smoke. Oh, and I know Angel is coming back home today so you can stop playing king of the jungle." Her snide tone grated on my nerves.

"I'm not playing shit. Now get the fuck out, Bree. You're wasting my time."

"You don't get to put me out," she squawked. I gripped her arm tight enough so she couldn't pull away but light enough so she couldn't claim I bruised her. Of course, she started screeching any goddamn way. "Get the fuck off of me! I know you heard me say I was pregnant, Smoke!" I knew Cress heard all the commotion but she didn't budge to break it up.

My girl.

"I don't give a fuck about you being twelve minutes pregnant, Bree. You gotta go." I tugged her to the front doors and shoved her outside.

"Bastard!" She shouted. Spittle from her mouth landed on my neck and I took a minute to compose myself before I spoke again. My head was starting to throb and my blood was buzzing.

I'd never hurt a woman but Bree was pushing me. Her hands flew up toward my face but she only managed to push my head back by driving the heel of her hand into my chin. I grabbed her slender wrist and placed it behind her back along with her other one. She fought against my hold but she couldn't get loose.

When she realized I outweighed her by about one-hundred pounds, she smashed the heel of her stilettos into my toe and pushed by me, heading back to the foyer. I hated calling women out of their names but I can't lie and say the word *bitch* wasn't on the tip of my tongue when pain started shooting up and down my leg.

I went after her, grabbing her arm again and pressing her against the wall. "What the fuck is wrong with you?" I growled.

"You're what's wrong with me. You're treating me like I don't have the right to be here!"

"You don't. You don't even live here. What the fuck is your problem?"

"Where is Cressida?" Her wide brown eyes darted around the foyer like Cress would pop out any second. I was shocked she didn't. I didn't blame her after seeing the way Bree lost her temper. "I don't even think she's here. You're a fucking liar and Angel is going to kill you if she's not here when he gets home."

"Don't make me carry you out to your car, Bree. Just go. Cress doesn't want to talk to you. Damn."

"Doesn't want to talk to me?" Her chest deflated and her shoulders slumped forward. I couldn't place the look on her face but it seemed sad and confused. I backed off her a little and eyed her incredulously.

"No. She doesn't want to fucking talk to you." I passed a hand over my hair and sighed. Bree was killing way too much of my time.

"Shit...do you think she found out about Angel?" She shifted from rubbing her non-existent stomach to hugging herself. She was probably saying something but I couldn't hear anything past her asking if Cress found out about Angel.

"What about Angel?" I asked, my brow lifted.

"About..." She looked up at me and said, "I'm pregnant with his baby. I didn't know how to tell her but…"

"What the fuck did you just say?" Cress's voice came eerily calm from the corner of the foyer. I didn't even hear her walk up. But there she was, one hand on her hip and fire in her eyes. I'd never seen her look so lit up with anger before. She was fucking gorgeous.

"Cress, I-I thought you weren't here." Bree took a step back because Cress's energy was too strong to confront head-on.

"Did you say you're pregnant with *Angel's* baby?" I looked down at her hands when she fisted them at her sides and saw the mood ring she always wore was pure black. "All these years…" Cress's voice shook while she composed her thoughts. "I've been confiding in you and telling you how controlling Angel was and how alone and trapped I felt. All these years I've been crying out and I thought I was crazy because you—my best fucking friend—always told me Angel was a good man and not to leave him."

"Cress, I'm sorry. I just…I wanted to be like you. Angel takes care of you and you're always complaining. He's so good to you and I wanted that. I didn't want to hurt you. I wanted to be taken care of too." Tears steamrolled down Bree's face turning into falling drops at her chin.

"You wanted to be taken care of?" Cress's face twisted into disgust. "What the fuck is wrong with you? He's abusive!" Her voice popped out loud and violent as she stepped closer.

Nasim let out a worried cry in the other room and I moved to get him and all the bags. While Cress tore into Bree, I shielded Nasim's face from the commotion, telling him his Mommy was doing great at handling her business. He clung to me, pressing his little face into my chest until I strapped him in the car seat.

When I went back into the foyer, I grabbed Bree's wrist and pulled her toward the door before Cress started throwing punches.

"You can have him, you simple bitch!" Cress shouted, throwing her wedding rings at Bree as I escorted her outside.

"You can sit here until Angel gets home for all I care. Just get the hell out," I grumbled, locking the door behind me.

"Cressida," Bree sobbed. "Please, let me explain!" I knew by the look on Cress's face that there wasn't enough explaining in the goddamn world to make her listen. I didn't bother waiting for them to argue more. I put the car in drive and peeled away from the house. I only had ten minutes to get Cress and Nasim to Boogie. I hated that I wouldn't have time to talk Cress down, but her being away from Miami and away from me and Angel was for the best.

When I pulled up to a gas station right on the edge of the Miami city line, Boogie was already there with one of Angel's men. I recognized him as one of the guys talking about jumping ship to Man's operation.

"Is he cool?" I asked, walking up to the two men. I left Cress in the car to get Nasim's things together and get him unstrapped from the car seat.

Boogie eyed me, then looked over at the man standing beside him. He was tall, slim, and had a gun tucked into the right side of his belt. Nobody else could see it but I knew it was there. I knew why he had on a shirt two sizes too big. I paid attention to the way he favored his right side over his left too.

"He's cool. Trust me. I know these men like the back of my hand. This one is loyal."

"Yeah…to who?" I quizzed, staring at him unflinching.

"What's up, Smoke? I'm Drew." He extended his hand for a shake and I looked at it then went back to talking to Boogie. I was leery of any man on Angel's team until he'd proven himself to me directly. "I'm not down with Angel anymore man. Most of us aren't but he has spies everywhere. It's hard to plan an exodus when you even have bottle girls watching you." Drew looked at me, his eyes pleading with me to believe he wasn't loyal to Angel.

Cress walked over to us with Nasim on her hip. Her champagne eyes swung from me to Boogie, then to Drew. "Hey," she said cautiously.

"What's going on, Cress? I'm going to have Drew run you to the hotel. He's good people. I trust him with my life." Boogie clapped Drew's shoulder harder than necessary and squeezed it. It was like he was giving him directions through that single gesture.

"Would you trust him with me and Nasim's life though?" Cress bit back. Her patience was thin and I liked it. Maybe she did let a little of my attitude rub off on her.

"I would." Boogie nodded solemnly.

"Listen…" I took my pistol out and tucked it in the bag hanging from Cress's shoulder. "If this motherfucker breathes funny or takes a detour, put a bullet in his skull from the backseat," I told her. She blinked wide eyes and thick lashes up at me.

"Jules…"

"You heard me," I said, not flinching. I glanced at my watch and said, "Now go. Call me from your burner phone later. Destroy this one now." I tapped her purse and she nodded, shifting Nasim to her other hip then digging out the phone and putting it in my palm. "You do it," I told her seriously. I wanted Cress to feel empowered even if breaking the phone was a small thing.

Cress put Nasim down and he stood wobbling on his own two feet while gripping my pant leg. Boogie, Drew and I watched her throw the expensive iPhone on the ground. The screen cracked in a spiderweb pattern right before Cress drove the heel of her shoe into the screen. It lit up and chimed, playing her ringtone for Angel. His face took up the screen in fragments interspersed with black squares from where the display was damaged.

Once she saw his face looking back at her from the ground, a rush of energy must have swept through her because she growled and stomped the phone again and again until it stopped ringing and went black. She tucked a sleek lock of hair behind her ear and looked around at the men staring at her in disbelief.

"Uh-oh," Nasim said looking down at the trashed phone.

"Yeah, uh-oh is right, buddy," I chuckled, picking him up. "I'm gonna miss you, King Nas." I kissed his forehead and he wrapped his little arms around my neck. "I'll see you tomorrow though. I'm gonna come see you and Mommy."

Boogie picked up the shattered phone and blew out a stream of air. "Shit, Cress. I didn't know you had it in you. You barely speak five words when I see you."

"That's because Angel won't let me talk to any of his men. The only ones he's ever trusted me around were Sam and now Jules." She caressed my name with her soft voice and I felt my dick threaten to get hard. Only Cressida had that kind of hold on me.

The more I thought about how much I loved her, the less I care about what anyone thought about me because of it. Yes, she was my brother's wife. Yes, she had his baby. Yes, I was head over heels in love with her. Probably always had been.

Fucking women was cool and all but I could always tell I was meant for something more. Something that wasn't empty. I knew whatever it was, it wouldn't be perfect and there'd be no fairytale ending or beginning…or middle for that matter. Now, I knew I was meant to be with Cress. I would pull down heaven and lift up hell to make sure she was mine.

I watched Drew place Cress's things in the trunk of a plain-looking Nissan and took note of the tag number. I walked over, leaned in so only he could hear me, and said, "You do anything to Cress or Nasim and I will hunt you for fun. Then when I catch you, I'll keep you in one of my hiding places as a pet. I'll come by and peel off strips of your skin until I'm tired of you, then I'll slit your throat." I backed up with a smile and slapped his back. "We have an understanding?"

He blinked rounded eyes and nodded silently. Besides the frequency of his blinks, I couldn't tell that he was shaken. It was a good quality to have. He needed to work on it though because the wet marks under his arms were giving him away.

"I hate leaving you," Cress said. Boogie was busy running around with Nas on his shoulders while Drew fought with the car seat in the back of the Nissan. I glanced around and pulled her closer to me with my fingertips on her hips.

"I know. I hate this shit too but it's better to keep you and Nasim safe. The other option is you sticking around and Angel doing something stupid. Then I'd have to blow the entire fucking city up and that wouldn't be good for anyone." I reached out and let my fingers slip through her hair.

"Oh god, please don't blow up the city." A soft laugh lit up her eyes and softened her regal cheekbones.

"Wait, you can't take the Lord's name in vain. Pastor Erickson would condemn you." I traced an invisible line down the front of her throat and watched her lashes flutter in response.

"I don't know if you've noticed, Jules but I'm not exactly the best preacher's kid. I kind of do my own thing and make sure to never mistreat people."

"And that's why I love you so much," I said, staring at her. "You care about everyone. Even me." I pressed a kiss to her forehead and I swear to fucking god I could feel our energies vibrate together in a constant hum of peace. Cress was my whole heart and I never paid attention because I was always focused on Angel.

"*Especially* you, Julien," she whispered, bouncing up on her toes and draping her arms around my neck.

"Got it!" Drew finally said, triumphantly pumping his fist in the air. "Car seat is good to go." He checked his watch and sighed. "We gotta hurry."

"I'll strap Nas in," Boogie smiled and the scar stretching down his face almost disappeared. You'd never know the type of shit he was into by looking at him.

I didn't care who saw me when I kissed Cress. What were they going to do? Tell Angel? It wasn't like I hadn't planned on doing that myself. "I'll call you when I get a minute and I'll try to get away to see you two. If I can't, I'll send you a message."

"What do you mean if you *can't*, Jules?" Worry threaded through her words.

"Nothing. Just enjoy yourself, okay?" I opened the door for her and she got in beside Nasim. I reached in and rubbed his sandy curls then told him to be good before tapping the roof of the car telling Drew to drive off.

"Wait!" Cress squeaked. The car halted then backed up to where I stood beside Boogie. The back window rolled down and she poked her head out, wild strands of golden stirring around her face in the breeze. "Julien, I love you. Thank you." I saw stars dancing in her pretty eyes.

"I love you too, Cress. And don't thank me. I'd do anything for you." I reached out to skim the apples of her cheeks. She looked up at me and smiled.

"I know. Your secret is safe with me." She winked and my goddamn heart nearly exploded with warmth.

"Secret?" I quizzed with a scoff.

"That the big bad wolf is really a puppy in disguise." She bit her bottom lip and it made me wish we were alone. I cleared my throat and tapped the tip of her nose.

"Yeah, okay. We'll see about that puppy shit when I see you later." I backed away from the car and they drove off this time for real.

"Not a fucking word, Boog," I said, walking to my car. He laughed and it was a bold, raspy sound.

"What? You thought I couldn't see what was going on between you and Cress? I knew the minute you sliced off those motherfuckers' nipples." He shuddered then rubbed his own chest through his shirt.

"Sometimes these assholes need a taste of their own medicine." I looked at my watch and groaned. "It's eight-fifteen. Let's head back to Angel's."

"Cool. I think we should meet Man before we meet Angel." I got in the car and Boogie got in beside me dropping his black backpack on the floor.

"Meet Man? You managed to find out who this sneaky motherfucker is?" I asked, shock evident in my tone. "Why didn't you tell me?"

"I'm telling you now, damn." He put his seatbelt on and reclined in the leather seat. "Man just has one request from you," Boogie said, staring at the road ahead of us.

"Oh? What's that?"

"Keep his identity quiet."

"That's it?" I chuckled dryly. "He's closing in on Angel's operation like a fucking ninja and the only thing he requests is anonymity?"

"That's it. He's going to need loyalty from you of course." Boogie's eyes flitted across mine.

"From *me*? Once I kill Angel, I'll hand over Rush and everything else to go with it. I want no parts of it after that. He should be asking for loyalty from you. You're sticking with Rush, right?" I pulled up to a stoplight and looked to him for an answer.

"Something like that."

"You gonna tell me how to get to Man or am I supposed to guess?" I asked him.

"Turn here and take Red Palm straight down."

"He's at your place?" I frowned, following his directions.

"Yeah, it's the safest place to meet," he informed me.

When we pulled up, Boogie turned to me and said, "He has a little bit of money for you. A thank you of sorts."

"I don't need to be paid. This is personal with me and Angel. It's deeper than money."

"I know. Still, you deserve it." Instead of getting out and going in the house so I could meet Man once and for all, Boogie reached in his black bag and pulled out two stacks of money, slapping them in my palms. "That's fifty-grand, Smoke." I looked down at the stacks and frowned, running my fingers along the green linen paper.

"You already working for this motherfucker, Boog?" Things were piling up around me quickly and I needed to know where Boogie stood. I still didn't feel like his loyalty had been compromised but I needed some kind of explanation.

"Smoke, chill." He pushed out a heavy sigh that seemed to fill up the quiet space around us. "Listen to me." We locked eyes and he continued, "I'm Man."

Silent bombs went off in my head. I looked at the stacks of money in my lap, then at Boogie and suddenly, it all snapped into place.

"*You're* Man..." I passed a hand over my face and let my head hit the headrest. "Boogie Man. Why the fuck didn't I see this shit a mile away?" Part of me was impressed that he was able to be so close to me yet keep something so huge hidden. The other part of me was angry with myself for such a huge oversight.

"I didn't want you to see it until now, Smoke."

"So, you using me to get Angel out of the way or what? What's the endgame, Boogie?" I narrowed my eyes at him to see if I could spot any other secrets in his eyes.

"Yes and no. I respect the fuck out of you, Smoke. The plan was never to use you. When Angel told me his little brother was getting out, I thought you'd make my job harder but turned out to be the opposite.

You cared about Angel but you didn't let him walk all over you. I knew eventually you'd have to separate from him because of the way he is. Because of how he treats people. How he treats *you*." Silence bunched around us making the car feel uncomfortably small. "It wasn't my place to say it before, but your brother talks shit about you like a dog. There's still no real reason for me to say this to you besides the fact that I want you to know who you're really dealing with."

"I know who I'm dealing with now," I said, my chest burning

with anger and pain. I didn't want to talk about the piece of shit Angel was anymore. I knew now and there was only one real way to rectify the situation. "So, let's go deal with this motherfucker." I drove away from Boogie's house and headed toward Angel's.

I knew he was home when my phone started blowing up. He called back-to-back and left several voicemails. Neither me nor Boogie said anything about him the entire ride. I'm sure we both had way too much shit on our minds.

I wanted to pick Boogie's brain. I wanted to ask him when he'd started usurping Angel's business and clients. I wanted to know how many men he had on his side. How many cops he had in his pocket. If he was going to take over Rush and do it the proper way, he needed to know what the fuck he was doing.

When I pulled into the driveway at Angel's, the door was wide open and I could see glimpses of him pacing in the foyer, a cigarette between his fingers and his phone clenched in his hand. I looked at Boogie and said, "You cool out here?" I honestly wanted to handle Angel one on one but I knew Boogie had his own gripes to deal with where Angel was concerned.

"For now. You know I'm here if you need any help."

"I know," I nodded then got out of the car. On the way to the front door, I realized that in the short time I'd known Boogie, he'd been more of a big brother to me than my own brother. Blood wasn't always thicker than water. That lesson seemed to be on repeat.

When I walked into the foyer, Angel stopped pacing and tossed his phone down with a clatter on the side table. "Where the fuck have you been, Smoke?" A vertical line etched between his brows showing his impatience. His blown-out pupils showed me he was high as fuck.

"Out," I said folding my arms across my chest. In my mind, I mapped out the location of every gun in the house and every weapon I had on my body. My knife was in a slim holster at my hip and my pistol was in my waistband.

"Out? What the hell were you doing out? Where's Cress and Nasim? You let my fucking family walk out? I should knock your big ass out for that shit. Where is my family, Smoke?!" Veins bulged from his outstretched neck. His wide eyes looked glassy and red like they'd pop out of his head any second.

"Safe," I snapped, my top lip snarling at the thought of him wanting to see Cress and Nasim.

"They're not safe unless they're here with me!" He thumped his chest and took a step toward me. "You're playing fucking games with me. Do you know who I am, Smoke? I could fucking kill you right now. I could put out an order to have you hit."

"Then do it, Angel." I dropped my hands to my side and took one long stride forward until we were chest to chest. Tension crackled and popped around us like live electricity. "You want to kill me so badly, do it."

He sniffed then wiped his nose on his tanned forearm before barking out a maniacal laugh. "You think I won't? Just because you're my blood you think I won't put a bullet between your fucking eyes?"

"I know you won't." I took the gun from the hiding place in the foyer and placed it in his hand. I dared him to do it. I knew he wasn't going to because killing someone on purpose takes a certain kind of darkness and lack of fear. Angel didn't have that. "Shoot me, hermano," I said.

"You're out of your goddamn mind, Smoke. I don't like the way you're talking to me." He looked at me but refused to raise the barrel and press it to my head. "Bring me my wife and son and maybe I'll forget about your outburst."

"I'm not bringing you shit. Cress doesn't want you anymore, Angel. She left."

"*Left?*" His laugh started low then built to a deafening sound that bounced off every surface. "Nah, she didn't leave. Cressida is a dumb bitch but she wouldn't..." My knuckles connected with his mouth and made a sickening wet sound.

"Watch your mouth when you talk about her," I growled over him, shaking out my throbbing fist. I didn't feel the pain, only the throb after the hit. Angel stood upright holding his mouth while blood trickled from between his fingers. "You like consistency, huh? Keep talking shit about Cress and keep getting hit."

"What I say about *my* wife has nothing to do with you!"

It does when she's my woman and not your fucking wife.

The words stayed in my head because I realized it wasn't the time to drop that bomb on him. Not yet. I wanted him to see his world crumbling piece by piece and it started with him realizing he had no more control over Cress.

"It does when she wants me to help her stay safe away from your ass." I jabbed my finger into his chest and he stumbled back a few steps. "Cress knows about you and Bree. She's tired of you abusing her. She wanted out."

"Fuck that bullshit. All I'm hearing is that my own flesh and blood helped my wife run away from home with my son! I paid you to guard them. What the fuck good are you?" He didn't sound like he was speaking to his brother. He sounded like he was talking to some stranger off the fucking street. It stung in a way I wasn't expecting.

"I did what was best for them. Not you. You need to take a step back and think about what the fuck you're doing with your life. You want to throw everything away because you can't get your coke habit under control?" Anger broadcasted from me strong and clear.

The last goddamn thing I wanted to do was kill Angel. Why the fuck couldn't he just step away from everything? Why couldn't he get help and go somewhere quiet and live life?

"Fuck you, Smoke! You don't know shit about me anymore. Since you've been locked away like a motherfucking animal, I've been changing. I've been growing." He paused and wiped away remnants of blood from his bottom lip. It started to swell and affect his speech. "You can't stand to see your big brother be the king of Miami. Or what is it, Smoke? You want Cressida? Hmm?" He was in my face. The blood drying on his lip and chin smelled faintly metallic and it made my blood hum. The hunger to kill was mounting fast and it wouldn't be good for Angel.

"I want you to open your eyes!" My voice thundered so loud

that the words scraped my throat coming out. We were now brother against brother. We were wild and untamed versions of ourselves. The energy was tight and loud like a siren wailing in the air. "You're going to lose everything if you keep acting fucking stupid! Your wife is already gone. Next is Rush. Then what, Angel? What are you going to do when all this shit vanishes and you're alone without a way to fuel your coke habit?"

"What the hell do you mean my wife is gone? She's coming back. You think I don't have ways to track her?" He laughed and shook his head, black strands falling across his forehead and sticking from the sheen of sweat.

"Look, take a step back from everything and just..."

"Just what, Smoke? Leave you in charge of my empire? The one I built from the ground up while you were rotting away in a cell getting told when to shower and when to sleep and eat? I guess that's the black side of you coming out huh? Prison mentality is nothing when you're half nigg---"

Another punch.

Another.

Crash. Crash. Crash.

My fist landed against his face so many times I think I blacked out. It was nothing like how movies and books describe. It was absolute nothingness. I was a robot working on autopilot. The only thing fueling me was hatred and pain. It dripped from pierced wounds in my heart. A heart I just realized I owned.

Before I knew what was happening, I felt something pulling me backward. Something strong but not stronger than me. My body moved forward and a roar grew inside of me like the gnarled bark of a tree.

"Smoke!" My name sounded far away. Submerged in water.

I blinked repeatedly until nothingness fell away and the scene in front of me unfolded. Crimson drops littered the once pristine marble in the foyer. The smaller drops led to a larger smear, then Angel's body lying motionless on the floor, face down.

"Smoke!" My name rang out again. That time I recognized Boogie's voice. "Come on, man. We gotta get you out of here."

"Is...he dead?" I asked, catching my breath.

"Nah, he's knocked the fuck out but not dead." I tore away from Boogie's grip and crashed my heel down on his spine as hard as I could. It was followed by a heavy kick to his ribs. Hard enough to crack them. His body jerked from the involuntary pain and a slow groan rolled from his bloody mouth.

"Let's go!" Boogie shouted at me while he stood in the doorway.

"Wait a goddamn minute. Let me grab my shit." I ran through the house and up to my room getting my laptop and some clothes. Enough to toss in my gym bag. After that, I went to the foyer and checked Angel's pulse.

He was still alive.

I ran a hand over my head and sighed. Nothing about beating a junkie's ass made me feel okay. I wasn't in control when I snapped though. Something else was driving. It was darker than I was used to.

"Yo, Smoke," Boogie called out again.

"I'm coming." It was only partially true. While Angel was knocked out cold, I was going to clean his ass out. "You want some of his personal stash?" I asked Boog over my shoulder.

"Hell yeah," he said with a nod. He knew I wasn't interested in the drugs so there was no threat to his upcoming organization.

I knew where all of Angel's shit was. He showed me everything when I got home. I remembered where his stash of coke was even though, at the time, I didn't know he was putting it up his nose for recreation. I thought he had it on him in case one of his men came up short and he had to make up the difference with his connect.

I went through the house popping safes and taking money and guns. I let Boogie have the extra drugs. It took us ten minutes to clean out the house. When we got back to the foyer, Angel was starting to stir. I didn't give him enough time to wake up fully because I knew we'd fight again.

On the way to Boogie's place, I remained stone silent. Too many thoughts were whirring through my brain. The one that kept bobbing to the surface was Cressida. I wanted to know if she was settled and if her and Nasim were okay.

"We'll check on Cress and Nas once we get moving. I don't think we should lay low at my place. Angel is going to have whatever men are still on his side crawling all around."

"Call a meeting. Outside of Miami. We need to see who's really down to ride with you and your organization," I said. Boog came to a stop at his house and cursed under his breath when he saw a car in his driveway that we both recognized.

"Smoke, can I talk to you?" Bree swarmed me the minute I stepped out. I wasn't in the mood for her sob story and I damn sure wasn't going to tell her where Cress was so she could stalk her and tell Angel.

"What the hell are you doing at my house, Bree?" Boogie stepped around me, handing off the keys to his house. Instead of standing there dealing with Bree's crazy ass, I went inside and left her fussing with Boog in the driveway.

Once I was away from all the damn squawking, I was able to think a little. I looked around the immaculately decorated house and shook my head.

This motherfucker was Man all along.

Well, shit, served Angel right to have his right-hand man take over his organization. Boogie would handle the business the way it needed to be handled. He wouldn't spiral and lose his grip on reality like my brother.

Even thinking of Angel as my brother now felt foreign. All my fond childhood memories turned hazy and dark. I was able to see all the times Angel fucked me over and used me when I thought I was helping him.

The sound of shouting broke my thoughts apart but I still refused to check on Boogie and Bree. He knew how to handle her crazy ass. I checked my phone to see if Cress called me from her burner but she hadn't. I did, however, have a new email from the offices at the Gemology Institute.

I wasn't the type of man to get nervous but something rushed through me when I saw the subject of the email.

RE: Certification Application

I glanced around the empty living room making sure I was alone before opening the email. My eyes ate up line after line of text until I got to the most important one.

You have been accepted into the Gemology Institute's gemologist certification program! Once your course of study is finished, you will be a certified gemologist and will be granted a certificate of completion.

I read it over and over just to make sure I wasn't seeing things but each time I read it, the words became clearer. I'd been accepted into the certification program. It was a hell of a lot better than the books I read while in prison. The ones Angel bragged about paying for every chance he got.

"She's going back to Angel's. That should give us some time to get the men together and you can tell them your plan." Boogie's voice snapped me out of my thoughts. I didn't realize the arguing had stopped between him and Bree. I was so caught up in being accepted into the gemology certification program that my mind blocked everything else out.

"Okay, cool," I said giving him a short nod.

"You do have a plan besides just handing me the reigns and shooting Angel, right?"

"Yeah, motherfucker I do," I assured him with a frown. We spent the next half hour clearing Boogie's stash from his house and moving it to one of his private locations. He knew Angel would be coming for him. It didn't matter if he knew who Boogie was. Angel knew Boogie wasn't doing his job and that was punishable by death but since he didn't have me to enforce the kills and he didn't have Boog, he would be scrambling. If there was one thing I knew about my big brother, it's that he wasn't a killer.

That was my area of expertise.

...

Chapter
FOURTEEN

Cressida

Nasim was knocked out on the bed. His little eyes were shut tight while he snored like he didn't have a care in the world. I wished I felt like that. Instead, I was going crazy. I kept looking out of the window every five seconds and checking the hallway to make sure Angel hadn't found his way to me.

I tried to relax but how could I when I knew my husband was probably in a murderous rage looking for me and Nasim? I ping-ponged back and forth between the bed and the small desk on the other side of the room. Sitting on the desk was the pre-paid burner phone I got after Drew dropped me off. I wanted to reach out to Jules but I had no idea if he was in front of Angel or not.

Every time I picked the phone up, my stomach swelled to accommodate the concrete knots pushing against the sides. I chewed the side of my lip and shut my eyes tight.

Just do it, Cress. Do it.

Without thinking about it anymore. I picked up the phone and sent a text to Jules.

Me: Checking in. Get back to me when you can.

I didn't want to say more than that in case Angel was lurking around somewhere monitoring Jules. I seriously doubted that was the case but my logical brain and my terrified brain were at war. After I sent the text, I stared at the phone waiting to see if he'd read it. Seconds after I hit send, the status of the text went from delivered to read and I let my shoulders fall a little.

Jules: Everything is good so far. Last I left him, he was knocked out in the foyer.

Me: Coke stupor or...

Jules: He caught a stupor from these hands.

I couldn't help laughing at his reply. Even when I was terrified out of my mind, he knew how to make me forget even if it was only for a second. Sometimes those one-second reprieves were everything.

Jules: You and lil man okay over there?

Me: He's knocked out. Everything is good. Will we see you later?

Jules: Of course. Stick by your phone and try to relax. I got you.

Those words were comforting even though I knew I had to want this escape from Angel more than Julien did. This wasn't his fight. It wasn't his mountain to climb. I had to make sure Nasim and I were good and that Angel could never touch us again.

I walked over to the bed after I was done texting Jules and stared at my son. My faith had been shaken since I married Angel, but looking at Nasim let me know that whoever was in charge of life knew I needed a reason to live when my own will ran out. True, I felt dumb and naïve as hell for getting caught up with Angel when I really wanted Jules, but there was nothing I could do about my past mistakes except learn to never make them again.

Once I knew Jules was safe and Angel wasn't around him, I had another person I needed to call. My throat tightened even thinking about dialing those numbers. I turned the TV up a little to give Nas some background noise while he slept, then I went into the bathroom with my phone and sat on the edge of the tub.

I studied my knees and looked at the scar on my left leg. I fell off my bike and scraped the hell out of my knee. I was determined to never ride a bike again but Trinity forced me to get back on my bike and ride again. She made me face those fears and told me I could do it even if I fell again.

I smiled and ran my fingers over the darkened two-inch scar then dialed Trini's phone number. I knew it by heart.

Nerves buzzed through my body making me feel nauseous. Each ring made my stomach twist more and more.

"Hello?" Trinity's voice came through clear and smooth and

my heart squeezed while my fingers spun the mood ring around and around.

"Um...Hey, Trini. It's me. Cressida. Please don't hang up." My words fell out all jumbled and disjointed.

There was a long pause on the other end. So long that I had to look at my phone screen to make sure she was still on the line. "Trinity?" I said, my voice wobbling from the weight of fear.

"Cress, is this *really* you?"

"It's me." I nodded against the phone. "I left him, Trini. I just...I wanted to tell you that. I left him. I'm in a hotel outside of Miami and Mom and Dad don't know so if they call looking for me..."

"I won't say a word," she said quickly. "Where's Nasim?"

"He's here with me. Knocked out."

"Wow. I don't know what to say, Cress. It's been a long time." She cleared her throat and I wondered if the same emotions that were tearing through me were clogging her throat. "I'm so glad you and Nas are safe and away from him." Another pause. "Are you leaving for good?" The apprehension in her voice was evident and understandable.

"Yes. There's nothing that could make me stay. I'm terrified but I'm done." The finality in my voice was shocking but it felt good and for once, I believed myself.

"I hope so for you and my nephew's sake. I really hope so. Do you need anything from me? Can I help?" Hearing her authenticity made my eyes burn with unworthy tears.

"No, Trini. Julien is helping. You remember him, right?"

"Angel's little brother, Julien? The one who had the crush on you in middle school?" The corners of my mouth curved at the tone of her voice. It took me back to the smell of Blue Magic and Pink Lotion on Sunday mornings when we were in our room and Trinity was making sure my hair was perfect for service.

"Yes, that Julien," I smiled into the phone.

"Are you sure he's really helping you? Why wouldn't he side with his brother? Unless..." Her voice faded away and my cheeks burned with what I knew would be her next question. "Are you fucking Julien, Cressida?" Her voice was a stiff whisper that pushed me to my feet. I opened the bathroom door and checked on Nasim. Still sleep. I left the door cracked and paced the floor.

"Yes, I am. But listen, hear me out," I begged. "It's like we both came to terms with who Angel was at the same time. I mean, I knew how he was and I was already working my way up to running away. I had a bag packed and everything but Jules..." I pushed out a soft breath. "Jules looked up to Angel like he was a god until he saw the same devil horns I wake up to every morning. We crashed together and it felt so right." I shut my eyes and let the memory of Julien's lips on mine wash over me. I saw his sexy face in my mind and mapped out the dark stars in his eyes.

"So, not only are you fucking Angel's little brother but you're in love with him too?" Julien's face vanished when Trinity spoke again.

"I am and I don't care what anyone thinks about it because for once, my heart isn't full of what-ifs. For once, I feel like I made the right decision. *Julien* is the right decision." The silence dragged on for several beats before Trinity spoke again.

"So has Julien realized that Angel is just a manipulative abuser who used him all the time?"

"He has. It was a painful realization and honestly, I know he's still struggling with it."

"Then how do you know he won't just take you right back to Angel? What if he decides blood is thicker than water?"

"I trust him with my life. I trust him with Nasim's life." Nobody else had to trust Jules but I did. I saw the truth in his eyes and his sincerity never wavered.

"Shit. I guess you trust him then," Trini said, a laugh clinging to the edges of her words. "Listen, I'm not trying to be overprotective but you have to understand how this looks to me. I've lost you so many times to Angel...I don't want this to be one more time." Tears made her voice thick.

"You won't, Trini. I promise. Not this time."

"Good because I love you and watching you get abused is painful, little sis." Her words landed like heavy stones inside of my chest. "I'd invite you and Nasim to my house so I could see you guys but I don't want to mess up whatever plans you and Julien have."

"We don't have any plans. He just wanted to get me out of Miami and out of Angel's reach." I couldn't tell Trini everything. It was better if she didn't know that I was laying low until Angel was dead and out of the fucking picture for good. The less she knew, the better.

"I still don't put it past Angel to have my house watched if he's looking for you."

"Me either," I muttered. I peeked out of the bathroom at Nas again then sighed. "Why don't you come by the hotel? Are you at home or work?"

"I'm at work. I can swing by for a little while when I get off." The excitement in her voice was contagious. By the time we got off the phone, I was grinning from ear to ear. I was finally going to see my sister after a year.

My cheeks were stinging when she sent me a text telling me she was on her way to my room after work. By then, Nasim was awake and bouncing off the walls with energy. I scooped him into my arms and kissed his chubby cheek.

"Aunt Trinity is coming to visit for a little while. The last time you saw her, you were only a newborn. Now look at you, walking and trying to talk." I pressed a kiss to the top of his sandy curls just as Trinity knocked on the door. Even though I knew it was her, I still looked out of the peephole with a stomach full of nerves.

When I pulled the door open, I wrapped my fingers around Trini's wrist and yanked her in before closing and locking the door. Once we were in front of each other, happy squeals rushed in front of the rib-cracking hug we shared. God, it felt good to lay hands on my big sister. To feel her again, to hear her voice, her laughter.

"I missed you so much, Trinity," I told her, smoothing her soft sandy hair and staring at her. Seeing Trinity was like seeing a celebrity for me. I only hoped this time nothing would come between us. I couldn't lose her again.

"Missed isn't even enough to describe how much I've thought about you and prayed for you, sis." She ran her fingers through my hair and shook her head while staring at me. "You look good."

"So do you." And she did. Her thick golden hair was brushed up into the neatest curly puff I'd ever seen and her edges were laid by the hand of God. I took in her emerald green pants, mustard silk blouse, and gold hoop earrings. She'd been doing well for herself it seemed. She got even more beautiful over the past year.

"Okay, that's enough fawning over you. Where is my nephew?" She walked all the way inside and grinned so hard I thought she would pop and turn into little bits of confetti when she saw Nasim cruising around the room.

We sat and talked for hours while Nas played. I told her everything that happened between me and Jules and she listened, reserving judgment. I told her about Bree being pregnant by Angel and she didn't even flinch. Then she did that big sister thing where they remind you of how they never liked that one friend you had in the first place.

I'd been missing real sisterhood in my life and now that I had Trinity back, it was time to heal.

...

Chapter FIFTEEN

Julien

"We're not calling a meeting at Rush. That's fucking stupid," I frowned at Drew who was for some reason, tossing out ideas like me and Boogie asked him.

"Why don't you make yourself useful until I call you?" Boogie said, dismissing Drew with a flick of his hand. "I have a spot," Boogie told me once we were alone. "I already put the word out to my men. The ones who are still with Angel need to hear from you so it won't look suspect."

I wondered how many of Angel's men thought Boogie was trying to steal business. I guess it didn't matter though. At the end of everything, those who were willing to switch organizations seamlessly would be alive and the others…well, they'd get to sleep in the ocean.

It didn't take me long at all to round up the rest of the men. I pulled in all the corner boys and the Rush employees who were a part of selling drugs around the club. In under an hour, we were all in one of Boog's storehouses. He'd already started to accumulate properties to stash products. From the looks of things, his setup was way nicer than Angel's. No, he didn't have the huge flex of touting Rush as his club but the quiet café we met at was much more lowkey.

There was no flash about the exposed brick walls or the ambient coffee and wine bar running the inside perimeter. The wide-open stage at the front of the café was the perfect place to address everyone seated at spread-out tables on the floor. I let Boogie do the talking while I sat in the audience.

I looked different from earlier when I'd dropped off Cress and Nasim. Now, I was in all black. A pair of jeans, a black hoodie, and black latex gloves. My body was thrumming, bubbling over with anticipation. It had been too damn long since I killed someone. The urge was so strong I could taste the metallic flavor of blood every time I inhaled. The same way you walk into a pizza place and can taste the crust, the sauce, the toppings…just from walking through the door.

I was practically fucking salivating.

Nobody questioned my presence in the audience. Nobody asked why I had on gloves. They all acknowledged me then focused on Boogie. That's how I wanted it. I hated being the center of attention. It made things tough when you wanted to kill someone.

"Me and Smoke called y'all here to have a discussion before Angel gets back to work." Boogie looked out at everyone then sat easily on the stool near the edge of the stage. "I know I'm not the only one who's noticed Angel's little habit," He rubbed his nose, then sniffed for punctuation and everyone chuckled and nodded. "I've tried to get him to cut back and so has Smoke but he's unhinged at this point and it's dipping into our product. Guess who's on the hook for all the missing coke?" He paused for effect and watched the faces in front of him.

A grumble went through most of the room. I paid attention to everyone who remained silent. Those were the ones who needed to be dealt with. I continued observing while Boogie spoke. He did an excellent job of weaving his words around them all so they understood what had to happen.

"I know a lot of y'all have been whispering about moving to Man's organization." That set off muttering and grumbling through all the men. Boogie watched them like a hawk. So did I. "Let me say this right now, whoever is honest will be rewarded. Whoever lies or chooses the wrong side of loyalty…well, you already know what your fate is. Choose wisely." He cleared his throat and stood up with a smile that told me he was ready to get the show on the road.

Uncertainty was thick in the air while Boogie paced from one side of the wide stage to the other. "How many of y'all have been talking about moving to Man's organization?" He looked out at everyone for the answer, and several of them lifted their hand or nodded. "Come on stage if you said yes," he told them with a big gesture. The only sound in the quiet space was the shuffling of feet onto the stage. "How many of you have already switched to Man's organization but are afraid to fully leave Angel?" More men joined him on stage.

"Last question." He flashed a deceiving smile. "Who wants to switch organizations?" A handful more stood and went to the stage. "That's it?" Boogie asked. "The rest of you motherfuckers are loyal to Angel?"

I watched each man who nodded and stood to my feet slowly. There were about eight guys left. Their faces were smug like they won some kind of prize. Honestly, in my eyes, they did win a prize. It wasn't a prize for them but it was a prize nonetheless.

I walked up behind the man closest to the back and plunged my blade into the back of his neck to disable him then I slit his throat. My fingertips buzzed when I sliced through his esophagus. I felt the warmth of his blood running over my knuckles even though I had on gloves. I pulled in a deep breath and moved on to the next man before anyone in the audience realized what was happening.

The men on stage saw though.

They tried to hide the horror in their eyes with masks and avoidance but I saw through that shit. They looked at me like I was a monster, like most people who had the privilege to witness me kill someone.

After slitting the second man's throat, the other men caught on. I made it to the third asshole and went straight for the carotid artery. I didn't have time to waste.

I would have loved to finish them off one by one with my knife but the situation called for speed and efficiency. I pulled out my pistol and knocked off three men with head shots. The remaining loyal subjects pulled guns on me but were taken out by Boogie before they got to squeeze the trigger.

"Now," Boog said clapping his hands together. "Anybody else want to declare their loyalty to Angel? Or are we all straight here?" His eyes had hardened to stony brown rocks.

"We're straight," they all said. It was a unanimous sound.

One of them spoke up, locking eyes with me and taking in my appearance. All black with blood-slicked gloves and shoes. I must have looked like something out of a nightmare.

"Is Smoke really Man?" He asked, trying his best to keep eye contact with me. He failed after a few seconds, dropping his stare to his shoes.

"No," I grunted from the middle of the floor.

"I am." Boogie held his hand out and the men broke out into conversation amongst themselves. Some of them already knew but most of them had no idea. "You saw the fate of your brothers who refused to leave a sinking ship. You want to be on that ship with them?"

"Nah, I'm good," he hurried to say.

"I don't give a fuck what ship y'all are on. I'm out." I usually liked to stick around and clean up my messes but everything in me wanted to get to Cress so I could check on her and Nasim. I hadn't heard from her since the first time she texted me.

For the first time in my life, I was worried.

Something was gnawing at me and it told me I needed to hear her voice. I needed to hear that she was okay. I hadn't heard shit from Angel all day. I already knew what to expect from him though. I'd started a war with my brother and he was plotting on how to get me. Nobody needed to tell me there was a price on my head after knocking him out in his own house and robbing him of all his cash, coke, and guns. Blood may have been thicker than water but it wasn't thicker than assault and robbery.

One of the stupid motherfuckers I killed in Boogie's café was probably put on the job to take me out since Angel didn't have anyone at his right hand anymore. That's what happens when you fuck people over. I had no idea what Angel's relationship with Boogie was but for your best friend to plot on your business and your life spoke volumes.

I told Boogie to have his new fleet of soldiers clean the mess up from the bodies because I had to go check on Cress. He nodded and told me he'd take care of everything and give me a heads up if he saw or heard from Angel. More than likely, he wouldn't. My brother was a goddamn coward. He probably wouldn't even show his face at Rush when the doors opened.

No. He'd be waiting in the wings to catch me slipping. That was the problem though, he thought too highly of himself and not enough of me. I didn't slip and I damn sure didn't get caught.

...

Chapter
SIXTEEN

Cressida

I was so full of joy after Trinity left that I was floating on a cloud. I couldn't remember the last time I'd been so happy or the last time I felt like myself. Falling in love with Julien, getting away from Angel, and reconnecting with my sister was all the food my soul needed.

After I gave Nasim his bath and watched him play happily with a few of his favorite toys I grabbed from the house, I got him dressed, snuggled next to his warm little body, and read him a story. I was addicted to the fresh powdery smell of him. I loved the way his little fingers curled around mine and how he tried his hardest to read along while I read to him.

Everything inside of me wished Angel wasn't his father. Nasim was such a light in my life. I wished his father reflected that. "Mama," Nas babbled up at me with heavy lids.

"Yes, baby?"

"Juuz?"

"No juice, Nas. It's bedtime," I said before kissing the top of his head.

"Juuz, Mama!" He repeated himself over and over until he was worked up into a fit of tears. Clearly, we were having a breakdown in communication. I even got his cup and poured a bottle of water in it and a splash of juice so he'd calm down. It didn't work. He shook his head and continued crying, "Juuz!"

In the middle of his epic meltdown, my burner phone rang and I answered once I recognized Julien's number. "I'm so glad to hear your voice," I told him, pushing strands of fallen hair from around my face. "Nas is having a fit. Maybe if he hears your voice, it'll calm him down."

"Is everything okay though?" He asked, concern in his words.

"Everything is fine, Jules."

"Juuz!" Nas squeaked, his tears stopped instantly. I looked at the phone in my hand and then back at my son.

"Wait a minute, Nasim. Were you asking for Uncle Jules?"

"Juuz! Juuz!" He bounced up and down on his knees, grabbing

for my phone. He only had a vocabulary of about three words but evidently, Jules was one of them.

I handed him the phone and put it on speaker. "Say hi, Nasim."

"Juuz!" He giggled.

"Hey, what's up, King Nas?" His deep voice put a stop to all the noise and I was flooded with relief. "You in there driving Mommy nuts?"

"Mama?"

"Yeah, the pretty lady. Your mama." I could hear the slight smile in Julien's voice and I nearly drowned in the gravel and grit of it.

"Juuz," Nasim cooed again. Jules couldn't see it, but Nas was giving the biggest gummy smile on earth with two little bottom teeth poking through.

"I love you too, man. It's bedtime okay? Sleepy time."

"Juuz. Bye-bye." Nas pushed the phone toward me and settled down like he was ready for bed.

"Bye. I'll see you later. I promise," Jules said with the same sincerity he always used. I put the phone to my ear and took it off speaker.

"You know all this time I thought he wanted juice?" It was easy to laugh once I no longer had a screaming child.

"I mean hey, Jules got the juice. He's not wrong," Julien laughed a little.

"Oh my god, you're horribly corny. I knew you were too good to be true." I pinned the phone to my ear with my shoulder and rubbed Nasim's back while he drifted off.

"Corny? Never," he scoffed. "You doing okay over there?"

"Yes, I'm fine. I miss you but that's it." My voice was soft and sweet and I realized I'd never spoken to my husband that way. Not even when he was going all out to court me. I fucking knew better. I knew I didn't love him. I blinked the thought away and kept talking to Jules. "Oh, I talked to my sister today."

"You did?" His tone was unreadable but it didn't do anything to mute my excitement.

"Yeah. I told her I was finally leaving Angel for real this time. I just wanted her to hear it from me. I didn't want her to worry when my parents inevitably came to her looking for me."

"Was she happy to hear from you?"

"She was. She came to the room for a little while but she left from work because we both agreed that Angel either had someone watching her house or he was watching it himself." Jules was silent on the other end and it made my stomach knot up.

"Cress, I wish you would have held off on seeing Trinity until I made sure Angel was gone. Completely gone. You can't put shit past him because he's a goddamn snake." He paused and took a breath. "I'm glad you got to see your sister. I know you missed her. I'm just…"

"Worried?" I asked.

"Yeah. It's a new feeling for me."

"Feelings are new to you period." I smiled a little and pulled my hand away from Nasim's back when I saw he'd fallen asleep.

"Can't argue with that. Listen, I'm headed to the hotel to

see you now. I don't feel comfortable leaving you and Nas there overnight alone."

"I have the gun, remember?" I quizzed, lifting my eyebrows.

"The kickback will knock you on your ass. You'll probably decorate the ceiling nicely though."

"Wow, fuck you, Julien."

"Hey, I'm just looking at things logically." His laughter died down a little then he said, "I'll be there in thirty minutes. Hop in the shower for me. I want to see those pretty curls." I touched my hair when he said it, and dammit if I didn't blush like a high school girl. "I'm trying to eat that pussy too. I missed my favorite meal this morning with all the bullshit going on."

Lord, Julien had me blushing all over the place. I nibbled on my bottom lip and pressed my thighs together. Everything pulsed in response to him.

"Wow, you're trying to make me wake up Nasim after I just got him to go to sleep?"

"I'll be quiet. I'm not the problem though. You're the loud one."

"Shut up!" I laughed into my hand trying to keep quiet.

"Oh my god, Jules! I love the way you suck on my pussy!" He said in an exaggerated high-pitched voice, mocking me.

"I do not say that shit, shut the hell up," I laughed a little louder and excused myself to the bathroom so I didn't disturb my child.

"I bet I could make you say it." His voice dropped a couple of octaves and my insides quivered.

"I bet you could too," I purred. "Okay, let me get in the shower before I combust."

"You do that, beautiful. I'll be there in a little while. Answer the door butt ass naked."

"No robe. No nothing?" I lifted an arched brow quizzically.

"Nothing. Just you and that sexy ass body."

"Boy, this body has been through childbirth. There's nothing sexy about it anymore." All I could hear in my mind was Angel laughing at me and telling me how I'd never go back to looking the way I did before I had Nasim. I was stretched out and lost my flat stomach.

"Cress, stop that shit. I'm not Angel. I'm not going to let you talk bad about yourself and I'm never going to talk bad about you so let's learn how to grow past that."

Grow past it.

He didn't tell me to get over it. He didn't threaten me within an inch of my life. He wanted to grow through it with me. Angel managed to pull the greatest trick of all time. Convincing everyone that Julien was the devil when it was him all along.

"Okay. Let's grow past it. I can't wait to see you. Everything is all tingly," I admitted as I turned on the shower.

"Oh yeah? I make you tingly?"

"Very."

"Can you show me where I make you tingly when I get there?"

"Absolutely."

"Good. I'll knock twice when I get to the door." He hesitated then said, "I love you, Cress." Those words made my mind go blank and my palms sweat.

He loved me.

It would never get old hearing Jules say those words. I knew earning his love wasn't easy and I was honored that he gave it to me and Nas so freely.

"I love you too."

"I know you do. I can feel it." There was no reason for me to be smiling from ear to ear like I was. I was running for me and my son's life and I was still married to a lunatic, yet I found a reason to grin and laugh and be joyful. If that wasn't a testament to the power of love, I didn't know what was.

I got in the shower and made sure to wash my hair. I wanted it to be curly again. It meant a lot to me that Jules helped me to straighten it but last night, I was still afraid of living with Angel and his mood swings. Now that I was away from him, I wanted to do things that made *me* happy. Even if it was something as small as letting my natural curls come out to play. I knew I wouldn't learn to be myself again overnight but small steps were still steps.

I checked on Nasim when I got out of the shower and he was still knocked out on the bed. I went into the sitting room and squeezed the water from my hair while it continued to curl and shrink. I rubbed myself down with vanilla and cinnamon oil and put my damp hair up in a puff while it continued to curl into spirals and ringlets. I wrapped the hotel's robe around my naked body and waited for Julien to knock twice while I watched TV. I was jolted out of a Fresh Prince rerun when I heard a soft knock on the door.

Knock. Knock. Knock.

My spine stiffened at the third knock. I stood and walked over to the door so I could look out of the peephole but the lock beeped and turned green. My eyes widened and I stumbled backward as the knob turned. I rushed into the bedroom and tossed the comforter over Nasim lightly enough so that it didn't wake him up.

My tongue was glued to the roof of my mouth but I still called out to the heavy footfalls making their way toward the back. I prayed that it was room service making a mistake or maintenance. Shit, I prayed that it was Jules and he forgot to knock twice.

"Jules?" I said quietly, picking the burner phone up from the dresser. A thick knot slid down my throat when I didn't hear an answer. I unlocked the phone and pressed Julien's number.

"I knew you were fucking him," Angel growled then walked around the corner holding a plastic key card between his long fingers. Fear seized my chest. The phone slipped from my hands as I regarded Angel's black and blue face. Julien must have beat the fuck out of him at the house. Good. He deserved every blow.

"What the fuck are you doing here, Angel?" I asked with a trembling voice.

"I came to get my fucking whore of a wife and my son." His blown-out pupils searched the room before landing on my face. "Where is Nasim?"

"He-he's somewhere safe. I didn't bring him," I lied trying to stall. Julien would be there in a matter of minutes.

"Bitch, you better take me to my goddamn son." He grabbed my hair and yanked me over to him. I refused to cry out in pain even though it felt like he was ripping my scalp off. I couldn't risk waking up Nasim.

With tears in my eyes, I watched the bed, making sure he didn't stir under the blanket. "Please," I whispered, trying to inch toward the sitting room with Angel's fingers tangled in my puff.

"Please what? Hmm? Please don't kill you for taking my son away from me? Or please don't kill you for thinking you could run away from me?" He yanked me toward the door and I said a silent prayer that he didn't wake Nas.

"Angel, please don't hurt me. I'll take you to Nas. Just…let me get dressed."

"Let you get dressed?" His top lip curled in disgust, then he barked out a harsh laugh. "So, what were you doing in here wearing just a robe?" He shoved my head and I stumbled into the couch falling onto my knees. I hit the floor with so much force, the carpet rubbed the skin off my knees. I bit down, rolling both my lips between my teeth so I didn't cry out.

"Were you waiting on Smoke to come in here and fuck you?"

"No, I swear. I just got out of the shower and…"

Slap!

My cheek burned and I felt the skin split instantly. I was stunned silent. Angel had never hit me before but I knew he was always capable no matter how much I tried to fool myself. I was too shocked to cry right then.

"You're lying to me *and* fucking my traitor of a brother?" He stood over me and pulled a breath deep from the back of his throat, then spat on me. The warm glob of saliva slipped down my cheek and stung when it hit the small gash he opened on my face.

"Let's go. You don't deserve clothes. You like being a whore so much, walk around naked." He shoved me out of the suite and into the hallway. Once the door closed behind us, he took the tie from my waist and slammed me against the wall. I prayed for someone to open their door and see or for Jules to walk off the elevator. The hallway was dead silent in response to my prayers.

Angel took advantage of my pain and tears and put the tie around my neck like a leash. I had to hold the robe closed so I didn't flash everyone in the lobby. He instructed me to keep my head down and not to speak to anyone on the way out. Thankfully, there weren't any people in the lobby because it was late.

When we got inside Angel's car, fear swallowed me whole. Now, I was alone with him. There was nobody to protect me. I would probably die in this car but at least I spared my son. I knew Jules would get to the room and take care of him.

"Oh, now you're crying huh, Cress? You weren't crying when Smoke had his dick in your mouth though, were you?!"

I *was* crying. It wasn't because of my guilt it was because I didn't get to kiss Nasim goodbye one last time.

"I can't believe I trusted y'all together." He laughed as he pulled off. "I should have known when he pulled that respectful shit. I should have *fucking known*. You just can't keep your legs closed." He stopped at a stop sign and looked at me. I was curled in the passenger seat, pressed against the window as much as I could. I wanted to put distance between us even in cramped quarters.

I had no way to defend myself against Angel. My bag and everything else was in the room along with the gun Jules gave me.

I wanted to murder Angel. A gun would have been my first choice but I refused to be his victim anymore. I would fight back however I could. I would fight back with my dying breath. I was done being abused.

Rage pumped through my veins mixing with fear. It was a potent combination that sent my heart rate into overdrive. I used the wave of adrenaline building in my blood to grab the steering wheel. We swerved into the lane beside us, earning horn honks. He looked at me like I'd morphed into an alien, then took his elbow and drove it into my nose. The pain was blinding.

I could only see the color gray and hear a high-pitched whine for a few terrifying moments. When my vision cleared, Angel pulled over and reach into the center console. The ominous barrel of a gun stared back at me when I blinked.

"Have you lost your fucking mind, Cress? You're trying to kill me! That's okay," he said, glancing around at the cars passing us by on the road. "I know how to settle you down." He caressed my swollen face with the gun and smiled wickedly at me, his face grossly distorted.

"Please don't," I begged when I saw him unbuckling his belt.

"You're doing a lot of begging for a bitch who tried to run us off the road. Nah, I know what you like. You need some dick. You can't keep your fucking legs closed. I need to treat you like the nasty bitch you are. Climb in the backseat." He aimed the gun at me and I hurried to climb between the front seats into the back. Everything on me throbbed in pain.

"I thought you wanted to go get Nas," I stammered, trying to put off the inevitable.

"I need to teach you a lesson first." He got out, and before I could reach for the door handle, he tore open the back door and aimed the gun at me, daring me to even try escaping. "You know, I thought I was being crazy going to Trinity's job and sitting out there. I thought it was a waste of time. Turns out, soon as you get away from me, you run straight to big sis. She led me to you, Cress.

I heard the little fake name you booked under and everything. After she left, I just sat in the lobby all day chopping it up with the staff. By the time I wanted to see you, all I had to do was go back to the lobby and tell them my wife forgot to give me an extra key to our room." He made a clicking sound and shook his head as he slid the gun along my collarbones. A sob shook me once I realized there was no way out of this. I was going to get raped and probably killed on the side of some non-descript road.

...

Chapter
SEVENTEEN

Julien

When I knocked on Cress's door and she didn't answer, my chest tightened. I waited a few seconds then knocked again.

Once.

Twice.

Nothing.

I pulled out my key card and used it to go inside. Everything was quiet. Too fucking quiet. Cress would have met me at the door.

I took out my gun and moved into the sitting area to look around. Nothing looked out of the ordinary at first glance, but I noticed the couch looked crooked.

Something happened.

My line of sight went straight to the floor where I saw the smallest drop of blood.

The fury that ripped through me had no words attached to it. There was no way to describe the flash that ignited in my chest. I moved into the bedroom and saw nothing out of place. The comforter looked tossed on the bed and Cress's things were sitting in the open closet. When I looked down at the floor, I saw her burner phone.

I picked it up with my free hand and looked through it. I was the last person she'd called around fifteen minutes ago. I checked my phone to see that I sure enough had a fucking missed call from Cress. I'd stopped at Target to get her a bottle of wine and to get Nasim a toy. I didn't hear it ring.

My thoughts shifted to Nasim. If Angel took Cress, then he must have taken Nas too. I sat on the bed and called Boogie. Before the phone rang, I felt something moving behind me. I ended the call and turned around, aiming my gun.

I quickly put the safety on when I realized how small the squirming thing was under the blanket. "What the fuck?" I stood up and pulled the comforter back to find Nas moving in his sleep.

My stomach sank.

Cress was in danger. There was no way in hell she would leave

Nasim unattended. My brain was working overtime.

Angel must have figured out where Cress and Nasim were and came to the hotel room. She probably opened the door thinking it was me. I wondered if she purposefully hid Nasim or if Angel didn't notice him in here asleep. Either way, she knew I'd be here soon so she knew Nas would be safe. I reached out and stroked his soft curls then put my gun away.

I kicked myself for trying to reason with Angel earlier. Back at the house, I could have dragged his ass out to the trunk and tied him up but something small and soft inside of me ached for my brother. I didn't want to kill him and I was putting it off for as long as possible. My stupid mistake could cost Cressida her life if I didn't hurry up and find them.

My phone rang like fireworks against the silence of the room. Nas fussed a little in his sleep and I placed a heavy hand in the middle of his back to settle him back down. I pressed the phone to my ear and answered when I saw Boogie's name.

"What's up, Smoke? Everything good? You called and hung up."

"Nah, Everything is far from good," I said, watching my nephew sleep. "We need to find Angel now. Not later. Not after shit has fallen into place. Now. He took Cress and I'm ready to burn Miami to the bones."

"Fuck. I'm on my way. You at the hotel?"

"Yeah." I ended the call and grabbed all of Cress's things from the closet. I looked at Nasim and tried to figure out how to move him without waking him up. Nerves took place of the rage for a minute while I scooped his little body into my arms. I'd never had to take care of him without Cress being around or nearby. I didn't want to hurt him or do the wrong thing. I sat him in the car seat and paused to stare at him for signs of waking. He stirred a little, turning his head but thankfully, he kept sleeping.

When I went to click the straps into place, his sleepy eyes opened and he looked around, no doubt trying to see where Cress was. "What's up, King Nas?" He whined and tried to sit up fully but his shoulders were pinned by the strap. "I know, you're looking for Mommy, right?" I clicked the buckle between his legs and moved my face closer to his. I kissed his forehead and he fussed.

"Mama!" He whined, opening and closing his fists.

"We're gonna go get Mama. We're going to bring your mother back even if I die doing it," I assured him, standing up. I handed him the toy I bought from Target and since it lit up and made noise, he settled down some to stare at it.

I met Boogie downstairs in the lobby and for the first time since I found out he was Man, he looked the part. He must have been at Rush when I called. He was dressed in all white slacks and a white button-down shirt, which was in stark contrast to his deep midnight skin. Two men I recognized from earlier tonight stood behind him, quietly menacing. The concierge behind the desk watched with wide eyes. Not at the fucking king pen in all white flanked by two men, but at me. Huge and hulking, carrying a baby in a car seat.

"Good evening, sir," he said tipping his head back to make eye contact. "Can I help you with anything?"

"No," I grunted my brows falling low into a scowl.

"Um, will the baby's mother…"

"Mind your fucking business," I issued the warning in a voice that shut the concierge up quickly. His cheeks flushed bright pink and he went back to looking at whatever was on the fucking computer screen in front of him. It was best he didn't poke or prod too much because I was feeling murderous.

"What the fuck?" Boogie frowned when he saw me carrying Nas in the car seat. "He took Cress but not Nasim?"

"She hid him, or at least I think she did." I walked past him and his men and went straight to my car. I already knew how to put the car seat in so that time, it wasn't much of a struggle.

"Where you think he took her?" Boogie asked, getting in the passenger side.

"I'm going to his house first. I'm assuming they didn't come through Rush." I looked to him for an answer and he shook his head no. "Cool. He's probably stupid enough to take her home."

"If he's at home then he's waiting for you to come. He's luring you in. We need to have more men follow."

I cut Boogie off mid-sentence. "I don't need anyone. The only reason I called you was because I wanted to know if Angel came to Rush. Now, I need you to keep Nas safe while I handle Angel. I'm tired of this shit." I sped through a yellow light and turned a corner speeding as I headed back to Miami.

I needed to get my mind right before I dealt with my brother so

I put on some Jay-z. His song *Lucifer* pumped through the speakers and I drove faster. I felt like Lucifer right then. Like I could swallow the world in hellfire.

If that was love, I didn't mind it.

If that was love, it burned hotter and deeper than the darkness that usually occupied me. I thought love would be roses and hand-holding. Nobody ever explained that love could be vicious with claws and teeth. That was the kind of love I had inside of me for Cressida. It was the kind of love that I would protect at any cost. Even my own life.

I pulled up to Angel's house prepared to die, but if I did, I was going to take my brother with me. "Take Nas away from here. Don't let anyone else touch him. Only you," I said locking eyes with Boogie. "I swear to god, Boog."

"I got him, Smoke. I'd never hurt Nasim." Sincerity rang out in his voice and his dark eyes. I nodded and got out of the car. I went to the backseat and opened the door to check on Nas. He'd fallen back to sleep holding the toy I got him. The image was burned in my mind. He was so innocent. He still had a chance in the world. I was going to make sure he got whatever he wanted in life by moving his bitch ass father out of his way. I kissed the top of his head and shut the door quietly.

"I'll call you when I'm done," I told Boogie as I pulled the black hood over my head and moved closer. I saw Angel's car in the driveway and lights on in the house. Good. I wanted him to be home. I wanted him to know that even in his own house, I would come in and take everything.

Nothing about the way I entered his home was quiet or stealthy.

He took Cress. I wasn't there to play ninja games. He knew I was coming for him so I made the announcement loud by sending bullets through the front door. I kicked it in after I shot around the keypad and fed the pistol more bullets while debris crunched beneath my feet.

I heard soft cries coming from somewhere in the house and I knew it was Cressida. My chest twisted. I moved past the foyer and looked around. I saw nothing in the living room or the kitchen. I looked everywhere on the first floor before moving upstairs.

The sniffles and cries grew closer as I marched up the steps.

"Cress?" I called out.

Nothing.

I walked into the bedroom and found Angel sitting on the bed, his elbows resting on his knees and his head hung low. Cressida was on the floor in a bruised ball. When I saw her, my heart ached. Her pain was my pain, amplified.

"Cress…" I kept my eye on Angel but I moved closer to make sure she was okay. I heard the soft whimpers again and I knew she was breathing. That was my main concern. I knew if I looked at her up close, I would take Angel's head off.

Angel let out a slow and low laugh while he sat there, refusing to look at me. I saw the gun sitting beside him but I doubted he'd reach it before I had him bleeding all over his bedroom floor. "I knew you'd come for her," he said finally lifting his eyes to look at me. I could tell he was high again.

"I'm glad you knew that." My teeth were clenched so tight my words sounded like concrete. Angel stood, not meeting my full height. He looked up at me and I hoped he saw the disgust in my eyes. I hoped he saw the hatred. We weren't blood anymore. We were something else. Enemies with childhood memories.

"I don't want to kill you, Smoke."

"You're not going to."

"But I am though. See, you fucked my wife." He grabbed his gun and I didn't move an inch. I wasn't afraid. There was no room for fear in my veins. Only rage and fury.

"She's not your wife," I said. "She was pressured into marrying you. Cress fucking *hates* you." I knew the smirk on my face pissed him off. I saw the fire in his eyes but he was a bitch and he knew if he hit me like he wanted to, I would break his face. I noted the bruises and swelling still present from his ass-whooping this morning. I guess it was time to finish things.

Veins strained against his neck and his forehead. I laughed a little and tucked my gun in my waist.

"You mad? You knew goddamn well she hated you. You married her because I liked her. You knew I liked her so you made your move while I was in jail, then you broke her so she wouldn't leave you. You're a bitch for that." I pressed the barrel of his gun to my chest and dared him to shoot. Even with a bullet lodged in my chest, I would still break his neck so Cress and Nas could be free.

"You know I'm the one holding the gun, right Smoke?"

"Fuck you and that gun. Shoot me or shut up." I butted up against the gun again and Angel drew in a deep breath from his lopsided nostrils. "That's what the fuck I thought." In one motion, I took Angel's gun and cracked him across the jaw with it. Blood splattered across the side of my face from the blow and I knew some of his teeth came out. I felt the unmistakable crunch of enamel through the impact.

Angel flew back on the bed and I heard a quiet squeak come from Cress on the floor. "It's okay, Cress. Don't move. I'll take care of all this shit. Can you breathe?"

"Uh-huh," she answered. It was a muffled sound with her face pressed against the carpet.

"Good. Did he…" I swallowed the thick knot in my throat at the thought of Angel hitting her or worse.

The way Cress sobbed in response to my question sent a red-hot coal sinking into the pit of my stomach. Anguish ripped through me at the thought of what she had to go through while I was on my way to her.

"It's okay, baby." I knelt down, still keeping an eye on Angel. I touched her soft curly hair and squeezed my eye shut for a moment. I needed a silent moment so I didn't put a bullet in Angel's head. That's not how I wanted things to happen. "Hey, look at me." I tucked a chunk of curls behind her ear and she turned her head so I could see her face and her eyes.

They were so swollen I didn't even know if she could see out of them. The delicate skin around her eyes was black and purple and there was a gash on her cheek. Bile rose in the back of my throat and fire swarmed my heart.

I couldn't kill him yet but goddammit I wanted to. It was beyond the humming and buzzing in my blood. Now, there was an inferno inside of me that I had to squelch.

"I got Nas. He's safe," I told Cress in as normal of a voice as I could muster. I wanted to pull her to me and cradle her. I wanted to fix everything and make all her problems go away.

"Thank...you." Her voice was so weak, I didn't want her to say another thing. Her lips were so swollen and split, I knew it hurt to talk.

"Don't say anything. Just be still. I got you." Angel shuffled around on the bed and I heard him before I saw him. He stood up faster than I anticipated and his foot crashed into my jaw while I knelt over Cress. I heard her frightened scream and saw her scurry backward, flattening herself against the wall.

I pulled myself up before Angel could muster up the coke-head strength to kick me another time. We were face to face like two kids again. We threw punches and blows like we were fighting for our lives. I knew if I let him overpower me, it would be the end and he knew the same thing.

I wasn't fighting fair though. Angel was a snake ass motherfucker so fair went out the window a long time ago. I backed him up against the window and pulled my knife fast as I could before another hit connected with my body. I pressed the blade against the side of his neck and he froze.

"What the fuck are you doing, Smoke?" His eyes were wide

with fear and adrenaline.

"I got this motherfucking knife pressed right against your jugular." I dug the tip of the knife into his skin and watched a dark rivulet of blood leak down to his shoulder.

"Smoke, get the fuck off me!" He roared and tried to get out of the hold I had on him but the way my forearm was pressed against his chest was like a bar of steel. I knew it. He was struggling to suck in breaths.

"I will sink this knife into your vein if you keep talking, Angel." I buried the blade a little deeper and more blood spilled out. My bones hummed and buzzed at the sight of it. I stared, fixated because I was spilling my brother's blood. This is what things had come to between us.

"You never planned to bring me into the fold with Rush and your organization, did you?" I asked, my nostrils flaring at the metallic scent in the air.

"I was. I swear to god, Smoke." Even hearing him call me that made me bristle. The very origin of that nickname was mean-spirited. "I needed to get some things squared away with my connect in Colombia. I had to build more trust because they think someone is taking their product. I had to let them know I was still trustworthy. See, that wasn't a trip for you to go on." He bared his teeth when the tip of my knife scraped against his skin and spilled more blood.

"You were using me like you always do. The same way you took five years of my life like it was nothing, Angel. You barely said thanks when I got out. You just put me straight to work."

"Exactly. That's how I show my thanks, hermano. I put you to work. I helped you make money." He paused to wince at the pain. "Listen, if this shit is just about me bringing you into the fold then I can do that. I can make you half-owner of Rush. The paperwork is in my office. We can pull it up and go to the lawyers tomorrow."

My eyebrows furled as I regarded him. "So, it's always been that easy, huh? Just set up an appointment with the lawyers and *voila*? You could have had this shit done before I even got out of prison if you were serious about us being equal partners. Instead, you fucked me over. Strung me along so I could do your dirty work," I laughed. It was a bitter taste on my tongue.

I saw Cress stand to her feet out the corner of my eye and I looked at her for a moment. Not long enough to give Angel any wiggle room though. She limped toward me and I saw how badly Angel beat her. There were dark, splotchy bruises flowering on her beautiful golden skin. Her bottom lip was split and her eyes were slits instead of the pretty almond shape I was used to.

Still…

She was beautiful. Her strength was stunning. Her determination not to be a victim was gorgeous. She was the portrait of fearlessness. She untucked the gun from my waist and aimed it at Angel's temple.

"I should fucking kill you!" She shrieked. "You bastard." Her words wobbled but she stood strong.

"Nah, don't kill him, baby." I leaned over and kissed the top of her head. "Let me show him how it feels to be helpless while you get the shit beat out of you." A crooked, dark smile hung on my lips. I pulled the knife from Angel's vein and tucked it away in my pocket, still smeared with blood. Blood that was damn near identical to mine. It didn't mean a goddamn thing to me anymore.

I slammed my fist into his face repeatedly until he slid to the floor. I didn't stop raining fury down on him until I realized he wasn't even grunting in discomfort anymore and his face was settled in a pool of blood leaking from various cuts and gashes.

"Is he..." Cressida's voice crept out whisper soft.

"No, he's not dead. I don't want to kill him yet." Our eyes met and I thought she was going to push back on my decision not to kill Angel. She didn't though. She nodded and set the gun down. "Give me five minutes and I'll get you out of here and cleaned up so you can see Nas."

"Where is he?" She asked, tipping her head down so I couldn't see her face. I lifted her chin gently and looked at her.

"With Boogie. He's safe. He woke up for a little while and I gave him a toy to play with. He went back to sleep on the way over here." Looking at her beautiful face swollen and bruised, hurt me in a place I couldn't describe. There was a constant ache in the corridors of my ribs even after I beat the living shit out of Angel. I thought that would help but it only dulled the anger.

"Can you have him bring Nasim here?"

"Now?" I asked, glancing at Nas's half-dead father on the bedroom floor.

"Now." Her words were heavy like stones sliding into place. Something changed inside of her after Angel hit her. I couldn't see it in her eyes yet but I heard it in her voice. I felt it in her energy.

I liked it.

I pulled my hoodie off and tossed it on the bed then called Boogie. I felt Cress watching me like a hawk the entire time. I reached out and pulled her onto my lap making sure to gently press her against me. I wanted her to feel safe. I wanted her to know that I would lay down my life and anyone else's who fucked with her.

"What's up, Smoke? You need anything?"

"Nah, I'm good. Can you bring Nas back to the house? Cress wants him now."

"Be there in a few." He ended the call and I got to work finding duct tape and zip ties for Angel.

Five minutes passed and I heard the door downstairs open and close. Heavy footsteps neared and I pulled my gun, aiming it down the stairway. "Chill. It's me." Boogie frowned as he marched up the steps carrying Nas in his car seat.

"How the fuck did you get here so fast, motherfucker?" I put the gun away and waited for him to answer.

"Goddamn, Smoke. This is how friendship works. You need something? I'm there. I never left. I don't leave my friends when they're in life or death situations." His dark eyes moved to something behind me. I looked over my shoulder and saw Cress standing there.

"He's waking up," she said, gesturing to Angel passed out on the floor in the bedroom.

"Fuck," Boogie hissed under his breath. He handed over a sleeping Nasim, and Cress thanked him.

"Thank you," I said sincerely to Boogie. He nodded then walked into the bedroom and assessed the situation.

"Jesus Christ, Smoke, you had zero mercy on him." He balled his fist up and put it against his mouth while he shook his head in disgust. Angel groaned and turned his head toward the sound. "Alright," Boogie said, looking at the supplies I'd gathered. "Let's wrap this cokehead motherfucker up."

"Wait…" Angel slurred out. Nobody in the room listened. I went straight to work with the zip ties. I got his hands behind his back while Boogie tied his ankles together. He groaned in agony a few times then passed out again.

"Where are you taking him?" Boog asked once he was hogtied on the bedroom floor.

"I have a spot," I said thinking of the mom-and-pop diner. "He can't stay there indefinitely but it's a start."

"I want to go with you," Cress said.

"Cress, you need to see someone to get you fixed up," Boogie said, looking her over with concern on his face. "I can call a private doctor."

"We can do that later. Let me try to fix myself up. I want to go with you to make sure he never escapes. I want to see him tied up with my own two eyes. I won't be able to sleep until I see it." Her voice trembled and her words were impaired because of how swollen her lips were but we both heard her loud and clear.

As much as I wanted to keep her safe and make sure she got medical attention, I knew she wouldn't let me leave her behind. I couldn't blame her after the way Angel stalked her and found her at the hotel. I still beat myself up over that. I should have hidden her better.

"I'll clean you up, Cress," I said, nodding toward the bathroom.

"I'll get Angel out of here. My trunk is big enough," Boog volunteered. He checked his watch, then hauled Angel by his bound ankles out of the bedroom leaving behind a splotchy streak of red. I watched for a few moments as Angel's head thumped down each step while he was dragged like a rag doll.

When I got tired of the dull thud of shoulders and skull against the steps, I grabbed some things from the linen closet and went back to the bathroom to tend to Cress's face. She sat on the sink as I wiped away dried blood and cleaned her cuts. She winced each time the cold peroxide hit her skin.

"I'm trying to be gentle," I told her, my brows drawn together. The last thing I wanted to do was hurt her.

"You're doing fine, Jules. Thank you," she said with a smile in her voice. "You don't give yourself enough credit. You know how to be gentle."

"You think so?" I asked, tipping my head to the side and cleaning the gash on her cheek. It was deep but not enough to need stitches.

"Absolutely. You're only gentle with me though."

"You're the only person worth being gentle with." I looked her over and felt my heart slip in my chest a little.

"I don't know what would have happened if you hadn't come

in when you did." She sniffled, trying to hold back tears but I didn't want her to. We were alone.

"Cressida," I said gently cupping her face in my hands. "Don't hide your pain from me."

"But I'm tired of crying. All the hell we've gone through and you haven't shed one tear. I don't want to cry either. Especially not over him." Venom laced her words.

"Crying doesn't make you weak. I love you because of how sensitive you are. How soft you are. I don't possess that shit but when I see it in you it's beautiful."

"So, you don't look at me as weak and stupid for letting Angel waltz into the hotel room?"

"It's not like you called him and told him where you were. Of course I'm not mad over that shit. I know my brother and I know he found a way to get to you."

"He followed Trini from work. He had a key card and everything and I thought..." Finally, the tears she'd been holding back fell down her cheeks and dripped from her thick lashes.

"You thought it was me," I said, knowingly.

"Yeah. I did." My jaw flexed involuntarily. "I tried to fight back. I tried to grab the wheel while he was driving but that's when he pulled over." I watched her shoulders shake with each gut-wrenching sob and that shit broke me down. I pulled her trembling body against mine and held her until the tears slowed down.

"He raped me, Julien. Once in the backseat of his car and once when we got back to the house. I screamed so much I thought my throat would burst into flames. I guess it pissed him off because he really fucked me up after that." Every single thing out of her mouth made me want to kill Angel. Rage ate me up and spit me back out as bones.

I had to make sure his death was slow and I had to make sure he knew what was happening. He deserved to feel every ounce of pain he put Cressida through.

Once I realized how much I loved her, I knew that all my life, I'd never really loved Angel. I tolerated him. I looked up to him but the love wasn't there. I had an obligatory sense of familiarity and closeness with him because he was all I knew growing up. It was easy for me to see that my grandmother hated me but Angel always hid his disdain with a suave smile.

I knew better now. That wasn't love. It was manipulation.

What I felt for Cressida and Nasim, was love. It was real and solid. I felt her pain when she cried and I wanted to take it all away no matter what the cost was.

"I'm so sorry, Cress. I'm so fucking sorry he did that shit to you and I wasn't there to protect you." I smoothed her messy hair back and kissed her forehead. "I'll make sure he never puts a goddamn finger on you again. I'll break every last one."

"Can I do it?" She sniffled and looked up at me, giving me a glimpse of those champagne eyes I fell so hard for. Something fluttered in my chest. It fucking fluttered.

Was that my heart?

Is that what it felt like to have your heart skip a beat?

"*You* want to break his fingers?"

"All of them," she said without an ounce of humor in her tone. I mulled it over in my mind and then nodded.

"I don't see why not. He hurt you with those fingers. Break those motherfuckers off if you want to, baby." She offered me the best smile she could. "See, that's why I love your beautiful ass."

"Because I want to break Angel's fingers?" She quizzed, tilting her head to the side a little.

"No, because you understand the darkness in me even if it's not always a part of you. You're the only person besides my mother who loves me for me."

"I was sure you were going to say it was the sex," she gave me another smile and I could see her warmth coming back slowly. Good. As much as I loved dark Cressida, I loved my golden girl even more. I was okay with being the darkness to her light. One couldn't survive without the other anyway.

"I fell in love with you over conversations and playlists and laughter. The sex didn't hurt though."

"I was about to say, don't lie, Julien Jean."

"I fell in love with you over conversations, playlists, laughter, *and* orgasms. Is that better?" She grew quiet but nodded her head while looking down at her fingers. A frown weighed my face down when I looked at her hands. "Cress, where's your mood ring?"

"He broke it. He said I was always wearing it and playing with it and he got so mad when he realized I didn't have on his wedding rings so, he snatched it off my fingers and stepped on it."

"He's a bitch for that. Don't worry though. I got accepted into the gemology certification program. When I'm done, I'm going to make you something even better."

"You got accepted? Jules, that amazing! I'm so happy for you and so fucking proud!" She wrapped her arms around my neck and the warmth of her love and pride melted into me.

That's why Cress was the love of my life. She was rooting for me even when she'd been beaten down figuratively and literally. She was sitting on the bathroom sink with a swollen and bruised face but she found it in her heart to be proud of my accomplishments.

After she was cleaned up and dressed, we all went to the mom-and-pop diner in the middle of nowhere with me navigating. Boogie tossed Angel in the trunk and started the cleanup process by the time Cress and I got out there so most of the hard work was already done.

Boogie and I worked alone to set Angel up in a metal chair in the middle of the tarp-covered floor. I had no idea how far Cress wanted to take her torture, but I was always prepared in case things got bloody.

Angel sat tied and taped to the chair while I held Nasim in my arms, trying to shush him back to sleep. Cress stood in front of Angel with her dainty hands anchored to her full hips. I missed seeing her mood ring more than I anticipated. I'd make her something better no matter how long it took.

"You sure you want Nas to see this shit, Cress?" I asked,

rubbing his back while he laid his head on my shoulder.

"Yes. He won't remember it outright but he'll always have an emotional memory of it and I want him to know his father was a piece of shit and that sometimes you have to take an eye for an eye no matter how peaceful you are." She stepped forward and the tarp crinkled under her feet.

Boogie opened a bottle of water and tossed it on Angel's face since he was still slumped over and passed out. It took a few times for him to sputter awake coughing and gasping. His gaze swung wildly around the dim area while he tried to orient himself. A string of garbled curse words fell from his swollen lips.

"Wake up, motherfucker," Boogie growled. He slapped his face a few times and Angel lifted his head with a heavy wobble. He could barely keep his eyes open. I swear to god, if I wasn't holding Nasim, I would have grabbed him by the hair and forced his head up so he could look into Cressida's eyes and see what the fuck he'd done.

Instead, I walked in front of him so he'd see his son and know that he wasn't even allowed that anymore. He didn't deserve to be a father to a kid as great as Nasim.

"You...motherfucking half-breed. Makes sense you'd want him to yourself. Black monkey see, black monkey do." A deranged laugh filled up the space. "I knew I should have never fucked a black bitch. I should have kept my bloodline pure and married a Columbian girl."

"But you didn't," Cress said with an eerie calm to her voice. I was amazed that she didn't haul off and hit him in the mouth. Maybe that was just my impulse. This part wasn't for me though.

This part right here was for Cress. She needed to take out some of the anger and pain Angel planted inside of her.

I swallowed my fury and handed her a pair of rusty bolt cutters. My time with Angel would come later. Now, it was Cressida's time to shine.

...

Chapter
EIGHTEEN

Cressida

The smooth cool metal of the bolt cutters was heavy in my hand. I don't think I'd ever held a pair before that moment standing in front of Angel tied up to a chair and helpless. I liked him like that. He could spew all the hatred he wanted but it didn't fucking matter.

I was in control for the first time. The realization halted me.

When I was a kid, my parents were strict and had control over everything I did. Hell, they controlled me while I was an adult too.

I had to go to the college they picked out and marry the man they thought was best. Whenever they weren't controlling me, it was Angel. Telling me how much I could and couldn't eat. How much money I could spend and where I could go.

My throat tightened when I thought about him forcing me to stop breastfeeding.

No. Fucking. More.

I wasn't weak or stupid or naïve anymore. I was tired and ready to do what the fuck I wanted to do without anyone telling me yes or no. So, I wasn't just going to break every finger Angel had. I wanted to cut them *off*.

I didn't care if I didn't have the stomach for it. I didn't care if I threw up right after I did it. I wanted to make a decision and carry it out no matter what the outcome. I'd found my backbone and I wasn't letting it go. Not even with Jules. I knew I wouldn't have a problem out of him though. He was not his brother.

I looked at Angel and saw the darkness dancing in his eyes. He wasn't high anymore but the cocaine lived in his system. He was that much of an addict.

"So, what, little Cressida is going to hurt me? Is that it?" He asked, spitting blood from his mouth onto the plastic tarp.

I realized I was waiting for someone to speak for me but neither Boogie nor Jules said anything. I was running the show. A thrill zipped down my arms and legs. "Yup. That's it. For now," I said with a smirk. It hurt like hell to smile after Angel hit me in my face like I was a grown man, but I'd never let him know it. He didn't deserve the satisfaction of knowing how badly I wanted to cry from the stabbing pain he inflicted.

"You must feel important now, huh, Cress? You're fucking my brother and you got him laying up in my house with my son playing daddy!" He roared and I flinched at his voice. The maniacal way he laughed at my flash of fear pissed me off.

I walked behind him where his hands were tied and taped and stared at his wiggling, grabbing fingers. They were searching for a way out.

I ignored his constant talking and shouting and glanced at Jules. He looked like he wanted to smash Angel's face...again. It was weird having a man who defended me and cared about what was said about me. I liked it. I *more* than liked it.

I knew it wasn't the right time but all I could think about was being in his arms. Feeling him pressed against me. Wanting him to touch me and knowing he only would if I asked.

Those thoughts propelled me to open the bolt cutters and press Angel's pinky finger between the jaws of the tool. He didn't ask if he could rape me or beat me and I wasn't asking if I could cut his fingers off.

I thought it would be a clean cut but I had to put more effort into it than I'd anticipated, which pulled horrific screams from Angel. The first scream made me cringe when I heard the snap of his bone. I thought that would be it but no, I'd only broken his pinky and not severed it. I opened the cutters then closed them again with more force. Blood leaked from the site and even though

Angel was screaming at the top of his lungs, I still heard the delicate pit-pat of crimson dripping onto the plastic.

It was such an odd thing to lock on to but it gave me the strength to keep cutting. One last snip and his pinky fell and rolled to a stop, nail side up. My stomach flopped and the room spun a little but I liked the sound he made when he was in agony.

"Cress, you okay?" Jules asked, walking around to inspect my handy work. I looked at him then at how calm Nasim was in his arms.

Me too, kid.

"Yeah, I just need a minute," I told him trying to steady my spinning head and lurching stomach.

"Okay! I'm sorry, Cress! I'm fucking sorry just don't cut any more of my fingers off. I swear to god, I'll go away and never come back," he babbled. I knew that was bullshit though. He'd never leave me alone. He had to die. That was the only logical outcome I saw for me and my son to have any semblance of peace.

Every plea from his lying-ass mouth pissed me off more and cleared my vision. I went in again, this time for a bigger finger. The one with the gold band on it.

Now that I knew how much force to apply when cutting off a finger, I was able to snip his ring finger off in two tries. I pushed out a triumphant breath when it fell, heavy and dead to the floor. After a few more high-pitched shrieks, Angel passed out from the pain. It was no fun cutting off fingers if he wasn't going to be awake to experience the torture so I dropped the bolt cutters.

"Is it getting to you?" Boogie asked, looking at me from his spot on the countertop. He was perched there, watching everything unfold with a wicked gleam of satisfaction in his dark eyes. Angel must have fucked him over too. That's what he did best.

"No, but I want him awake when I cut off the rest."

"My girl," Jules chuckled. "Your mommy is a badass," he told Nasim.

"Language," I scolded playfully.

"You just cut someone's fingers off in front of him and you're fussing at me about my language? Priorities, baby." Goosebumps blanketed my arms when he called me baby.

Shit, maybe I was as dark and twisted as Jules. I was standing there with my husband's fingers at my feet while I looked at his brother with hearts in my eyes. Still, it felt right, and I refused to ignore my intuition anymore.

"Whatever," I scoffed, tossing a playful hand in the air. I went to twist my mood ring around and remembered Angel broke it and my heart slipped in my chest a little.

"I'll make you something better," Jules assured me without me even having to say a word. Boogie hopped down from the counter and looked at Angel, chuckling.

"I have a spot I can move him to unless you want to finish things here, Smoke." I noticed that even though Boogie was a boss in his own right, he looked to Jules for confirmation. He respected the hell out of him and I understood why.

Jules was quietly strong. He exuded so much power and presence that I had no idea how he was able to play second fiddle to his brother all his life. When he entered a room, everyone noticed.

They were either scared or curious. I used to be both. Once I got to know him, I was just intrigued and I probably would never cease to be intrigued by him. He was enigmatic.

"Nah, pack him up and hold him. I want to make sure Cress gets her face looked at and she needs to settle down from everything. Gag him." Julien tossed one last glance at his brother then went to put Nasim in the car seat. "Tell everyone at Rush something believable. I trust your judgment." At that, both me and Boogie looked shocked. Jules didn't trust anyone's judgment but his own. "Why the hell are y'all looking at me like that?" He quizzed, handing Nasim a toy.

"You trust my judgment?" Boogie said, rubbing his chin.

"Yeah. Some reason I shouldn't?"

"No. You know I got your back, Smoke. It's just nice seeing you finally trust someone."

"Don't let that shit go to your head old man," Julien joked.

"Never that." I sensed the friendship blossoming between them and it was nice. Jules was changing and he didn't even realize it.

"Get him bandaged up and put him somewhere soundproof," Jules said to Boogie.

"Oh, trust me, I have the perfect place for this motherfucker." Boogie rubbed his hands together and then got to work.

...

It had been a few days since I chopped Angel's fingers off in that abandoned mom-and-pop diner. I didn't miss him at all where ever he was. I was busy healing, learning to unwind, and not be in a constant state of survival.

I refused to sleep in the bedroom I used to share with Angel. Instead, I slept beside Jules in his room. We decided that for a while, we'd stay in Angel's house to make things look normal. After Angel's disappearance died down, we'd move into a place of our own. I couldn't wait. Being reminded of the constant control and abuse between these four walls was hell on my anxiety.

"Alright, I got King Nas down after like three damn stories and making his light-up shark dance for five minutes." Jules came into the bedroom looking worn out. He told me to take a bath while he put Nasim to bed and I jumped at the chance for some alone time.

When he came back into the room, he pulled his t-shirt over his head and fell backward on the bed, staring up at the ceiling with his hands behind his head. His chiseled, tight abs were on display for my viewing pleasure and I definitely gawked.

I hadn't been feeling like myself since Angel raped and beat me like I was nothing. Even still, every time I was in a room with Jules, I couldn't help the way my body reacted to him. I'd been too scared to do anything besides kiss and cuddle but the way he looked lying in front of me turned my most private places wet.

"I don't know how the hell I went my entire life without that little boy. He's a lot to deal with but I miss him every night after he goes to sleep." Hearing him say things like that only made me want him more.

My eyes skated down his body and stopped at the stupidity-inducing V-cut at his hips pointing to the line of dark hair just beneath the waistband of his sweatpants. I couldn't help fixing my stare on his impressive dick print. Even soft, I imagined wrapping my lips around him and sliding his dick in and out of my mouth until he came down the back of my throat.

The thought turned my knees to mush.

"You alright, Cress?" Jules lifted his head and stared at me with intense mahogany eyes. I nodded then moved closer to him. He sat up when I approached, rubbing his palms down his handsome face. I knew he was tired but he was fine as hell and I needed him more than I wanted to admit.

I needed his closeness. I needed to feel him deep inside of me so I could forget the way Angel felt. I wanted to drown in Julien with all his darkness and float away from the life I used to have.

I sat on his lap and his hands found my waistline immediately. His long fingers squeezed then traced the lines of my hips through my silk robe.

"I'm fine," I told him.

His eyes fell shut as he buried his nose against my neck. "You sure?" His palms slid down to my thighs where the robe fell open naturally.

"Yeah. I just…need you." I couldn't keep my hands off his granite chest. "Why don't you have any tattoos on your chest?" I quizzed out of nowhere. I had to ask a question to stop my mind from running away. I'd end up mauling him if I didn't slow down.

"I don't know," he shrugged. "Maybe I'll put your name right here." He pressed my hand against the left side of his chest then lifted it to kiss my palm…then my wrist.

"You'd get my name tattooed on you?"

"Why not? I only tattoo things on my body that will forever mean something to me. You mean the world to me, Cress."

"You have to stop saying things like that. I already want to jump on you and you're not helping."

"You want to jump on me?" God, that arrogant smirk of his was so sharp and clean it sliced through my fear. As much as I wanted Jules inside of me, I wondered if he still wanted me after what his brother did.

"Maybe." I shrugged. Jules gripped my hips tight and stared into my eyes like he was trying to read the pages of my soul. "I'm tired of reliving the way Angel hurt me."

I straddled him and pressed my weight down. His dick thickened immediately and the pressure on my clit felt deliriously good.

Pain and anger flashed in his eyes. "I hate knowing what he did to you. But I hate that you have to think about it and relive it even more. Let me erase him." He spoke between slow warm kisses along my throat. My hips moved organically, rocking and grinding against his fat dick.

"I want him gone," I panted. "I don't want to think about his hands on me or his mouth or…" I didn't get to finish that sentence because Jules flipped me over and settled between my legs like a rock sinking into a river.

"I'm going to leave my mark all over your perfect body, Cress," He growled right before pulling my earlobe into his mouth and tugging with his teeth. Prickles of honeyed pleasure blanketed me as I squirmed beneath his bulk. "There won't be any more room for him to exist once I'm done with you."

I couldn't respond with words because the way his mouth worked my flesh only allowed for moans and ragged, animalistic breathing.

Julien's teeth scraped my collarbones on the way down to my breasts. He sucked and bit and licked with so much hunger...

No.

It was something deeper than hunger. It was the need to claim and possess. I opened my legs wider and he growled with his tongue flattened over my nipple. He thrust his erection against my bare pussy and another nasty moan floated from my lips. I felt every bruise he left behind. Each one flowered on my skin accompanied by heat and electricity.

"Oh my god, Jules," I cried out, rubbing the soft waves of his hair, dragging my nails along the back of his neck. He kissed and licked a sultry song down my ribcage before reaching my stomach and kissing every imperfection I knew was there.

The way he handled me didn't raise insecurities though. Instead, I felt cherished and honored. Jules worshipped me through his lips and tongue and I blessed him with the slick wetness between my thighs and the way I called his name.

My toes curled when he kissed my inner thighs nibbling and pulling his teeth along the silky skin there. By the time his lips connected with my clit, I was a puddle.

He took his time, moving slowly around my aching bundle of nerves before going in for the kill. He slurped and sucked gently at first, then he applied pressure and my back arched off the mattress to absorb more of the pleasure he was doling out.

I clamped my thighs against his ears and he forced my knees apart while he grumbled with my pussy in his mouth. The vibrations went straight to my core and I thought I would crack open and rain down diamonds.

"Julien," I said, my hand splayed on top of his head while he licked, sucked, and probed. "I'm…about to…"

"Come in my mouth, Cress. Paint my fucking tongue." He kept the pressure right on my clit as he slid two long, sturdy fingers inside of me. I wasn't thinking about anyone else but Julien right then. There was no reliving my ex-husband. There was no fear. There were only waves of orgasms crashing into me while Julien's fingers curled to massage my g-spot and his mouth alternated sucking and licking my clit.

He only let up after he'd had his fill. I didn't get to dictate that. Once he was full, he knelt up on the bed and watched me try to find my soul while he gripped his cock through his sweats.

"Look at that pretty ass pussy." He said before freeing his dick and stroking it. "So fucking wet." He bit his bottom lip and I thought I would come all over again. "Let me watch you play with it, Cress." His eyes ate up every gentle stroke and slip of my fingers as I rubbed my throbbing pussy. I jolted each time I grazed my sensitive clit.

"Goddamn," he said, shaking his head. "All of that is mine." His fist moved up and down his shaft. I wanted him inside of me so bad

I was one step away from pleading for the dick.

"It's all yours Julien," I purred.

"It'll be mine forever." With one hand above my head, bracing his weight, the other hand guided his thick swollen head inside. He dipped in then pulled out and I wanted to cry.

"Fuck me, Julien," I demanded, my hips lifting greedily.

"Listen to you. Nasty and bossy. I like that shit. Say it again, baby." The look in his eyes said he wanted to eat me alive and I would let him. I would let him do almost anything he wanted right then.

"Fuck me, Julien," I said again, pinching my nipples.

"Like this?" He quizzed sliding in, spreading me as he pushed. My eyes fell shut at the deep and full pressure of his thrust.

"Yes!" I gasped when his strokes turned hard and violent. "Oh god, yes!" He lifted my ankles onto his shoulders and leaned down so he had more control. His dick slipped deeper between my walls and I felt wetness lick the insides of my thighs and kiss the curve of my ass.

"You know how much I fucking love you?" He asked in my ear as he drilled into me.

"Yes, I know. I know, baby." I didn't recognize the throaty voice that came from my mouth.

He sank his teeth into the side of my neck and I cried out. It felt so good. It anchored my mind and body, forcing out memories of being hurt and abused. I felt the love pouring from Julien. He wanted to please me. He wanted to comfort me.

I felt it from my hair follicles to my toenails. He filled my body up but he filled my heart and mind too. Emotions swallowed me whole and tears rolled from my eyes into the hollows of my ears.

I couldn't tell if I was crying because of the much-needed release or from the way Jules worked his hips to hit places I didn't know existed inside of me. Either way, I was his. I didn't want anyone else ever touching me. The way that man fucked me... made love to me...healed me. It was unmatched. I couldn't ever see putting another man in his place.

My body convulsed involuntarily with a climax that rattled my ribs and left me breathless. I wasn't expecting to come so fast or so hard but Jules did things to my body I couldn't explain. Being with him was a fresh experience. Fresh like citrus in the spring. He made me feel new.

"Fuck, Cress...why is your pussy so good. So wet. Oh my god." He groaned with the next thrust and I felt his dick go rigid inside of me. It throbbed and swelled, nearly splitting me in half. His orgasm spilled into me, hot and slippery. He let loose a string of curse words against my hair while his breathing returned to normal.

After he eased out of me, he pulled me close and kissed the top of my head. We laid there like that in comfortable silence for a while. I found the rhythm of his breathing and heartbeat so soothing that I fell asleep. His presence put me out like a light.

...

"I'm going to visit Angel today. You wanna come?" Jules looked at me over his shoulder after he finished the breakfast I made for him. Scrambled eggs with cheddar, toast, bacon, and grits. The way he fucked me last night warranted an immaculate breakfast.

"How are his um…nubs?" I shrugged my shoulders not knowing what to call Angel's newfound lack of fingers.

"Boogie found a private doctor who stopped the bleeding and gave him antibiotics. I instructed him not to give pain medicine though. I want him to suffer." The words rolled off his tongue so effortlessly and I didn't flinch. I wanted the same thing.

"Me too." I finished my cup of coffee and put it in the dishwasher. Jules wrapped his arm around my waist and pulled me against his chiseled body.

"Listen to you. Went from being golden to being onyx."

I tipped my head to the side and said, "What does that even mean?"

"Well, at first you were my golden girl. Shiny, brilliant, soft. Just like gold. Now?" He shook his head and kissed a trail down my bare shoulder. "Now, you're like an onyx stone. Dark with streaks of light but still nobody can tell what the fuck is going on in your head."

"I like that description," I told him, turning in his arms so that I could see his handsome face. God, that man was fine.

"It fits you." He tucked his bottom lip between his teeth and grunted as his eyes took a leisurely stroll down my body. "You know what else fits you?" Without warning, he lifted me onto the counter. I let out a yelp as I held on to his shoulders and wrapped my legs around his waist.

"What else fits me, Jules?" My grin stretched from one ear to the other.

"My dick." His warm palms slid up my thighs sliding around to my back.

"Stop being nasty. Nasim is going to wake up any minute and..."

"And we have the monitor right there. We can see and hear him when he wakes up."

My nightshirt was on the kitchen floor in the next second. The breeze in the house made goosebumps flutter across my skin but the way Jules touched me made them melt away again.

I tossed my hair back in a half-curly half-straight cascade that Jules gripped tight at the base of my neck. There were no more words. Only heat simmering into my skin and sliding down my spine, pooling between my hips.

I reached beneath his waistband and stroked his stiff dick, trying to wrap my fingers around the rigid shaft. I wanted to lick it. Spit on it. Trace every vein with my tongue until he was groaning and growling like an animal.

Jules had other plans though.

One thrust and he was fucking me, pulling erotic sounds from my open mouth. I dug my heels into the top of his ass and pushed him deeper even though it stung. I couldn't explain the delicate balance between pain and pleasure that I'd learned to love with him but it drove me wild.

"Fuck, Cress. Your tight little pussy is about to make me come hard as shit." Jules dug deep and paused while he kissed and sucked on my lips one at a time. I slipped my tongue into his mouth and he nibbled on it while fucking me slowly, pushing so deep I moaned into his mouth.

His pace picked up and gravity disappeared in the pit of my stomach. I was floating. His name was a chant falling like raindrops from my lips.

Deeper.

Harder.

Suck.

Lick.

Groan.

"Jules, I'm coming!" My voice swiped the ceilings as tendrils of silky heat and wetness poured from me.

"Shit me too," he muttered. His movements turned jerky seconds before he shot into me. It was a flood of warmth that I welcomed with nail marks on his back.

A frantic knock on the door pulled us apart abruptly. Jules pulled up his pants, tucking his wet dick away, then moved to the foyer. I heard him grab his gun and a knot formed in my throat.

Could Angel have gotten out?

What if he came here to hurt me or Nas?

"Is Cressida here? I need to talk to her. I haven't heard from Angel in almost a week." The sound of Bree's tears forced a rush of air out of me that I didn't even know I was holding in. I'd take anything as long as it wasn't Angel. Bree, I could deal with.

I fixed my clothes and grabbed the baby monitor before rushing to the foyer. My body was still buzzing from fucking Jules. It gave me a high I wasn't expecting. Or maybe the high came from knowing Angel couldn't control and hurt me or my son anymore.

Either way, I was ready to put Bree's backstabbing-ass in her place.

"Why are you here, Bree?" When I walked up, Jules had her backed against the wall. He didn't lay a finger on her but his body was enough of a cage to keep her contained. Nobody in their right mind would try to get around his broad, chiseled body. Every time she moved and tried to look around Jules, he blocked her and his muscles flexed under his smooth skin. My throat tightened at the sight of it.

I blinked away the lust clouding my brain and glared at Bree. "Where is Angel? Please tell me, Cress. He's going to be the father of my baby and I haven't seen him in days and it's worrying me sick." Tears clogged her voice and rolled down her cheeks but they had zero effect on me.

"You think I give a fuck about you being worried sick? You sat there and watched me get financially and emotionally abused. Then you gaslit me the entire time just so you could fuck Angel. Now, you show up here at my house wanting sympathy and understanding? Girl, fuck you." I motioned for Jules to step aside and he did without question.

"Cress, without Angel here, you're all I have. Please listen to me." She clasped shaking hands together under her chin and begged me with teary eyes.

"Fuck. You. Bree. Have your baby alone. I don't know where Angel is and I don't give a fuck. I hope he stays gone. Now get out of my house." We stood there, staring at each other for a few beats. Finally, she turned on her heel and muttered something about me not being a real friend and finding Angel on her own. I flipped her off when she walked out and Jules slammed the fucking door.

"Is she going to be a problem? She's talking about finding Angel on her own," he asked once the front doors were locked.

"No. Bree is a leech. Once she gives up looking for Angel, she'll move on to the next stupid motherfucker who can give her money and stability." I shook my head at the woman she turned out to be. Every time I thought about how Bree told me I was being crazy for crying over Angel and how stupid I was for wanting better, my cheeks prickled with heat.

Everything made sense in hindsight. She was the only friend Angel let me have because he knew he could use her to control me. Bree was just as bad as him and honestly, they deserved each other.

I refused to let her occupy space in my head anymore. I wasn't going to think about her or her baby. If Nasim wanted to have a relationship with his sibling when he got older then that would be up to him. I was washing my hands of the entire situation.

...

Chapter
NINETEEN

Julien

B oogie's hide-away house way out in the middle of nowhere was the perfect place to keep Angel. He was relegated to the shed in the backyard. It was a decent-sized area made of concrete and metal. Boogie even took care to have the shed sound-proofed. He must have known it would be used for murder and torture at some point. I couldn't wait to have my own spot so I could construct something similar.

Before Cress and I came to check on Angel, she left Nasim

with Trini who smiled from ear to ear when she saw me. She even hugged me. I still wasn't used to physical contact from anyone besides Cress, so it was a stiff one-armed hug she got back but it was something.

"Oh, my fucking god…" Cress's words came out between dry heaves as I pulled open the shed door letting the cheery Florida sunlight spill into the dark space.

"What? He's not getting top-notch treatment in here."

Holding her nose tight she asked, "So he can't even go to the actual bathroom?"

"Nah. He doesn't deserve a bathroom. I mean unless you want to take the zip ties off him and show him some kindness." Cress shot me a look that could have knocked out an elephant so I backed off.

"It stinks, that's all." Her words were short and muffled by her hand over her mouth.

Angel stirred in the corner at the sound of our voices. His feet shuffled and the chair he was tied to groaned under his weight. I walked over and took a look at his bandaged fingers.

"Well, I can tell you don't have an infection. The only thing I smell in here is shit and piss." The smell was enough to make the strongest man's stomach roil, but I refused to react. The putrid smell of Angel's waste was an inconsequential part of his torture.

"Fuck…you, Smoke," he grunted out, trying and failing to struggle against the tape and zip ties that bound his wrists.

"Yeah, I know right? It's fuck me but you're the one missing fingers and tied to a chair in a shed." I shook my head and walked closer. The stench wafting off him was suffocating. "How's withdrawal going, big brother?" I tipped my head to the side and looked at his sweat-drenched face in the slices of light falling from a window near the roof. His eyes were starting to look normal. Now, I could see the hate and the pain in them.

When I looked at Angel, I no longer saw the brother I looked up to my entire life. I saw the manipulative, lying, abusive piece of shit he really was. Better late than never.

"Look, either kill me or let me go, Smoke. This shit is cruel." His voice cracked when he finally decided to look at me.

"I can't do that, Angel. How long did you string me along? How long did you give me fake-ass support and lie to my face? Huh?" My voice jumped in volume and he flinched at the booming sound. "How long did you abuse Cressida and scare the shit out of her? But you're asking me for sympathy? Fuck that. You can suffer."

"Please...I'm sorry for everything." His frantic eyes searched until he found Cress, who was standing in the corner with her arms wrapped around herself. "I'm sorry, baby. You know I love you. I-I'm Nasim's father. He needs his father in his life."

Luckily, his plea fell on deaf ears. Cressida rolled her eyes and scoffed, making her way to me. My arm instinctively looped around her waist.

Mine.

I would protect her from any and everything.

"Julien will be a better father figure to him than you ever could.

I hope your death is slow and painful. I'll be here to watch every second of it." Her smile was icy.

"You're going to let this backstabbing motherfucker raise my son!" Angel's voice exploded and I tightened my grip on Cressida before drawing my fist back and smashing it into Angel's reckless mouth.

"You need to learn how to talk to women. It's okay. I have plenty of time to teach you how to watch your mouth."

"I'm…sorry," he sputtered, spitting blood on the concrete floor.

"I'll be back when you learn some fucking manners." I turned and headed for the door with Cress in tow. Angel let out a pained cry from his chair.

"Please! Don't leave me in here!" It turned into a roaring chant that became muted once the heavy door slammed shut.

Once Cress and I were inside Boogie's house, I looked her over, trying to pluck apart her quiet demeanor and impassive face. "You okay?" I quizzed, pulling her closer to me on the couch.

"Yeah, just a little shaken up," she admitted, draping her legs over mine.

"Was it hard for you to see Angel like that?" My knuckles brushed her collarbones.

"Oh, you thought I meant shaken up from seeing Angel? No. Well, yes but not how you're thinking. I'm shaken because I *didn't* feel any pity. I felt nothing. I thought I would feel bad or nauseous or…something. The only thing that bothered me was the smell but I even got used to that after a few minutes." She trapped her bottom lip between her teeth and I couldn't stop staring.

After everything we'd been through, Cressida was more beautiful to me than she'd ever been. I was just as attracted to the swirls of marbled darkness running through her as I was to her warmth and light.

I pulled her plump bottom lip from between her teeth and leaned over to kiss her. To suck on that fucking lip because it was so perfect and juicy. The way she whimpered against my mouth made my dick hard in less than a second.

"I love that you weren't phased," I told her, gripping her jaw and making her focus on my eyes.

"You don't think something's wrong with me?" She glanced up with those big champagne-colored eyes and my cock twitched again.

"Nah. There's nothing wrong with you." I adjusted my growing dick before pulling her on top of me. "You're perfect, Cress."

"You're just saying that because you want to fuck me." A devilish smile crossed her kiss-swollen lips.

"I'm saying it because it's true. I can fuck you whenever I want to. I don't need to sweet-talk you."

"Oh, really?" When she tipped her head to the left, silky hair tumbled down her shoulder and I grabbed a fistful. "What if I told you no?"

"No? I don't do no." I pushed her sundress up around her full hips, exposing the blue panties underneath. The heat pouring from her pussy was driving me insane. If I didn't get inside of her, I was going to lose my shit.

"So, you're going to take it?" She batted those long lashes at me and I was helpless.

"We both know you're going to give me that pussy *willingly*." I tugged her panties to the side and pulled out my hard dick.

Cress tried to playfully hop off my lap but I wasn't having that shit. My hand darted out and snagged her dainty neck before she could move too far away. I put her right back where she was and she gasped.

"I must not be choking you hard enough if you can still gasp like that," I grumbled, tightening my grip. Her greedy hips rocked back and forth in response. "Now, tell me to take it," I growled with my lips pressed against her ear.

When I let her throat go, my hands went to her hips to guide her rhythmic rocking. I needed her pussy sliding against my dick. When we connected, electricity zipped through my core. She must have felt it too because the moan she let out was sexy as fuck.

"Tell me to take it, Cress." My hungry mouth kissed her throat.

Lick.

Bite.

Suck.

"Take it, Jules. Fuck me." That's all I needed to hear. I pushed inside her without any romance. She needed to know how intense my feelings were for her. I wanted to show her over and over. "Oh my god!" She whimpered with her head tossed back.

"Good girl, Cress." I slapped her ass then dug the tips of my fingers into her soft cheeks. "Now, ride this dick. It's yours." I slipped the straps of her dress down, exposing her full tits and plump, pebbled nipples. They were at the perfect height to pull into my mouth so I sucked and licked them one at a time while she rode me.

It didn't take long for her to find the right rhythm. The way her ass bounced up and down made my fucking toes curling against the soles of my shoes. I knew I wouldn't last long. Not with the way she moaned and called my name.

When I felt her walls tighten around my dick, I let out a tortured groan and tried in vain to hold her hips still so she wouldn't move anymore. She shuddered on top of me, shutting her eyes and biting her lip while an orgasm washed over her.

"Oh…god," she trembled. The next languid stroke from her wet pussy had me ready to explode. I came unglued listening to her soft, needy moans and the way her ass sounded clapping against my thighs once she picked up her speed again. I let loose a low moan as my dick jerked and flooded her with my seed.

We were both spent. Heavy breathing and slow movements made me feel drugged. I always felt like that After I fucked Cress. She was more potent than anything Angel used to sniff up his nose.

"So, let's not tell Boog we fucked on his couch. I'm sure he'd be pissed," she giggled, pulling up the straps of her dress. I cracked a half-smile and nodded lazily.

"Yeah, let's keep that between us." I leaned over and kissed her forehead then stroked her cheek with my thumb. Her skin was satin beneath my touch. "You know I'd never let anything happen to you, right, Cressida?"

"I know," she smiled.

"You know I'm serious about us, right? This isn't a fling." I couldn't pretend like she didn't have me wide open. It was an unfamiliar feeling that was unwelcomed before but now, it anchored me. The love I felt for her let me know I wasn't dead inside.

I was still dark and twisted. To everyone else looking at me, I was probably still an unforgivable monster but I was different with her. With her, I was the skull *and* the rose. I was life and death. Murder and beauty.

...

While Cress got much-needed sister time night with Trinity, I went to Rush to handle business with Boogie. The club was packed as usual and from the looks of things, business was still being conducted even though management had changed.

I greeted everyone I knew with a quiet head tilt as I made my way to the red-illuminated stairs leading to what used to be Angel's office. There, I found Boog and a few of his men sitting around chatting.

"What's good, Smoke? How'd things go at the crib?" He stood and slapped hands with me before motioning to his boys to give us privacy. They filed out, closing the door behind them.

"Things went as expected. He's still sobering up. Going through withdrawals." Flashbacks of Angel's eyes flickered through my head and I felt nothing. There was a hollow space where he used to reside in my mind. I didn't feel remorse or pity. I felt peace.

"When do you think you'll be ready to finish him off? He's stinking up my shed," Boog laughed but I knew there was gravity behind his smile.

"I'm not ready yet," I told him honestly.

"Is it too much for you to handle? I know how you feel about him now but he's your brother."

"Nah. He's not my brother. A big brother wouldn't string me along or treat me like I was beneath him. A big brother wouldn't let me waste five years of my life only to come home to empty promises and bullshit. Angel is nothing to me now." My jaw flexed but it was the only signal of my anger.

"So, what's the endgame, Smoke?" Boogie leaned forward, resting his elbows on the large glass desk he sat behind.

"I need him to understand first. He won't until he's done with withdrawals. I need him to know with a clear, and sober mind why things came to this ending." I stared at the wall. There was a painting of a gold, diamond-encrusted crown on a black background.

Angel wasn't the king anymore. Rush was no longer his kingdom and I was no longer his loyal subject or his jester. Whatever the fuck he used me for over and over, I wasn't that shit anymore. Things had changed.

I'd changed.

"I didn't come here to talk about him though. You let me handle that motherfucker. I wanted to talk to you about Rush," I said.

"We're still on track for the transfer," he told me.

Once Angel was out of the picture, me and Boog started transferring Angel's businesses over and putting them under the name Brandon Ellis. Boogie's legal name.

His dark unreadable eyes watched as I pulled an envelope

from my pocket. I sat it between us on the desk and said, "The new shareholder's agreement came to the house yesterday and it has my name on it as an equal partner right beside your name, *Brandon*." I lifted an eyebrow and Boogie laughed a little.

"What's the problem, *Julien*? You don't want to be my partner with Rush?"

"I don't want any parts of this fucking club, man. I want to..."

"You want to design jewelry. I know. You're going to make big fucking money once you complete your certification. Still, Rush wouldn't exist without you. You came up with the idea for the club in the first place and Angel was supposed to put you on as a partner and he never did. As your best fucking friend, it's my job to right his wrong."

I stared at the envelope on the desk for a few beats before meeting Boogie's eyes. "I don't need pity."

"And I'm not giving it to you. This is rightfully yours. You can be a silent partner. You don't have to touch a fucking thing. This just ensures you'll get half of the profits and you can make decisions. Who else am I supposed to trust with shit like this?"

"Not me," I grumbled, running a palm over my waves.

"Why not?"

"Because running a business isn't for me. I'm not cut out for that shit. It's not how my mind works."

"Listen to yourself, Smoke. You want to design custom jewelry. You want to be your own boss and make your own lane but you don't want to run a business?" His eyes crinkled at the corner and the dim lighting in the office caught the impressive scar on his face.

"Working for myself isn't running a nightclub though," I reasoned with a shrug.

"You're full of shit and you sound like Angel."

My hackles raised and I sat up a little straighter, squaring my shoulders. "I'm not like him at all," I frowned.

"No…but that's him speaking through you. Angel has become the negative self-sabotaging voice in your head telling you that you can't do things. Nothing is stopping you from making this money. We split Rush fifty-fifty. You can stay silent or make moves. I trust you. So, what's up?"

His words hit me hard and fast.

He was right.

Angel had worked his way into my head after a lifetime of him telling me I was stupid. I was a killer. I would never be as good as him.

None of that was true but I was letting it dictate the way I made money and decisions. I didn't have to run drugs to own half of Rush. It was still hard to let Angel's insidious words go. They were threaded into me.

If I wanted to kill him, I couldn't just do it physically. I had to kill the version of him that lived in my head too. I knew Cressida would have to do the same thing. It's the reason why there was no other woman for me. Nobody else endured Angel the way we did. Yeah, we took different routes but the result was the same. Two broken people at the hands of Angel Delgado.

I cleared my throat and said, "Okay, fuck it. I'll stay on as a partner." It wasn't a cure-all for the way my brother fucked my head up and twisted my self-image, but it was a start.

A half-smile lifted one side of Boogie's mouth and he extended his arm for a handshake. "Welcome aboard, partner. Let's get this money."

"Let's get it," I said shaking his hand.

...

I walked into laughter and conversation between Cress and Trini. It felt good to hear her laugh. The warmth that she'd planted in my chest always came to life when she was near. It was a nice contrast to the cold darkness I was used to.

"Hey!" Cress chirped, popping up from the living room couch to give me a kiss. My arm automatically wrapped around her waist. I lifted her off the ground as our mouths crashed together. I didn't even know I missed her until she was pressed against me.

"What's up?" I smiled after setting her down.

"Oh my god. Did Julien Jean just *smile* voluntarily?" Trinity asked. She looked so much like Cressida but in her own way. Her skin was a few shades darker and she was thicker than her sister but other than that, they shared nearly every feature.

"I smile sometimes," I shrugged, sitting down on the couch. Cress went to sit beside me but I pulled her onto my lap. Her proximity was as close to peace as I'd ever gotten.

"You smile when you see Cress," Trini pointed out with a knowing grin. "You know what? I'm not mad at it though. At first, I was kind of side-eyeing my sister for being with you but..." She eyed me then sighed. "You can't help who you love and you can't help when you love them. Plus, I don't get the same abuser vibe from you that I got from your brother."

At the mention of Angel, Trinity's smile slipped. "Where is he anyway?" She quizzed. Her voice was quiet like he'd pop out of a hiding space any moment.

"Don't know. Don't care," Cress sighed.

"I beat his ass. He took off," I told Trinity. She eyed me for a long while before pursing her full lips together and grunting.

"So, you just beat him up and he ran away? You really think that's going to work? You're in his house with his...wife, technically, and his son. He's not going to leave it alone. I need to make sure my sister and nephew are protected." I saw the worry in her brown eyes.

"He's not coming back, Trinity." I wanted her to leave it alone after that but she was fiery.

"How can you ensure that he's not coming back? He practically runs Miami. Someone like him isn't just going to vanish." She waved her hand in the air and her gold bangles clanked softly.

"I killed him." My voice was flat and my expression was void. Trinity blinked with an open mouth, unsure of what to say next. I felt Cress stiffen in my lap and I gave her thigh a comforting squeeze.

If Trinity was going to keep pushing her line of questioning then I wanted to give her an honest answer. She knew Angel well enough to know murder was the only acceptable way to keep him from Cress and Nas.

"You're serious, aren't you?" She almost whispered.

"As a motherfucker." I held her gaze and neither of us blinked.

"Trinity, listen," Cress started, holding her hands out. "Please don't say anything."

"Cress, stop." Trinity shifted in her seat and looked at me briefly before turning her gaze to her sister. "I'm not going to pretend to be perfectly cool with what Julien just said but honestly there was no other option." Her throat dipped when she swallowed and I knew she was having a tough time accepting that she was sitting across from a killer.

Even though Angel wasn't dead yet, telling her I killed him sounded better than telling her I was holding him hostage and torturing him until I felt it was time to end it. She'd definitely be uncomfortable then.

"Julien, you did what you had to do. I'm not holding anything against you and I'm not saying anything to anybody. I'd kill him for Cress and Nas too."

We all sat in silence for a while before I finally spoke. "Thank you, Trinity. I know hearing something like that isn't easy."

"It's not but what else could be done? He was a monster." She shrugged her shoulders with ease as if the weight of everything was settling in and she was adjusting.

We all had a few drinks after that then Trini headed home after sneaking in a kiss to a sleeping Nasim. I hung back and watched Cress hug and kiss her sister. I watched the way her eyes lit up when she laughed and the way her unconditional love for Trini wouldn't let her leave without one more hug.

I realized I loved everything about Cressida because she was the opposite of me but I was starting to see where we were alike too. The more I unveiled about her, the deeper I fell. It was scary but I knew she wouldn't betray me. She wasn't Angel.

"I'm glad you got to spend some time with Trinity," I said once we settled in bed to watch TV. Cress pressed her warm body against me, resting her head on my chest.

"Me too. I'm glad Nasim is getting to know her now. He needs his auntie in his life."

"And you need your sister." My hand slid down her back then slipped under her nightshirt. She looked so damn good wearing one of my t-shirts to bed. It hung on her frame like it would a kid playing dress-up. Cress was a grown woman though and she'd come along so beautifully.

"I do. I need her. I need Nasim. I need *you*." She lifted her eyes and watched me. A hazel stare that melted through my cinderblock heart. I only melted for her though.

"The feeling is mutual, Cress." I skimmed her plump bottom lip with my thumb and watched her eyes smolder with want. "See, that look is going to get your pussy eaten. Stop playing."

"Is that supposed to be like a threat?" Her giggle was so fucking sexy.

"I don't do threats. You know that. I hunt then I kill." I grabbed her sides and tickled her ribs a little making her laughter pop out bright and bubbly.

"So, are you going to kill me now, *Smoke*?" She lifted a perfectly arched eyebrow at me like she was throwing down the gauntlet and she knew I'd pick that shit up.

"I'm going to kill your pussy." I stole a kiss. It was possessive and direct. I tasted her tongue, sucking on it before biting her bottom lip, making her moan. My dick throbbed in my underwear.

"Sit on my face," I told her, sliding down in the bed so I could lay on my back. I thought she would protest or laugh it off but my girl climbed on my face like I told her to and I was going to reward the fuck out of her for it.

I hummed against her thick pussy lips and she trembled. I felt her bracing against the headboard because she already knew I was going in for the kill. She wasn't wrong.

I spread her open so I could lick and kiss all around her clit. I realized she didn't need direct stimulation to come hard. So, I teased her first. She was so damn sweet, I could have feasted and gorged myself on her all fucking night.

She wasn't sweet like sugar. Cress was sweet like a flower. I tasted her freshness, her unique flavor. I licked her petals before devouring them in hopes that I could harness some of her beauty and let it sustain me forever.

Her moaning reached a fever-pitch after I'd left marks on her thighs and slipped my tongue inside her entrance. She was primed and ready by the time I wrapped my lips around her stiff bundle of nerves. "Ju…lien!" Her moans broke my name apart into fragments as she rained on my face. I kept light suction on her while her hips bucked involuntarily and her spine went stiff.

The headboard creaked from how hard she gripped it. I forced orgasm after orgasm from her until she curled forward and her moans turned to helpless whimpers.

When she fell over, she rolled onto her stomach still shaking. I wasn't about to let her get any recoup time. I climbed on top of her, just like she was. I nudged her leg up and slapped her round ass with my dick. Pre-cum smeared across her pretty golden skin and a sense of pride flooded me.

Cressida was mine. My woman. My partner in crime. My best fucking friend.

I buried my cock inside of her with that feeling consuming me and she sang my name like a goddamn angel. I held both her hands with mine while I pounded her wet pussy hard and deep. Currents raced through my body the longer I stroked her. I pressed my lips to her temple and kissed her before saying, "You know this pussy belongs to me forever, right?"

"Yes, baby. Forever."

"I love you, Cress." The admission spilled out of me. I was helpless against it. I'd never been vulnerable in my fucking life, but I was right then.

"I love you too," she moaned with her face in the pillows.

I knew what people meant when they talked about making love now. I was definitely fucking the soul out of Cress, but the feelings I had for her were the reason behind it.

A tingling swell of pressure ballooned inside of me and I felt my dick twitch with the need to release. "Shit, I'm about to nut so fucking hard," I muttered into her soft hair. Cress squeezed and squeezed until we both came in a shower of curse words and heavy panting.

Afterward, she laid her head on my chest while I stroked her hair and soaked in the feeling of having someone who loved me. Someone who I loved even more.

"I didn't know it was possible to feel like this," she said quietly tracing the rose tattoo on the back of my hand.

"Like what? Satisfied," I chuckled.

"Yeah, but also so in love and secure. I know I have a lot of work to do before I unglue Angel from my brain but being with you helps so much." She sat up to look at me. Sex-tousled hair fell down her shoulder and the side of her face. She glowed like a star and she was all mine. It still baffled the fuck out of me.

"I don't want you to think I'm using you as a crutch, Jules but you have no idea how nice it is having you in my corner."

"I know." I brushed a chunk of fallen hair behind her ear. "I feel the same way. We get each other in ways nobody else would understand. Shit, to everyone else, I'm still a monster. You see past that though and you get me.

Nobody has ever gotten me before. I thought Angel got me. That shit was an act. But you? You're real and I can feel that shit. I think that's why it was so easy for me to fall." When I looked at her again, she had tears in her eyes. It made my throat tight.

"Oh my god," she chuckled, tears lodged between her words.

"What?" My brows fell low on my forehead.

"That was beautiful, Julien. Especially coming from you. I know how hard it is for you to express yourself. Knowing you felt safe enough to pour your heart out in front of me means more than anything." She took my face in her small hands and made me look at her. "I got your back forever." Sincerity and truth sparkled in her teary eyes.

I knew right then that no matter what happened, I was going to marry her. I never wanted marriage before but hell, I never wanted any of the things Cress had shown me before she came along.

I was a different man now because of her and I wasn't mad at it. I wasn't fighting it anymore either. I would love her out loud the way she deserved. I would help her raise Nasim and show him what a real man looked like. I'd be whatever she needed from me because she showed me both sides of myself.

The skull and the rose.

...

One month later...

The smell coming from Boogie's shed wasn't as bad today. Someone must have hosed it out and sprayed Angel down. I kept him locked up and had a doctor tend to his fingers so he wouldn't die. He was fed once a day and whenever someone came in to hose him down, he was held at gunpoint until it was all over but he was allowed to stand while still restrained.

I wasn't taking any chances.

"Smoke, what's up?" He looked at me, squinting from the sunlight spilling in.

"What's up, Angel?" I pulled up a stool from the other end of the shed and sat close to him. The faint smell of urine and feces greeted me. "You eat today?" I asked, looking down at the short pile of plates by his foot.

"Nah. Not hungry." For the first time in a long time, his eyes looked normal and he didn't spew insults. Over the weeks, he'd been coming down from the drugs in his system and every day he acted more civil. I couldn't tell if he was accepting fate or healing from withdrawals.

It was probably a little of both.

"Okay," I said with a shrug.

"How's Rush? You and Cress always come in here and stare at me but you never talk."

"I'm not coming here to talk. I'm coming to see if you're done with withdrawals. Looks like you're pretty much done."

"I'd do a fucking eight-ball right now if you handed it to me," he chuckled dryly.

"I didn't come here to offer you a goddamn thing."

"Where's Cress? She's usually stuck to your side." He glanced behind me then back to my eyes.

"She's coming." Cress was finishing up a phone call with a daycare center that offered her a job. She went to enroll Nasim so she could start looking for jobs and they noticed how all the kids in the place were drawn to her. The director jokingly offered her a job but once she found out Cress was about to start job hunting, the offer became real. She had an interview right after we left from seeing Angel.

"Y'all married yet?" A snide smile lifted the side of his mouth.

"Nah. You're still alive."

"You plan to remedy that, Smoke?"

"I do. You knew that though." I pulled out a pack of his favorite cigarettes from my pocket and lit one for him just as Cress walked in. I rested the cigarette between his lips and he took a long pull, shutting his eyes.

"It smells less like shit in here today. Drew must have hosed him off," Cress sighed. She'd come so far from when she first stepped into the shed. Now, she was used to the stench and Angel's empty threats.

Today, he didn't seem as hostile. That meant it was finally time.

"You asked how Rush is doing," I said, squinting through the haze of gray smoke that filled the area.

"Yeah. What's new? Did you tell everyone I got killed by my connect?"

"Actually, I did," I smiled. "And Boogie, who is the new co-owner of Rush, along with me, told your connect that you'd been taken care of. Luckily for him, they were getting tired of your bullshit and they were planning to take you out anyway."

"You were wearing out your welcome with them. They were tired of you using their shit instead of selling it," Cress added, sitting on my lap.

"Listen to you. Wow. Fucking my brother must have given you some confidence, huh?"

"You have no idea. But mainly, it's the fact that I don't have to worry about being beaten, raped, and controlled on a daily basis."

Her words were sharp and cold. I saw the moment they sliced through Angel's exterior. His nostrils flared and he took a long, extended drag of his cigarette. The tip glowed an angry orange-red.

"I didn't hit you until you thought you could leave me," Angel countered.

"And I still ended up leaving you." Her top lip curled in disgust. I rubbed her thigh and slid the tip of my nose along the shell of her ear.

"Why? I gave you everything, Cress. A nice house…you didn't have to work, you had designer clothes, shoes, and bags." He took one last pull of the cigarette then I took it from him and sat the butt onto the floor. I extinguished the glowing ember with my shoe and rubbed the back of Cress's neck, gripping it.

"You controlled me. You belittled me. You didn't give me shopping sprees, Angel. You gave me an allowance and a shopping list. If I deviated you took everything from me. You made me eat the foods you wanted me to eat. You didn't allow me to be free because you knew I didn't love you and I'd run the first chance I got."

"If you didn't love me…why marry me, huh?"

"Because I didn't know how to think on my own. I let my parents choose my life. *They* wanted you. *They* loved you. *I* just went on a date with you. Biggest, stupidest mistake of my goddamn life. I don't regret it though because I got Nasim out of it."

"Don't let him forget me, Cress. That's the last thing I'll ask of you. Don't let my son forget me." His eyes turned sad and for the first time, I saw actual pain ripping through him. Good.

"He will forget you, Angel. He won't have to know what a

disgusting person you were. That's the best thing me and Jules can do for him." She stood from my lap then leaned down to kiss my forehead. "I'm leaving. You need this time with your brother. He's already dead in my mind. Watching you kill him won't even matter to me at this point." She flashed the prettiest smile before leaving the shed and shutting the door.

Angel looked gutted. The expression was quickly replaced with anger. It blazed bright in his eyes. "Cressida!" He roared at the closed door. "Don't you fucking walk out on me!" He tried to stand but he was secured to the chair so he just ended up scooting across the floor, dragging metal against the cold concrete.

"She's gone, man." I sighed then stood to my feet.

"I guess this is what you wanted huh? Me out of the way so you could have her all to yourself. So you could have my fucking son!" He tried to free himself again but it was no use.

"You made this happen, Angel." I stooped down so that I was eye to eye with him. "You set all this shit in motion because you only cared about yourself. Because you couldn't be honest if your life depended on it. You thought you had me in your pocket and that I was just going to follow behind you blindly." I laughed but it was humorless.

"So what, that means you kill me? Your only brother!" Veins bulged against his skin, snaking from his temple down to his neck.

"Maybe a normal motherfucker wouldn't kill his only brother but see…I'm not normal." I tilted my head to the side and smirked. "You used to remind me of that all the time, remember? You told me how much of a savage I was. How much of a monster I was. So, no hermano, a regular man wouldn't kill his only brother for betrayal and lies but a savage monster would."

"I never meant any of that shit I said about you, Smoke. I-I said it because I knew you had the potential to be better than me and…"

"I *am* better than you!" I boomed, standing to my full height. "I'm none of the things you called me. I'm none of the rotten seeds you planted in my head, Angel. I'm. Not. Smoke." In one fluid motion, I pulled my knife out and extended the blade. "I'm Julien. You could never even call me by my real name. I'm done being what the fuck you wanted me to be."

"Please, hermano. I love you." Tears shone in his eyes but they did nothing to the depth of darkness swelling inside of me. Tears wouldn't save his life.

"It took all this time for you to finally love me? Damn shame. I guess it's fair though. It took me all this time to realize who the fuck you really are."

"Smoke…I mean, Julien, you've taken everything in my fucking life just let me live and I promise I'll never bother you or Cressida."

I waited for him to finish talking, then I plunged the tip of my blade into his throat, right below his Adam's apple. His eyes went wide with shock as blood leaked down his chest. "You'll never stop lying to get what you want," I said, holding the blade in place.

Angel tried to respond but it only made more blood pour from him. "I took everything from you. *Me.* The monster. The incompetent one. The one ending your life," I said against his ear.

I twisted the knife deeper into his throat and he gurgled, eyes still bulging. I let my eyes fall shut as I listened to his last breaths.

My blood hummed and my fingers buzzed with pleasure. This was supposed to happen. It needed to happen. There was no way Angel could live, no matter how much I wanted to ignore it.

Now I had Cressida and Nas. I rightfully owned half of Rush. I was free to do what I wanted when I wanted to do it. I was my own man, finally.

After Angel bled out, I realized I wasn't the person he shaped me to be anymore. Smoke died with Angel in that shed.

I was Julien Jean.

And that was enough.

"Is everything done in here?" Cress's voice was soft and quiet as she walked in. I'd been sitting on the stool close to Angel's body, watching his life force drain from him and lost track of time.

I blinked away the haze and looked at her. With the light shining from behind her, she truly looked like an angel.

"Yeah. It's done. Finally."

"You want me to call Boogie for the cleanup?" She asked me.

"Nah, I want to do this one myself." I stood up and moved to the table near the door. There were paper towels and bleach that I used to wash my knife off.

"I'll help," Cress announced, tipping her chin up.

"You don't have to."

"I *want* to. This is like closing a chapter for me too, Jules." She had a point, so I didn't argue with her. I got to work cutting Angel free and wrapping his body in a thick plastic tarp while Cressida cleaned the blood. I'd taught her not to use bleach but peroxide instead. We needed to break down the enzymes.

We worked silently, side by side with me securing the body and her scrubbing and washing. I laid Angel in the corner because I would come back once the sun had gone down and get his body so I could dump it in my favorite spot.

"We'll come back when it's dark?" Cressida asked after we were done.

"Yeah. You know the routine." I draped my arm around her slender shoulders and we left.

After we drove around listening to Biggie and Jay-z to clear our minds, we ended up at a drive-through getting burgers, fries, and milkshakes. I pulled over at a park and we sat on a picnic table and ate like we were starving.

The only sounds between us were our mouths moving and chewing. After my last bite, a burp belted from my mouth without my control and it was the thing the broke the silence between us.

Cress laughed so hard she hiccupped which made me lose it. Before I knew it, we were doubled over with laughter, leaning on each other for support while our shoulders shook and we gasped for air. My laughter settled down naturally but Cress's melted into genuine tears. She didn't have to explain why. I already knew.

"He's finally gone, baby," I said, pulling her into a hug. I squeezed her so tight, I thought I might break her. I realized I needed that embrace too.

"He's gone," she whispered against my chest. "Oh my god…" Her sobs were quiet and I wanted to give her privacy but I couldn't let her go. "It feels so surreal. I didn't know how heavy his energy weighed on me."

"Me either. I'm in a weird space but I don't regret it." When Cress looked at me, I wiped her tears.

"Good. I don't want you to regret it because I damn sure don't. He didn't regret anything he did to you or me." Her voice was firm when she spoke that time. The tears were drying and her expression was turning to stone.

"You're right about that shit," I grumbled, grabbing my milkshake. Cress grabbed hers and we both took long sips. Something about the sweet cold sensation on my tongue helped bring me back to the moment instead of my mind replaying Angel's angry eyes.

"You wanna go with me when I drop him off?" I asked, already knowing the answer. She was my ride or die. She would want to go.

"Of course. Trinity wants to spend time with Nasim anyway. We can ride out."

"Champagne?" I asked.

"Hell yeah. Let's make it an event. We deserve it."

She was right about that shit. I couldn't explain the weight that was lifted off my chest knowing Angel was gone and that I'd done it personally. Once Cress was done with her milkshake, she slid closer to me and I couldn't help tugging on her springy curls. I was glad she let her natural coils free. She looked the most beautiful like that.

"Jules, don't pull my hair. You know what that does to me."

"Nah. I'm unaware," I smirked.

"Unaware my ass."

"What about your ass? You want me to slap it? Bend you over and fuck it? Or should I eat it?"

"You should stop being so nasty." She shoved me but I didn't budge. Instead, I gripped her wrist and pulled her against me. I couldn't help stealing a kiss from her. "Julien," she hissed when I pulled away.

"What? We have the entire park to ourselves."

"I'm not wearing a dress and it's still broad daylight. Anyone could see."

"So, you're telling me these leggings don't pull down?" I slid my finger beneath the waistband of her leggings and she smiled big and bright for me.

"Stop," she gritted out from between clenched teeth. Another smile was brewing beneath the surface though. "I'm going to throw the trash away and then we're getting back in the car." She said it with so much authority but the lust in her eyes was evident. I knew exactly what time it was once we were in the car.

We didn't exactly run to the parking lot but we definitely had some fucking pep in our step. I ducked into the backseat first, then Cress climbed in after me. Our lips crashed against each other in a tangle of heat. Lips, tongues, and an accidental bump of our teeth, all showed how much we needed this release.

I wasn't sure exactly how I got her leggings down and hanging from one ankle but once I did, she straddled me, panting and rocking against me like if she didn't fuck me, she would die. The feeling of her hot pussy grinding against me almost made me dizzy. I couldn't get my dick out fast enough.

Cress kissed a line from my jaw to my neck while I pulled her panties to the side and found her wet heat thrusting upward. We both melted into a long groan.

Cress slid up and down my dick like it was her personal stripper pole and I was just along for the ride. I slipped my hand under her shirt and bra to squeeze and tease her nipples, making her bounce even faster. I wasn't letting her do all the work though. I thrust my hips upward, digging into her while she whimpered and fucked me back harder.

It was raw. It was cathartic. It was everything we both needed.

"Fuck, Jules you feel so good," she said while bracing herself on my shoulders. The car rocked with our movements and I knew anyone walking by could hear the nasty sounds coming from both of us but I didn't care and I was sure Cress didn't either.

"So do you, baby." I pulled her thick hair and she gasped. The intense need to come filled me up until I could barely stand to feel Cress fucking me the way she was.

Goddamn.

"Come for me, beautiful," I said, trying hard to keep it together. I wanted to watch her unravel. It was the most beautiful thing I'd ever experienced and it never got old. I pulled her close to my mouth and found her neck with my lips and teeth. She was sweet and soft. I couldn't get enough.

"Julien!" She cried out, digging her nails into my shoulders. The small pricks of pain were enough to keep me focused on not flooding her with cum.

"Oh my god." She shuddered.

I felt the first wave of her climax. She tightened around me and I maintained composure but that second wave took me out.

"Fuck, Cressida…" I dragged her name out while I held her full hips in place. She stayed there on top of me while I pulsed inside of her over and over until my balls were drained and I thought I would fall the fuck asleep right where I was.

"Damn," she said, slowly climbing off my still sensitive dick. "I never knew sex could be so therapeutic."

"Oh yeah. I definitely have therapy dick," I joked with a lazy smile. She tossed a soft punch at my chest in response.

For a while, we sat there, cracking jokes and laughing with a newfound ease. It felt like the sky opened and we could finally breathe again. Nothing was perfect, but I couldn't picture them being any better than that moment with her. Sweaty, satisfied, and happy in the backseat.

...

The night air coming off the water was chilly and I saw Cress hugging herself while I steered the boat. I pulled off my black hoodie and tossed it at her. "I told your ass to bring a jacket. You wanted to be cute," I fussed.

"Whatever. I didn't think it would be this cold." She slipped her head inside the hoodie then her arms before letting out a content sigh. "Thank you."

"Uh-huh," I muttered, shaking my head.

When we reached the perfect spot where I knew the gulf stream would carry Angel's body, I killed the engine and stood still for a few moments while the water made the boat bob up and down. "You ready to do this?" Cress asked me.

"I'm ready." I couldn't think of anything I wanted to do more. I was ready to be done with Angel once and for all. I hefted his body into my arms one last time then I let him slip over the boat's edge and into the inky black water. A small cluster of bubbles rose to the surface before the ocean swallowed him whole and carried him out of sight.

That was it.

He was gone forever.

"Wow," Cress sighed, leaning against me. "It's…over. Just like that."

"Just like that," I repeated.

"I feel so…at peace." Her smile was gentle but sure. "What do we do now?" She asked.

"We drink this fucking champagne, then we tell the rest of Miami that Angel got killed. After that, me and you are free to start a new life together. The life you deserve." I squeezed her shoulder and she grinned up at me, her pretty eyes sparkled even in the dark.

"The life *we* deserve," she corrected. I couldn't argue with that so I agreed with a kiss on her forehead. We steered back to the docks after celebratory drinks. We were ready for a new chapter.

A new life. It would still involve death and beauty but betrayal wouldn't ever be an issue again.

I couldn't choose my family by blood but I could damn sure choose the family I wanted to love and I chose Cressida and Nasim.

I'd choose them every time, over and over.

...

Epilogue

Julien

Five years later...

"I know I'm running late but I'm on my way," I told Cress.

"Julien, you were supposed to be here a half-hour ago," she sighed into the phone. I could almost see her rolling those pretty eyes. We were having an intimate get-together for her birthday but I had to stop by my store to pick up her gift. I wanted to make sure it was perfectly polished.

After becoming a certified gemologist, I used money from

Rush's profits to take on an apprenticeship with the go-to celebrity jeweler in Miami. I learned more under Mr. Chung than I did in any of the classes I took. He showed me how to craft using the basics. He taught me how to put my heart into every piece I made and it paid off because, after two years, I was able to open up my own custom jewelry shop, Jean's Jewels, and pull in clientele I never thought I'd be able to snag.

Once I grabbed Cress's birthday gift from the safe, I hurried my ass home to my wife.

When I walked into the house, Trinity was the first person to greet me. Well, her round, eight-month pregnant belly was the first one to greet me. She was a close second.

"Took you long enough." She rolled her eyes but then broke into a big smile and held out her arms for a hug. Since I couldn't get too close, I opted for a belly rub.

"What's up, Trini?" I bent over and said, "What's up, Trini's belly?" She shoved me playfully as I made my way into the living room where the birthday girl was.

I watched her silently for a few seconds. She was the brightest person in the room. I may have been a little partial but that's how I saw it. She was laughing at something Boogie said to her and the way she tossed her head back and let her thick curls fall made me want to put everyone out so I could fuck my wife. I had to behave though.

When she finally noticed me, I saw the sharp gasp she sucked in before excusing herself from the conversation with Boogie and rushing into my arms.

"Baby!" I lifted her off the floor and spun her in a circle while her arms were locked around my neck. "Oh god, I missed you so much," she said in between kisses.

"Get a goddamn room," Boogie called from the couch.

"Uncle Boog, watch your mouth." Nasim's little voice came from somewhere but I couldn't see him.

"You see this? Y'all just let your son talk to me any kind of way," Boogie fussed.

"Daddy!" Nas squeaked when he laid eyes on me. I knelt down and he crashed into me out of nowhere. "I thought you were going to miss Mommy's birthday."

"Nah, you know I'd never miss Mommy's birthday." I stood up, holding him even though he was getting tall at five, almost six years old. "Where's your sister?" I asked him, searching for the only woman who had me completely wrapped around her finger. Well, her and her mother had me wrapped up like a damn Christmas gift.

"She went potty," Nas said, smoothing his hand over my hair.

"Well, go get her. You can't leave your sister, lil man." I put him down and he ran up the stairs screaming his sister's name.

"Jewel! Daddy's home! Stop pooping and come on!" The entire room laughed at his carefree outburst.

Not many people came to celebrate Cress's birthday but the people that mattered were there. Trinity and her husband Calvin, Boogie, Drew, and a couple of other guys from Rush, and of course Nasim and Jewel. I liked that no matter how many people knew us, our circle was small. These were the people I'd chosen as family and they hadn't let me down once.

"So, since Julien is here now, can we sing happy birthday and cut the cake?" Trinity asked, rubbing her belly.

"Your hungry ass just wants to eat," I countered, moving into the kitchen.

"And?" She frowned while poking out her lips.

"Let my baby eat cake. Y'all know she's eating for two," Calvin laughed.

"But how are you demanding to eat cake on *my* birthday?" Cress asked with a faux attitude. "It does look amazing though," she marveled once we were all around the island. Staring back at us was a rich chocolate cake with lush, red strawberries running around the border.

"Jules, did you get this?" Cress quizzed, glancing up at me.

"Nah. When I went to order the cake, Trini said it was taken care of," I told her with a shrug.

"Then who…" Cress's voice trailed off as she looked to her sister for an answer.

"Mom and Dad sent the cake," she confessed dropping her shoulders. Cressida rolled her eyes and scoffed at the gesture. She hadn't spoken to her parents in five years and she made it clear she didn't want to.

"I know you cut them off, Cress but they wore me down and I was emotional and…" Trini stopped to exhale. "I'm sorry," she finally said.

"It's fine just…don't do this shit again. Cut off means cut off. If they think they can get to me through you, they'll keep trying."

Over the years, Cress had really come into her own. It was sexy as hell watching her grow. She went from working at Nasim's daycare to owning two centers of her own. We never had to pay anyone to watch our kids and I was forever grateful because I didn't trust anyone and Nasim and Jewel were my entire world.

"Okay, okay. I'll respect your boundaries," Trinity promised with her hand over her heart.

The sound of four little feet padding into the kitchen stole my attention. When I looked to the doorway, I saw Nas holding Jewel's hand with a smile on his face. "I got her," he announced proudly.

"Good job, Nas," I said giving him a thumbs up.

"Daddy!" Jewel ran over to me as fast as her three-year-old legs would carry her and I scooped her up in a big bear hug. She was so perfect. She had Cress's champagne eyes but everything else was all me. Dark wavy hair that was hard to tame, along with my nose, lips, and cheeks. She was my twin in nearly every way.

"Okay, *now* we can sing and cut the cake. The gang's all here," I said, kissing Jewel's temple.

The cake couldn't get served fast enough for Trinity. She vanished once she got her plate. I didn't see her resurface until it was time for Cress to open her gifts. I waited everyone out. I wanted my gift to come last.

She knew it too.

After she swooned over the gifts from the kids and all our friends, she looked my way with excitement brimming in her eyes.

I saw the way she bounced up and down in her seat waiting. Her fingers instinctively went to the spot where her mood ring used to be and I felt my stomach sink a little.

It had been five damn years and I still hadn't come up with a suitable replacement for her mood ring. Whenever she got excited, her fingers still found that bare spot and rubbed.

I walked over to her and pulled a small black ring box from my pocket. Her hands flew to her mouth as she tried to contain herself. She knew exactly what I was about to give her.

"Damn, Cress. I haven't seen you this excited since I proposed," I smirked. It had been three years and being married to her still was my biggest achievement.

"Julien Jean, I swear to god, if you don't give me my present..." Her knees jumped up and down while she tracked my every movement.

"I'm about five years late with this gift, but it's not because I forgot or pushed it to the back burner. I'm five years late with this gift because every time I tried to create it...I couldn't get it right. I tried every year but it still didn't capture the way I felt that day at the carnival when I won it for you." I heard Trinity make a soft swooning noise behind me.

"When I won that ring for you, I remember thinking you were the most beautiful girl I'd ever seen. You made me forget how dark life was. You wrapped me up in the moment."

The rest of the room faded into static and the only person I could see right then was Cressida. When it was just us, I didn't mind emptying my heart.

"I was finally able to capture that feeling and put it into a mood ring I'm proud to put on your finger." I opened the box and handed it to Cress. It felt like every ounce of air was sucked out of the room while I waited for her response.

I spent months working and reworking the mood ring. The stone was hand-carved in the shape of a rose. I could have made it flat but that didn't work. Not for her. She wasn't flat. She was multifaceted. The rose was cut into a 3-d figure that sat in the middle of a gold band and anchored with two small, solid-gold skulls at each side.

"Oh...my god. Julien. This is amazing." She plucked the ring from its box and slipped it onto her naked finger. "I can't even find the words right now." I heard her voice thicken with tears before I saw them in her eyes. "I've missed my ring for so long and now..." She shook her head and admired the way it looked on her finger. Shit, I admired it too. I put in a lot of hard work to make it perfect. "It's so fucking stunning."

"Mommy, watch your mouth," Nasim warned. Everything came crashing back down on me like a ton of bricks. I just poured my heart out in a room full of people.

"Sorry, baby," she laughed a little then focused on the ring again. "Thank you, Jules. You have no idea how much this means to me." She hopped up and launched herself into my arms.

"Aww, that's so sweet!" Trinity cooed, holding on to Calvin's arm.

"Yeah, sorry y'all had to hear all that," I said with a sheepish grin.

"Sorry for what?" Boogie grumbled. "We're all family up in

here. We all know you love your wife."

He was right. Of course, everyone knew how much I loved Cress but Boogie was right about us all being family. Sometimes, I still fell into the old way of thinking. I still heard Angel telling me I wasn't smart enough or good enough.

I was forever a work in progress. Having a real family in my life made the journey easier though. Being loved by the people who loved me was a feeling that I would never get tired of.

The End

OTHER BOOKS BY DANIELLE JAMES

Twisted

The Twisted Series (Books 1-6)

Flowers Behind the Gates Series:

Flowers Behind the Gates

Sleeping Monsters

Power Trip

Death of a Rose

Garden of Secrets

LUCY Duet (Books 1&2)

Naughty R&B (A six story anthology)

Have Mercy

Dangerous Territory

Tortured Whispers

The Monarch Room

The Moreau Estates

Wisteria

Nocturnal Sins

BOMB

Margot

Trust Issues

Defect

Honey Sugar

ABOUT THE AUTHOR

Danielle James is an independent romance author who has published over thirty titles. She writes bold stories for bold readers while always placing the journey to love at the center of her books. James currently lives in Virginia with her husband of nine years, her two children, and their dog.

Made in the USA
Monee, IL
16 July 2021

73753151R00226